Some people will stop at nothing to be famous . . .

Simon has been Molly's best friend since university. But he also has a fatal attraction to straight men and when this leads to a devastating betrayal of Molly's trust, their friendship seems beyond repair.

Distraught, Molly turns to Lilia, an eccentric ex-cabaret singer with an extraordinary past. But Lilia has plans for Molly. She will break her and remake her, turning her into a superstar.

And for Lilia the question isn't what would she do to make Molly famous, more what wouldn't she . . .

Julian Clary is one of Britain's most loved entertainers. His memoir *A Young Man's Passage* was a *Sunday Times* bestseller. He is the author of two critically acclaimed novels: *Murder Most Fab* and *Devil in Disguise*. He lives in Camden and Kent.

Also by Julian Clary:

Non-fiction
A YOUNG MAN'S PASSAGE

Fiction:
MURDER MOST FAB
DEVIL IN DISGUISE

DEVIL IN DISGUISE

JULIAN CLARY

EBURY
PRESS

3 5 7 9 10 8 6 4

Published in 2009 by Ebury Press, an imprint of Ebury Publishing
A Random House Group Company
Copyright © Julian Clary 2009
First published in hardback 2009
This edition 2010.
Julian Clary has asserted his right to be identified as the author of this work under
the Copyright, Designs and Patents Act 1988.

Devil in Disguise is a work of fiction. In some cases true life figures appear but their
actions and conversations are entirely fictitious. All other characters, and all names of
places and descriptions of events, are the products of the author's imagination and
any resemblance to actual persons or places is entirely coincidental.

'Is That All There Is?' Lyrics by Lieber / Stoller. Copyright 1966 Sony/ATV Music
Publishing LLC. All rights administered by Sony/ATV Music Publishing LLC. All
rights reserved. Used by permission.

Permission to reprint lines from 'Lilac Wine' by James Shelton granted by Warner
Chappell Music Ltd. The lines from Kurt Weill's gravestone are from 'Bird of Passage'
by Kurt Weill/Maxwell Anderson, permission granted by Warner Chappell Music.

The Random House Group Limited Reg. No. 954009

Addresses for companies within the Random House Group can be found at:
www.randomhouse.co.uk

A CIP catalogue record for this book is available from the British Library

The Random House Group Limited makes every effort to ensure that the papers used
in our books are made from trees that have been legally sourced from well-managed
and credibly certified forests. Our paper procurement policy can be found on:
www.randomhouse.co.uk

Mixed Sources
Product group from well-managed
forests and other controlled sources
www.fsc.org Cert no. TT-COC-2139
© 1996 Forest Stewardship Council
FSC

Printed and bound in Great Britain by
CPI Cox & Wyman, Reading, RG1 8EX

ISBN 9780091927356

To buy books by your favourite authors and register for offers visit
www.rbooks.co.uk

Very special thanks to Kirsty Fowkes, my editor, whose confidence and enthusiasm never wavered.

Thanks also to Andrew Goodfellow and Gillian Green at Ebury, Hazel Orme my copy editor, Eugenie Furniss my agent, Allan Rogers for his knowledge of torch songs, Nicholas Reader, Paul O'Grady and Barb Jungr for their advice, Ian Mackley for staying away and Peter and Carol for feeding the chickens.

And, of course, Valerie, who answered my sighs with her own.

For Jackie

PART ONE
2001

PART ONE

2001

Chapter One

Molly carefully painted her nails blood red, three vivid stripes on each neat oval to make a flawless finish. As the polish hardened, she gazed down admiringly at her hands. She had looked after them well: the skin was soft and moisturised, the cuticles a healthy pale pink with no breaks or hang-nails. When she sang on stage that night, these hands would sweep and flourish expressively around her, enhancing her performance and conveying the required emotions with skill and subtlety. They were tools as valuable as her voice, and must be treated with respect. She lifted each one in turn to her mouth and gave it a little kiss, rather like a cat might with its paws. A pity, really, that her role required her to wear gloves.

Her hands might be her best feature but the rest of her, she knew, scrubbed up well. She had a pretty, plumpish face, with regular features that carried heavy stage makeup well, and her dark-blonde curls gave her the look of a cheerful country lass not overly concerned with matters of grooming or personal hygiene. She was fleshy and voluptuous. Her cleavage, when pushed up and powdered down, could heave and pant fetchingly as she filled her lungs with air – she had noted the admiring looks of her fellow performers, unable to resist the occasional furtive glance. She had a hefty rump and Rubenesque thighs, but these were usually hidden under the full-length robes that most of the musicals and operas she was cast in required her to wear. Her boyfriend Daniel said she had an hourglass figure. He lusted after her naked body, ripe breasts and big, wobbly thighs, and he would kiss them, bite them, part them at every opportunity.

As Molly waited for her nails to dry, she went through her usual pre-performance ritual, making a conscious effort to think with gratitude about her life thus far. It was a trick her social worker had taught her when she was growing up in the children's home in Liverpool. Positive thinking. The glass must always be half full, not half empty.

I'm twenty-three, she thought. I'm in my prime. I'm earning a living doing what I love – singing. It might be small-time at the moment but who knows what plans Fate has waiting down the line? Nobody hung out the bunting when Cilla Black was born but she made the big-time – and how! If she can do it, why not me?

It was simply a question of willpower and determination, of being in the right place at the right time.

Molly felt a sense of destiny hovering about her. One day she would be a successful recording artist or a West End star; for now she was honing her craft with a third-rate weekly touring company. She wasn't proud. Community centres still had stages, and the punters still came to hear singing, even if it was in places as uninviting as Chatham, Port Talbot or Swindon. No matter. Sooner or later, things would change for the better.

And there was Daniel, a handsome painter and decorator with a sexy Cockney accent. He had helped her to her feet when she'd slipped over in the street on her way to an audition almost a year ago. He picked her up in more ways than one. After a few dates and some rampant, adventurous lovemaking, she had moved in with him. She loved him with all her heart and he loved her too. Professionally and in her personal life everything was hunky-dory.

'Thank you, God,' she said aloud, her voice still carrying a strong trace of its original Scouse accent. 'I'm made up. Work, sex, love. Cheers!'

As if by way of an answer, the Tannoy in her dressing room crackled into life: 'Ladies and gentlemen of the Midlands Operetta Company, this evening's performance of *The Mikado* will begin in five minutes. You have five minutes. Thank you.'

It was Saturday night, the last performance in glamorous Stevenage. After the show it would be time to pack her things away and move on. Next stop, Northampton.

Oh, shit! thought Molly, staring at her own wide blue eyes in the mirror. Digs. I've forgotten again.

She scolded herself as she gave her makeup one last check and straightened her thick black wig. She never remembered to arrange her accommodation for the next stop on the tour, and by the time she got round to it, all the best places had been snapped up by other, more organised members of the cast and crew.

Oh, well, she thought, as she needlessly added a touch more blusher, comforted by the soft cool touch of badger hair. I'll worry about Northampton tomorrow.

She said goodbye to her perfect nails, pulled on her pink, elbow-length gloves and headed for the stage.

Two days later Molly was wheeling her battered, dark-blue suitcase up the pathway of Kit-Kat Cottage in a village called Long Buckby.

The theatrical-digs list for Northampton had been dismally short and, because she had left it so late, all the cheap and cheerful rooms near to the theatre were taken. In fact, she had been unable to find anything suitable at all.

In desperation, she called the Derngate Theatre and spoke to a very helpful stage-doorman called Roger. Once he'd heard that she was about to be reduced to sleeping in her dressing room and washing herself and her smalls in the hand-basin, he'd come up with Kit-Kat Cottage's phone number. 'It's not on our proper listings because it's so far out most people don't want to stay there. It's a bus journey or two into town.'

'I've got a car,' she said quickly. 'Tell me more.'

'I don't know much about it, if I'm honest. No one from here has stayed there for ages. They're an elderly couple making some cash out of their spare room, I think, and the old girl had theatrical inclinations once. A bit eccentric. Do you want the details?'

'I'm all ears,' Molly said, her eye-liner pencil poised over a crumpled envelope.

So here she was. It was late spring, and either side of the pathway leggy daffodils and grass in need of a trim brushed her ankles. It wasn't really a cottage at all, she noted, but a pre-fabricated bungalow, pebble-dashed in the same pea shingle as the path, giving an all-over mottled blond-caramel effect. Either the gravel or the Tarmac underneath it was giving off a curiously restful metallic scent in the afternoon sunshine. She heard a bee buzzing on a nearby rose.

This is nice, she thought, taking a deep breath of fresh, country air. She had spent all her life in the city where everything was concrete, glass and asphalt, and had only ever peered at green fields from train windows. The closest she'd got to a farmyard animal was doing panto with Jim Davidson a few years ago.

The path led to a small, pointed porch open to the elements. On either side there were generous bay windows. Both sills, she could see, were crammed with ornaments: ceramic ballerinas, glossy china Siamese cats, even a wax owl-effect candle, all facing outwards to the path. Behind them, shielding any further investigative glimpses into the rooms inside, hung startling cerise-pink lace curtains.

Hmm. It's all a bit Blackpool, thought Molly. But if that was the worst that could be said for the place, she was in luck. The relentless weekly searches for somewhere to lay her head had forced her to lower her standards, as far as aesthetics were concerned. She could cope with anything as long as her room was clean and her bed comfortable.

She rang the bell and heard a cheery ding-dong inside, which made her smile. There followed two low barks and a woman's voice saying something soothing but unintelligible. A moment later the door swung open, and revealed her landlady, or at least the top of her head. A full crown of henna-red hair greeted Molly. 'Mrs Delvard?' she ventured.

Slowly the scarlet head tilted upwards and a pale, powdered forehead appeared, followed by perfect painted eyebrows, milky green eyes, with matching emerald eye-shadow, a button nose and unnaturally flushed lips. The old lady was wearing a dark-blue, heavily embroidered kimono that had clearly seen better days; the slow raising of the torso, like a geisha girl recovering from a stately bow, was mesmerising.

'*Wilkommen*!' she breathed, as soon as she was upright. 'You must be Molly. Do come in. But, please, do not call me Mrs Delvard. I am Lilia.'

'Thank you, er . . . Lilia,' said Molly. From that accent, the old lady was obviously German. She hadn't noticed it on the phone, but it was only slight, so perhaps that was why. As she stepped into the hallway, she inhaled a strong jasmine scent and noted the old framed theatre posters on the walls and the bunches of dried roses hanging upside-down. It was all strangely familiar. She had met dozens of aged theatrical landladies during her few years of touring. They were often retired from 'the business' themselves, and loved nothing more than to reminisce about their glory days. She hoped Lilia was of this ilk, as she enjoyed hearing tales of high jinks and hilarious acting mishaps from productions gone and long forgotten.

'Follow me, please,' Lilia said, leading Molly down the hall. She had an elegant walk, Molly observed, but with a hint of an arthritic limp. As Molly parked her suitcase, the old lady steadied herself on a chair as she passed it and winced in pain.

Poor old thing, Molly thought, filled with sympathy. Despite the glamour of her appearance, her joints were obviously weary.

'I expect you are tired after your journey. Sit down, please. I will bring tea,' said Lilia. Her voice was low-pitched, attractive and lived-in; its owner sounded as though she'd seen a few things in her time.

'Thank you,' said Molly. 'That would be lovely, but I don't want to put you out, love. Would you like me to help you?'

'No, not at all, my dear. It is good for me to move about. I have been sitting here all afternoon lost in an old movie on the television. I am a little stiff, that's all. I need to come back to reality.' She gave Molly a warm, sad smile, then left the room slowly and with some effort. Soon there were the sounds of a kettle being filled and crockery being arranged.

Molly looked about. Despite the bright sunshine outside, the lounge was gloomy and cluttered. It was a small room and the battered, dark-red-chenille three-piece suite was too large for such a modest space. An old-fashioned vanilla-coloured enamel fireplace squatted modestly against the chimney-breast. Above it, an incongruously grand full-length portrait of a beautiful red-haired woman, wearing a sapphire-blue dress, a cigarette holder between her fingers, gazed down at the clutter, framed by ox-blood-red flock wallpaper. A large television sat in the window bay, which was surrounded by dark-pink velvet curtains complete with a scalloped and fringed pelmet. At either side of the chimney-breast there were deep alcoves. The shelves in the one nearest to Molly heaved with a collection of lace fans, ostrich feathers in a crystal vase, photographs of Lilia in her prime and several more recent pictures of the present-day Lilia, hugging a large black-and-tan dog. There were no shelves in the furthest alcove, but instead a wooden upright chair. Molly gave a little cry of surprise when she realised a man was sitting there in the shadows.

'Oh, I—Sorry, love, I didn't see you there,' she said, with a nervous laugh. He didn't respond, didn't even look at her. She raised her voice and stepped sideways a little so that she was in his field of vision. 'Hello. I'm Molly.'

There was still no response. He was a thin, elderly man, completely motionless and, she got the impression, unaware of her presence. It felt too strange to stand there staring at him and saying nothing so after a moment she tried again. 'I'm going to be staying here for the next week,' she said, as though she was talking to someone with a hazy grasp of English or a hearing impediment.

Still he gazed silently into the distance.

She pressed on: 'I'm an actress and singer. I'm in a tour of *The*

Mikado – you know, the Gilbert and Sullivan opera. I'm Yum-Yum.'

He remained oblivious to her. What on earth is wrong with him? she wondered. Without thinking, she opened her mouth and began to sing softly:

> 'Ah, pray make no mistake,
> We are not shy,
> We're very wide awake,
> The moon and I.'

She stopped, and although the man didn't say a word, he turned his head slowly in her direction. His sad, watery eyes looked beyond her into eternity.

'Poor love,' said Molly quietly. She sat down on one of the armchairs and the two of them waited in companionable silence.

A moment later Lilia carried a tea tray gingerly into the room. As well as a pot, cups, milk and sugar, there was also a huge fruit cake and the old lady tottered slightly under the weight of it all.

Molly leapt to her feet. 'Here, Lilia, let me help you.'

'Thank you, my dear. So kind.' Lilia handed her the tray with a smile and lowered herself into a chair with a heavy sigh. 'That's better.'

Molly placed the tray on the table and hovered uncomfortably. 'Shall I pour?' she asked.

'Please do,' Lilia said quietly. 'I'll have mine white with no sugar.'

Molly poured the first cup, noting that there were only two cups and saucers, and two plates and forks. 'Nothing for . . .?' She indicated the silent figure in the alcove.

'Oh, goodness, no!' said Lilia, with a chuckle. 'My husband, Joey, by the way. I tried putting tea and cake in the food-processor for him once, but he wasn't interested. He only seems to like those little tins of baby food and purées of steak and kidney pudding or the Bombay Palace Special.'

No further explanation of Joey and his catatonic state was forthcoming, so Molly finished pouring the tea and slicing the cake, then handed Lilia her cup and plate before sitting down herself.

'So,' said Lilia, briskly, as if only now could she get down to the business side of things, 'I would like to welcome you to Kit-Kat Cottage. I hope you will enjoy your stay here. Your front-door key is there, on the table. Breakfast is included in your tariff and you are welcome to share my meals for a small extra charge, or provide your own food and use the kitchen. Just let me know what you'd like to do. I used to charge for the phone as well but you youngsters all have mobiles now so there's no point. You can come and go as you please, and there's a television and radio in your room. I do not go to bed early so don't worry about disturbing me when you come in late at night. I will make you some cocoa, if you like, or perhaps a small brandy would be good for your throat. I used to sing myself – not opera, like you – but I found a drink afterwards, brandy or schnapps, very acceptable.'

'Thank you, that's really kind of you,' said Molly, pleased. She'd been in places with far meaner attitudes and more restrictive rules than this. A cosy brandy at the end of a long show sounded just right. 'And while I think of it . . .' she reached into her pocket for a crumpled envelope '. . . here's my rent. Eighty pounds for the week, as we discussed on the phone.'

'Gratefully received!' said Lilia, accepting the envelope and slipping it into her kimono. 'There is plenty of hot water, have all the baths you want. I bathe my husband in the evenings, after *Coronation Street*. It is a rather tortuous process involving winches and so on, and can take up to an hour. Such a bother! But it has to be done at least once every two days or he starts to smell of Parmesan cheese. I don't know why old men should smell so much but they do.' She shrugged. 'Another of life's mysteries. Old ladies, as everyone knows, smell pleasantly of lavender and biscuits.'

'It must be very hard for you,' Molly said, grateful that she would be out at the theatre at that particular time. 'And is your husband . . .?' she ventured, not sure how to ask what Joey's complaint was.

'He had a stroke, the doctors say, two years ago. He's been like this ever since. That's why I call him Joey. It's a bit like having a budgerigar in the room. His real name is Michael.'

'Oh. I see.' Molly couldn't decide if naming your husband after a budgie was an act of cruelty or simple desperation. Was Lilia unkind or just trying to make light of a sad situation?

'Of course, you do not wish for life to turn out this way but marriage is, as they say, for better or worse. I just get on with it. It is not easy at my age, but there it is.' Lilia gave another world-weary smile.

Molly felt a wave of sympathy for her. 'You're doing a fine job. It must be difficult.'

'I married Michael in the seventies. There is our wedding picture, up on the shelf. You can see for yourself we were a gorgeous, glamorous couple. I was a star then, and he was my partner, my manager, my lover and my friend. But he's Joey now,' said Lilia, her voice quivering. 'I had to separate the two. Michael was a fascinating man: erudite, smart, inspiring. And Joey? Silent, staring . . . incontinent. Locked in his own head. Michael would have hated such a fate.'

Lilia gazed fondly at her husband, who continued to stare, motionless, into space. Molly shifted awkwardly, wondering how to fill the silence. She placed her empty cup and saucer on top of the plate, put them back on the tray, and said brightly, 'That was lovely, Lilia, thank you.' By way of concluding things, she wiped the corners of her mouth with her middle finger and smiled.

'I will show you your room now,' said Lilia, tipping her teacup to slurp out the last drops.

'Okay, then,' Molly said, relieved. She was keen to get settled in and have some time to herself. She needed to phone Daniel and let him know she'd arrived safely, and Simon would be waiting to hear from her too. It was her custom to ring him on the first night in new lodgings and tell him what they were like. He loved hearing about her landladies, the more eccentric the better. Lilia would be right up his street. 'Now, I'd better—'

'There is one more thing,' interrupted Lilia, raising her hand to silence her new lodger. 'There is someone else I want you to meet. The real man of the house.'

'Who's that?' asked Molly.

'My boy. My best boy. Heathcliff.' Her eyes sparkled. She raised her voice and called towards the door. 'Where are you, Heathcliff? Come to Lilia!'

The door opened and a large, muscular Rottweiler, the size of a lion, pushed his way hurriedly into the room and headed straight for Lilia, panting with excitement. With his rear legs still on the ground, he raised himself in the air like a stallion, his front paws as big as table-tennis bats, one on each of Lilia's shoulders. His impressive tongue licked her ravenously from chin to forehead as she cooed and giggled girlishly. 'There, there! My love puppy, my baby, my gorgeous, handsome man!'

'He's . . . beautiful,' Molly said, trying not to recoil at the sight of the enormous tongue lapping the old lady's face, taking the powder and paint with it.

'Yes, he is! And gentle as a baby, so don't be frightened. Down, Heathcliff, down. Now. Come along, Molly, we will go and find your room.'

Heathcliff sat down on the hearthrug, two syrupy spindles of saliva escaping from either side of his mouth.

'Good boy,' said Molly, tentatively, but Heathcliff never took his eyes from Lilia.

Chapter Two

Somewhere in his mind Simon realised it was risky to pour himself a third glass of *vino rosso di Sicilia*. It was only five o'clock in the afternoon, after all. The first mid-afternoon 'snifter' had seemed harmless enough. He told himself he deserved it. It was a pick-me-up, no less, after a traumatic sleepless night. Pick him up it had. It had given him such a spring in his step, he'd decided without much ruminating that a second was in order. This had also gone down the hatch so smoothly and quickly that he had wandered into the kitchen, empty glass in hand, and was contemplating the third. The shot in the arm that the first drink had given him had faded. The second had allowed a brief reprise, but had been annoyingly fleeting. He needed that third, yearned for it and desired it so strongly that his feet were almost tapping with impatience.

A dark recklessness coursed through his veins, and he snatched the bottle from the counter as if some invisible figure might take it away from him. 'Fuck it!' he said, pulling out the cork he had stuffed back into the neck in the feeble pretence that he wasn't going to drink any more. He knew the outcome of this game because he had played it before. Many times. Why did he pretend he could enjoy just one drink when one was never enough? And why did he wake each morning promising to have a wine-free day only to relent mid-afternoon without so much as a struggle? He would finish this bottle and very probably go to the off-licence for a second. He could always find a reason to indulge himself, and once the bottle was open it was game over. He didn't even bother toying with the notion of restraint, these days.

It's not my fault, he told himself, as he glugged the ruby liquid into his wine glass. I need some comfort. I blame Molly. After all, it's been two and half months now, and how on earth am I supposed to cope for all that time without her? It's no wonder I need the odd drink. I've been discarded, and it's the only comfort I can lay my hands on.

For the last few weeks his drinking had been getting just a little worse and he was sure it was because, without Molly, he was unravelling. She was his best friend, his soulmate. She had abandoned him to go cavorting around the country in some dreadful show and his increasing intake of alcohol was the consequence. Usually he and Molly spoke at least twice a day and met up almost as often. When she was between jobs they practically lived together, spending hours in cafés, endlessly chatting, always able to amuse each other and never bored in each other's company. Without her, he was lonely. It was as simple as that.

He looked at his watch. Molly was going to call him as soon as she had settled into her digs in Northampton. It was her custom to ring him during the afternoon that she settled into a new place so that they could have a giggle over the latest hole she was staying in – another of the little pleasures they shared. But if she guessed he'd been drinking, he knew what would happen. Disapproval would creep into her voice, and she'd very often cut the conversation short, as if there was no point in talking to him in his inebriated state, and he would be left feeling more deprived than ever.

Hopefully, she'd phone soon. He looked again at the glass of wine in his hand, luscious and inviting. He was dying to sip and savour it, roll it over his tongue and swallow it. He could just about hold himself together on three glasses of wine, as long as he enunciated clearly and didn't start rambling. Four glasses and he was liable to start going on about the BBC, the Post Office, the DSS, British Gas or any other organisation that drink seemed to transform into the enemy *du jour*. Both he and Molly knew very well that if he started ranting, he was most definitely pissed. If she didn't call soon there would be no point in answering the phone.

The third glass of Sicilian red was risky, therefore. He was still sober enough for lucid self-recrimination, not drunk enough to be lost and pain-free. It was the tipping point.

With the glass in hand, he wandered into the lounge and sat looking out of the window across the railway tracks towards Camden High Street.

Simon had met Molly on their first day at Goldsmiths College in London when they were both freshers, starting out on their university lives. The welcome meeting had just begun in the college theatre and Simon was sitting in the back row, listening intently to the head of the English department, who was explaining how they were all on the threshold of an exciting new future. The door behind him flew open and a rather flustered Molly crashed through it. 'Sorry I'm late!' she announced, in a breathless Liverpudlian twang. 'I had the wrong room. I've been sat with a load of geeks in Geography!'

Simon stared at her. Immediately she turned her head and saw him. She gave him a grin and headed straight for the empty seat next to him, plonking herself down without ceremony. 'Have you got a tissue, mate?' she asked, in a loud whisper. 'I'm sweatin' like a bloody 'orse 'ere. I've just run the one-minute mile in these.' She showed him the big stacked heels on her boots.

'Not easy,' Simon agreed.

'You can say that again.' Molly rifled through her bag and pulled out her information pack. 'Now – what have I missed?'

'Quiet, please, at the back!' called the head of English crossly. Simon and Molly exchanged looks and snorted quietly.

They were friends from that moment on. It was only natural that they should go straight from the welcome session to the cafeteria where, over what claimed to be chilli con carne, they filled in their course-option forms identically, thus ensuring they'd be attending all the same seminars.

'Shall we opt for Dickens or Sylvia Plath?' Simon asked, wrinkling his nose and chewing the end of his Biro.

'Sylvia Plath. No contest. I can't be doing with Dickens – all them Mr Fartpants and Mr Chuzzlepricks. Drives me insane. Plath is much easier, just bumble-bees and bell jars. Then she had the good sense to top herself. Didn't go on and on and on, like Charlie boy.'

'No contest, then,' Simon agreed. 'What's next?'

'Medieval poetry or the complete works of Piers Morgan?'

'Medieval poetry,' they said simultaneously.

She's fabulous! Simon thought. He was already falling in love with her, if in a strictly platonic way, and that was a very novel experience indeed. He had never mixed with girls much, as his boarding school had been all boys and his life afterwards, in the years before he'd decided to come to university, had been decidedly male-centric. He'd thought that was the way he liked it, but there was something about Molly's extraordinary energy and her throbbing vibrancy that drew him to her. She was larger than life, a big girl with fabulous cheekbones and a cascade of dark blonde curly hair piled on top of her head and trailing halfway down her back. She wore men's shirts and jackets but always with a chunk of impossibly large diamanté on the lapel and bold, punky makeup. Simon, who was tall and willowy and rather delicate, complemented her look, and they were soon inseparable, always together in the refectory or the college bar, laughing, whispering about something or clinking their glasses to toast their brilliant futures.

They were rather disdainful of their fellow students, whom they perceived to be over-studious and boring, at least in comparison to themselves. They were the arbiters of style in their world, and gossiped indiscreetly about those around them, creating witty but disparaging nicknames for all and sundry, 'Anorak girl', 'Psoriasis Boy' and 'Hunky Hughes' being just a handful of examples. They gave each other knowing looks and spoke in coded catchphrases. They were far too caught up in their own fabulousness to bother much with course work or writing tedious essays.

Apart from their looks, behaviour and exclusivity, something else that drew everyone's attention to them – whether they were interested or not – was Molly's habit of letting out screeching, ear-piercing soprano notes anywhere and everywhere she went. Simon thought it was hilarious. Sitting in the bar or walking down the corridor she would, without warning, launch into an aria or an obscure line from one opera or another, culminating in a glass-shattering top C that would stop all conversation, all movement around her. Once delivered, she would give a grand wave in all directions and carry on with what she had been saying or doing before this impressive musical interlude. Simon thought she was amazing and wonderfully talented, even if some of the other students found Molly's habit a little less enchanting than Simon did. Some even took to wailing like fighting cats when they saw her. But Simon loved attention of all kinds, even the negative variety, so he and Molly saw it as further evidence of how special they were.

The bubble they had created for themselves was impenetrable by others, a two-person tent made from the Emperor's new clothes, with no zip, no buttons, no means of removal. They were utterly dependent on each other, their emotional well-being knitted fast together. Simon loved this dangerous new co-existence, and he was thrilled and excited by Molly.

The only thing that might have come between them was men. But in that first year at university, Molly was recovering from a broken heart and still pined for her lost love. Many were the evenings that they opened up the vodka and Molly got nostalgic, telling Simon over and over again about Jezza and how much she loved him. Usually she'd end up weeping in an alcohol-fuelled crying jag, wondering why Jezza didn't love her any more.

'Because he's a fool, that's why. You're an extraordinary creature, a tropical flower among the weeds of womankind. He couldn't handle that. Most men, sooner or later, want to be in charge. They want their woman at home scrubbing the doorstep and making their dinner. You were never going to do that.'

'No, I bloody wasn't!'

'Well, there you are, then. You were too much for him to handle. Besides, you have me now,' Simon would say, hugging her and stroking her unruly curls. 'You don't need men any more.'

'It's not quite the same, though, is it?' Molly would sniff. 'I have needs, you know, and you can't pretend you can do anything about those, can you?'

'No,' Simon said honestly. 'I can't. But I do love you, Molly. You can get a shag from anyone, but you'll only get true love from me.'

Then Molly would get all emotional and cry and say she loved him too, and no man would ever come between them.

No man ever had, either. Yes, Molly had fallen in love plenty of times, once she'd managed to get over Jezza, and when she did, it would cause an irritating hiatus in their ongoing devotion to each other, but in the end she always came back to him. The men in Simon's life never seemed to last much longer than a few hours, so there was no problem from that side of things. It was Molly and Simon, together for ever.

Simon took another large slurp of his wine. Of course he and Molly were going through a rough patch at the moment – another reason for the medicinal administration of Sicilian red. It was all because of the dreary builder, Molly's latest love interest and rival for his attention. It was a bore, that was all, having to think about it, talk about it and deal with it – Daniel this, Daniel that, Daniel all bloody day long. Simon really couldn't be doing with the way Molly threw herself into her relationships. He dreaded hearing the catch in her voice when she announced there was a new, perfect man in her life because he knew what it meant: the sparkling eyes, the dreamy expressions, and the endless breathless gush. She couldn't just date someone once a week, take it slowly and let things develop. No, she always had to be devoured by the new lover, investing all her emotional well-being in a romantic ideal that, sooner or later, turned sour. And she never seemed to learn her lesson. Why, within a month of meeting this Daniel she had given up the lease on her own flat and moved in with him! Just like that, if you please. It was all too cosy and too sudden. There weren't enough hours in the day for Molly to devote to Simon *and* her latest beau, and it was always the squeeze who got her attention. It was unfair, Simon thought. They had vowed to go on life's journey together and, in his frequently intoxicated opinion, Molly was breaking her promise. Simon's love for Molly was eternal, but it was far from unconditional. She must, at the very least, be available to him.

Simon knew he was having a bitter and twisted moment. Perhaps he was already a little drunker than he'd realised. But he couldn't help it – he felt deeply neglected.

He was still staring out of the window, now feeling rather cross, when the telephone interrupted him. He put the almost empty wine glass down on the table and took a deep breath. Yes, he decided, he was sober enough to speak. He picked up the receiver.

'Hiya, chuck!' came Molly's familiar greeting. 'How's tricks?'

'Oh. Yes, hello there.'

'You all right?' Molly asked. There was a pause and then she said, 'You on the sauce?'

'No, no. I was deep in thought, that's all. How's Northampton?'

'I think it's all right, actually. My landlady's German, claims to have been a huge star in her day. All silk dressing-gowns and heady perfume. Very *Sunset Boulevard*. You'd love her. Her name's Lilia – bright orange hair and heavy makeup. Traditional bungalow affair: knick-knacks everywhere, photos of the good old days, lots of pink, lots of lace. My room's okay – clean and no used condoms or filthy knickers under the bed like the last time, so that's a plus. Masses of doilies and china ladies but that's all right, I don't mind that. Sheets and blankets on the bed, not a duvet, and gold-brocade scatter cushions. She's got a huge slavering Hound of the Baskervilles called Heathcliff, and a sad old husband who's had a stroke and can't move or talk. Sits like a statue in the corner of the room, poor love. It's ever so sad, Si. I haven't had the full story yet, but I intend to – the place is dripping with posters and photos. I bet she's had a fascinating life.'

'Fabulous,' Simon said slowly, concentrating on not slurring. 'You must investigate fully.'

'Oh, I will, God love her.'

'Are you ever coming home?'

'Last week now, then I'm on my way. I can't wait. Have you missed me?'

'I feel like a cheese sandwich without the pickle. I'm inconsolable. I may not last until the weekend.'

'I miss you too, something shocking. Whenever I go away, you get yourself into trouble. Talking of which, have you heard from your married man?'

'No,' said Simon, dismissively. 'Nor do I expect to.' This was not a subject he wanted to talk about, as he was rather embarrassed by his weeping and wailing of a few nights ago when Molly had called from Stevenage. Drunk as a skunk, he'd howled down the phone, said he couldn't live without Justin, that he was going to do something silly – all the usual histrionics Molly had heard many times before. Suddenly he felt a little hypocritical over the things he'd been thinking about Molly and her love life: if he was honest, he had to admit that she had put up with her fair share of listening to the same old nonsense from him, just on a slightly different theme. 'I don't particularly care if I never hear from him again, actually.'

'I see. You've changed your tune a bit. I thought you were about to get the noose out if he didn't answer your text.'

'No. It has no future. Justin has a wife and child. There's nothing I can do about that.'

'Well, the other night you were all for presenting yourself on their doorstep, intent on breaking up a happy home.'

'I thought better of it,' said Simon, pained at the memory of his dramatic, drink-induced threats.

'I'm glad to hear it.' Molly sounded relieved. 'I was a bit worried you were going to make an arse of yourself.'

'I don't actually know where he lives, so there was little chance of that happening.'

'Take my advice, hon, and give Justin a miss, eh? That way madness lies.' She was being gentle with him now, not pleading but softly cajoling. Perhaps she was aware that he'd had something to drink, but the door of sobriety was still ajar and it seemed that she wanted to get her foot through it while the going was good.

'Hmm,' Simon muttered.

'Time to move on. Agreed?'

'I thought he was the One . . .' Simon trailed off and sighed heavily. He could feel himself getting maudlin. Justin had been divine, a chartered accountant with a mean streak and well-cut suits that set off his broad shoulders. He'd talked scornfully about gays, leered at big-breasted women and said all poufs revolted him, but he didn't mind Simon sinking to his knees to administer the relief his huge erection so clearly needed.

'The One?' said Molly, incredulously. 'Come on, Si, I don't want to be mean but let's talk facts, shall we? If there is a "One" I think it's highly unlikely that you'll meet him at two o'clock in the morning behind a clump of trees on Clapham Common, chuck. And if you do, it might be for the best if he wasn't busy, in his spare time, being a loving husband and father. I'm not Claire Rayner, but your ideal partner may well turn out to be gay.'

'I don't *like* gay men!'

'Oh, Jesus, here we go.' Molly sounded exasperated.

They'd been through all this before. Molly had tried to understand, she really had, but he knew she was still mystified by his preference for straight men – even if the very fact that they were willing to have sex with him might indicate that they were not really of that persuasion at all. His proclivity had been chewed over as a curiosity and pondered as a tragedy many, many times over the years. No solutions had so far presented themselves.

'You know what I'm like, Molly. I can only sleep with a man under specific circumstances. If he's straight!' Simon said helplessly.

'This is madness, Simon!' Molly raised her voice. 'You've got to stop this or you'll lead a life of never-ending misery and frustration. I love you, and all I want is for you to be happy.'

Simon paused for a moment, then hung up.

Chapter Three

Being an only child often implies that one is cherished, if not a little spoilt, but this wasn't true in Simon's case. His parents had married late in life, and both were in their early forties when he was born. He had wriggled into their lives either before they were ready or after it was too late. Whichever way you looked at it, things were not quite right. He got the distinct impression that his mother and father had stopped at one child because their first experience of parenthood was so bewilderingly disappointing. They had never seemed much interested in him or in anything he had to say. Tired smiles greeted his childish questions, and their answers were always designed to terminate any further line of questioning. 'Run away and play, Simon,' had been the refrain of his childhood. He bored them, he realised, and the best thing he could do to please them was go to his room and amuse himself.

His parents were so polite and indifferent that he felt like an unwanted guest in his own home. It had been no surprise when he was sent to boarding school at the age of seven – there was a distinct air of relief in the house in the days leading up to his departure. But even when he arrived home for the holidays, it was to resentful looks, pained expressions and whispered asides. By the time he was a teenager, it was like coming to visit two elderly strangers with whom he had almost nothing in common. They peered at him and feigned interest in his future, often suggesting he go back-packing.

Damaged as he was by such a loveless upbringing, Simon was intelligent enough to feel hard-done-by. Inevitably he looked for attention elsewhere. He had been sent to a boys' prep school and later to a Catholic public school deep in the country. In the classroom, and more significantly, the dormitory, he sought and found the popularity that was missing at home. His cruel but uncannily accurate impersonations of the teachers had his classmates enthralled and, encouraged by their giggles, he found ever more outrageous expressions of his subversive, ultimately angry personality.

His attention-seeking continued after lights out, and was not unsuccessful. Word of his skill and compliance in the arena of darkness travelled to the bigger boys and soon Simon's nights were most eventful. Although sleep was a tedious necessity, it became clear that there weren't enough hours in the night. To satisfy all the demands upon his services, Simon was soon keeping appointments in the afternoons as well. When the school gardener sought to confirm the saucy rumours, it was just a matter of time before Simon was expelled. The greenhouse had not been a wise choice of venue.

Back home, his parents were able to add reproach and disdain to their gallery of expressions. Even false smiles were now a thing of the past. Simon could do nothing right. But with the good grounding of an expensive education, he sailed through his A levels at the local college. The morning his results arrived, and his parents looked at him with their usual blank-eyed indifference as he announced his three A grades, he packed his bags for London, not caring where he went, simply keen for a great adventure. After a couple of days at King's Cross station, he met some other desperadoes and moved into a surprisingly civilised squat in Waterloo. Soon he had his first job, as an usher at the Old Vic theatre, selling programmes and ice creams from a tray in the interval. The uniform was bottle green and Simon decided he looked particularly dashing in it. It was not taxing work but he enjoyed it.

He sent his parents a postcard with his new address, but didn't phone home and heard nothing from them. His new left-wing friends soon radicalised him, and he became a fully paid-up member of the Socialist Workers' Revolutionary Party, forever going on protest marches and to sit-ins. He had his eyebrow pierced and wore his hair so short it was only one step away from a shaved head. Such a look, with his lean limbs and soulful, bright blue eyes, made him a popular addition to London's gay scene. In fact, it was his eyes that people always remembered. They could sparkle across a crowded dance-floor and lure prospective lovers into his orbit. Once there, and given their full, heavenly, mesmerising voltage, any boy or man was his for the taking, seduced by the sadness that swam in their depths. He would take them home, have sex with them and turf them out in the morning. More often than not, they kept coming back. Something about Simon touched them, made them return for another look into his soul. Even hardened gays, who'd had all the tenderness fisted out of them, would declare themselves awash with love – who'd have thought it after all these years? – and they would try to nurture similar feelings in Simon, who was having none of it. He never seemed to fall in love with anyone, no matter how much they aroused or amused him. He didn't much mind – it was just the way he was made.

This was a learning period for Simon. He discovered his own powers and also his own desires. These included gay sex but not, rather confusingly, gay men. He was bemused by this knowledge for some considerable time and chewed it over as if it were a particularly difficult clue in a cryptic crossword, pondering several solutions. Could he possibly be a woman trapped in a man's body? Was sexual realignment the answer? This he dismissed instantly. He was perfectly happy with what God had given him, and therefore definitely not in the wrong body. Even if surgery and hormones were going to make him attractive to 'real' men, it was too high a price to pay.

Another option might be a life of chastity. Simon surprised himself by thinking long and hard about this. Some of the Benedictine monks who had taught him at boarding school had seemed genuinely serene and holy, and he would dearly have liked to escape from the eternal discontent that followed him around like a lost puppy, and to lose the discontent in his eyes that everyone commented on. Could it be transformed into piety and compassion for God's suffering on the cross? It would be a long and unlikely journey from atheist revolutionary to the monastery, though. He knew deep down that he didn't have a vocation for a spiritual life. It wouldn't ring true.

The final and equally unsatisfactory option was to confine his interests to straight-acting gay men. There were plenty of those around and they were, or so they liked to think, barely indistinguishable from their straight counterparts. Certain bars and clubs in London were designed especially for them, done up like a construction site with lots of corrugated iron and empty beer barrels. These men – or MEN, as they no doubt thought of themselves – certainly looked the part, favouring biker jackets and Dr Marten boots. They stood around in alcoves staring into the distance, glowering at all and sundry. If he followed them into the darker recesses at the back of the club, he could have quick, rough sex with them and no questions asked. It was almost like the real thing – but not quite. Simon saw straight through the posturing of these men. They were just silly, self-deluded queens and they failed to satisfy him on any level.

The solution to this delicate conundrum came in the shape of a lorry driver.

Simon had taken on day work as a parcel-delivery man for a few months, and one afternoon he had stopped at Clacket Lane service station on the M25 to stretch his legs. He wandered aimlessly along the grassy verge until he found himself in the section reserved for articulated lorries. A huge black truck with several pictures of topless women stuck to the windscreen loomed before him. As Simon approached, the driver flashed his lights three times and leant out of his window. He felt a flutter of excitement in his stomach: here was a real man, a lorry driver wearing a greasy T-shirt and three days' stubble! The driver indicated that Simon should hop in. Once inside he drew some grubby curtains across the windscreen and, without a word, climbed between the seats on to a small mattress area behind. By the time Simon had negotiated his way through to him, the driver had unbuckled his belt, undone his flies, and presented Simon with a very impressive cargo indeed. The sex was quick and unceremonious and fulfilled all of Simon's wildest fantasies.

The knowledge that straight men were often not as straight as they seemed liberated him and set him on a heady voyage of discovery, one that sometimes resulted in the odd black eye but more often in delightful, exquisite encounters with men whose wedding rings only added to their attraction.

Simon's enjoyable adventures as a sexual rover were rudely interrupted when he received a letter from his father telling him some sad news. His mother was very sick with cancer. 'It's at an advanced stage, I'm afraid, and the doctors are not at all hopeful. Do you think you could come and see us?' he suggested.

Simon sighed at the inconvenience, but thought, upon reflection, that he ought to pop home.

A small stone of misery had resided somewhere inside Simon's chest cavity for as long as he could remember. It was so real and permanent he felt sure it was of tangible, solid form. It would still be there, indestructible, after his cremation, nestling among the silken ashes like a Fabergé egg. At a loss to explain its origin, he had a tendency to graft reasons onto his melancholy. When, as a boy, he was told the story of Christ's death for our sins, he put his misery down to the collective misery of mankind. And when the family cat died suddenly, he wept for weeks, not out of genuine grief for the bad-tempered feline but because he felt like crying, and here was a bona-fide reason to do so. Earthquakes reported in the news, abducted children or even the sad state of the nation's economy were also declared causes for Simon's all too apparent unhappiness.

When Simon, living in the squat with his new anarchist friends, received the letter telling him his mother had cancer, the stone of misery began to throb, invigorated by the news and its potential. He had no difficulty in sitting by his mother's bed every day for three weeks, blowing his nose and wiping the tears from his eyes.

'He's heartbroken, poor boy,' said the nurses to each other. 'He must love his mother to bits. Look at the state of him.'

Simon wasn't exactly indulging himself but he knew, deep down, that this crying and carrying on was little to do with his dying mother. He felt it anyway, always had, and now it was being fed, thriving like the cancer.

When his mother eventually died – her last words to him were 'Canada seems nice' – Simon stayed with his father for a week and was the star turn at the funeral, breaking down as he read a Christina Rossetti poem, shaking hands and passing around sandwiches with red eyes at the house afterwards.

'Look after each other,' said the relatives, as they filed out later. 'It's just the two of you now.'

The next day, while his father sat in the lounge drinking a bottle of whisky, Simon put his mother's clothes into bin-liners and took them to the local charity shop. When he got home, the whisky bottle was empty.

'I'm going to sell the house and move to a bungalow in Dorset,' said his father, as if he was announcing that he planned to take an overdose of paracetamol.

'Okay,' Simon said cheerily. 'I'm going back home to London tomorrow. Keep in touch.' And he left the next day, certain that he would never see his father again.

Simon returned to the squat, his day job delivering parcels and his nights in the soft, dark corridors of the theatre, armed with ice creams and ready change. One day he was driving through New Cross when he saw a handsome denim-clad youth with a rucksack flung over his shoulder entering an old Victorian public lavatory. On impulse, he parked his van and followed him. Inside it was empty, apart from the youth who, as Simon entered, was just zipping up his flies and moving from the urinal to the sink to wash his big rugby-player's hands.

Damn. I'm too late, Simon thought, as he took his place at the now-vacated trough. He stood there, nevertheless, looking encouragingly towards the boy, who was wiping his hands dry on a paper towel. He was aware of Simon's intense stare, and took his time, carefully drying between each finger. Just before he left, he turned and gave a knowing smile.

Disappointment is all part of the game for a gay man on the cruise. But for Simon, the sad sight of seeing such a beauty slip through his fingers amounted to heartache. The pain spread down his arms and up his neck until an audible sob caught in his throat. If only he'd got there quicker he might have been lucky. The boy had appeared to know what he was after and had seemed almost amused. Who was he? Should he follow him? Should he wait to see if the boy came back? All these thoughts made Simon's heart beat faster. He stood there, waiting, hoping for the sound of footsteps, but hearing only the drone of traffic from New Cross Road.

That night as he lay on his mattress in the squat, fantasising obsessively about the one that had got away, he remembered something. On the back of the boy's rucksack there had been a label. Simon closed his eyes and concentrated. Yes. He could see it clearly now. It read 'Goldsmiths College'.

By the next morning he had decided his future. He drove to Goldsmiths and picked up an application form. With his first-class A level results and agreeable personality, he would surely be offered a place there. He chose English literature as his subject, a kind of tribute to his mother, who had enjoyed a good read.

And then he met Molly.

As soon as Simon and Molly's lives intersected, the value of true friendship was suddenly revealed to him. It was a revelation. His schoolmates had always bored him, however much they sought his company, and he'd had neither the desire nor the opportunity to get to know girls before, but Molly had a presence and allure that was both fun and decidedly feminine. He was somewhat in awe for the first time in his life, feeling that, in some obscure way, he had met his match. She was funny and theatrical and could make a simple walk down the corridor into a memorable experience. Molly, in turn, seemed to be drawn to his dangerous disregard for other people's opinions and his brooding, unpredictable personality. They spent hours talking, mostly about themselves.

It was a few weeks after they had first met at uni, and the pair of them were walking through Greenwich Park on a chilly autumn afternoon, just as darkness was beginning to fall.

'What makes you tick?' asked Molly.

'Misery,' said Simon, without hesitation. 'It's my natural state.'

Molly looked at him curiously. 'Really? You don't seem so miserable to me.'

'That's because I'm happy at the moment, comparatively. Fate led me here, you see, to be your friend. Thank goodness for lust.'

'Eh?' said Molly, puzzled.

Simon told her about the denim-clad youth with his fateful rucksack and the encounter in the lavatory. 'Those few seconds in a public toilet where nothing much happened but a smile had far-reaching consequences. But for that moment I would not be at university and I would not have met you,' he finished solemnly.

'Well,' Molly said. 'Praise be for your thriving hormones.'

'I think the story rather vindicates my entire lifestyle,' said Simon, grandly.

'I'd have been lost without you here,' said Molly. 'And the boy with the rucksack? Have you seen him again?'

'Not a sniff. How annoying is that?'

'Look on the bright side. It gives you something to be miserable about.'

'True. Otherwise I'd have to go looking for someone else to moon over. I need a hit of misery every morning the moment I wake up or I can't function. It's like snuff to me. Do you think there's something wrong with me? It's not normal, is it?'

'What's normal?' asked Molly, questioning the question. 'I think all intense feelings should be regarded as precious.'

How clever of Molly, thought Simon, to put a positive spin on even the darkest of thoughts.

Already there was an understanding and acceptance between them that neither had ever felt before. During the first few weeks they had been busy laughing and impressing each other with their wit and style. Now, having established that they were on the same wavelength, brothers and sisters in arms, they trusted each other to know their innermost secrets and fears. Molly had mentioned that she'd spent her childhood in a children's home, but Simon hadn't pressed his new friend for more information. 'What was it like?' he asked now. 'Growing up in a home with no family?'

Molly stared out over the green parkland and thought. Then she spoke – matter-of-factly and without a hint of tragedy. 'Not as bad as it sounds. I had a happy childhood, I'd say. They did their best. I was fed and clothed and I had loads of friends. It was all I ever knew. There was no abuse, if that's what you were wondering. It was all very proper. Sometimes you'd get close to the workers there but they'd have to back off. They weren't really allowed to be properly tactile. Against the rules. I was always a needy child. As if that's a bad thing at six years of age.'

'Why weren't you adopted?' asked Simon.

'They did try, but I had this idea in my mind that my mother would come back for me one day. Every few months, prospective parents would come and leer at me as if I was a leg of lamb in the butcher's window, but I was having none of it. I did my best to put them off. I pulled ugly faces, swore like a trooper, developed sudden bouts of incontinence. I even bit one woman who kept stroking my hair as if I was a doll. But some folks were so desperate they still wanted me. They'd have taken home a rabid ferret. When the social workers asked me if I'd like to go and live with a couple in their posh gaff in Chester, where they could be my new mummy and daddy, I said, "No," most emphatically.'

'They didn't make you?'

'They couldn't. I'd have run away. I spent a few weeks with foster-parents occasionally, but I saw to it that I was sent back to the home. To me, those foster-homes were a holiday, nothing permanent.'

'I longed to be adopted,' said Simon, imagining the glamour of auditioning new parents, perusing their bank statements and asking if they had a swimming-pool.

'I didn't. I was staying put in case my mother wanted me.'

'And did she?'

Molly's voice went very low and quiet. 'No, as it happens.'

'Do you know who she was?' asked Simon, gently.

'I remember her,' said Molly, with the first echo of sadness in her voice. 'People thought I wouldn't because I was so young when I went into care, but my memories from before then are a lot more vivid than people assume. When you're five, you take in a great deal. She was called Susan, and she had brown hair. She cried a lot. Screamed when they took me away. I can still hear her howling my name as they bundled me down the stairs and into a car. Two policewomen were holding her back, gripping her wrists.'

'Why, though? Why did they take you from her?'

'That I don't know. I was hungry all the time. I remember that. She obviously wasn't coping. A five-year-old's memory, vivid as it is, doesn't really deal in facts, just feelings and emotions. I don't know if it was drugs or what. I was at risk, that was all the authorities needed to know, so they took me away.'

They sat on a bench high on Greenwich Hill, looking down at the elegant white pillars of the old Royal Naval College.

'And your father?' asked Simon, his ears freezing in the frosty air.

'That's a complete blank,' said Molly. 'He doesn't feature at all in my memory. There's a whole scenario that I made up when I was about thirteen to comfort myself. I decided that my mother worked in a flower shop and he was a married man who came in every Friday on his way home from work to buy roses for his wife. They fell in love and began an illicit affair, and she got pregnant with me but didn't tell him. To stop his wife suspecting, he still came in every Friday for her roses, and my mother, in her jealous misery, would press her hands into the thorns and smear the stems with her blood. Because there were other people in the shop they had to remain civil and polite, but they gave each other sad, passionate looks as she rang the till and handed him his change. Then he left the shop and, because he was crying, stepped into the road, right under the wheels of a bus.'

'How terribly tragic!' exclaimed Simon.

'Yes, it was,' agreed Molly. 'Then, of course, I was born. Just imagine. It was 1978. Susan was an unmarried, not to say broken-hearted mother, struggling to cope with her grief, and it all became too much for her.'

'Did she take to drink?' asked Simon, caught up in the drama of the story.

'Worse than that. Drugs.'

'No!' said Simon, horrified.

'I'm afraid so.'

'It was the only way to numb the pain, I expect,' concluded Simon.

'That's what I told myself,' said Molly, turning her bright eyes on her new friend. Her tone changed to plain and brutal. 'On the other hand she might have been a common prostitute and my father some sweaty car mechanic.'

'I think it was quite different. Your father was a visiting Hollywood star with a penchant for sordid sex in a lay-by,' said Simon, countering her dejection with some flighty energy. 'After a hard day's filming at Pinewood your soon-to-be father indulged himself with a spot of kerb crawling . . . He was stunned by your mother's beauty and paid an extra fiver to take his pleasure without the protection of a condom. Stardom's in your genes!'

Molly laughed. 'So my mum *was* a prostitute, not a flower-seller?'

'No,' Simon said hastily. 'She was a beautiful girl down on her luck, who couldn't resist the power of your father's fame and sex appeal.'

'Well, that would never happen.'

'Why not? It's just as likely as your story. Why shouldn't it?'

Molly looked thoughtful, then beamed at him. 'You're right. Thank you, Si. Somehow you've just made the world a better place for me to live in.'

'It's a great pleasure,' said Simon, taking Molly's gloved hand and giving it a squeeze. 'Any time you're feeling sad about the world just come and see me. I'll confirm your worst fears.'

'You can turn sweaty car mechanics into film stars,' said Molly.

'It's a gift,' agreed Simon, with a shrug.

Chapter Four

'That one,' said Simon.

'With the broken nose? Surely not.'

'Yes. Him. I simply have to have him.'

Simon and Molly were drinking in the student-union bar, settled in a corner seat where they could study everyone coming and going. It was eight o'clock in the evening and they had been there since they'd decided not to bother with a lecture on the metaphysical poets that had been scheduled to start at three. After a couple of glasses of wine, Molly had felt rather squiffy and switched to water, but Simon was downing the half-price cider like there was no tomorrow. As they had become closer, it had dawned on Molly that Simon's drinking was excessive. They went to the pub most days between lectures and he could easily manage two pints of lager to her modest half. In the evenings, if he wasn't getting pissed in the student bar, he was off to Soho, doing much the same thing. His drinking seemed inextricably linked with his reckless pursuit of unlikely sexual conquests. Now he was staring at the bar, where some members of the college rugby team were having a post-training drink. He was transfixed by one particularly rugged individual.

'I think he's too rough,' said Molly, a note of caution in her voice. 'He looks as if he'd beat you to a pulp as soon as look at you.'

'Mmm . . .' said Simon, shuddering with pleasure at the thought. 'Now you're talking.'

'You'll end up like Joe Orton if you're not careful.'

'It wasn't rough trade who took a hammer to him, was it? Look. He's having another bottle of beer.'

'He just burped!'

Simon sighed. 'He gets better.'

'Well, he's doing nothing for me.'

'Go and talk to him. Find out his name for me.'

'I'm not procuring for you! Ask him yourself. But you're barking up the wrong tree, honey. In fact you're in the wrong bloody forest. Those blokes are red-blooded heterosexuals to a man – look at them!'

'The boundaries of male desire are not so easily categorised. The fact that he's just been pumping iron or laying into a punch-bag or whatever they do in the gym means testosterone is pumping around his gorgeous body. He's also halfway through his third bottle of Becks so his judgement is affected.'

'He'll need more than a couple of jars to mistake you for a page-three girl, Simon.'

Simon stared at her. 'Believe me, I know. Everything will work out very nicely. I'm going to the bar. Are you ready for another exciting glass of fizzy water?'

'Yes, please. Try and show some restraint. He'll swing for you if you proposition him. I don't want to spend the rest of the evening escorting you to A and E.'

Simon stood up, cleared his throat and sauntered his way to

the bar, a foxy glint in his eye. Molly watched her friend, drunk and reckless, as he stalked his prey. The rugby player was sitting on a bar stool, his chunky thighs spread wide. Simon slipped in beside him, waving his five-pound note at the barman while the boy, oblivious, carried on laughing and joking with his friends. Molly watched as Simon placed his order, then tapped his quarry's shoulder. He half turned to Simon, then swivelled round to face him and they shook hands. A friendly, animated conversation took place. The barman then delivered Simon's cider and Simon clearly offered his new friend a drink, which was accepted and a further order placed. Then Simon turned and nodded towards Molly. The rugby player looked over. She gave a weak wave. Simon must then have said something very funny indeed as the boy let out a loud, hard laugh, before giving Simon a slap on the shoulder. She saw him blink slowly at this, savouring the touch as if he were a lame man touched by the Messiah.

Molly smiled to herself. Despite her reservations, which were not moral in any way – rather, old-fashioned concern for Simon's physical well-being – it was hard not to get involved in the excitement. There was never a dull moment with Simon, and she had a ringside seat. To anyone else watching, they were just two lads having a drink at the bar, but she had privileged information. She knew of Simon's carnal desires, his determination to seduce and devour the poor broken-nosed innocent. Her friend was completely focused, she could see. It wasn't a whim or a bet, this slow, calculated entrapment. It was clearly of great importance to Simon. The longer the build-up, the greater the prize.

Her own emotional needs were quite different. Endless one-night stands had no appeal for her. She craved the tenderness of real lovemaking, with the emphasis on 'love'. She wanted a partnership: the knowledge that he would be there tomorrow, that he cared for her and would look out for her. The fireworks of sex and lust were just part of the package.

Simon was now talking earnestly to the boy and holding up one finger. His companion nodded in agreement and called to the barman, as Simon tore himself away and hurried over to Molly. He spoke quietly and urgently in her ear, like a double agent imparting vital information: 'Nick King. Second year geography. Hooker. We're going back to his to smoke a spliff.'

'Oh. Are we?'

'Me and him. You've got an essay to write.'

'No, I haven't. Why can't I come too?'

'Because I told him you have herpes.'

'You what?' Molly said, outraged.

'Only joking. But, darling, you do understand, don't you? I sense fire in his loins. The gods are smiling on me.'

'I feel as if I'm watching some poor lamb go to the slaughter.'

'He smells of soap, chewing-gum and lager. A potent combination, I'm sure you'll agree.'

'How do you think he's going to feel in the morning?'

'Sore, hopefully.'

With that, Simon kissed her goodnight, pulled her to her feet and propelled her in the direction of the door.

'Bye-bye, baby!' she sang, as she left the bar.

Simon didn't turn up for the morning lecture. He was waiting for her in the refectory afterwards, though, and looked disgustingly hung-over.

'I hope it was worth it,' said Molly, tutting, as she looked him up and down.

'Let's go to the pub,' was Simon's reply.

'You've got the same clothes on as yesterday.'

'I may never wash again. The Rosemary Branch is calling me.'

Molly laughed and stood up. 'Come on, then, you old lush. Let's go and get tanked up once again.'

But a few drinks later, although Simon was drunk and his mood euphoric, he still wouldn't spill any beans about the presumed success of the previous night with Nick.

'So. How was he?' Molly asked.

'I never kiss and tell,' said Simon.

'Ah! So you kissed him!' declared Molly.

'Darling, I didn't go back to a hall of residence in Catford to look at his etchings. My lips are sealed, though.'

Try as she might, Molly could get no more details from him.

'All too sordid for your unaccustomed ears, I'm afraid,' Simon would say.

Occasionally Molly would be out with Simon and, if the mood took him, he would fixate on a random man in a crowd. It could happen in a nightclub, a crowded train or even a supermarket queue. A predatory look came into his eyes and she only had to follow his gaze to see a handsome off-duty soldier, unmistakeable with his regulation army haircut and well-ironed civvies, or a gum-chewing East End hoodie. Anything might happen in the next few moments. It was not unknown for Simon to abandon her alto-gether. More often than not he would go off for a few minutes and return sniffing indifferently, as if he was a market shopper and the produce well below expectations. 'Now, where were we?' he'd ask.

Simon's view of Molly's more conventional approach to romance was decidedly dismissive. Her first boyfriend, Jezza, had also been an inmate at the care home in Liverpool. They had been inseparable and moved into a flat together when she was sixteen, she had told him, but Simon stifled a yawn. 'How nice for you,' he said. 'Did you curl up together on the sofa to watch TV and eat food covered with breadcrumbs?'

'Well, yes, we did, actually,' replied Molly, rather chagrined that such a significant relationship in her life was clearly failing to hold Simon's interest.

'I thought as much. And did you sleep under a cheap Paisley duvet cover and acquire a kitten by any chance?'

'You're awful and I don't know why I like you. We had a canary.'

'You were nesting. Making the home you never had. Feeling grown-up.'

'I loved Jezza, Simon. Why must you belittle that?'

'I guess convention nauseates me.'

'It's your love life that's nauseating to most right-thinking people!'

'Let's not call it a love life, Molls. A series of unlikely fleeting triumphs, yes, but I have no dealings with love.'

'I do.'

'I know that.'

'I loved that boy. I'd have done anything for him.'

'Aw. I'm filling up. So where is he now?'

'I was at sixth-form college, studying hard for my A levels. He robbed an off-licence with some mates of his. He got five years.'

'So you'd do anything for him except wait?'

'I would have waited, but he told me not to.'

'So much for love. What happened to the canary?'

'It flew out of the window.'

'It all worked out quite well, then.'

*

Although they were enjoying themselves hugely at college, Simon and Molly had to face stern reality when it came to their dismal academic performance. Their course work – what little they did of it – was marked with withering scorn by their tutors. Eventually, at the end of the second term, they were called in to see the head of English, who told them that the university was not a holiday camp and unless they concentrated their efforts he saw little point in them continuing. Afterwards they sat in the refectory and tried unsuccessfully to jolly each other along.

'I'm sure Goldsmiths will be very quick to take all the credit once we're rich and famous. That man's a nasty, vindictive old fool,' said Simon.

'They'll be naming the library after us one day, mark my words,' said Molly, less vehemently. She was a little more worried about her future. After all, she had come to university to get a degree so that she could make her own way in the world. Without it, what would she do?

'If he thinks we're wasting our time here maybe he's right. Let's take our talent elsewhere.'

'Really?' Molly was wide-eyed. 'You mean . . . leave?'

Simon shrugged. 'Why not?'

She considered it. She knew that Simon's approach to life was much freer than hers. He'd arrived on a whim and perhaps he would leave on one too. The prospect of university without him was too grim to contemplate for a second.

'Come on, Molly.' Simon's eyes were sparkling. He had sensed adventure, she knew. 'You're fabulous and talented and you don't need an English degree to be a star. And I certainly don't need one. I have other, rarer qualifications. Let's chuck this in. It's been fun, but real life is waiting for us out there. Let's go and get it.'

'But where shall we go?'

'To Hollywood!'

'Hollywood?'

'All right, then, Cricklewood.'

'To the pub, more like!' Molly laughed.

'Come on, then. Are you game?' Simon widened his eyes, daring her to seize the day.

'Yes,' she said decisively. 'I am.'

'Good. Then let us offload. Amen.'

There and then they emptied their bags of anything to do with course work, leaving books and files and pens on the table, and hooted their way out of college for ever. As a parting gesture, they stood on the steps by the main front door and did a dozen Tiller-Girl high kicks. With each one, Molly gave an operatic note full vent. Then they ran out of the gate, glad to be gone, thrilled to be free.

As dramatic and exciting as that moment had been, reality kicked in when they had to move out of their halls of residence and hand back their grants. But they did their best to keep their bubble inflated. Simon contacted some pre-university friends of his who told him of a room going in a squat at Elephant and Castle. He and Molly moved into it together, sleeping top to tail on an old mattress in their sleeping-bags. It was cold and squalid but they kept each other laughing, determined as ever to triumph in the end, reminding each other through chattering teeth that they were special, destined for greatness, sure to succeed.

Nevertheless, the exultation they had felt at abandoning their university education did not last for ever. Life in the Elephant and Castle squat was no fun, and when their fellow squatters got deeply into drugs, it was so boring that they decided to move on. Simon found them another, better place to live, in a large

Victorian mansion in Lorrimore Square, Kennington, where they occupied adjoining rooms on the top floor. It was an established squat, run collectively with weekly house meetings. There was even a cleaning rota and a house kitty for toilet rolls and tea-bags. All in all, it was a very friendly and well-organised community. Nine other people lived in the house and the general atmosphere was one of New Age niceness, and respect for each other and the property they were 'looking after'.

'This is dead nice,' said Molly when they first went to look at it. 'Makes a bit of a change from the dog shit and used needles we're used to.' She'd been becoming a little depressed in their last place, wondering if she'd made a really serious mistake in leaving university. The improvement in their standard of living restored some of her usual cheerfulness. They moved in as soon as they could.

Simon and Molly spent a week splashing the walls with white paint and making novelty tables and chairs out of old orange boxes and bits of hardboard.

'It's all about lighting,' said Molly, when she brought home a small red-painted lamp with a fringed shade. It cast a warm pink glow around her room. Simon opted for a bare blue-tinted lightbulb.

'I guess the time has come to stop talking and get on with it,' said Molly, one evening, as they sat in her room, she with a cup of tea, Simon drinking a can of Special Brew.

'That sounds rather ominous.'

'We've got to do something, though. Don't you agree? We're running out of money for a start.'

'Can't we just be fabulous wherever we are? Or is that too gay?'

'You're all talk and no knickers, you are.'

At least Molly knew what she wanted from life. Singing, as anyone within earshot could testify, was her main interest. But what were Simon's plans exactly? He was undoubtedly clever and perceptive, but how did he intend to apply these talents? His vision of a marvellous life involved no career or particular prosperity. If he was to take a piece of paper and write 'Interests', alcohol and anonymous sex with straight men would have been at the top of his list. 'I suppose I could become a Welsh politician,' he joked, 'or I might be the reincarnation of Truman Capote,' he added, a glimmer of seriousness just detectable in his tone.

When Molly was faced with an empty purse she was far more practical and dynamic. 'Well, I'm getting my glad-rags on tomorrow. I'm taking my sheet music with me into town and I'm going to march confidently into every bar or restaurant that has a piano and ask if they want a singer. Or a waitress. Or a barmaid.'

'If that's my cue to say I'm coming too, forget it.'

'We can't live on fresh air. Or drink it.'

'In that case I shall make my weary way to the DSS and sign on.'

Molly found work almost immediately as a singing waitress at Joe Allen's in Exeter Street, a restaurant popular with musical-theatre types. Simon's dole money was not enough to keep his bottomless glass full so he reluctantly phoned his contacts at the Old Vic and got part-time work as a backstage dresser.

'Pulling down some West End Wendy's trousers six nights a week is not my idea of a fulfilling life,' he announced, after his first night.

'Neither is dipping my thumb into Christopher Biggins's gravy, but needs must,' replied Molly.

Most nights after work, Simon would go drinking. He would have a couple in the pub next to the stage door, chatting with the wardrobe girls and the front-of-house staff. Then, after a while, he'd say, 'Time for me to slip into the night,' make his way to Soho and spend a few hours touring the gay bars and clubs. Simon had various 'drinking buddies' – friends he only ever saw in these places, after dark and under the influence. Some evenings Molly would meet up with him when she finished at Joe Allen's. Their nights out together could get quite wild, if the wind was in the right direction, but he always steered clear of his drinking pals on those occasions. They were part of a world to which he couldn't take Molly, much as he would have liked to.

Simon was always Molly's biggest fan. When she sang for the diners at Joe Allen's he would often turn up after his shift at the Old Vic and lean against the bar, listening intently while keeping a firm eye on the gentlemen's latrine. He alone would holler and cheer when she finished a number and, emboldened by drink, he would often shush a particularly noisy table and tell them to show some consideration for the poor girl singing her heart out by the piano. Simon watched Molly's confidence as a performer grow and soon he suggested she get an audition song ready.

'Audition song?' said Molly, rather taken aback.

'Yes. It's time you offered your services to the professional theatre, don't you think?'

So one night at Joe Allen's, when someone approached Molly after hearing her act and asked if she would be interested in auditioning for a musical, she was all ready. Better than that, she got the job, playing the stripper Tessie Tura the Texas Twirler in *Gypsy*, singing 'You Gotta Get A Gimmick'. It was hardly the West End – four weeks' profit share in Milton Keynes. It turned out there was no profit but lots of sharing. Still, Molly returned with an agent, a list of auditions to attend and a boyfriend called Paddy, a musician who played sax in the *Gypsy* band. Within a few weeks she had a part in the National's production of *Candide* and had given up her room at the squat to move in with Paddy. Simon was invited over to their love nest in Wimbledon, but it wasn't to his liking. He thought Paddy was a crashing bore who smoked too much dope, but he could see Molly was smitten.

Simon seemed perfectly content to stay on at the Kennington squat until the day he lost his job at the Old Vic. He'd made the mistake of having a few Bacardi Breezers between shows one afternoon. Bacardi always had a particularly strident effect on his mood, so when the company manager ticked him off because he was ten minutes late for his evening call, Simon picked him up and threw him down the stairs. The man was not badly hurt and decided not to involve the police – on the condition that Simon was fired on the spot.

Simon never considered getting another job. He signed on and he had somehow convinced his doddery father that he was still a student, now studying for a PhD on Albanian theatre practitioners. He moved to a new squat north of the river and, between the dole money and the cash his father sent, he was able to support himself and, more importantly, his drinking habit, which, without the restraining influence of Molly, was considerable. He had his first drink of the day earlier and earlier, and ended the night drunker and drunker. It became commonplace not to know what he'd done or how he'd got home.

Simon and Molly still met frequently and spoke on the phone, especially once they both had mobiles (even if Simon's pay-as-you-go was always running out of juice), but she was not there to see the state he was in when morning dawned. She scolded him if he sounded hung-over, but she didn't know the half of it and Simon was careful to hide it from her.

If anything they were more affectionate with each other on the telephone than they had been when they lived in each other's pockets.

'I love my Molly!' Simon would declare several times a week.

'Are you missing me?' Molly would ask.

'I feel like the Marquis de Sade without a whip. And how is life in the cosy seclusion of heterosexual coupledom?'

'Apart from your and my forced estrangement, it's fantastic. Paddy has issues with athlete's foot, but no one's perfect.'

'That's why I prefer my men to keep their shoes on.'

'Paddy is gorgeous and kind and I love being with him,' said Molly, dreamily.

At this point Simon always lost interest in the conversation. Hearing about the walks hand in hand on the common, Paddy's prowess in the lasagne department or their pet names for each other made Simon want to heave.

'The thing is,' Molly was saying, 'because he goes to the gym three times a week there's an awful lot of laundry.'

'You don't say?' remarked Simon. 'I have a lot of laundry too, but that's mainly on account of all the bodily fluids I'm drenched in by the time I've strolled innocently home through the park.'

'Thank you for sharing that, Simon.'

But only ten months later things went wrong with Paddy. While Molly was away appearing as the Good Fairy in *Sleeping Beauty* at Brighton's Theatre Royal, Paddy fell in love with one of his private pupils. Molly moved in with an actress friend of hers called Jane, and there was much weeping and wailing down the phone to Simon.

'Well, look on the bright side,' he offered. 'You'll never have to eat lasagne again.'

Molly choked. 'Your flippancy isn't funny at all sometimes. I've got a broken heart here! I thought I was going to spend the rest of my days with Paddy. . .' She dissolved into tears.

'Listen to me,' counselled Simon. 'There are bumps and bruises in all walks of life. I let this real beauty slip through my fingers the other day at the swimming baths. I was devastated. I could hardly roll my towel up afterwards. But I dealt with it. Move on, I say. Next! Don't let the bastards get the better of you.'

'I'm trying,' said Molly.

'Let's exorcise him with a trip to Soho. Meet me at eleven o'clock at Revenge.'

While Molly's career was blossoming, Simon's energy went into maintaining his 'interests'. He didn't aspire to anything, as long as he could feel the first flush of intoxication, which swept over him like bleach on a greasy floor every time he had a large glass of Chardonnay. That was what Simon lived for. The liberating douche. That, and urgent sexual gratification.

'It sounds horribly primitive,' said Molly, when he tried to explain it to her.

'It is,' agreed Simon.

'And I worry about you. I worry that one day you'll meet the straight man who takes real offence when you make a pass and decides to duff you up.'

'I've had the odd unfortunate encounter but I can run fast. I want you to understand. You like safe, steady men and I like dangerous, unsteady men. Each to their own.'

That Christmas, Molly gave Simon a St Christopher medal with his initials engraved on the back. 'To keep you safe on your travels,' she told him. Simon laughed, but he promised to keep it with him just in case.

Molly soon acquired another boyfriend and entered into another, what he called 'warts-and-all', relationship. And then another. Simon would meet them, shake their hands limply and suffer their company at the occasional party, but he was resolutely cool with them. He much preferred to meet Molly alone because he hated to see how needy and loved-up she got, forever leaning into her boyfriend for a reassuring peck and gazing longingly at him across a crowded room if they should be separated for more than a few seconds. It never rang true to Simon. Molly was a vivacious, sexy woman. Why was she squandering her charisma on these dreadful men? She devoted so much energy and emotion to each relationship that she must be exhausted! Given how predictable the eventual outcome was, it didn't seem like a wise investment to Simon. If that was the price you had to pay to get a cup of tea made for you in the morning and have someone to rub your feet when they were sore, it wasn't worth it.

One night the following spring they fell out of Heaven nightclub at three in the morning and Simon insisted they go for a stroll by the river. Molly was more street-wise than Simon, but they linked arms as they walked over a deserted Charing Cross Bridge and were soon sitting on a bench by the inky Thames just in front of the National Theatre. Everything seemed incredibly peaceful. They could see and hear traffic crossing the bridge to their left and the distant whoops of other late-night revellers. Even faraway sirens seemed just a part of the great cacophony of the metropolis.

'Do you ever wonder where we'll be in ten years' time?' asked Simon. 'Or twenty? Or thirty?'

'We'd be in our fifties,' said Molly, sounding appalled at the very thought.

'Grey hair and grey skin,' said Simon. 'If we've been successful in life we'll be trying to cling on to what we've achieved, fighting off young pretenders. If we've failed to make our mark we'll be full of self-loathing and disappointment.'

'That depends at which point you give up on life, I guess,' replied Molly, resting her head on Simon's shoulder as she looked at the streetlights reflected in the water.

'I imagine it's a gradual procedure,' said Simon. 'Preceded by a period of self-delusion. I've always thought the ageing process is far worse for beautiful people.'

'Are there any preparations I should be making?'

'I somehow think you'll manage,' said Simon tartly.

'Well, there's no shame in getting older. It happens to everyone.'

'It does. But there's no one so self-aware as a homosexual. We tick off every day, watching for decay – little signs of death. We welcome them home like stray dogs. It's thought we party more than other folk because we have no breeding responsibilities. We don't live in supportive family groups so we seek and satisfy our human social needs through the so-called gay community. We're also the lucky dispensers of the mythical pink pound, so it's assumed we can afford to go out swinging from the chandeliers every night of the week.'

'Yes, you're all loaded,' said Molly, enviously. 'You're never seen in the same cap-sleeved T-shirt twice.'

'None of that's true!' Simon sounded agitated. 'I'm not out

every night to interact with our gay, lesbian, bisexual or trans-gender brothers and sisters. I'm out every night because I'm a sex maniac.'

'Always out on the sniff,' said Molly.

'It rules my life.'

'I know it does. From an outsider's point of view it seems like torture.'

Simon sighed. 'I'm so glad. It would be awful if no one noticed how much I suffer.'

Even through his jacket Molly felt Simon's shoulder muscle tighten. She lifted her head and peered at her friend. Simon, nostrils flared, was staring with the intensity of a gun dog towards a shadowy area under the bridge. 'What is it?' she asked.

'A man!' said Simon, incredulously, as if this were an endangered species. 'Tracksuit bottoms, a tattoo on his neck and he seems a bit drunk.'

'Oh, Lord, no,' said Molly, wearily. 'Not at this time of night, surely?'

'I'm going over to investigate,' announced Simon, resolutely, never taking his eyes from the target. 'You stay here.'

'Simon!' said Molly, indignantly. 'It's half past three in the morning! You can't leave me here. It's not safe.'

'I'll only be a few yards away,' said Simon, over his shoulder, by this time already several steps from her.

'Simon, no!' shouted Molly, but he carried on, disappearing into the shadows under the bridge.

Chapter Five

The morning sunlight came streaming in through the faded cotton curtains of Molly's bedroom in Kit-Kat Cottage. She had slept comfortably and woken up happy, until she remembered her conversation with Simon the night before. She'd been shocked and hurt when he'd hung up on her. He must have been drunk, she thought, or well on his way to getting there. He was such a worry. She'd seen his drinking getting heavier and heavier over the years, but she was convinced it was entirely because of his consistently tragic love life. They were so close that it made her almost as miserable as it made him.

If only Simon could restrict himself, as Molly knew some gay men did, to furtive, fleeting encounters with these allegedly heterosexual alpha males, it would be all right. But in the years Molly had known him, Simon had got himself into a repetitive cycle of intense excitement followed all too swiftly by wrist-slashing misery. Now she dreaded hearing about his latest love because she knew for sure exactly where it would lead. She knew that she'd got over-involved with relationships herself in the past, and been depressed when things didn't work out, but at least her affairs of the heart were in with a chance. Simon only lusted after the unattainable. If, as had happened once, the man of his dreams fell for Simon too, and decided to give up his 'straight' ways and embrace a committed relationship, then Simon, of course, went off him instantly. The men he desired had to be straight and be seen to be straight. A wedding ring was a particular turn-on, a child seat in the car a plus. A sniff of homophobia in the mix and Simon was in heaven.

Quite how it all worked – how Simon managed to get into these men's trousers – was a grey area. As far as Molly knew, there were two methods of attack. Sometimes Simon would target a particular man, slowly but surely seducing him, igniting his curiosity, then pouncing once the grooming process was complete and sufficient alcohol had been administered. The other, less time-consuming option seemed to involve relieving men already in a state of some arousal, be it in cinemas, saunas, toilets or parks, the any-port-in-a-storm scenario. Darkness seemed to help things along.

In either case the outcome was always doomed. Love could not flourish in such circumstances. Simon was aware of this. As he had told her himself, with infinite sadness in his voice, love grows towards the light, and the glow of a Benson & Hedges behind a rhododendron did not suffice.

Molly sighed and put her worries about Simon out of her mind. She would deal with all that when she got back to London next week. In the meantime there was the weekly challenge of working out how the shower operated. Some she'd come across seemed more complicated to master than flying a helicopter.

She took her faded avocado-green towel from the chair where it was neatly folded, put on her dressing-gown and padded across the hall to the guest bathroom. It was a tiny space, with only a lavatory, a miniature basin the size of a sandwich box and a plastic shower as narrow and claustrophobic as an upright coffin. After several attempts, Molly managed to open the door, which suddenly folded in two like a trouser press. Squeezed inside, she looked at the various buttons and levers, mystified. After several exploratory jabs, she pressed a small frosted orange button and, with a sound like a lawnmower, the shower churned into action. Several lukewarm jets fell like light rain. She moved an important-looking lever downwards and the flow increased until it hissed and steamed, scalding hot. It seemed that in this particular model of shower, the temperature was inextricably linked with the water pressure, so if she wanted to shower, the only answer was to stand patiently under the equivalent of a dripping umbrella or lose her skin under a boiling torrent. She chose the umbrella. Washing the soap off took ages, but she managed in the end, dried herself and got dressed.

It was nine o'clock – exceptionally early for theatre folk – when Molly ventured into the kitchen. It was empty, with no sign of Lilia or her husband. A selection of breakfast cereals was lined up on a shelf like library books, each one decanted from its cardboard box and put into secure see-through Tupperware containers, and the labels from the original packaging Sellotaped to the tops. Molly chose Somerfield's own-brand muesli, and poured some into a bowl. She saw the milk jug on the table and went to pick it up, then noticed an envelope, with her name on it in sweeping handwriting, propped against it. Inside she found a tasteful retro drawing of a black-headed seagull with the words '*Bonne Chance!*' printed underneath. On the reverse was written, 'Wishing you the greatest of success in Northampton, and a happy stay at Kit-Kat Mansion, Lilia xxxx'.

Ah, that's nice of her, thought Molly, smiling. She was touched by the old lady's thoughtfulness. She would take the card with her and stick it to her dressing-room mirror. There weren't many on it – one from Simon, a lovely big one from Daniel, a small white one from her agent, which had been stuck to a bunch of flowers on the first night of the run, and a few from actor pals who remembered these things. But where other people had cards from their family, Molly had none – just a good-luck charm on a leather band from her favourite social worker that she always draped round her dressing-room mirror.

She finished her breakfast alone. By the time she left Kit-Kat Cottage, there was still no sign of Lilia and the house was silent. Even the huge dog seemed to have vanished.

The drive to the Derngate Theatre in Northampton took about twenty minutes through pleasant countryside, affluent villages and past the Althorp estate, home to the Spencer family. Molly was there by nine forty-five, ready to start rehearsals at ten. She parked her battered old Nissan by the loading dock at the rear of the theatre, took a small plastic holdall from the boot and walked round to the stage door.

Just inside, a man sat in a cosy little room with a sliding-glass window on to the corridor. He was in jeans and a faded Sex Pistols sweatshirt, reading a magazine with a steaming cup of tea by his side. Molly knocked on the glass and he got up, came over and slid back the panel.

'Hello, chuck. I'm Molly Douglas. You must be Roger. We spoke on the phone the other day and you were good enough to get me those lodgings at Kit-Kat Cottage.' She gave him a big, warm smile, the one that always seemed to win her friends. It was important to be friendly – the stage-doorman was a personage of great influence and importance. He would gossip about her to the other theatre staff, and any rudeness or diva behaviour could result in deep unpopularity. A stage-doorman who was on side, though, oiled the machinery of life. He would pass on any letters and messages she might receive, send up flower deliveries and tell her, via the Tannoy, if visitors or admirers were seeking admittance to her dressing room. Best of all, he would relay the spiciest gossip and the best titbits of scandal.

'Oh, yes, Molly Douglas,' said Roger, consulting a list of names. 'That's right, I remember,' he replied, polite but wary. 'How are you getting on there?'

'Very well, thanks. No problems so far, anyway.'

'Good. Welcome to the Derngate. Dressing room four is on this level, just down to the left.' He passed a key, with a battered wooden brick attached to it, through the sliding-glass window. 'That's to stop you taking it home with you,' he added.

Molly judged him to be in his mid-forties and of Mediterranean origin, although he spoke with a north-London twang. His hair was short, and speckled pleasingly with grey just above his ears. His eyes were like an eagle's, large and brown and darting around, taking in everything about her.

'The dressing rooms are nothing special,' he continued. 'You'd think they'd spend a bit of money on them but it's a dump, love.' He shook his head wearily.

'Oh, never mind. I've got some incense with me,' said Molly, lifting her suitcase.

Roger wrinkled his nose. 'Can't stand incense. Makes me retch.' He shut the sliding window, picked up *Take A Break*, buried his nose in it and paid no further heed to the leading lady. I'd better tread carefully with that one, thought Molly. She pushed her way through a couple of fire doors and walked down a narrow, windowless corridor made of breeze blocks. Dressing rooms one to five were on the left, the doors painted navy blue. Access to the stage was on the right and the toilets were between rooms one and two, and four and five.

No en-suite, then, thought Molly, grimly, stopping outside dressing room four. She turned the key, left it in the lock and went in.

Her very first entering of a new dressing room was always an important moment for Molly: she felt it was vital to her performance and to the emotional fabric of the coming week. She put down her bag and stood in the middle of the room, looking about her, inhaling the previous occupant's stale perfume and a whiff of disinfectant from the sink in the corner. There was a sagging metal single bed against one wall, its thin mattress covered with a tired pale-blue candlewick counterpane. Opposite this were two mirrors, a white Formica counter that ran the length of the room, and two grey plastic chairs. At the far end, opposite the sink, there was a long, narrow window. The curtains were rough and woolly, a *mélange* of messy grey and dirty turquoise. Ventilation could be achieved by pulling a lever at the side, which, Molly noted, would tilt open the louvred glass slats.

She lifted her holdall on to the counter and set to work, personalising the cell-like room, as she did every week on tour, to give consistency and comfort to her travelling lifestyle. First she pulled out a dark-green Indian throw, heavily embroidered with beads and tassels in bright orange and purple, and laid it over the bed. She added a small, matching satin pillow, then set her incense holder on the counter and lit two sticks of sweet and sultry Nag Champa to give the room a thorough spiritual cleaning. She rang a little silver bell, waving it elegantly to tinkle across the floor, then as high up as she could reach and, most particularly, in all the dark corners where unhappy spirits might linger or bad vibes lurk.

Next she took out a very small wooden electric lamp, hand-painted with tiny roses and topped with a camp fringed vanilla shade, which she plugged in and turned on. She placed her small portable radio in the middle of the bench and turned that on too. The sensible tones of Radio 4 filled the silence. It was the last five minutes of *Book of the Week*. Molly listened with half an ear while she set out her makeup just so in front of the mirror. Then she turned off the harsh overhead strip lighting and switched on the bulbs round the mirror. The room was transformed: the lighting was now soft and harmonious, it smelt delicious and looked homely and cheerful.

'There!' she said to herself. 'Northampton, I'm ready!'

Monday was always the technical-rehearsal day when the actors, the band (three tired, disillusioned musicians and a lot of click-tracks, frankly) and the technicians got used to the new space, rehearsed their cues, sound-checked and walked through the show, making sure of their entrances, exits and any alterations, such as a raked stage, that they needed to take note of.

Having completed her dressing-room routine, Molly wandered to the Green Room to make a cup of tea and see who was about. A dear old actor called Peter McDonald, cast in the title role of the Mikado, was sitting at the dirty Formica table drinking coffee out of a polystyrene cup and reading *The Times*. He was in his seventies, dapperly dressed as always in a beige linen suit and pale green tie. He was vaguely known by the public from a popular series of the late sixties, *The Butler*.

'Morning, Miss Molly. I trust you're keeping well?' he said, his tone implying that a certain Dunkirk spirit was required under the circumstances of the location.

'Yes, thank you, Peter, as well as can be expected.'

'Are your digs satisfactory?'

'Yes, I think so. Yours?'

'A poky little arrangement ten minutes' stroll from the theatre through perilous terrain, but somewhere to lay my head. I shall survive.' He gave Molly a telling look and shuddered discreetly.

Molly smiled at him She was fond of Peter, who was a seasoned repertory actor, and they had spent some happy hours in each other's dressing rooms discussing the other actors or the latest theatre and its crew. Peter went some way to filling the gap that Simon left, although he was no gay best friend. Despite his camp playfulness, he was divorced with two grown-up daughters.

'Now, Miss Molly,' he said, putting his paper down, 'are you excited? Because I am! Just a week! One week more. One little week to go.'

'I know. Wonderful, isn't it? If my wedding day dawns brightly many more times, I'll go bonkers.'

Peter rolled his eyes. 'And if I hear "Three Little Maids From School" ever again after Saturday, I won't be responsible for my actions. It ran through my head all last night. Sheer torture.'

They smiled conspiratorially. The last week was often the hardest to get through. The cast were all desperately tired of each other, the show had lost what little energy it had once had, and no one thrilled to the sound of the score any more, not even the paying public. It was work, plain and simple. Molly had both enjoyed and endured the experience but she would be glad when it was over, and she knew that Peter was tired of this uninspired production and the rigours of touring. 'We've all had enough now, haven't we?' she said.

Peter glanced over each shoulder, as if someone might hear him, and nodded conclusively. 'I really don't know how much longer I can put up with this shit!' he cried, in tones of queenly dismay, then lowered his voice. 'I don't want to name names,' he whispered, 'but there's a certain Pish-Tush in this show who is full of Pooh-Bah!' His face twitched with irritation. 'I'll say no more.' He relaxed again, picked up his paper and studied the crossword in *The Times*. Molly was well aware of the rivalry between Peter and the middle-aged actor called Duncan, who played Pish-Tush, which often spilled onto the stage. Duncan took great delight in blocking Peter's spotlight during his big number, and Peter's revenge was to flap his sleeves distractingly whenever Pish-Tush had an emotive line. The two had first crossed swords sixteen years ago in a production of *Lord Arthur Savile's Crime* in Norwich, and were sworn enemies. The result was a mini soap opera within the not-uneventful plot of *The Mikado*.

'It'll soon be over. You'll be home before you know it, back in your bachelor flat in Southampton.'

'Alone!' said Peter exultantly. 'But still alive!'

The door to the Green Room opened and the stage manager, Kenny, stuck his head round it. 'Everyone to the stage, please,' he said. 'We're starting the tech in three minutes. Call to stage!'

'And she gets on my nerves too. Runs this show like we're all on a school trip.'

'Kenny is Nurse Ratched, more like,' said Molly, flicking off the kettle and abandoning her tea-making preparations.

'And we're all lunatics in the asylum,' said Peter, tossing his newspaper across the room and standing up with a groan. 'Come on, let's go.'

The actors gathered on the stage, discreetly eyeing up the locals who were sitting about on the side. The company toured with its own sound and lighting operators but the stagehands and scene-shifters were employed by the theatre.

'They look as if they'd be more at home in a garden centre,' muttered Peter to Molly, looking at a couple of portly men with faded black polo shirts tucked into their trousers. A group of three younger men were loitering on some piled-up packing cases. They wore black too, but they were cool and sexy in dark jeans and crumpled T-shirts. 'They're dolly, though,' he added breathily.

The tech started with a general introduction of the main players and the stage crew, but the boys on the packing cases weren't considered important enough to get a name-check.

'Okay, people!' called Kenny, in his best school-mistressy voice. 'Could I *please* ask everyone to give me their full *attention* for the next couple of hours? I know it's tedious, but the sooner we get started, the sooner we can all break for lunch. Let's work together.'

'I'd rather be locked in a lift with Dennis Nielsen than work together with Duncan ever again,' hissed Peter, standing at the back with Molly.

'Right, could we have the Titipu men and Nanki-Poo standing by, please?' continued Kenny. 'Everyone else off-stage, ready for entrances.'

'I'm ready for a large gin,' said Peter, under his breath.

Molly's eye was drawn to the boys as the technical rehearsal began. When she, Pitti-Sing and Peep-Bo came tottering out of the wings for their first entrance, she watched them from the corner of her eye. Not only were they good-looking in a rumpled, stubbly way but, she noticed, when she was standing in the wings opposite, that occasionally one would let out a groan. It seemed they were playing some sort of cat-and-mouse game of endurance, wherein they would all sit in professional silence until one suddenly punched another on the thigh or upper arm, and the unlucky recipient would involuntarily whimper with discomfort and surprise. Eventually the stage manager told them to stop mucking about and they sat motionless and moody, with bowed heads.

When she emerged from the opposite wing after completing a scene, she found herself a few feet away from the subdued youths. On impulse, she went over. 'Hiya, boys. I'm Molly,' she said brightly.

They looked up, their eyes resting appreciatively on her chest, and mumbled their hellos. The tallest one made the introductions. 'I'm Sam. Er . . . he's Marcus, and that's Michael.'

'Well, I'm pleased to meet you,' said Molly. She was always friendly with the crew and loathed the way some actors treated them, as if they were unworthy of acknowledgement. She gave them a cheeky look. 'I saw you getting told off earlier. If you can't be good be careful, that's what I say.' With that she punched them all in quick succession, Sam and Michael on the arm, and Marcus, a brooding, fresh-faced cherub, saucily on the thigh.

'Ouch!' said Sam, as the other two moaned loudly. They stared at her in surprise for a moment, then laughed at her impudence.

Kenny spun round angrily on his swivel chair. 'Sssh!' he said. 'Can I please ask you to be quiet over there.'

'Sorry, Kenny,' Molly said quickly. 'My fault.'

Kenny tutted and swung back to position at Prompt Corner.

Molly made a guilty face, then giggled naughtily. 'Apologies for that, lads,' she whispered. 'I'll make it up to you. I'd better go. I've my big scene coming up.' The next time she emerged from the wings, she was disappointed to find they'd gone.

The first night in a new town was always quite gruelling. The theatre would be packed and the local dignitaries would attend – the chain-gang, as Molly called them, because no one who had a mayoral chain of office could resist wearing it out – and it was 'press night', with the Northamptonshire local papers out in force. After the show, the cast were obliged to attend a 'mix and mingle' with the theatre club audience, who had paid over the odds for such an opportunity, in the stalls bar.

'Ugh!' said Peter, as he sailed past Molly in the wings just before the finale. 'It's shake and fake night. Cold sausage rolls and warm Chardonnay, no doubt.'

He wasn't wrong. The theatre manager, a bow-legged lesbian called Bertha, grasped Molly firmly by the elbow the moment she entered the bar and steered her round the room, introducing her to a succession of tight-skinned, overdressed ladies and their tired-looking husbands. It was nice enough to be complimented on her performance and her singing but it was wearing to have to answer the same questions time after time. Luckily, Bertha got her a glass of the warm Chardonnay to help things along, and once she'd shaken hands with everyone she was required to meet, she managed to slip away. Bertha was busy on the balcony smoking her pipe and chatting to a woman in tweed.

Back to the bar, pronto! she thought, as she'd been clutching an empty glass for too long. She passed Peter on the way. He caught her eye and raised his to heaven. He looked rather glamorous, with the remnants of his heavy Japanese makeup still emphasising his eyes. She lifted her glass questioningly to ask if he wanted another, and he nodded vigorously, then turned his attention back to the little old lady who was chatting away to him, oblivious.

She got to the bar, pushed her way between two men and found herself standing next to young Marcus, who was looking distinctly bleary.

'Nothing stronger than a shandy for you, my lad.'

'Course not, Molly,' said Marcus, a sparkle in his intoxicated eye, which hovered, Molly observed, well below her neck. 'Great show. Nice set of lungs you've got.'

'Thanks. Glad you enjoyed it.'

Marcus shrugged. 'It's not really my type of thing, if I'm honest. I prefer films.' He grinned at her. 'But you were cool.'

'I do my best.' She ordered two extra large glasses of Chardonnay. 'Are you boys having a good time?'

'We're sitting over there, getting as much of this free booze as we can. Wanna come and join us?'

Molly passed Peter his wine and looked at the rest of the crowd, all the stuffy types talking importantly to one another. Then she saw Sam and Michael huddled round a table at the far end of the bar, laughing with each other while they waited for Marcus to get back with the drinks. 'You know what?' she said recklessly. 'I would. Come on, I'll carry that pint for you, if you like.'

Molly spent the remainder of the evening joking with Marcus and the other boys, teasing them and horsing around. She felt guilty because she knew she was supposed to be mingling and being charming but, really, she'd done her bit, hadn't she? Once she was actually enjoying herself, though, it all came to an abrupt halt. The free wine was swiftly withdrawn at eleven thirty and the bar shutters pulled determinedly down soon after. Bertha could be seen circling the room like a sheep-dog, slowly rounding up the crowd and pushing them towards the exit.

A few too many Chardonnays over the limit, Molly said good night to her new friends and tottered to the stage door where she asked Roger if he'd be so kind as to order her a cab home.

He made a quick phone call, then said, 'It'll be ten minutes. If you want my advice, you'll keep talking to the driver on the way. They're rubbish round here, sometimes fall asleep on the job.'

'Oh, right,' said Molly, trying not to sound tipsy. 'I shall engage him in conversation, then.'

'I would,' said Roger. 'You're going to Long Buckby, Lilia Delvard's place. Pick a topic that'll last, that's my tip. Which rules out my sex life.'

'Yes, love. Thanks again for giving me the number.'

'Well, I wouldn't want you sleeping on the streets. I hope it's bearable there. It'll be all right for a week, anyway. I know Lilia. She's an odd fish but she's one of us. She put on her own show here a few months ago.'

'Lilia did?' said Molly, more than a little surprised.

'Yes,' said Roger, rolling his eyes. 'It didn't go too well. She hired the whole place on a Sunday night. I think it was supposed to be some kind of comeback. Self-delusion, of course. She thought people would remember her from a hundred years ago.'

'Oh dear. I feel sorry for the old thing,' said Molly. 'I bet it was her big night, too.'

'She only sold fifty-eight tickets, and twenty of those were special needs.'

'God, that's awful. Poor Lilia!'

'Poor me!' retorted Roger. 'I had tickets for Ronan Keating that night, and I had to bloody work. Your cab's here.'

Chapter Six

It was almost midnight when Molly alighted outside Kit-Kat Cottage. She hadn't needed to keep the driver awake by talking: he'd talked to her non-stop for the entire twenty minutes. 'I was going to be an actor myself, years ago, but it's no life, is it?' were his parting words.

The lights were on at the cottage, and Molly fancied nothing more than the promised nightcap so she hung her cardigan over her bedroom-door knob and knocked gently on the lounge door. There was a hurried rustling within, followed by a long pause. She knocked again, and said, 'It's Molly. Shall I come in?'

'Ah! *Molly*!' Lilia's muffled voice exclaimed, as if she had been expecting someone called Nelly. 'Do come in, my dear!'

Molly opened the door and stepped inside. She glanced towards the alcove, but Joey's chair was empty. Then she registered the hot fug in the room. Despite the sultry evening, the gas fire was on full blast. The dog was lying on the hearthrug, panting, and Lilia sat smiling in her armchair, looking a little flushed.

'Sorry to bother you, Lilia,' Molly began, fanning herself with one hand as she spoke, and wondering if perhaps she should have gone straight to her room.

'Not at all, my dear!' said Lilia. 'Back from your triumphant first night? Come in, sit down and let us toast your success.' A bottle of brandy and two glasses stood ready on the table. 'Please pour us each a drink.'

Molly went to the table obediently and uncorked the bottle.

'How did it go?' asked Lilia.

'Oh, you know. Fine. I did my best.'

'Good. I hope for your sake that was the case,' said Lilia. 'Beware the *Northampton Gazette*. They can make or break a career.'

Molly handed her a glass of brandy and sat down opposite. Her landlady's stockings, she noticed with surprise, were rolled down round her ankles. 'I'm ever so bored with *The Mikado*, to be honest. I'm much rather hear about you. Tell me about your singing career, Lilia,' she said earnestly. 'Please?'

'Oh.' Lilia looked away. 'You cannot really want to know. It was such a long time ago.'

'I'd be interested. Really,' said Molly. 'I bet it's fascinating.'

Lilia looked bashfully at Molly. She exhaled through her nose, seeming to contemplate the wisdom of telling her story. Finally she spoke. Molly sat back, cradling her brandy glass and listening intently.

'I was the great singer, Lilia Delvard,' the old lady began. 'The Céline Dion of my day, only not as horsy. Here. Look. This is me.' Lilia stood up and reached for a framed photograph from the many on the shelf. She showed Molly a black-and-white picture of her barely recognisable younger self.

'Beautiful!' said Molly, admiringly. 'Foxy lady!'

'This was 1950, I think, at the Café de Paris.'

'Did you perform there?'

'Well, I wasn't cleaning the toilets. I was a star,' Lilia said matter-of-factly.

Molly studied the photograph. A young, elegantly dressed woman stood with her back to the camera, her neck bejewelled and her head turning, almost as an afterthought, towards the lens and her limpid eyes inviting, as if beckoning someone to follow her to the adjoining boudoir.

'My image was rather *femme fatale*,' Lilia explained. 'I was German and the war was not long over. I could hardly pass myself off as Julie Andrews.' Both women laughed lightly at the image. 'I went the other way. I wasn't Miss Squeaky Clean, like dear Julie. I get a Christmas card from her every year still. Just can't seem to shake her off. I became the German Temptress, sultry and moody and difficult to predict. If anyone dared to talk during my set, I would stop singing and stare until they were embarrassed into silence. It was said that I was the only person in London who could shut Princess Margaret up.'

'You sang for Princess Margaret?' asked a breathless Molly.

'She was one of my biggest fans.'

'What did you sing?'

'Bitter ballads, mostly. "Moon Over Alabama". Brecht, of course, Kurt Weill. "I'm A Stranger Here Myself", "September Song". "*Cuando Vuelva A Tu Lado*" was about as upbeat as I was allowed to get. My signature song was "The Man That Got Away".'

'I love it!' said Molly, enthralled, looking from Lilia to the photo and back again. 'You've still got the twinkle in your eye,' she said sincerely. 'Wow. What an amazing thing to have done! Did you make any recordings?'

'That is a sore point!' Lilia chuckled at the memory. '"Fever" was to be my hit song, but Peggy Lee came to see me one night and the next thing I knew she had released it.'

'Really? Did she know you were going to do it?'

'I told her myself over martinis at Goldenhurst. We were staying at Noël's for the weekend.'

'What a bitch!' said Molly, indignantly.

'Eartha Kitt was the worst. You only had to hum a tune in the lift and she'd nick it.'

'No!' said Molly.

'As for Sarah Vaughan!'

'What did she do?'

'We shared a dressing room once and I had hiccups. Half an hour later she goes on stage and starts all this scat singing!'

'She was famous for her scat singing.'

'After that she was,' Lilia muttered. 'I invented it. I was the first. It still rankles.'

There was a slightly awkward silence. Molly handed the framed picture back to Lilia, who took it, and said, 'Shall we have another brandy?'

'Yes, please.' Molly got up to do the refills.

After a moment's thought, Lilia said, 'I've just had a wonderful idea. How about I throw a little after-show supper for you and the rest of the cast on Thursday night?'

'Oh, Lilia, that's so sweet of you. But I wouldn't want you to go to the trouble—'

'Not at all, my dear. Just a few little nibbles and some *Cava*. To tell you the truth, I'd love it.'

'Well, I'm sure they'd all be delighted to meet you.'

'I remember Peter McDonald when he was on *Dixon of Dock Green*. And *The Butler* was my favourite show.'

'He's a really lovely man.'

'Then I hope he will accept the invitation. Leave everything to me.'

'It's very kind of you, Lilia. We're all far away from home and it's our last week. It would be great to have a bit of a get-together.'

'Then it is settled. Thursday night is open house at Kit-Kat Cottage. Here's to you,' said Lilia. They clinked glasses and smiled at each other.

It must have been about three in the morning when Molly was woken by a light tapping on her door.

She sat up and turned on the bedside light. The tapping came again.

'Hello?' said Molly. 'Who is it?'

'It's Lilia. May I come in?' Her voice sounded shaky and weak.

Before Molly could answer, she saw the doorknob turn. Lilia, in a faded pink calf-length nightgown with bluebells jauntily dotted all over it, came silently in and shut the door behind her. 'Forgive me,' she said. 'When Joey wets the bed, I sleep in this room.' With that, she moved determinedly towards the bed, lifted up the blanket and hopped in before Molly had said a word. Then she turned on her side so that she was facing Molly and pulled the blanket up round her shoulders. 'Turn the light out, Molly, dear,' she whispered. 'I am one tired old lady.'

Molly was speechless. In her semi-conscious state she did not have the strength to express her discomfort, so she dutifully flicked the switch and lay down, staring into the darkness and trying to come to terms with the unexpected presence in her bed.

Her hopes that sleep would envelop her swiftly and completely were unrewarded. She was tense and stiff and her eyelids fluttered open again the moment she instructed them to close.

Lilia's breathing, on the other hand, was slow and heavy.

Molly turned on her side, facing away from her, but the movement seemed to disturb her bedmate, and Lilia snuggled closer, snaking a sinewy arm round her waist. With two sleepy grunts and tugs she was spooning Molly from behind and breathing hot, decaying breath on the back of her neck.

Molly lay rigid and uncomfortable, until at last sleep rescued her.

Molly awoke the next morning with a dull, pulsing headache. Lilia was no longer beside her and she was alone with her Chardonnay-and-brandy hangover. She tried her best to revive herself under the trickle of water from the shower, then got dressed. When she went into the kitchen Lilia was sitting at the table in her usual silk arrangement, buttering a thin slice of toasted pumpernickel bread. 'Good morning, Molly!' she said cheerfully. 'I have a glass of water and two aspirin ready for you.'

'Oh, thank you, Lilia. I think I need them.' She wondered whether to mention the curious incident in the night time but decided against it. Perhaps it would be best if I just forget about it, she thought, and hope to hell that Joey doesn't wet the bed again.

Lilia gazed at her wisely. 'The trouble with brandy is it's very difficult to stop at one glass. Or so it would seem in your case. Anyway, it is done now.'

Molly glanced around the room. There was no sign of Joey or Heathcliff.

'It is still too early for the men,' Lilia said, as if she had read her mind. 'Please sit down and I will make you coffee.'

'No, don't get up. I'll sort myself out,' insisted Molly.

'Really?'

'Really.'

'You're a lovely girl, Molly. Such a nice change. I had Toad of Toad Hall here last Christmas. He thought I was his personal handmaiden,' said Lilia, taking a bite but continuing to talk nevertheless. 'He had me grinding beans, stirring coffee, spreading organic anchovy paste on gluten-free crispbread. Such a carry-on.'

'Goodness!' said Molly. 'You'll have none of that trouble with me, I can assure you.' She went over to the Welsh dresser and helped herself to some muesli, then turned to sit down.

'While you are up, my dear,' said Lilia, halting her in her tracks, 'could you pop me a piece of bacon in the pan?'

'Of course.' Molly put her bowl on the table and set about her task. She lit a ring on the gas stove and placed the frying pan on top of it. She opened the fridge and reached in for the bacon.

'The eggs are in there, too, as you're in the vicinity. Scrambled, if you wouldn't mind.' The old lady's lips made a quick cat's cradle of pouts and smiles, finally selected the smile and gave it full vent.

'Of course I don't mind,' Molly said, glad to help. It must be nice for Lilia to have someone to do things for her for a change, and if frying a bit of bacon and scrambling some eggs made her happy, she was glad to do it. 'So I take it Toad was a bit of a pain. Some actors are like that, you know. Really precious.'

'Mmm.' Lilia looked mournful. 'Poor Toad of Toad Hall. He went down with food poisoning on the Tuesday. He was Toad of the khazi for the rest of the week . . . He must have got it from some kebab he ate between shows.'

Molly laughed. 'Poor Toad!'

'Indeed,' said Lilia, joining in the laughter. 'Missed his press night. Terrible business. But you look very well. Hung-over, but well.'

'I'll feel better once I've had my muesli,' said Molly, feeling a little nauseated by the smell of bacon. She mixed the eggs and heated some butter in a pan, lifted it off the gas and swirled it round. She boiled some water to make a fresh pot of tea and put a plate under the grill to warm. When the bacon and eggs were done, she served Lilia from the right-hand side like a proper waitress and finally sat down to her own neglected breakfast.

'Thank you,' said Lilia. 'This looks delicious.' She picked up her knife and fork and cut the bacon into pieces. She piled the scrambled eggs on top, and gave it all an encouraging shuffle just as Heathcliff padded sleepily into the room.

'Ah! There you are, my precious,' said Lilia, placing the plate on the floor beside her. 'Molly has made your breakfast! Isn't she a darling?'

After Heathcliff had finished his bacon and eggs, Lilia disappeared into her bedroom to get Joey up. Molly, finally enjoying her muesli and a cup of coffee, heard her humming 'This Can't Be Love' as she went about her task.

Molly washed up the plates, then scrubbed the saucepan, and put them all neatly on the Welsh dresser. When she'd wiped the grill, she went to her room and called Daniel on her mobile phone.

'Molls!' he answered. 'Are you ever coming home?'

'Last week away, I promise. Home on Sunday. I can't wait, I miss you too.'

'How's the show going?'

'All right. Michael Ball's coming to town to do a concert in a few weeks' time. I think most people in Northampton are saving themselves for that. Can't say I blame them.'

'They're only human,' said Daniel. Then he said yearningly, 'Please come back. I want you – I need you! I've been sniffing your underwear, that's how desperate I am.'

'Dirty pervert,' laughed Molly. 'Wherever are you? It sounds very noisy.'

'That's because I'm hanging off a ladder three storeys up somewhere in Dulwich.'

'I suppose phone sex is out of the question, then?'

'They take that kind of thing in their stride here in Dulwich. Might be dangerous, though. I'm hanging on to the scaffolding with one hand and the phone's in the other.'

'Oh, well. We'll just have to wait until the end of the week.'

'Looks like it. Shame.'

'That poor mattress. Battered rotten.'

'Can't wait.'

'Can we have roast beef and Yorkshire pudding when I get home, please?'

'Only if you promise to prod the joint the moment you walk through the door.'

'It's a deal.'

'I love you,' said Daniel.

'I don't think anyone's ever told me that from up a ladder before. I love you, too.'

'See you Sunday.'

'My mouth's watering.'

''Bye, sweetheart.'

After she'd disconnected, Molly sat and smiled for a while, feeling the warm glow of love creep over her as comforting and luxurious as scented bathwater. It had been hard to be away from him for so long, but the reunion would be all the sweeter for that.

A little later she went back to the kitchen to make herself another cup of coffee. Joey was in his wheelchair, a plastic bib round his neck. Lilia sat stock still beside him. She held a finger to her mouth as Molly came in. 'Sssh!' she said softly. 'My starling is paying a visit.' She nodded towards the draining-board where a bright-eyed bird was perched on the edge of a fruit bowl. He was quite big, a good four inches tall with black eyes. His back and wings were a shimmering mixture of bottle-green and purple. The starling eyed Molly fearlessly for a moment, looked towards the open back door to check his escape route. Then, obviously deciding that he posed no danger, he took several healthy pecks at a Conference pear. 'He's a hungry boy!' whispered Lilia.

'He's fantastic!' breathed Molly, not wanting to scare him.

'Oh, yes,' agreed Lilia. 'He comes to see me every day. He waits in the garden until I open the door. He's very fond of Joey. I think it's because he doesn't move. Then when I go to the shops he follows me to the bus stop and waits there for me to return. He hops along the garden walls just ahead of me.'

Having had his fill of pear, the bird embarked on a quick hop-skip around the room, then flew out of the open kitchen door.

'Have a nice day!' trilled Lilia.

'You're like Mary Poppins,' said Molly, laughing.

'Next time, I hope you will meet my little thrush, who also comes calling. Now, then, where was I?' asked Lilia. She scooped up some porridge with a spoon and resumed feeding Joey, who looked not at her but at Molly, his eyes more alive than they had been when she had first seen him in the lounge. Molly sat down at the table and smiled warmly back at him. It felt surprisingly intimate to be there with the two of them, witnessing their morning ritual and the starling's visit. 'Do you mind if I stay?' she asked.

'Stay?' said Lilia, pausing in her task.

'Here. In the kitchen with you both.'

'Oh.' Lilia spooned up some more of Joey's breakfast. 'We don't mind at all, do we?'

'Thank you,' said Molly. It was warm and cosy, with the sun shining through the window and Heathcliff asleep on the lawn – it almost felt like being part of a proper family. She daydreamed that Lilia and Joey were the grandparents she'd never known and that by some extraordinary chance she had ended up in their home, to be welcomed and loved and looked after. Molly glanced over at the old man in his wheelchair. Was Joey trying to tell her something when he looked at her? There certainly seemed to be more in his expression than the eerie blankness she had seen the other afternoon.

Lilia wiped Joey's mouth with a wet flannel and offered him a plastic cup half full of what looked like very milky tea. He looked gratefully at his wife, who murmured, 'There, then. That's better.' She turned to Molly. 'You see what a mother hen I am? Starlings, thrushes, husbands, lodgers – I take care of them all.'

'You really do,' said Molly.

'I see only the good in people, in animals, trees, nature. I understand that we all have our place in the world. We are all God's creatures.' She finished feeding Joey his last spoonful, then licked the spoon herself, gave his mouth a final, gentle wipe with the cloth, then put it on the table. 'As far as I can work out, we have two main functions on this earth. There are two imperative instincts all living creatures are born with. Can you name them?'

Molly frowned, trying to come up with the right answer. 'Er, let me think . . . Is one eating? And reproduction?'

'Almost. Love and survival. That is what drives us. In fact, they feed off each other. After all, there is no point in surviving if we cannot feel the heightened emotion of love, and there is no point in being in love if we aren't going to survive to enjoy it. We need both, and we have both. Cheers!' Lilia raised her cup of coffee to Molly. '*Auf dich*!'

'Cheers!' said Molly, who didn't have anything to toast with, but didn't like to say so. Lilia's so wise, she thought. I can definitely learn something from her.

By the time Molly arrived at the theatre at six, she felt back to her old self. She'd had a nap in the afternoon, which had revived her nicely. She greeted Roger warmly at the stage door. 'You're a glutton for it, aren't you?' he said, passing her the dressing-room key through his window. 'You were fairly pickled last night, but if you want a return match, I'm game.'

He slid his window shut before she could answer, leaving her puzzled as to what he was going on about. She shrugged and headed off down the corridor.

In her dressing room, she lit a stick of incense, opened the louvred windows to let in some fresh air and turned on her lamp. Finally she flicked the switch on the radio. It was the news, so she turned the volume down to a comforting, well-educated blather from the corner. On her way to the Green Room for a cup of tea she passed Marcus in the corridor. 'Hiya,' she said brightly. 'Did you feel as awful as I did this morning?'

'I wasn't too bad. I can drink loads more than that and still feel fine,' he replied, with a grin. 'By the way, Molly, can't wait to have a go with your *frikadeller*. Sounds like a right laugh.' He loped off down the hall without stopping.

Another one being odd, thought Molly, surprised. What did he mean, *frikadeller*? Was it something I said last night and forgot about? Oh, God, did I get so drunk I've had a memory lapse?

The only person in the Green Room was Peter McDonald, wearing a black T-shirt with the words 'Nobody knows I'm a Lesbian' printed on it.

'Evening, gorgeous,' said Molly. 'How are we today?'

'We're half asleep. I fear there are students living above me and there was a lot of thumping music and general high jinks going on when I got home last night. I hardly slept a wink.'

'That's a job for Rentokil. You can't put up with that. Have you complained?'

'Indeed I have. I was given directions to the nearest Travelodge.' Peter raised his eyebrows at her. 'No need to tell me about your accommodation. I'll find out on Thursday, will I not?'

Molly was just pouring hot water into her cup, but she stopped and turned to Peter, baffled. 'Eh?'

'You're having an "At Home", I see, after Thursday's show. Everyone welcome.'

'But how on earth did you know?' Molly said. She'd been planning to tell them all about Lilia's offer of an after-show party during the interval, and sound out how many people might be interested in coming.

'It's on the noticeboard. I've already put my name down.

We're having schnapps and rollmop herrings and your landlady, the fabulously named Lilia Delvard, no less, is going to be there in person.' He laughed witheringly.

'Oh,' said Molly. 'I'm so glad you can come.'

'I'm rather looking forward to it,' said Peter, slyly, before returning his attention to the newspaper.

Molly finished making her tea, added the milk and gave it a bit of a stir. 'I'll just go and have a look,' she said casually, and headed out with her mug.

The noticeboard was adjacent to the stage door. A letter from Equity, the actors' union, was displayed, wittering on about minimum wages, and there was a dog-eared notice from the theatre about health and safety. A letter typed on pale pink paper was pinned to the middle of the board:

Attention!

Miss Molly Douglas invites you to Frau Lilia Delvard's world-famous *salon* following Thursday evening's performance.

After a light supper of schnapps, *frikadeller*, gherkins and rollmop herrings, Miss Delvard herself may be persuaded to perform some of her most famous numbers.

Places are limited, so please put your name below and see Molly for directions to Kit-Kat Cottage, Long Buckby.

Quite a few people had already signed up for the event: Peter, Roger, Renata (who played Katisha in the show and was a middle-aged actress of the Joan Collins ilk, with quite a lot of what might be called 'go' in her still), the wig mistress Christine and the three stagehands, Sam, Marcus and Michael. Some of the cast had yet to arrive at work and Molly had a feeling that most would be too intrigued to stay away.

Just then Roger appeared behind her. 'You know what actors are like when there's an offer of free food and drink. Bloody gannets. Still, I can never say no myself.'

Molly laughed a little uncomfortably. 'What I don't understand is how this notice got up here at all. Lilia only told me she was planning a party last night.'

'Oh, she came in this afternoon,' Roger said. 'She flew in, pushed that into my hands and asked me to pin it up for her, then dashed out. She must have been parked on the double yellow outside. I thought I caught a glimpse of a car anyway – it was one of those special tall ones with room for a wheelchair in the back.'

'What time did she come in?'

'About half three.'

Just when I was sleeping, Molly realised. 'She needn't have driven into town, daft old dear. I'd have put it up for her.' She stared at the notice again. It was odd to see her name up there like that, as though she'd written the invitation herself.

Roger gazed at her. 'Everything all right at that place?'

'Oh, yes, yes, absolutely fine,' Molly said at once. 'Lilia's a sweetheart. I love her to bits.' She had a flashback of the old lady climbing into her bed and snaking her arm round her waist. That hadn't been quite so pleasant. She shook her head. She'd resolved to forget about it. After all, Lilia needed some allowances made for her age, eccentricity and faded-star status.

'As long as you're sure. She's a funny one.' Roger sniffed. 'You be careful, that's all. One young lady who stayed there said she was treated like a glorified home help. You'll be painting her toenails green and trimming her manky old minge before the week's out, if you're not careful. I hate to tell you but I've seen it all before.'

'Oh, no,' Molly said stoutly. 'She's been fine with me. Completely fine.'

Roger fixed her with a beady stare. 'From London, are you?'

Molly nodded.

'Thought so.' He sniffed. 'I used to live in London. I was on the stage door at the Vaudeville for years, but I gave it all up and moved away just over a year and a half ago. Got so damn sick of that place – the people, the noise, the dirt, everything . . . and when I met my partner, we decided it was time for a fresh start. So here I am.' Roger rolled his eyes. 'Glorious fuckin' Northampton.'

'Don't you miss London?'

'Naah. Not really. I think I'm made for the quieter life.'

Molly smiled and nodded but she couldn't imagine living anywhere but the big city. She was hit by a jolt of homesickness. Don't worry, she told herself, only a few more days and then I'll be home with Daniel and all this will be forgotten.

Chapter Seven

Simon woke up late and lay for a long time staring up at the cracked ceiling and raking through the events of the night before. Once he'd got a fairly clear idea of what he'd been up to, and had managed to get control of his shaking limbs and aching head, he rolled out of bed and headed to the kitchen for restorative tea.

He still felt guilty about hanging up on Molly the previous Sunday, but he knew it would be all right. They were prone to these lovers' tiffs. It was painful to endure but always eventually resolved itself. She would call him or he would call her. All would be well in the end. Neither Simon nor Molly could live for long without the company of the other. It was unthinkable. How strange, then, that they were so different. Simon felt none of Molly's desire to work and succeed. Ambition didn't grip him at all. He liked to waft through life like a leaf on the breeze. He was far too interested in the twists and turns of fate, the random nature of all human transactions, to consider trying to control or steer his course in any chosen direction. What would be would be.

Despite its freedom, the reality of Simon's life was rather dull. Apart from Molly, he had few friends outside the gay scene. His life consisted of recovering from one 'big' night and preparing for the next. When his father had died and he had inherited several hundred thousand pounds, he had bought his current flat on Hampstead Road in Camden Town. It looked exactly like a squat but he owned it. Even with a bit of money in the bank, his lifestyle didn't change much, although he had long since stopped attending Socialist Worker meetings. He drank a lot and slept a lot, saving his energy for his late-night prowls around the parks, cinemas, canal towpaths and night buses of the metropolis. He lived off the remainder of his inheritance, vaguely aware somewhere in the back of his mind that he was chipping away at his bank balance, and one day the supply of cash would run out. Well, once it was spent he could get another job as a dresser, if he had to. Oh dear, thought Simon. I must be sobering up if I'm thinking about working. Yuck. Now, what shall I do this evening? I wonder if Charles is popping into town for a quick one.

He sent Charles a text. A reply came back immediately: 'Meet me in the Brief Encounter at eight.'

After a quiet afternoon, a shower and the application of a little Hide-the-Blemish to cover the red blotches on his face, Simon set out to meet Charles, walking south down Hampstead Road towards Soho, a journey he had made many times before, to meet Charles and Roger for another night of gaiety.

But, of course, Roger won't be there, he realised, with a pang of sadness. He still missed Roger, even after all this time. He'd been a part of Simon's life for so long that when he'd moved away, it had left a gap that was hard to fill.

In his younger days, Simon had had many friends but gradually his circle of chums had shrunk as they settled into relationships, moved away, or simply got bored with the pursuit of drunkenness and sex – Simon had heard that such a feeling could encroach as one matured, but as he'd never felt anything vaguely like it, he couldn't understand how. As the flightier friendships had petered out and vanished, he'd been left with his two best friends, Charles and Roger, who seemed as enamoured of getting utterly plastered as he was. He'd been meeting them in dark corners of pubs and nightclubs for years to drink and scout for men, and they'd stuck together while lesser men came and went from the scene. Yet in the many hours they'd spend together since they'd first met, they'd discussed little of real importance and knew only the scantiest facts about each other.

Charles seemed a rather lost soul, originally from San Francisco and not planning to return. He worked as a civil servant for the tax office and lived in Croydon, but was evidently able to perform his duties on the computer despite several late-night forays each week into Soho. Roger was the stage-doorman at the Vaudeville Theatre on the Strand and lived in a room above the Lemon Tree pub, next to the stage door of the Coliseum. Of the three, Roger was the one forever seeking a new chapter in his life. 'I'm sick of this crowd,' he'd say, week after week. 'The same tired old faces.'

'That boy over there isn't tired or old,' said Charles. 'He's fresh meat. Looks German to me. I wonder if he'd like to drive up my *autobahn*?'

'What's the point?' complained Roger. 'I don't want to be someone's holiday romance. They can fuck off. I've got more self-respect than that. I want a boyfriend.'

Roger craved permanency, yet his consistent and unwavering cynicism about life in general seemed to prevent him attaining his goal. Every passing male between the ages of twenty and sixty was given the once-over, assessed on the spot for their suitability and usually found to be sub-standard.

'Not husband material,' Roger would say, after the cute barman had given him his change. 'Too young. And I'm sorry, but I'm not moving in with a man who has a Betty Boop tattoo on his arm. I don't care how good-looking he is.'

'He's only served you a drink,' Simon pointed out. 'He hasn't, as yet, expressed an interest in becoming your life partner.'

'I saw the look in his eye,' said Roger, indignantly.

'So did I,' said Simon, under his breath.

Nevertheless, they would all chat and moan and provide companionship of sorts for each other. There was never any suggestion that their friendship would lead to anything more, although Charles had once made a half-hearted pass at Simon when they were both feeling particularly desperate. Simon was quick to put his cards on the table. 'I'm afraid I don't do gays. I'm saving myself for the night bus home. It's Destination Neasden. Need I say more?'

'Aha!' said Charles, not in the least bit offended. 'I think it's much the same on the Croydon bus. Boys will be boys, after all. Message understood.'

One night when he and Simon were out together, Roger declared he was going on the pull and left Simon at the bar. He returned a bare three minutes later with what Simon could only describe as a novelty pensioner in tow. 'This is Freddie,' Roger announced. Soon they were kissing passionately, and within twenty minutes, he and Freddie had disappeared into the night together. Left alone at the bar, Simon found himself a comfortable spot and settled in for a night on his own, followed by a little jaunt on Clapham Common to finish things off nicely. He could survive without his cruising chum.

But it seemed that true love had finally come Roger's way, and it happened with lightning speed. The following week, he said that he was moving in with Freddie and, furthermore, that he was relocating to the Midlands.

'He's everything I've ever wanted,' said Roger, misty-eyed.

'You mean he lives in sheltered accommodation and he's got some Viagra?' snapped Simon. 'I've never heard such nonsense!'

'You can't move in after just a week,' objected Charles.

'He's the One,' said Roger, as if he was proclaiming the winner of a talent contest. 'All I can say is, you know when something's right. I only hope it happens to you one day. You can't stay on the scene for ever, you know. Sooner or later you become a sad old fucker. So long, losers.'

With that, he left. It was going on for two years now, and no one had heard from Roger since, but none of them were the type to keep in touch with each other. He must have changed his phone number as well, for when Simon did send a casual text enquiring after his health, there was no reply. Simon was surprised by how much he missed his old friend but, after all, they'd spent many years drinking and cruising together. Of course he wished him well and cheered him on – he was all for people getting what they wanted, good for Roger – but now it was just him and Charles.

Simon arrived at Brief Encounter on St Martin's Lane to find Charles had got there first and was already finishing a bottle of beer. Simon ordered his, and in no time at all, they were on their fourth lager each.

'What do you say to a change of scene?' asked Charles.

'Like where?' Simon said warily.

'Let's give the Two Brewers in Clapham a go. The trade can be a bit rough south of the river, but that's TV researchers for you. It'll make a change from all the sour-faced queens in here. Talk about minty! When I asked the barman for a bottle of Becks he looked at me as if I'd told him I had a button mushroom instead of a penis.'

'I'm game,' said Simon, who knew the Two Brewers from his days in nearby Kennington.

They finished their drinks and wove their drunken way down the street to Leicester Square tube. Simon bumped into a lamp-post and Charles said it was a ridiculous place to put one in the first place. On their way to the tube station Simon stopped at a cash machine. His credit, he realised through his lager haze, was now just six hundred pounds. Within a month he'd be broke. He felt a mixture of panic and relief. Maybe the next chapter of his life was just about to begin. He drew out fifty pounds.

The Two Brewers was crowded and rowdy, but the atmosphere was happy and the music camp. Simon and Charles managed to secure two bar stools and settled in for another big night. It was several hours and a good four or five pints later when someone shoved a leaflet into Simon's hand. It was an entry form for a drag talent competition the following Thursday at a pub in north London.

'I might go for this,' slurred Simon.

Charles blinked dozily at him. 'A drag competition? But you've always hated drag queens, haven't you?'

'Yes. But there's only one way to overcome a prejudice. Embrace it. I might be the one to convert myself.'

Charles peered hard at the leaflet, cross-eyed. 'Looks fantastic! Go on, do it.'

'I will. Barman, do you have a Biro?' So drunk he could hardly write, Simon managed to fill in his name and telephone number. Under the section entitled 'Drag Name' he paused for a moment, then scrawled 'Miss Genita L'Warts'. He slipped his entry into the box provided and ordered another drink. Clapham Common was just up the road and he could hear it calling him.

Chapter Eight

On the night of the party at Kit-Kat Cottage, there was quite a buzz at the theatre. Apart from post-show drinks at the pub or in the theatre bar it was unusual for the company to enjoy a social event together. Plans were made for Peter, Renata and Christine to travel to Long Buckby in the car with Molly, while Sam, Michael and Duncan would go with Roger, which meant they'd be a little later as Roger had to wait half an hour after curtain down for the night-shift person to take over his duties at the stage door. Marcus would travel there on his motorbike.

'Your car appears to be a Nissan arrangement,' commented Peter to Molly, as they had their traditional coffee in the green room before the show. 'Are leather seats too much to hope for?'

'Velour, chuck,' Molly said.

'Oh, the horror!' said Peter. 'I may break out in hives.'

'Perhaps you'd better not come, then. I wouldn't want you to suffer.'

'Oh, I'm so looking forward to it!' exclaimed Peter. 'I guess I'll just have to endure in silence. I may bring a roll of clingfilm. I'm sure you'll be the perfect hostess once we get there. I'm contributing a bottle of Laurent Perrier. Rosé, naturally.'

'Very acceptable,' said Molly. 'Lilia and I went to Sainsbury's this morning. We've even upgraded from *Cava* to champagne, I hope we've got enough for you all.'

'So do I. I've been saving myself,' Peter informed her.

Later, as Molly was applying her makeup, Christine came in with her wig, a heavy dark Japanese-style hairpiece with the traditional chopsticks through the bun.

'Hiya, sweetheart!' she said, in her pleasant, reassuring voice. 'Bet you're glad you're about to see the back of this thing. One more matinée and evening show after this and you're done.'

'Gosh, you look nice!' said Molly, admiringly. Christine was always well dressed, usually in soft, velvety fabrics cut low at the front to make a feature of the lotus-flower tattoo springing from her cleavage. Tonight she was in a bottle-green wraparound dress with a grey cashmere pashmina tied at her waist, gypsy style, and silver strappy sandals. She had made herself up with pink, glittery lips and shimmering black eyes. She wore copper earrings the size of bangles and, as ever, looked cool.

Christine was pleased. She stole a quick glance at herself in the mirror. 'Thanks. I thought I'd make an effort for our proper night out.'

'I do hope no one's going to be disappointed,' said Molly. She closed one eye and applied a thick dark swoop of liquid liner along the lid. 'It's a buffet and a few drinks, not *Sunday Night at the London Palladium*.'

'The invitation sounds very sophisticated. Pardon me for asking, but is Lilia famous?'

'A living legend in some circles. She's retired now, of course.'

'Sounds fabulous! I can't wait. I'll meet you after the show,' said Christine, as she closed the door behind her.

Molly stared at her white made-up face and painted little rosebud lips. 'What's got into everybody?' she asked her reflection. 'You'd think they'd never been to a party before. It's not the Oscars, for Christ's sake. I just hope Lilia can live up to the billing.'

Such was the anticipation among the cast that they raced through the show, knocking almost five minutes off the running time. The moment the final curtain fell, Peter turned to Molly. 'I'm going to have a quick shower and a facial scrub. I'll meet you at the stage door in exactly eleven minutes.'

In fact he was there in nine, dressed in a fresh blue gingham shirt, face gleaming and hair carefully blow-dried into the skeleton of a quiff. Renata was in a white linen trouser suit, still in full Oriental stage makeup. She said she had a bit of a headache and wasn't sure if she should come.

'Please come, Renata,' said Molly. 'Lilia is so looking forward to meeting everyone. You'll love her.'

'Very well,' she said, sounding pained. 'Just a brief hello. We have a matinée tomorrow. There's going to be a terrible whiff of peardrops from the stalls.'

'All the more reason to have a bevvy. Come on, let's go to the car.'

Renata always needed to be coaxed into coming to the pub or even into the dressing room for a glass of wine after a show but then, when she'd had a couple of sips, she was the life and soul. Molly wanted Renata to be there because she was a mature woman and a theatrical, and she thought Lilia might appreciate her.

Christine arrived in a flurry of smiles and excited giggles and got into the back with Peter. Renata sat regally in the passenger seat and Molly drove. Once they were out of the city and into the winding country lanes, threaded with clusters of houses and villages, Peter said, 'I wouldn't fancy this drive every night. You need your wits about you in the pitch dark.'

'I rather like it,' said Molly. 'I've seen starlings and pheasants, rabbits – even some sort of falcon the other morning.'

'Treacherous in the winter months,' rejoined Peter, knowingly.

'Well, it's not winter, is it?' said Molly, slightly exasperated. 'It's September and we're only here a couple more days.'

When they eventually parked outside Kit-Kat Cottage, Peter peered out of the window. 'Is this it? I was imagining some sort of quaint latticed-window affair. This is your bog-standard modern little bungalow.'

'I think Lilia has fallen on hard times,' said Molly, feeling defensive. Kit Kat Cottage now seemed like home to her and she didn't like the critical edge in Peter's voice. 'It could happen to any of us.'

'Tell me about it,' said Renata, quietly. 'I was Peter Cook's plaything once. Now I'm touring the provinces and attending parties in bungalows. How are the mighty fallen!'

'Well, you're right, I suppose, Molly. And I can't really boast about my little *pied-à-terre* come to that,' said Peter, sounding a little kinder. Perhaps he'd seen Molly's expression of hurt and realised it was time to water down the theatrical bitchiness a little.

'Shall we go in?' said Molly. She had a distinct sense of trepidation about the evening ahead. If only Simon were here. He'd know how to keep them in check. But, as far as she knew, he and she weren't even speaking at the moment so she'd have to manage alone.

They got out of the car and stood in a line on the garden path as Molly fished in her handbag for the keys. Heathcliff barked gruffly from within.

'Is there a dog?' asked Peter, wary. 'Only I'm not very good with them.'

'It's only Heathcliff,' said Molly, soothingly. 'He's a big old softie.'

She opened the door, greeted Heathcliff – who took one look at the visitors and padded off to Lilia's bedroom – and led everyone into the empty lounge. The table was heaving with food and there was a strong smell of vinegar and Scotch eggs. Champagne glasses were lined up on top of the piano, with small, neat schnapps glasses gathered around them like day-old chicks with hens.

'I'll put the bags and things in my bedroom,' she said, making a quick collection. 'Do make yourselves comfortable.'

'Lovely spread!' said Christine. The three guests eyed the food hungrily. Everyone was always starving after a show. 'I guess we'd better wait for the others.'

'Yes, of course,' said Renata, with admirable restraint, although she couldn't stop staring at a pork pie.

'Sod that,' said Peter. 'Those stagehands look as if they haven't eaten for a week. They'll inhale this lot. Let's tuck in while we can.'

Molly left them to it and took the coats through to her room. She had just dumped them when the doorbell rang so she headed for the front door. Marcus came in first, flushed from his open-air ride, followed by Duncan, Sam, Michael and Roger. Molly led them into the sitting room and there were cries of mock surprise and joy as they all greeted the colleagues they had seen less than an hour ago, albeit in a theatrical version of Japan. Peter pulled his bottle of Laurent Perrier from a plastic bag with a flourish. 'What we need is some of this!' he declared. 'Sam, will you pass the glasses round?'

Molly brought out two more bottles of Sainsbury's own champagne and urged everyone to help themselves to the buffet while she popped the corks and started filling glasses. Soon the hum of conversation and the clink of cutlery on china plates filled the room.

'All right, Duncan?' Molly asked, as she did her best to circulate in the crowded room.

'Mmm. I've no idea what I'm eating but it's delicious,' he said, spraying filo-pastry crumbs.

'That's the story of your life,' said Peter, tartly.

Renata had downed her champagne and was eyeing an elaborate glass bottle on the mantelpiece.

'Peppermint schnapps,' Molly informed her. 'Have some!'

'Peppermint?' demurred Renata. 'I'm not sure.'

'Good for the digestion.'

'Is it? Well, maybe just the one . . .'

Sam, Marcus and Michael were huddled in the alcove, drinking from cans of lager and somehow sharing a single armchair.

'Now, boys,' said Molly, as she passed, 'sorry there are no kebabs, but this is all healthy fare, so don't be shy.'

'Is it Arabic?' asked Michael.

'I'm not eating sheep's eyeballs!' said Sam, and the three fell about laughing.

'Arabic? What are you talking about?' Molly pointed over at the table. 'Rollmop herring? Dumplings? Gherkins and pumpernickel? You need to learn a bit about world cuisine, boys.'

Roger slid round in front of Molly.

'Hiya, Rog,' Molly said brightly. 'Like a top-up? I've got some bubbles left if you're interested.'

Roger ignored the offer. 'This is very odd,' he stated. 'Where is Lilia?'

'I don't know, actually. She said we should start without her if she was still getting ready.' Molly looked at her watch. 'But she must be done by now. I'll go and knock on her door.'

'I mean, what sort of party is it where the hostess doesn't even show her face? She's not Elton John, for fuck's sake.'

'She's here, don't get your knickers in a twist.'

'Well, go and get her. We could do with some entertainment around here. I'm not being funny but to be perfectly honest with you, I'm bored.'

Molly put a placatory hand on his arm. 'Okay, Roger, I get the message. Calm down, have a drink and I'll see what's keeping Lilia.'

As she excused herself, pushing past everyone, she felt a little flustered and her smile was somewhat strained. Roger had managed to sour the mood for her, but perhaps he was right. It *was* odd for Lilia not to be present at her own party.

She shut the sitting room door behind her just as Renata was letting out peals of laughter and Duncan was raising his voice to Peter. She took a couple of deep breaths in the corridor and knocked gently on Lilia's door, which wasn't on the latch. Heathcliff growled menacingly from within.

'It's only me,' said Molly. 'Just checking that you're all right.'

'Ah, Molly,' said Lilia. 'Do come in. It's rather dark in here.'

Molly pushed the door open and stepped inside. She could see nothing but darkness for a moment, then made out Lilia's silhouette framed against the window. She was sitting on the edge of the bed, and her left arm was moving slightly. Seconds later Molly realised Lilia was stroking Joey's forehead. The old lady was wearing a floor-length, ruby-red sequined gown, which shimmered like ectoplasm in the gloom.

'The guests have arrived, I hear.'

'Yes, they're having a great time. Are you coming to join us?'

'I do apologise. Joey will not settle.'

'Is there anything I can do to help?' asked Molly, eagerly. 'Shall I make him a cup of tea?'

'No liquids at this time of night. The only answer may be to increase his medication.'

'Why don't you bring him to the party? It's only next door.'

'They might confuse him with the rollmop herrings. I'd never forgive myself if he was accidentally eaten.'

Molly snorted, more with surprise than amusement. 'Lilia, that's awful! Come in and enjoy yourself. You look beautiful.'

'Not a particularly convincing compliment as I'm sitting in the dark, but thank you. I shall endeavour to make an appearance shortly. I feel . . .' She hesitated, her voice trembling very slightly. Then she continued. 'I feel – unsure of myself. Nervous of meeting all your young friends.'

'Oh, you don't have to feel like that. They'll like you, I promise, and you'll love them. You're just like us.' Molly was overcome with pity for the poor old lady who had wanted to have a party and impress the theatre folk but was now too scared to show her face. Molly went to the bed and knelt down next to it. 'I don't have a mother. But if I did I'd feel very proud if she was like you.'

Lilia bowed her head, and Molly heard a quiet sob. 'This is such a Disney moment,' said Lilia. 'Crying is the least I can do.'

Molly got up, then sat on the other side of the bed so that Joey's skinny, withered legs lay between them. She took Lilia's hand and clasped it to her chest. 'You are a star, Lilia. Never forget that. Come and have some champagne. Meet your public.' Molly released her hand and the two of them hugged, forming an arc over Lilia's supine spouse.

Molly returned to the lounge, poured more drinks and reassured everyone that the hostess would be with them shortly. The excitement was on the brink of souring if Lilia didn't appear soon. It was now almost half past one, and the stagehands were restless and keen to go now that the beer had been drunk. Peter was getting positively militant with indignation. 'What is this? I've never waited so long for someone to make an appearance in all my life! I mean, you've done your best as a warm-up act, girl, and good on you for trying, at least. But don't you think it's time you served up the main course?'

'Lilia will be here any moment,' Molly said, as winningly as she could. 'Come on, Peter, just a few more minutes. Have another drink. I've kept a bottle of champagne back just for you.'

With Peter placated, Roger sidled up. 'You want to tell Lilia to get a move on,' he murmured. 'I hear rumblings. Renata's getting very loud. That peppermint schnapps is going down as if it was a can of Lilt. And Duncan's been giving Peter death stares for the last twenty minutes. Unless something distracts them soon, they'll be wrestling each other to the floor. Christine appears to be rolling a joint and I can feel one of my heads coming on. You'd better do something.'

'All right!' said Molly, feeling desperate and wondering what on earth she *could* do.

As if on cue the door swung open and everyone fell silent. An intriguing shadow came through the door first, and then a magnificent Lilia, head held high and steady, her hair fashioned into a fox-red candyfloss halo, her dress glimmering and gleaming in the light. Her hands were resting on her hips. She surveyed the room. '*Wilkommen*! I'm so glad you could all make it.' She bowed.

After an awkward pause Duncan started the clapping and soon everyone joined in. Renata let out a couple of appreciative whoops. Peter passed Lilia a glass of champagne and shook her hand, suddenly rather bashful. 'A magnificent gown you're wearing this evening, Miss Delvard. Thank you for having us to your lovely party.'

'Thank you,' said Lilia graciously. 'I wore this dress when I appeared at Carnegie Hall. Tom Jones asked me to marry him that night.'

'Really? That's amazing!' said Peter. 'Tom Jones has been married for years, hasn't he?'

'Or was it Liberace? I forget.'

The rest of the visitors swirled around her.

'Allow me to introduce myself,' said Renata. 'I'm Renata Maxwell. Contralto and Katisha in *The Mikado*.'

'Ah! A young Lauren Bacall!' declared Lilia, which went down very well.

'So thrilled to meet you,' Renata gushed. 'I'm looking forward to hearing you sing.'

'We shall see,' said Lilia, waving her hands in front of her as if bothered by a fly.

'Fantastic makeup!' said Christine, bobbing up and down in front of Lilia like an exuberant child.

'Thank you,' said Lilia. 'I learnt makeup application during my time in Hollywood. Have you heard of a film called *Cleopatra*?'

'With Elizabeth Taylor?'

'That's the one. I was Libby's stand-in.'

'Wow!' exclaimed Christine.

'She's a sweetheart. Never well, though. Even then. It's me you can see in all the Nile scenes. Miss Taylor had a bout of intestinal hurry. We were so alike no one ever twigged.'

'I can see the resemblance even now,' said Christine, admiringly.

'It helps if you half close your eyes and look at my left profile.' Lilia turned her head obligingly.

'Oh, yes!' said Christine, excitedly. 'It's uncanny!'

Lilia glided a yard away from her and tapped Roger on the shoulder. 'So glad you could come, Roger. And many thanks for placing the invitation on the noticeboard for me.'

'Always happy to oblige,' said Roger.

'The Derngate holds a special place in my heart. It was a very memorable night.'

'I'll say,' said Roger. 'Lots of people are still talking about it.'

'I'm sure,' said Lilia, nodding. 'Now, pass me a fork, would you?'

Roger handed her one from the table and Lilia tapped the side of her champagne glass to gain everyone's attention.

Molly had been hovering at her shoulder, entranced by her landlady's charm. She had spoken to almost everyone. Now Molly stood back to bask in her star quality.

'Thank you, thank you,' Lilia began. 'May I thank you first, most sincerely, for making the trek out here into the wilds. It means a great deal to me that you took the time and trouble.'

A gentle spatter of applause rippled through the room. Lilia paused, waiting for it to subside before she continued, 'I am very touched.'

'I'll say,' muttered Roger. Molly gave him an angry nudge.

'The showbusiness world, I thought, had forgotten me,' continued Lilia, oblivious. 'But then Fate brought the beautiful Molly to my door. In the few short days she has been here she has shown me such kindness. And now, tonight, she brings me new friends – all of you!'

'Will you sing for us, Lilia?' asked a rather intoxicated Renata. 'It would be such a treat.'

'I will, if you insist, delve briefly into my glorious past.'

'Hurrah!' said Peter, raising a glass.

'Spare us,' murmured Roger. 'Trust me, I've been here before.'

'I would like to begin with a song written for me in 1950 by James Shelton.' Lilia cleared her throat and stroked it with her hand. She closed her eyes and opened her mouth. At first there was nothing, then a low, steady I-sound. It got louder until, like a paper plane taking off, Lilia launched herself, unaccompanied, into the song.

> 'I lost myself on a cool, damp night
> Gave myself in that misty light
> Was hypnotised by a strange delight
> Under a lilac tree.'

Lilia sounded a little tremulous, but this added poignancy to her rendition. It was slow and regretful. As she sang her voice grew stronger and she opened her eyes. She didn't just sing the song, she acted it, gaining intensity, her hands grasping in front of her at a bottle-shaped hallucination. She warbled through a second verse, then a third, and ended on a long, deep vibrato note.

'Bravo!' shouted Peter, when she finally ran out of breath.

'More!' cried Renata. 'It's divine.'

'She's got the auditory equivalent of beer goggles on!' hissed Roger.

'Thank you so much,' said Lilia. 'And now – 'Peel Me A Grape'!'

Halfway through this number Duncan joined in on the piano with some jazzy chords. By the end everyone, except Roger, was keeping the beat with finger-clicking, while Molly and Renata hummed backing harmonies.

'What is this?' asked Roger. 'Sing-along-a-Granny-o?' But no one paid any attention to him and Lilia didn't seem to hear his catty remark.

Another bottle of schnapps was opened and passed round, as Lilia continued to entertain her guests with 'Honeysuckle Rose', 'May I Never Love Again' and 'Old Devil Moon'.

'Frank Sinatra told me he preferred my version of that song to his own,' Lilia told them afterwards.

By now Peter's enthusiasm had waned and he tapped his watch, looking worriedly around the room. 'This is all very lovely, but has anyone seen the time? Almost half past two!'

'It's not exactly Ronnie Scott's, is it?' said Roger, quietly, giving Molly a meaningful look.

'I shall finish with some Kurt Weill,' said Lilia. 'I think I just about have the energy. After all, these are the songs written by the man I believe to be my father.' She left a pause for this impressive fact to sink in. The medley was comprehensive, from early obscure songs sung in German right through to 'Mack The Knife'. The audience were fading by the end, although Molly was mesmerised, her eyes shining with pride and admiration. The final applause was consequently a little tired and short, and Duncan, Peter, Roger and Renata jumped up almost immediately to indicate the end of the evening. Sam and Michael were soundly asleep on the sofa while Marcus was staring into his beer can.

Lilia raised her voice. 'Again, thank you all for coming. I leave you with the words carved on my father's gravestone:

> ' "This is the life of men on earth,
> Out of darkness we come at birth
> Into a lamplit room and then
> Go forward into dark again." '

With that she bowed to the room and swept out, with only Molly clapping now.

'My poor cat'll be starving,' said Roger. 'Come on, I reckon I can fit everyone in my car, if Sam goes on the back of Marcus's bike and Duncan sits on Peter's lap.'

Everyone stood up and headed out, mumbling their thanks. The front door slammed and feet hurried down the gravel path. There was a loud guffaw and stifled giggles, then the sound of car doors and an engine being started. Finally it zoomed off into the distance and there was silence.

Chapter Nine

Simon had forgotten about the drag competition as soon as he'd posted his entry in the box. A couple of minutes later he had staggered out of the pub and headed to Clapham Common to try his luck with the shadowy figures who lurked there. When Jimmy, the manager of the pub where the competition was to be held, called him a couple of days later to confirm his appearance, he was more than a little baffled. Fortunately he was on his second glass of Veuve du Vernay and therefore in a rather good mood.

'Did I really fill in an entry form? Good heavens! I blame the lager in the Two Brewers. I'm sure it was off. I ended up having sex in a skip that night with the captain of the Lowestoft rugby team. At least, that's who he said he was – Charles said he recognised him from the menswear department at Bentalls. Typical.'

'You were swallied,' said Jimmy, in his thick Glaswegian accent. 'You're Genita L'Warts, apparently. But if you'd like to withdraw, I'll understand, aye? We willnae send the police round.'

'I cannot, for a moment, imagine myself appearing on stage. In drag. It's unthinkable. I'm never drinking again.'

'That's a shame,' said Jimmy. 'Genita L'Warts is a great name.'

'I was very drunk. I'd have signed up for the Foreign Legion if you'd put the form in front of me. No, I don't think so, thanks all the same.'

'The prize is five hundred pounds and first dibs at the after-show buffet.'

'Really?' There was a pause. Then something seemed to possess Simon. 'Count me in. I'll be there,' he blurted out.

'You sure now?' said Jimmy. 'There's no pressure. . .'

'Oh, yes, I'm sure,' said Simon, firmly.

'Brilliant,' said Jimmy. 'Be there by nine and the show starts at eleven.'

'You can depend on me,' said Simon, and hung up. He stared at the phone with a kind of excited horror. What had he done? He'd never felt the slightest desire to be a drag queen, and now he was going to be in a competition. It was daring and different. Well! he thought. This calls for a bottle of *Cava*.

The next day, Simon paced round his flat thinking and smiling. He felt more excited and invigorated than he had for ages. In the hallway he looked at himself in a mirror and tried to imagine what sort of woman he would make. 'Genita L'Warts,' he said quietly, several times. 'Who the devil are you? Friend or foe?' He giggled.

Suddenly he had a thought and opened a cupboard in the hallway where he began pulling out the broom, the Hoover and assorted junk. 'Aha!' he said at last. 'I knew it was somewhere.' He pulled out a large roll of two-tone purple and green shot silk that he'd pinched from the Old Vic on the day he was dismissed. He'd concealed it under his coat imagining he'd make some fabulous curtains with it, but had never quite got round to it. His experience in the wardrobe department had taught him a fair bit about how costumes were made, and now it was time to put those skills to the test. Holding one end, he flung the roll down the hall, then draped himself in the gorgeous fabric, turning this way and that to allow the light to shimmer over the silk. Still swathed in it, he went back to the lounge to pour himself another drink. 'Genita, Genita,' he murmured, between sips.

Where does one begin? he thought. Here was a creature conceived in the final throes of drink-induced stupidity. Now he had to flesh her out and produce some sort of performance in record time. A thought flashed into his mind and he couldn't stop himself speaking it aloud. 'A vile, vindictive, unstable woman, though rather fabulous with it.'

Whoever she was, she liked a drink, certainly: the bottle was empty in no time. 'Greedy bitch!' he declared.

He started work on his dress at once.

During the hours that Simon sat alone and sewing, he began to meditate upon Genita and who she was, like a broody seagull doggedly nesting high up on a craggy cliff, sitting on her clutch of eggs in stormy weather, willing them to hatch. It was not until he felt an ache in his cheeks that he realised he was smiling. The creative process – the sewing of the dress and the dreaming up of a new persona – had energised him and gladdened his heart. He felt alive about something other than sex for the first time in his life. He was happy!

Well I never, he thought. I'm all of a flutter and there's not a cock in sight.

It was a different sort of excitement too, not the tingle in the loins or the blood-pumping readiness of the predator moving in on his prey: it was a prouder, deeper, more soulful excitement. As Genita L'Warts took shape in his mind, he felt the empowerment a sculptor must feel when he's chipping away at bare rock, making something new and unique. He had three days to prepare, to conceive and develop his *alter ego*. He didn't go out once in that time, apart from a few trips to the off-licence to buy bottles of Grey Goose vodka. Only the best for Genita.

The more he drank, the more Genita thrived inside him, like an air bubble in a spirit level.

'Who are you?' he asked.

'Just a visiting friend,' replied Genita, through the very same lips. 'Nothing to be concerned about. I shall be performing at the Black Cap on Friday. Don't fret about it. I'll take care of everything. Vitriol and filth, that's what they want at the Black Cap and that's exactly what they're going to get.'

'They'll love it,' said Simon, convinced that his appearance would be awesome.

'I don't want a wig,' continued Genita, once Simon had replenished her glass with Grey Goose. 'I only wear turbans. If you shave your head it'll be a boon. My eyebrows are black and extend like antlers way above the hairline. My makeup is extreme, some would say grotesque. The dress is fine but needs some sequins and crystals sewing on . . . This vodka's terribly weak. Are we on rations, or something?'

Simon added an extra slurp to the glass.

Genita took a sip. 'Ah, yes,' she said. 'Now, where was I? My performance – the first of many, I trust – won't be for the faint-hearted. I intend to call a fist a fist. If you get me well oiled enough I'll take care of everything. I'm a tart with no heart. No one messes with me.'

Simon felt the alcohol overpowering him and lurched towards his unmade bed, even though it was only eight o'clock in the evening.

'I shall let you rest,' said Genita. 'I will still be here when you wake up. Shall we say nine thirty? Threshers closes at ten and you're perilously low on Grey Goose.'

Simon sank into a deep slumber, only to awake suddenly at the appointed hour as if someone had tapped him briskly on the shoulder. He rubbed his eyes, picked up his debit card from the bedside table and set off down the high street to the off-licence, pausing to be sick in a public bin outside Argos. Genita must be obeyed.

It took Simon two days to turn the stolen fabric into a regal, full-length gown with a matching turban. It was loosely based on a dress he had helped to make for Gertrude to wear in the Old Vic's production of *Hamlet* a few years back. Charles, in a rare appearance outside the bars of Soho, came to Simon's flat to help with the fittings, then dashed to the Oxfam shop to get some glittery black shoes and to Boots to acquire makeup. When the costume was ready, they had a dress rehearsal.

'You look divine!' cried Charles, when Simon emerged in his full get-up. 'Like a vision. But have you thought about what you're going to do on stage? You can't just stand there like a straight man in the Vatican. You need to do something. Perhaps you could mime to Eartha Kitt singing "Monotonous"?'

'Genita doesn't mime,' said Simon, firmly, looking himself up and down in the mirror. He felt slightly alarmed at what he saw, at how strangely familiar she seemed. He had become the very antithesis of what he sought: a drag queen. A strange feeling came over him, a rare combination of excitement and self-loathing.

'Who is Genita?' asked Charles.

Simon closed his eyes. 'I am possessed by a dark and daring spirit. John Leslie and Bette Davis rolled together in one terrifying package,' he replied. A sombre silence descended on the pair.

'I feel a little nervous for you,' said Charles, at last.

'Don't worry. Genita will be wonderful. She's promised me, and I believe her.'

On the night of the competition, the dressing room at the Black Cap was crowded with jittery amateur drag queens, squealing with excitement and smoking nervously. Simon staked his claim to a far corner and hung his dress on a light fitting. He was icy cold towards his fellow competitors, variously attired as Dannii Minogue or Dame Edna Everage, or others he couldn't quite recognise. He unpacked his makeup and had a swig of vodka from the silver hip flask he had inherited from his father. Genita fluttered inside him like a moth in a lampshade. It would not be long now before she was released.

'Touch my frock with that cigarette and I'll save you the trouble of going to Bangkok for a sex change. *Comprendo*?' he said, to what could only be a very unconvincing Davina McCall looky-likey. 'And if you think Davina would be seen dead in a cheap top like that then . . . you're probably right.' Is this me speaking or is Genita here already? he wondered.

'I'm not supposed to be Davina!' said the naff queen, indignantly. 'I'll have you know you're looking at Penélope Cruz!'

'Pass me the bucket,' said Simon.

According to the list on the dressing-room door, Simon was to appear seventh, right after an act called Maud Boat. He sat down in front of the mirror and gazed at his reflection. Already he looked quite different: that afternoon he had carefully and ceremoniously shaved his head. Now he set to work. Starting from the nose and working outwards, he applied a pale foundation to his face and smoothed it outwards from the nose to the ears, forehead and beyond; then he powdered himself liberally. He rubbed soap into his eyebrows and reapplied the foundation, causing them, to all intents and purposes, to disappear. Now his entire head was a blank canvas.

I look like a corpse, he thought.

He started with the eyebrows, painting a steady arch from the inner point of the original, just above the bridge of the nose, up and out like a swan's wing. He repeated the procedure on the other side. Next, the eye sockets were similarly exaggerated to run parallel with the brow and also coloured black, the outer edges of each eye fanning out luxuriously like feathers. A white pencil ticked between each quill enhanced the effect. Long, thick black eyelashes added another dimension.

He moved to his mouth, using a deep red pencil to create a severe pout, although the outer edges were turned slightly upwards to add a knowing, cheeky touch. Once the outline was complete, a gash of Russian Red lipstick was applied and topped with matching Kryolan glitter. The original outline was then redrawn with black. Now his mouth was a shimmering cushion of lush stickiness.

He dipped a brush into white iridescent powder, stroked it along his cheekbones and added a cold grey shading immediately underneath. The final touches were a whisper of pink blusher dabbed either side and two beauty spots, one under Genita's right eye and the other on the left jawline, just an inch below her lips.

Face done, Simon took off his shoes, trousers and T-shirt and folded them neatly. Wary of leaving anything on show in a dressing room filled with queens, he rolled them up, placed them in his holdall and zipped it shut. Next he put on two pairs of extra thick tights – even though his legs would not be on show – and released his dress from the plastic cover it was restrained in. A couple of his rivals gasped at the sight of it.

'Oh, my sweet Jesus!' lisped someone, from the other side of the room.

'Get her!' said another. 'I thought this was amateur drag, not Vivienne Westwood's spring collection!'

Simon ignored them and stepped into the dress. 'Would you be so kind?' he asked Penélope Cruz, who was busy snorting a line of cocaine from a Woolworths mirror.

'I've got a terrible case of the runs,' she said, as she fastened the back of Genita's dress.

Simon settled himself down to wait, staring at his reflection from time to time, completely satisfied with it. Eleven o'clock came, and he watched with serene indifference as, one by one, each hopeful tottered nervously on to the stage and was greeted with cat-calls and jeers by the drunken crowd. Here was an audience ready for a real star. Genita swelled inside him and the contractions started. Instead of gas and air, Simon took vodka and tonic in liberal quantities. One by one the acts returned, bedraggled and forlorn. The only one who had been mildly well received was a Madonna tribute with exploding tits. 'How predictable,' came Genita's voice from somewhere within. Simon wiped the sweat from his brow and repowdered.

Finally it was time.

'Ladies and gentlemen,' shouted Jimmy down the microphone, 'please welcome on stage – Miss Genita L'Warts!'

Genita swept on to the tiny stage and stood there, shimmering in the follow-spot. She peered at her audience disapprovingly, as if they were youths caught sniffing glue in a bus shelter, and took a swig from the vodka bottle she held tightly in one hand. Eventually the crowd quietened, but still Genita didn't speak. She took an air-freshener out of her handbag and sprayed the people at the front. Finally she lifted the microphone to her lips and spoke: 'I am Miss Genita L'Warts, the patron saint of homosexuals.'

Chapter Ten

It was the morning after the party. Lilia was sitting at the kitchen table when Molly came in for her morning muesli. She gave her a warm smile. 'Good morning, sweet child,' she said, in a girlish voice. 'I am concerned that I kept you up late last night with my performance.'

'Oh, Lilia,' said Molly, crossing the kitchen and grasping her hands. 'You're not to worry about me. In fact, I want to thank you for such a wonderful evening.'

Lilia released her hands and folded them in turn around the younger woman's. They smiled at each other.

'Goodness!' said Lilia, letting Molly go, then clapping once. 'Such kindness on an empty stomach. And you have a matinée to perform in a couple of hours. Have a cup of coffee.'

Lilia sat while Molly ate her breakfast and the two of them talked over the previous night and what a success it had been. 'It quite makes me long for the old days.' Lilia sighed. 'When I was the *chanteuse du jour*, a star of the cabaret. But it's too late for me now.'

'No, it isn't,' Molly said loyally, though of course she could see that Lilia was now past her songstress days. The show the previous evening had been enjoyable but the old lady's voice was quivering and rather ropy, taking a visit round the note rather than to it.

'Do you really think so?' Lilia's eyes sparkled a little.

'Of course,' Molly said, remembering Roger's story of the failed comeback. I mustn't encourage her too much, or she'll do it again, poor love, she thought. And she shouldn't waste her money and get her hopes up all over again. She said quickly, 'You should ask your friends round and do some little performances for them. Have some more soirées. Maybe a spot of singing in the village pub.'

'Huh!' grunted Lilia. 'I'm not that desperate. Those old women in the village, they don't understand me, or art, or beauty. They think I'm eccentric. They laugh at me. What they don't know is that I am alive and they are dead. And I have lived more in a single year than they have in their entire lives!'

'I want to hear more about it,' Molly said eagerly. 'I want to hear about your amazing experiences.'

'You shall, dear Molly, you shall. Are you back late tonight?'

'No – I'll come straight home after the evening performance. I'll bring us a bottle of wine, if you like, and we can sit down and have a good talk.'

'But I'm sure you have better things to do. Drinks with your friends, a visit to Northampton's finest club, Manhattan Nights . . .'

'Don't worry about that,' Molly said, waving away Lilia's concern with one hand. 'I'd much rather be here with you. I'm leaving on Sunday and I still haven't had the chance to hear your story.'

Lilia looked at her with watery eyes. 'You'd really like that?'

'Of course I would. I can't think of anything nicer.'

'You're so kind to me,' Lilia said, looking as pleased as a child promised an ice cream.

When Molly left, Lilia followed her to the front door almost anxiously. 'Do you really want to hear all about my life, Molly?' she asked. 'I would understand if you'd rather be with your friends.'

Molly bent down and gave her a hug. 'Of course I do.'

'Thank you, my dear. You've made me very happy,' said Lilia, bobbing up and down a couple of times with enthusiasm. This she achieved by bending her knees; a younger woman would probably have jumped lightly on the spot. 'I will await your return.'

Everyone at the theatre seemed a little subdued, tired out by their carousing the previous night.

'Thanks for the party,' said Peter, when he and Molly met in the Green Room. 'Five hours' sleep and I still look like Dale Winton. I'm a walking miracle.'

'Thank you for coming,' said Molly. 'Isn't Lilia fascinating?'

'A game old bird,' said Peter. 'And she can still warble a tune, I'll give her that.'

'Lilia has soul. She sings in a way only people who have lived a life can.'

'You must find out what her story is,' said Peter. 'She might be related to Leslie Joseph.'

'I'm going to. It's my last chance tonight. After tomorrow, I'll probably never see her again.'

'Or me.' Peter shrugged. 'Showbusiness is a funny old world, isn't it? We all get thrown together in the most random of ways. Some people we attach ourselves to, others we can't wait to let go of.'

'I know what you mean,' said Molly.

That night Molly left straight after the curtain call, barely stopping to take off her wig and makeup. On the way home, she picked up a bottle of good, full-bodied Chilean Merlot from an off-licence. It seemed a suitable drink, somehow.

When she got back to Kit-Kat Cottage, the bungalow seemed quiet and dark. Then, as she shut the front door behind her, she heard Lilia call from the lounge, 'Molly, my dear, you're home.'

'Yes, and I've got the wine. I'll just fetch some glasses.'

In the lounge, Lilia was once again wearing her silken kimono, stretched out along the red sofa and awaiting her audience. Molly poured them both some ruby-red wine and handed Lilia hers. They chinked their glasses together.

'To you, Lilia!' said Molly, brightly.

'Thank you, my dear,' Lilia said modestly.

When Molly was settled, she gazed at Lilia, who seemed to be waiting for a question to prompt her into speech, so she said, 'Was your childhood a happy one?'

Lilia perked up at once. 'It was very exciting. I practically grew up in the dressing room of the Metropole. And the Nelson and the Theater des Westens, in Berlin. My first toy was a lipstick. Yes, I was happy.'

'Were your parents actors?'

'Not exactly. They were a slightly different breed. Cabaret people, performers, innovators. Berlin in the thirties – you cannot imagine it. I am coy about my age, but I was there – just. I remember it in flashes, as a child would, not intellectually.'

'What do you remember?'

'My mother, mostly. She was getting ready to go on stage. Dark eyes, and glowing white skin. She would smoke nervously, and pace up and down. She would kiss and hug me as if we were never going to see each other again, with tears of regret in her eyes. Then she would leave me. Alone. She would only be gone for half an hour, then she'd come back in and smoke some more.'

'Was your mother as famous as your father, Kurt Weill?'

'Some believe my father to be Kurt Weill, but I do not!' Lilia said emphatically.

'Oh!' Molly was surprised. Hadn't Lilia herself said that Kurt Weill was her father? She asked reasonably, 'Well, who are the "some"?'

'Academics, musicologists. People of note. It has never been proven. In fact, I threw it in for effect. If you say Kurt Weill was your father before you sing one of his songs it heightens the experience for the audience. They think you're channelling or something. I'd say Cliff Richard was my father if I thought it would help.'

'You devil!' said Molly, laughing at the old lady's audacity.

'Ah, an old cabaret trick.' Lilia chuckled like a wise owl. 'Nancy Sinatra, Liza Minnelli, Prince – everyone does it at some stage of their career . . .'

'So who is Lilia Delvard?' asked Molly, relishing the sound of the name. 'And who was your real father?'

Lilia leant back on her pillows and a dreamy look came over her face. She seemed to be reaching back into the far-distant past and her earliest memories. Then she began in a soft, musical voice, her German accent more pronounced, 'I am the daughter of Otto Falckenberg. He was the director of the Academic-Dramatic Union in the Berlin of 1901. Apart from being my father, he was the sire of modern cabaret in all its variations. Along with artists, painters and students, he was protesting against the strict morality of the time, the censorship by the government and interference of the police. With a group of like-minded artists, he formed a group called Die Elf Scharfrichter – the Eleven Executioners. They were young and ambitious and angry!' Lilia's voice quivered somewhat. She paused to take a breath and steady herself. 'They hired a room at the back of an inn and decorated it with grotesque masks. To avoid harassment by the authorities, they called themselves a club and played only to invited guests. Their first performance began with a discordant song from the Eleven Executioners, during which they threw their bloody robes at the audience. Next came *chansons*, recitations, puppet plays, dramatic pieces and literary parodies, all written and performed by this innovative group. They acted vicious sketches about their betters and sang dangerous satirical songs. As you can imagine, they were all the rage. It had never been done before. No one had seen anything like it. A breath of fresh air. A *tour de force*. A sensation. The beginning of a new era, a new means of expression, of resistance, of liberty!' Lilia looked Molly gravely in the eyes. 'But change was afoot. The Eleven Executioners were soon to become twelve.' Lilia tapped herself on the chest. 'And then thirteen.

'One afternoon during rehearsals a beautiful woman entered the room. She was tall, with black hair parted in the middle, falling to her shoulders, framing her pale, angular face. Her eyelids were heavy, her lips full and red, and she was extremely, almost painfully thin, but with the pride and arrogance of a thoroughbred foal. She was the most bewitching creature Otto Falckenberg had ever seen.' Lilia paused for a moment, as though fighting a strong emotion. Molly guessed she didn't want her feelings to get in the way of the narrative – it was obvious that she needed to tell her all this. Somehow Molly felt she understood.

Lilia went on, 'The woman's name was Marya Delvard and in my opinion she was the most important female cabaret artist of the twentieth century. She was also to become . . . my mother.'

Molly gasped and reached across to take Lilia's hand. Lilia sniffed, took a handkerchief from the side of her chair and wiped her eyes, even though they were tearless.

'This is beautiful!' breathed Molly. 'It's like a Radio 4 play.'

'It is dramatic and florid, perhaps, but this is the only way I can tell it to you,' said Lilia, regaining her self-control. 'I have told this story to myself so many times, it is like a book to me.'

'Please carry on,' begged Molly. 'What happened next?'

Lilia cleared her throat. 'The moment he clapped eyes on her, Otto knew he had to have her. He called a halt to the rehearsals, jumped down from the stage and introduced himself as the director of the Eleven Executioners.

'Marya shook his hand and said, "I know who you are. I saw the performance last night and thought you were of interest. I have come to offer my services to you. My name is Marya Delvard and I am a friend of Frank Wedekind. He has written a song for me to sing. I think it will suit your show very well."

'Otto asked her if she had the music with her and called for the pianist. My mother was a sensation from the moment she stepped onto the stage. For a woman to be so bold and so powerful was a rare thing in those days. At once, Otto made her a part of his performance, and later concentrated only on her when they fell wildly in love with each other. The two of them became definers of the cabaret – they really led the way for the re-emergence of the suppressed decadence of the Berlin underworld. Otto was brilliant, talented, inspired. His stage shows drew the great intellectuals, thinkers and writers. He was one of them. Marya was a brittle beauty who personified intelligent excess, indulgence and liberation, for their own sake. She was never seen in daylight and it was said she had cocaine for breakfast and lettuce for lunch. God only knows what she had for dinner. Schapps and cigarettes, probably. Despite her slight frame it is said that no one noticed she was pregnant with me until she gave birth while singing "The Lavender Song" during a matinée.'

They both took a sip of the ruby wine and sat in silence. Lilia stared intently at the wall. What will be next? thought Molly.

Lilia said at last, 'That is why I could do nothing but sing myself. You do understand that, don't you, Molly? It was in my blood. It was my birthright. I'm a creature of the stage, just as my parents were before me. There was no other calling I could follow in life, even when they had long gone.'

'What happened to them?' Molly whispered.

Lilia closed her eyes and said nothing for a long while. Then she sighed and opened them again, fixing Molly with her watery green gaze. 'I cannot tell you that yet, my dear. Perhaps another time. It is too painful for me. Too difficult.'

'Of course. I'm sorry.' Molly gazed at the floor, feeling awkward.

'Don't worry, my dear, you haven't hurt me. That particular pain is so familiar to me now, it is a dull ache that I hardly notice. I've had other hurts to take its place.'

'Tell me about your life, your career,' begged Molly. 'I would dearly love to hear about them.'

'Not now. Let us talk about the future,' said Lilia, brightening suddenly. 'Enough of the past.'

Molly felt slightly shell-shocked. To jump from Lilia's early childhood straight to the future was quite a leap.

The old lady continued, 'You see, now I find myself preoccupied with the end of my story, not the beginning. I know I am old and my life may be edging towards some kind of conclusion, but I need a final flourish. Do you understand?'

'Yes, I think so. The last act?'

'I can't be doing with just fading away.' Lilia seemed worried. A little distressed, even.

'You have a lot of life yet to live, Lilia,' said Molly. 'A bang, not a whimper – is that what you want?'

'Exactly. Look at poor Joey. He lies in his bed or he sits in his chair. I feed him and I clean him, until one day – what will happen? His kidneys will fail or he will turn blue or he will die in his sleep. After the life I have had it is bad enough that I now live in a bungalow – I have always despised them! This must not be my fate.'

'What is it you'd like?'

'I don't know. But I will tell you this much. Old age makes me reckless. I do not stop and worry about the consequences of things any more. My mother's genes, perhaps. I give in to my desires.'

Molly poured more wine. She raised her glass, signalling another toast. 'To a happy future!'

Lilia, though, did not lift her glass to meet Molly's. She looked bemused. 'Happy?' she said. 'Spare me that. I gave up aspiring to happiness as a child. No. I see my life as a film. I only want it to be a good one, that's all. Happy doesn't come into it.'

Silence fell. Lilia's eyes drooped.

'Are you tired, darling?' asked Molly. She must remember that Lilia was an old lady, born in the nineteen thirties.

'Yes, my dear. Terribly.'

'I've been an exhausting guest, I do apologise.'

'Oh, no,' said Lilia. 'It does me good to talk about it. But let's leave it there. Suspended. The shows, the champagne, the cabaret.'

Molly smiled and collected the now empty glasses. 'Come on. Time to turn in.'

Lilia looked relieved. 'Yes, an excellent idea. Help me up, Molly, would you mind?'

Molly offered her a crooked arm and led her out of the lounge to her bedroom door, where they said a fond goodnight.

How much more was there to tell? wondered Molly later, as she lay in her bed. What had been the fate of Lilia's parents? How had Lilia's own cabaret career come about? And how had she ended up married to Joey and living in a bungalow in Northampton?

I bet she won't have time to tell me before I go on Sunday. How frustrating. I expect I'll never know.

Chapter Eleven

On Sunday morning Molly awoke with a thick head and no recollection of how she'd got home the night before. She decided it was best to lie there and think for a while, without even opening her eyes. Despite her hangover, she smiled to herself. It was important to conclude a run with a good party. She hated those prissy shows where everyone rushed off within half an hour of the final curtain. A rollicking knees-up appealed to her Liverpudlian sensibilities. It concluded things properly and *The Mikado* could now be filed in the recesses of her mind as the show that had received a memorable send-off. She couldn't quite remember how it had ended. She had fuzzy memories of them all dancing around the empty stage to something pounding out of the sound system, and there was even the faint recollection of Peter yelling and screaming, then some kind of punch-up with Duncan . . . She must ring him later and get all the gossip.

Funny to think she'd never be dressing up as Yum-Yum again – at least, not in the same way and with the same people.

And *The Mikado* would now be for ever associated with the extraordinary Lilia. She had grown very fond of the eccentric old woman who had lived such a vivid and varied life. But Molly also knew that in showbusiness you got to know people very well, swore undying love and never heard from them again. You were always on to the next show and the next gang. Lilia, of course, wasn't part of the company, but she was part of the experience, and it was time to move on.

Finally she opened her eyes.

'Oh, my God!' she said involuntarily, her voice croaky and not at all ready to be used.

The first thing she saw was a body lying next to her, and a mop of brown hair on the pillow.

Of course. That was how she had got home. There was the battered leather jacket on the end of the bed. Marcus, the cute, teenage, stagehand, had offered her a lift on the back of his motorbike. Or had she demanded one? Oh dear. She had a sudden recollection of screaming at the top of her voice as they drove through the sleeping village of Long Buckby.

Then once that had found a chink through the armour of her hangover, several others came bustling through. Her arms round Marcus's slender waist, reaching down to his crotch as they drove through the darkness, Marcus parking outside and helping her to stagger up the gravel path. Molly reached down and touched her knee: yes, there was the fresh graze from where she had fallen over. And then – oh dear. The next bit was truly mortifying. She had refused to let him go until he had given her a kiss. No, not a peck on the cheek – that wouldn't do. She wanted a proper French kiss. Right now, or she'd scream her tits off – that was what she'd said. And poor, embarrassed Marcus had obliged. His lips had been cold from the ride home, but they were soft and tasted of cider and cigarettes. She had held the back of his head, pressing him towards her, and her tongue had explored the depths of his mouth as if it was trying to lick her palm through his skull.

Eventually he'd pulled away and said, 'Jesus!' but she had grabbed a clump of his thick hair and pushed him roughly forward again. The second kiss had gone on and on, and she had writhed and moaned, grabbed his hand and pushed it up her skirt. Eventually, with her knickers round her ankles and Marcus's fingers still inside her, she had managed to get her keys out of her coat pocket. Then she and Marcus had gone noisily down the hallway and swiftly to her room. Marcus's muscular young body and eager manhood . . .

Enough. She covered her mouth in horror. She would never drink again.

There he was. She peered over his shoulder and looked again at his youthful face. He was sleeping soundly, breathing softly with his lips just parted and his impossibly long, doll-like eyelashes resting on his soft cheeks.

Molly solemnly shook his shoulder, said a polite 'Good morning' and explained, while looking directly into the dilated pupils of her lover's dreamy eyes, that it was time for him to get dressed and leave. No, it was not possible for him to visit the bathroom. He must be very quiet.

She enjoyed watching him dress, noting with an erotic thrill the absence of underpants, and responded with a Scarlett O'Hara smile when he leant over her for a final, roguish kiss. She inhaled the sexy smell of his distressed leather jacket and stroked his hair one last time. 'Sssh!' was her last communication. Marcus slipped silently out of the room, out of the bungalow, on to his motorbike and away.

As soon as he was gone, Molly wiggled back down under her

bedcovers, closed her eyes and tried her hardest to go back to sleep. Maybe when she woke up she could pretend the sordid incident had never happened. She felt regret. Her longed-for reunion with Daniel was somewhat sullied. But now she was awake, her mind was racing and full of memories of the night before that made her squeak with a combination of embarrassment and pleasure. In the end she gave up and dragged herself out of bed. At the window, she drew the curtains. Lilia was shuffling down the garden path with Heathcliff at her side. As Molly watched, she paused and the dog stopped next to her. She muttered something soft and held his big, square head in both her bony hands, blowing him a kiss. Heathcliff gazed up lovingly at his mistress and she looked back at him tenderly.

That overweight Rottweiler is really a form of therapy, thought Molly. The affection she lavishes on him – he's probably what keeps her going.

Molly took her time in the bathroom. She didn't want Lilia's final memory of her to be a rough, hung-over one. She washed and conditioned her hair, exfoliated her tired skin and drank glass after glass of water. Makeup was liberally applied. By the time she appeared in the kitchen, she had a deceptively healthy glow, a radiant smile and fresh, peppermint breath. 'Morning, Lilia!' she said perkily.

Lilia was sitting in her usual place at the kitchen table, Heathcliff standing patiently at her side, as if he was waiting for his cooked breakfast.

'Molly! Good morning, my dear. Do sit down. I have put a cushion on your chair. It is nice and soft. I was pottering in the front garden this morning and I met young Marcus. These country boys are the same the world over, don't you find? So feral.'

'Our last-night party got a little wild,' said Molly, helping herself to some muesli, then sitting down. 'Thanks for the cushion.'

Lilia leant forward and said confidentially, 'I was once buggered by a Viennese taxi driver.'

This startled Molly, and she stared at her landlady for a long, awkward moment, unable to prevent herself from visualising it. Then she said, 'Poor you.'

'Not at all. It was the most liberating experience of my life. As I opened my mouth to scream, my soul fluttered out and away. It was gone for a week. Happy days. So, you see, I understand the extraordinary power of sex. And the tenderness it can leave in the nether regions afterwards.'

Molly wasn't sure how to respond to such a surreal revelation at breakfast time. She decided to bring the conversation back to more mundane matters. 'I'm back to London this morning, Lilia, as soon as I've finished packing. Thank you so much for having me to stay here. I've had a brilliant week with you. I really can't thank you enough.'

'Yes,' said Lilia. 'You are saying all the things an English-woman deems correct. The perfect guest. I have enjoyed your company also.'

'I'm glad.' Molly wondered if there was any orange juice in the fridge. She was craving something sweet. Her hangover wasn't holding up well.

'No doubt Daniel will be pleased to see you?' said Lilia, the question loaded with sub-text. Lilia knew all about Daniel and most aspects of Molly's life. She had slowly but firmly prised every-thing out over the days Molly had been at Kit-Kat Cottage. When they'd been shopping in Sainsbury's for the after-show party,

Molly had told Lilia everything about her lonely childhood, failed university career and determination to make it as a musical actress.

'He's busy working, I expect,' said Molly breezily, stirring her muesli intently but unable to consume a spoonful without the very real risk of retching.

'I hope you will keep in touch with me,' said Lilia, suddenly. Her eyes seemed to search Molly's face for a positive response.

'I intend to,' said Molly. 'You've taught me a great deal. I leave here a wiser girl. A Lilia Delvard graduate.'

Lilia turned to stare out of the kitchen window. 'Not a sign of my starling or my dear little thrush. It is a dreary day. When it is grey and raining it is hard to remember what the sun feels like on your skin. But if you try very hard you can remember.' She turned and focused on Molly. 'Do not forget the things you have learnt here. I have tried to impress you, Molly, not because my ego demands it, but because I have suffered. There needs to be a payoff. A wise and illuminating conclusion that benefits the world I leave behind. I don't know why I chose you, but I feel somehow we are connected.'

'You're being very solemn and serious for this time of day,' said Molly.

'I may never see you again,' said Lilia. 'I want you to remember me as a cabaret artist, not a silly old German woman. Cabaret. That has been my life. I was born into it, as I have told you. It runs through my veins and is more than just a few songs and a threadbare feather boa. Please remember me, tell others about me. Don't let me vanish into obscurity – not entirely.'

'I won't,' Molly promised.

'Good,' said the old lady, allowing a big sigh to billow out of her mouth. She seemed satisfied.

Half an hour later Molly had packed her cases and loaded them into the car. 'Goodbye, Lilia, and take care,' she said, hugging her and kissing her on both cheeks.

'I will, my dear. And you – I wish you all good fortune. You are a special girl. I am sure that great things await you. I hope I see you again one day.'

'God bless!' said Molly, with finality, and wheeled her suitcase down the gravel path towards the gate. She felt a slight twinge between her legs and resolved to stop at the nearest shop for some cranberry juice.

Molly was at home in London by lunchtime. After Lilia's gloomy, cluttered bungalow, the flat she shared with Daniel seemed bright, sunny and minimal by comparison. It was nothing special, just a second-floor, one-bedroom arrangement in a cheaply built nineteen-seventies block in a nondescript side-street off Tufnell Park Road, but it was affordable and bright, with laminate flooring and Ikea furniture.

Everything was neat and clean: Daniel had obviously made an effort. On the kitchen table there was a 'Welcome Home' card – a picture of a cat asleep in a basket by a coal fire, a bowl of milk at her side. Inside, in Daniel's slanting, masculine writing, it said: 'Molls! You're home at last! I'll be back around six and will show you how much I've missed you. There's a present in the fridge. Love you, Daniel xxx'.

Ah, bless, she thought lovingly. She could guess what the present was. She propped the card on top of the microwave and pulled the fridge door open. Champagne and white chocolate truffles. Her favourite. Next she took her case into the bedroom.

The sheets were clean and the carpet had been hoovered. It was good to be home. She unpacked, put some laundry into the washing-machine, made a cup of tea and sat down to open her letters.

Before she did so, she allowed herself a contented sigh and a long sip of tea. It was always a joy to be in her own space after a long, intensive period of work. Having spent all day every day of the last month cooped up in the theatre and her few spare hours locked into Lilia's strange world, it was lovely to have her own things around her.

It always surprised her how quickly she readjusted to her old life, and how swiftly the work routine and the people she had been with faded from her consciousness. Actors and dancers who told you every intimate detail of their lives, laughed and cried with you, discussed their dreams and aspirations with you and hugged you tightly on the last night, vowing to meet up in town and resume the deep friendship you had embarked on, were swiftly forgotten. It all meant nothing. The tight-knit family group was, seasoned pros understood, merely for the duration of the contract.

It was a similarly unspoken rule that any affairs and liaisons that might occur while on tour or during the run of a play or panto were of little or no consequence. What happens on tour stays on tour. Everyone in the theatrical world knew that. Outsiders didn't, unfortunately. If you were a teacher or an estate agent or an office worker, intimate encounters in the workplace would not be as inconsequential. There was not the built-in escape at the end or, indeed, the abundance of suitable locations, such as dressing rooms with handy day-beds. And theatre people had the added temptations of working in the evenings, the after-show parties with liberal amounts of booze, the frisson of on-stage relationships where the boundaries between acting and reality might so easily become blurred and confused. Not to mention the occupational hazard of fragile egos needing reassurance and the occasional touch of comfort . . .

These were Molly's vague thoughts as she drank her tea. She was determined to dissolve the niggling twinge of guilt she was feeling about her night of lust with Marcus. Daniel wouldn't understand that theatre folk operated under different moral rules and she had no intention of trying to explain it to him. She couldn't even say she particularly regretted what she had done. It would be a private memory that no one knew about. Only Lilia – and she was miles away, safely in the past now. If anything, her love for Daniel had been intensified by the experience with Marcus. Or so she told herself.

The one person she could share absolutely everything with was Simon. Their silly falling-out was, she had no doubt, just temporary. They hadn't spoken since he had hung up on her the day she had arrived in Northampton. It wasn't unusual for them to behave petulantly with one another. Once, they hadn't spoken for six months, after Simon called Molly an interfering busybody and she told him he was a bitter and twisted queen, incapable of sustaining a relationship. Their reconciliations were always accompanied with fresh declarations of eternal friendship, plans for turkey-baster babies and a blissful old age together somewhere fun and unexpected, like Las Vegas or Casablanca. Molly resolved to call him later, after she'd had a nap. The hangover was just a faint ache now, but she had time for a rest and a bath before Daniel came home.

Chapter Twelve

Simon had marked in his diary the date of Molly's return to London and was half expecting her call. Their reconciliations were always full of affection and laughter. He had missed his soulmate more than he cared to admit. It was all very well drinking with Charles and cruising on his favourite commons, but he never felt quite as happy as he did when he was with Molly. No one else amused or understood him like she did.

He sat in the Sunday-morning sunlight that poured through the windows of the flat, illuminating the dust and the empty bottles piled up by the fireplace, staring at the phone and wondering what to do. Not only did he want to hear all about the tour and everything that had happened in Northampton but he couldn't wait to share his exciting news with her. Things had been moving apace since Genita's last stage appearance, and he knew Molly would be staggered, excited and delighted by what had happened. But he was very aware that he was the one who had hung up on her, rather unforgivably. He was still feeling guilty about it. She only ever wanted the best for him. It was very bad behaviour to throw that back in her face and act as though she was the one in the wrong.

Should I make the first move, he wondered, or should I wait? Perhaps she's still cross . . . But that wouldn't be like Molly. She was always quick to forgive even his worst tantrums. He decided to wait until Monday, to give her time to have the passionate reunion with Daniel she was no doubt enjoying at that very moment, but he couldn't last any longer than that.

When the phone rang at three o'clock, he knew at once who it would be. He snatched it up with an eager 'Hello?'

'Si, it's Molly. I'm back in London.'

'Are you, now?' he said, unable to disguise his pleasure at hearing her voice again. 'And how was Northampton? As glamorous as ever, I trust?'

'I had a very odd time. I can't wait to tell you all about it.'

There was a pause. Simon rubbed his fingernail along some dirt embedded in the edges of the telephone table. 'So I'm forgiven?'

'Well . . .'

'I'm sorry about that little snit I was in,' he said quickly. 'You know I didn't mean anything by it, don't you?'

Molly laughed. 'Oh, Si, I do know. Let's forget it. How have you been?'

'Rather busy, thank you for asking.'

'Good. Er, busy doing what? Your usual nocturnal activities?'

'Not really, no,' said Simon. 'Listen, I have so much to tell you. Can we meet up somewhere?'

'Not today. Daniel's coming home in a minute for roast beef and Yorkshire pudding.'

'I've never heard it called *that* before.'

Molly giggled. 'How about tomorrow? Lunch at Delancey's?'

'I'll be there at one o'clock sharp. Longing to see you!'

'Dying to hear your news!'

When Simon put the phone down, he felt restored and happy. In just the right mood for his first glass of something.

Delancey's was a favourite lunch spot of theirs, an unpretentious French bistro in Camden Town that was open all day, and they had spent many a long, lazy afternoon there. The waiter recognised Simon when he arrived just before one, and ushered him to his and Molly's favourite corner table. When she arrived a few minutes later they flung their arms round each other and hugged. When they finally sat down, there were tears of pleasure in their eyes.

'How blissful it is to see you,' said Simon. 'We must never, ever fall out again.' He called to the waiter, 'Champagne, please!'

'I am *so* pleased to be home,' said Molly, wiping her eyes with a napkin. 'You're looking so handsome!'

'Are you glad the tour's over?'

'Oh, yes. It wasn't my most memorable job, but I was missing Daniel, and missing you, of course.'

Simon's smile became a little fixed at the mention of Daniel, but he thought it wise to refrain from saying anything catty so early in their reconciliation.

'So tell me,' continued Molly, 'what's the big news?'

Just then the waiter arrived with the champagne in an ice bucket, and Simon maintained an enigmatic silence until their glasses were full and the man had withdrawn.

'To you!' he said, raising his glass.

'And to you, my dearest friend in the world!' replied Molly.

'Now then,' began Simon, 'take a look at this.' He plopped something on her empty plate. It was a glossy leaflet advertising a fun-packed night at the Black Cap, a pub just north of Camden Town. The main photograph was of an extraordinary creature dressed in a black sequined power jacket with matching mini-skirt and turban. The makeup was extreme – glamour gone mad – huge black eyes sweeping up to the forehead and pouting lips encrusted with glitter. The words, in a jaunty pink font with stars dotted above and below, read: 'Live on Stage – the Drag Scene's newest sensational discovery MISS GENITA L'WARTS! Friday night. Be there or be straight!'

Molly wondered why he wanted her to read this information. Then she looked again at the photo. 'Oh, my Lord!' she shrieked, with surprised amusement. 'Simon! What *have* you done? Is that you? *You* are Miss Genita L'Warts?'

'At your service, bitch.'

'Oh. My. God!' Molly screamed again.

'It's all happened rather quickly.'

'I'll say. You were swigging the whisky and pursuing a happily married man the last time we spoke. Suddenly you're a cock in a frock with the career prospects of a young Danny La Rue. What happened?'

'Well, you see,' said Simon, lowering his voice as if someone might overhear, 'high as a kite I signed up for the amateur drag night at the Black Cap. Just for a laugh. The next day I'd forgotten all about it, but they phoned and told me I was to turn up the following Thursday and I had a five-minute slot. I was sober then and something about the challenge appealed to me. Suddenly I was possessed by a dark, daring and, if I say so myself, hilarious spirit.'

'Oh, Simon! Whatever happened next?' exclaimed Molly.

'Well, my *dear*, Thursday dawned and Genita was feeling

supremely confident. I strode out on to that stage and I fucking slayed them!'

'Good for you. What did you do exactly?'

Simon could see that Molly was struggling to understand his extraordinary news. He had never expressed any interest in performing before: Molly had always been the star turn and perhaps he had detected just a teaspoonful of chagrin in her tone. 'Well, that's just the thing. I haven't the faintest idea. She just babbles away. It's almost as if I talk in many tongues.'

'Do you sing?' asked Molly, and took a gulp of champagne.

'No, don't worry. Not yet, anyway.'

'I'm not worried, Simon, just asking.'

'Genita doesn't sing – at least she hasn't yet – and she certainly doesn't mime. She'd be deeply offended by the very suggestion. She just raves at the audience mostly, spouting vitriol and filth, crossing every line and crucifying every taboo. She knows no bounds.'

'Simon, I'm so pleased for you,' said Molly, genuinely excited. 'You're a hit!'

'Well, yes, it seems I am. A large fish in a small pond, that's all, mind. After that first gig – I did twenty minutes instead of five and a ten-minute encore – they stormed my dressing-room door to book me again. Since then every gay pub in London has been calling me up and asking for my services. It's madness!'

'Amazing, Simon. Congratulations. I can't believe it's all happened so quickly.'

'I'm going to have to find an agent or a manager, I guess.'

Molly was gazing at the leaflet, still rather shocked. 'I'd better come to the Black Cap next Friday, then.'

'I'll put you on my guest list. Word has it the Pet Shop Boys are coming, and I've heard a whisper about Simon Fanshawe, but let's not get our hopes up.'

'Are you earning heaps of money?'

'Darling, I am hot, hot, hot. Trouble with these gay bars, of course, is they try and fob you off with a couple of drink tokens and first dibs at the cold buffet. Makes me sick.'

'So no, then?'

'Well, not as yet. Give us a chance. I'm not doing it for the money, am I? I just seem to have stumbled on something that works. I have every intention of being a flash in the pan. When you see Genita, you'll understand. She's so barking that it's not really a commercial proposition. She's never going to fill the Albert Hall or be on tea-time telly. It's a bit like I'm channelling some weird, dethroned Egyptian empress.'

'Why do you say that?'

'Because that's what I feel. She's regal, bitter and enraged. If I hadn't been stone-cold sober when I went on stage I'd swear it was the rantings of a drunken queen.'

'Heavens.'

'I'm serious, Molly. I really don't know what's going on with me. It's a bit like a blind person suddenly being given the ability to paint amazing, disturbing pictures. The most probable outcome is that she'll disappear as suddenly as she arrived.'

'I'd better come and see you sharpish, then.'

Simon wasn't sure, but it seemed as if Molly was slightly more comfortable with the idea that his success might be short-lived. 'Consider yourself at the top of my guest list! I have this feeling that one day I'll walk on stage and I'll just be dreary old me again. It's a terrifying thought. I'll retreat to my dressing room in a hail of beer bottles and the compère will have to make an announcement: "Miss Genita L'Warts has left the universe."'

'I never, ever imagined you'd be a performer, Simon,' said Molly, sipping her champagne. 'I don't know why. I'm so excited for you.'

'You don't mind, do you?' He had to be sure he wasn't treading on Molly's toes by taking to the stage. He couldn't bear it to come between them.

Molly put down her glass and looked aghast at her friend. 'Mind? Darling, I think it's fantastic! I always knew you were a star but I thought it would be through art or writing or politics.' She picked up the leaflet and held it up to Simon. 'This is fantastic, chuck. Seriously brilliant.'

'I guess I was just a bit worried that I was invading your territory in some way.'

'Don't be daft,' said Molly, with a laugh. 'I'm a jobbing actress. I operate as part of an ensemble. You are a product.'

'Am I?' asked Simon. 'Is that good or bad?'

'It's good. Very good,' concluded Molly. 'Now, let's order – I'm starving.'

Chapter Thirteen

'You are coming to see Genita, aren't you?' demanded Simon, when he called on the Monday. 'I'm at the Black Cap on Friday, remember? And I've put three tickets on the guest list for you, so no excuse.'

'I'm dying to see you,' Molly said truthfully. 'Of course we'll be there.'

She had decided to ask her actress friend Jane to come with her and Daniel to watch the show. Jane had been out of work for so long it was debatable if she was still an actress at all. As a consequence of this she was inclined to be a little miserable, but Molly was fond of her. It had been at Jane's flat that Molly had found refuge after the Paddy débâcle and Jane, although she wasn't a girl to go in for relationships, had been kind and sympathetic. Another contributing factor to Jane's low spirits was her looks: she had what one can only call a characterful face with straw-blonde hair and voluminous cheeks. Her figure was pear-shaped and she dressed in ill-advised tight clothes that did her no favours. It all made life as an actress challenging, in a profession full of good-lookers. Her last job had been five years ago, for a BBC drama in which she played a psychologically disturbed prisoner, mainly sitting in the background, swaying.

Poor Jane, thought Molly, she could do with a night out, especially since she got turned down for that *Crime Watch* reconstruction job. It would cheer her up to see Simon in action, and there would be scant opportunity for her to be too intense or maudlin.

On the night, Molly was full of anticipation and experiencing the odd sensation of preparing to see Simon on stage. It was normally Simon who sat in the audience dutifully watching his best friend in one show or another, and Molly was still a little stunned to find they had swapped roles. Daniel had to go home after work to shower and change, so she met Jane in Ruby in the Dust on Camden High Street for a quick bite to eat before the show. Jane was quite perky. She'd had a Tarot consultation a month before, she said, and the card reader had announced that Jane had special healing powers that were being cruelly wasted, so she was now doing a part-time course to hone and develop them. She had a vision of her future, she said, where she worked in an alternative-medicine clinic, curing the sick and giving hope to the terminally ill. (She added that she had a particular affinity with animals – she had stroked a Staffordshire bull terrier in Eltham High Street the other day and he had immediately stopped limping.)

There was certainly a new spring in Jane's step, Molly conceded, although the quiver in her voice remained.

'What is important,' said Jane, seriously, 'is that I rein myself in. I'm currently learning to switch my powers off when they aren't required. A trip on a bus or the tube can be painful for me. I can very easily be overwhelmed by the physical and mental malfunctions that surround me, you see. I was in John Lewis the other day and I was quite sure the man in front of me had a brain tumour. I wondered if I should I tell him.'

'And did you?' asked Molly.

'I walked away and immediately locked eyes with a woman in the early stages of emphysema. I just had to run out of the store and go home to meditate. I did some long-distance healing for both of them and I'm pretty sure I cured the emphysema. Mind you, it took it out of me. I slept for fourteen hours afterwards.' Jane looked exhausted just thinking about it.

'It sounds very draining. And acting? Any news there?' asked Molly, hoping to steer Jane back to common ground.

Jane shook her head. 'I can see why I thought I wanted to be an actress in the first place,' she said dismissively. 'I wanted to draw people towards me, to communicate with them and move them. But I didn't understand that I was searching for my place in the world. My acting aspirations were misplaced. Now I have a proper function. I offer healing, not mere entertainment.'

'Yes,' said Molly, after a pause, aware that her own chosen profession was now considered small fry. 'I'm glad you've discovered your destiny. Shall we order?'

The dinner that followed was something of a battle of wills. Molly wanted to keep the conversation light and fun, while Jane's new-found path in life seemed to disallow anything frivolous. Molly told a few amusing Kit-Kat Cottage anecdotes, but Jane only wanted to hear about Lilia's bad joints so that she could send forth some kinetic healing rays.

Molly was mightily relieved when Daniel arrived, his dark curly hair still glistening from the shower, wearing a dashing grey cashmere crew-neck and black jeans. He looked particularly handsome by candlelight, she thought happily, watching a soft vanilla-gold highlight flutter on his cheekbones and his strong, twitching jaw. Daniel smelt of soap and deodorant and drank beer straight from the bottle. He was fit and he knew it. He squeezed Molly's hand under the table as they listened to Jane's earnest ramblings, and she could tell he was getting impatient with her. When she launched on to another speech about human suffering and physical frailties, he interrupted, 'Give it a rest, will you, Mother Teresa? We're after a good night out. Lighten up!' His voice was reasonable but determined. 'Have a beer, why don't you?'

'I'm sorry if I'm boring you,' said Jane, then she sniffed the air. 'Do you have suppressed anger? That can be very bad for you.'

'For you and all,' muttered Daniel, and Molly decided they should make their way to the Black Cap. A change of scene was called for. She saw now that it had been a mistake to bring Jane and Daniel together and expect it to be a tranquil mix. They were in very different moods and it was impossible to alternate her responses to each of them successfully. She ended up being serious with Daniel and playful with Jane, and soon both of them were morphing into one sulky companion.

The Black Cap was very busy, an assortment of young and older gay men five deep at the crowded bar, but quite a few lesbians, too. There was a buzz of excitement in the air and already people were gathering at the far end round the small stage, staking out their patch, ready for Genita's performance, even though there was a good half-hour to go.

Molly and Daniel had been there quite a few times before, attracted by the late-night drinking on their way home from the West End and the vaguely amusing, if old-fashioned, drag shows. Daniel always attracted admiring glances and even the occasional drunken approach, but he was good-natured about it. He did his best to indicate that he wasn't gay by hanging his arm round Molly's shoulders and kissing her affectionately between sips of his drink.

'More than just the regulars in here tonight,' he said, when he eventually returned to the girls, clutching two bottles of Becks and an orange juice for Jane.

'Rammed, isn't it?' said Molly. 'Do you think this is all for Simon?' She looked at the crowd, wondering if he really had this much pulling power.

'Let's move down to the front a bit, shall we?' said Jane. 'I think there might be an ingrowing toenail in the vicinity. And I sensed a painful expression of self-hatred in someone standing very close to us.'

Molly and Daniel perused their neighbours as if they were trying to spot a sniper.

'It might be that geezer over there,' said Daniel, nodding towards a stooped man in his fifties with a well-cut suit and tired eyes.

'Isn't that Peter Mandelson?' asked Jane, squinting.

'Don't be silly,' said Molly. 'As if he'd come here on a Friday night.'

They moved down and found themselves a good spot near the front of the stage.

Between every song, the resident DJ announced that Miss Genita L'Warts would be appearing live on stage very soon, and each time the crowd whooped and hollered.

'Simon's cracked it before he even comes on,' said Daniel, impressed. 'Good on him.'

Molly smiled at him, admiring his generous spirit. Simon hadn't always been as pleasant as he might have been towards

Daniel on the few occasions when they'd met previously. She'd explained that Simon was very protective of her and inclined to be territorial, and Daniel had said he quite understood and had no problem with him. Nevertheless, it was good of him to come along, show his support for Simon's new venture and be so positive.

Jane wasn't saying much now, but had assumed a haughty air of melancholy while she gazed about her at the throng.

'At least she's shut up,' said Daniel, quietly, into Molly's ear as he nuzzled up against her. 'When's Simon on?'

Molly consulted her flyer. 'It says ten o'clock. But it's past that now, and no sign of anything happening.'

The stage was still in darkness. Perhaps to build up the anticipation, the DJ kept saying Genita would be on after the next track and then the next, until the crowd were baying for her. When he did this trick for the fifth time some butch lesbians started to chant, 'We want Genita! We want Genita!' The sentiment spread through the now-packed pub like a Mexican wave until the offending music could no longer be heard.

At last, the spotlight wobbled into action on the red velvet-effect curtains and the DJ finally announced that the moment they had all been waiting for had arrived.

'She's here, she's queer, get out of her way!' he screamed, above the whoops. 'Are you ready? Are you sure? Can you handle her? The patron saint of gay, lesbian, bisexual and transgender folk is among us! Please go wild for the one, the only MISS GENITA L'WARTS!'

The follow-spot did a figure-of-eight across the stage as the curtains parted and 'Don't Cry For Me Argentina' thundered through the speakers. Genita L'Warts stood in a cloud of dry ice centre stage, dressed in an ice-white hologram sequined evening gown with a matching satin matinée jacket and a skullcap turban, parodying the balcony scene from *Evita*.

Molly gasped, unable to take her eyes off the incredible apparition in front of her. Somewhere under the gown and the makeup was the Simon she knew and loved, but he was only just discernible. It was like looking at a photograph of a loved one after a child had scribbled over it with coloured crayons.

'Christ!' breathed Daniel, frankly stunned.

'Gen-ita! Gen-ita!' screamed the crowd, while Genita soaked up their adoration, her huge painted eyelids glittering as she observed them with a sardonic, superior gaze. Her glistening lips pouted and sneered alternately. Eventually she raised her hands to calm them. She was serene and in control. The throng quietened, and she rasped out the opening lines to 'Don't Cry For Me Argentina'.

My goodness, thought Molly, Simon's actually singing!

But Genita stopped after the first half-dozen lines, and enthusiastic applause broke out. She silenced it with another wave of her gloved hand. Then she addressed the audience.

'Good evening, to all my gay and lesbian people, arse bandits and cock dodgers alike. I am among you, your very own Genita L'Warts, patron saint of queers and licky lesbians everywhere.' From somewhere in the crowd came a drunken bellow. Genita turned and stared at the offender. 'Shut the fuck up or I'll come down there and risk getting rabies. I have lowered myself to appear before you tonight for one reason only – cold, hard cash and free fucking booze! Why else would I bother, I ask you?'

Every time Genita insulted her audience, they roared with laughter, which in turn appeared to infuriate her all the more.

'Will you shut up?' More noise. 'Right, that's it. You're all an absolute disgrace. Unless I get complete silence right this second I'm walking off stage never to return. Security! Security! I am a sophisticated artist, not one of the tired old addled drag queens you're all used to puking up in front of! Silence! I said silence!' Genita was like a school mistress and the audience her naughty children.

'You really are a disgusting bunch,' she continued. 'How you think you're going to pick anyone up dressed like that, I can't imagine. It's like being at a boot sale.' And so she went on, haranguing them with bitter insults, incensed by their laughter.

Molly had never seen an act like it. As Simon had said, there was no real substance to the performance: there was a vague attempt at 'The A to Z of Gay Etiquette' but Genita didn't get beyond B (A was for arse wipes and B for buggery) before she became distracted and spent at least twenty minutes repeatedly telling the audience to be quiet, while her insults moved from the general to the particular, as she selected individuals to attack. Some lesbians at the front were picked over like an old chicken carcass: their hair, clothes, lifestyle – everything about them was ridiculed. Then a young disco dolly in a cap-sleeved T-shirt caught her eye, and he was hauled up on stage for a dressing down that was as cruel as it was thorough.

'You poor, sad, insignificant little gayboy,' said Genita, finally pushing him off her stage. 'As your patron saint, my heart breaks for you. How unkind can nature be? Pig ugly, zero dress sense, buck teeth and a skin complaint. No wonder you're gay. I guess your tiny brain worked out that that was the only way you were going to get a fuck.'

Somehow the relentlessness and vehemence were hilarious.

Molly and Daniel were doubled up with laughter and even Jane had tears of mirth in her eyes. When Genita finally left the stage, after her second encore, Jane announced grandly that laughter was good for the soul and Simon a very gifted, if unusual, healer.

Indeed, the audience was buzzing with happiness. No one understood quite what they had seen, but they knew they would never forget it. Some sort of comic miracle had taken place. How could someone be so entertaining for almost an hour when the great bulk of their 'material' simply consisted of telling them to shut up? A great calm spread among them, in direct contrast to the demanding, even angry chanting that had been going on before Genita's performance.

'Oh, my God,' said Molly, awestruck. 'I had no idea. None!'

'Who would have thought he had it in him?' Daniel said, shaking his head. 'I'd never have guessed.'

'He obviously finds his *alter ego* very *freeing*,' observed Jane.

'It's that or the glitter lipstick,' agree Molly, who was also impressed by how beautiful Simon looked in full drag. He'd always been a handsome boy but he made a ravishing woman.

'I've got to say it, he was brilliant!' declared Daniel.

'I haven't laughed so much for ages,' added Jane.

'Out of this world,' said Molly, feeling very proud of Simon. The creation of Genita L'Warts, so wildly unexpected, seemed to liberate her dear friend. The bitterness and cynicism that he had always carried around him was turned into a positive thing, somehow, through his bizarre creation. Simon had stumbled upon something new and fantastic purely by chance. Molly felt, as did everyone else, that she had witnessed a performance of comic genius. 'Let's get another drink and then go backstage to congratulate him. I'm rather shell-shocked.'

'Not for me,' Jane said, picking up her coat. 'I think I've had all I can take for one night. Give Simon my love and admiration though. 'Bye.' She kissed them both and started to push her way to the door. She turned back just long enough to say, 'You might find that ingrowing pubic hair is fine now, Molly,' and then she was gone.

Once Daniel and Molly had fought their way to the bar and been served, they crossed the dance-floor to the toilets where they'd been told the dressing-room door was. A bouncer stood outside, shaking his head sternly at a gaggle of excited queens who were trying their best to talk their way into the inner sanctum.

'But I *love* Genita!' one was saying. 'I just need to tell her that.'

'Sorry, mate, no can do. She doesn't want to see you,' explained the bouncer.

'But I *love* her!' the queen persisted, near to tears.

'That will do. Make your way back to the bar now, please,' came the firm response. The bouncer then placed a hand on each shoulder and spun the anaemic queen round. 'Off you go,' he said, giving a push in the right direction. More protestations followed, but no one was getting past.

'Perhaps we shouldn't bother him,' Molly said. 'He doesn't seem to want any visitors.'

'We're not any old visitors,' Daniel said obstinately. 'Leave this to me.' He shouldered his way through to the bouncer, with Molly huddling behind him. When they got there, he said confidently to the bouncer, straight man to straight man, 'We're Molly and Daniel, mate. We're on your list.'

The bouncer glanced at his clipboard and knocked on the

door, announcing their names in a deep voice. A squeal of delight from within was all it took, and to the excited murmurs of those left waiting, the door was opened and Molly and Daniel were admitted.

The dressing room was tiny, consisting of an old school desk with a rectangular mirror, mottled with age, propped up on it against the wall, lit by a rusty Anglepoise lamp. Simon was alone, slumped in front of it, a wad of cotton wool in one hand and a tub of Cremine in the other. He had removed the makeup from one eye but not the other. As the door closed he eyed them in the mirror. He let them speak first.

'Simon, you were fabulous,' said Molly. 'Congratulations.'

He smiled and stood up to hug his friend.

'Brilliant, mate,' said Daniel.

'Thank you,' Simon said softly, more or less ignoring him. 'I'm feeling very weak. Do sit down. I think there's a bottle of wine somewhere.'

'We're all right, thanks,' said Molly, raising her bottle of lager. They sat behind him on two grey plastic chairs. There was no window and it smelt of damp and cheap cosmetics.

'Not much of a dressing room,' said Molly.

'It's a fucking horsebox,' said Simon, wiping his other eye several times in quick succession. He then poured mineral water over a fresh piece of cotton wool and dabbed his eyes and cheeks.

'They loved you out there – really!' said Molly.

'I know they did,' said Simon. He sat back in his seat, as if he was only able to relax now that he had removed the eye-shadow and lipstick. 'They loved Genita, anyway. Quite a mystery, isn't it? She's not a very lovable character.'

'A woman with balls, though,' said Daniel, with a jovial, admiring chuckle. 'Folks love that.'

'Do they?' Simon sighed.

'Listen, honey,' said Molly, moving in front of Daniel to give Simon a big, affectionate squeeze. 'If it ain't broke, don't fix it, pal. All you've got to do is carry on.'

Simon hugged her back and exhaled loudly on her fleshy shoulder. 'But I don't know what I do, Molly. As soon as the turban goes on, I become this harridan of filth. I'd never speak to that young lad like that in a million years when I'm myself. He can't help his buck teeth, poor soul.'

'That's why they love you,' said Molly, breaking out of the hug for a hearty laugh. 'You're fab, that's all you need to know. And I love you, so there.'

The mood was broken by the bass tones of the bouncer vibrating through the wooden door: 'Lucy Cavendish from the *Evening Standard*, Kate Moss and Immodesty Blaize would like to pop in and say hello.'

'Just a minute,' said Simon, trying to be cool but clearly excited at the prospect of meeting a burlesque star and a super-model. 'Be right there!' he called. 'Tell Kate and Immodesty they're very welcome.'

All three stood up, and Daniel said, 'We'd better be going.'

'Yes,' agreed Molly, 'I'll call tomorrow, Si.' She held his face between her hands and pulled him towards her for an affectionate smacker on the lips. 'Night, hon, have a good one.'

She took a step back and it was Daniel's turn to say goodbye. He opted for one of those manly semi-hugs, which turn out to be three vigorous slaps on the back followed by a quick withdrawal. 'Night, mate,' was all he said.

As soon as the dressing-room door was opened, an octopus of arms reached in and desperate voices called out, 'Genita!' Daniel had to force a path through against the tide.

Just before the door closed behind them, Molly turned to give Simon a final wave. He was looking at himself in the mirror, staring intently and wiping his cheek with a tissue.

Then Kate Moss brushed past, blocking her view.

Chapter Fourteen

It was five o'clock in the morning before Simon got home. Kate and Immodesty had whisked him away to a party in Primrose Hill, where Kate had told everyone what a huge star he was about to become and the Cristal champagne just kept on flowing. When he finally collapsed on his bed, drunk but excited, he knew that that night he'd crossed a bridge to a new world. Something unexpected but rich in possibility glittered before him. He had the chance to go into the place that so many longed for. When people put on makeup, dressed up and went out on the stage, what did they want? To be adored, desired, loved and fêted. That had happened to him! It could go on happening. He could become . . . *famous*. Rich. His life could be about performing. He could spend half his time as Genita, the woman never lost for words, brilliant, caustic, extraordinary . . .

Was this what he wanted? Fame and adoration had really never featured in his plans for himself. His ambitions had always been more basic. If he was honest, they still were. Earlier in the evening, back in the dressing room at the Black Cap, something rather unexpected had occurred, and it was only now he was alone that he had time to contemplate it.

Daniel.

There had been only a fleeting second of eye-contact while he was talking to Molly but Simon had felt a fatal twinge, a stab of excitement just below his navel. After that, all was lost. As he talked, he had noticed from the corner of his eye that Daniel's gaze was still focused on him. He wiped a trace of lipstick from the corner of his mouth to his chin, glanced across to Daniel's hands, which were clasping his pint glass, then up to his heavy-lidded, smiling eyes. Their gaze had locked for an instant before he'd looked back at Molly.

That was all it had been, but now Simon relived it and the swell of excitement returned. He knew this sensation well – the delightful conflagration of lust and the possibility of passion sparking into flame. He shouldn't, but he would. A sudden feral resolve possessed him. He would make it his business to see more of Molly and Daniel and discover where this new challenge led.

Simon fell into a deep sleep. When he awoke, head thumping, dry throat croaky and sore, there was a strange brown stain on his pillow that he realised must have come from his mouth. Well, that sometimes happened after a particularly big night. He staggered into the kitchen and drank some tap water from a dirty, tea-stained mug. He returned to his bed and dialled Molly's number. 'So Kate and I are the best of friends,' he said teasingly.

'You sound rough,' said Molly. 'Just woken up?'

'Yes, but I feel wonderful.'

'So you should. Congratulations on last night, Simon. Fantastic.'

'Thank you. You and Daniel had a good time, then?'

'Brilliant, yes.'

'Good. I'm so pleased. I wouldn't want to speak too soon but I think you may have finally found a boyfriend I approve of.'

'Wonders will never cease. You've got a job and my fella gets the thumbs-up.'

'Listen – I've got a night off. I'd like to take you both out to dinner.'

'Ah. That's really kind of you, but we're already going out. It's our anniversary.'

Simon's lips tightened but he managed to keep his voice light. 'How nice! Why don't I come along?'

'Well,' said Molly, clearly unsure, 'I think Daniel wants it to be just the two of us, you see.'

'Oh, nonsense! I haven't seen you for months and I want to celebrate too. How's about I pay?'

'Well, it's not really—'

'I insist. I can be a surprise for Daniel.'

'Any other night we'd love to, honestly. It's just that we've made plans. He's taking me to Joe Allen's.'

Simon's mood curdled. 'Oh, okay. Some other time.'

'I'm sorry, Simon.'

'Never mind. I have to go. Speak soon,' he said petulantly, and hung up. He realised that he was cross with Molly for getting in the way of his seeing Daniel again. How naughty I am! he thought, amazed at himself. Daniel is Molly's boyfriend. She adores him. There's no point in seeing him again: he belongs to her.

But he couldn't deny what he felt. The flutter of excitement in his chest – such a relief from the constant ache of misery: he was impatient for another viewing of Daniel. His bad lustful angel sat on his shoulder, telling him that it wouldn't matter if he just *looked* at him again – would it?

Daniel and Molly would be in Joe Allen's later, toasting their love over a romantic anniversary dinner. What was to stop Simon turning up and joining them? If he ordered a bottle of champagne as soon as he arrived, they could hardly be so rude as to ask him to leave. And what harm could it possibly do? He only wanted to look, he told himself again. Would Molly begrudge him that? Of course she wouldn't!

He spent the rest of the afternoon lazing about, managing to change his sheets and the stained pillowcase, thinking over and over again about Daniel's beautiful eyes staring into his.

Before he went out, he had a bath and ate a bowl of Heinz spaghetti – his favourite since he was a child. He dressed to the nines in a three-piece suit with a lavender shirt and a white tie, then headed into town. He started his evening in Soho, arriving at Revenge around seven o'clock. He was on his second pint when Charles sauntered in.

'Well,' Charles said, raising his eyebrows, 'the prodigal returns.'

'The prodigal is just passing through,' replied Simon. 'Having a last glance at his sad, sordid life as it used to be before he swans off to richer, more glamorous waters.'

'Get you,' said Charles. 'You've won a drag competition, not been voted President of the fucking United States. Now buy me a drink before you leave us.'

'They don't sell Cristal in this dive, so will a pint of lager do?' said Simon, grandly.

'Very nicely, thank you.'

They spent the next couple of hours bitching and drinking, until Simon announced he must be off.

'Take care, dear one,' said Charles. 'Love you, wouldn't wanna be you.'

'You've been . . .' Simon searched for the words. 'Well, you've been. Let's just leave it at that.' He nodded goodbye and headed for the door.

'See you on the way down,' called Charles.

Simon enjoyed his walk in the fresh autumn air and arrived at the restaurant in Exeter Street at half past nine. The place was packed, as usual, and there was a queue of about six people waiting for tables to become available. Simon brushed past them and came face to face with the maître d'.

'I am a surprise guest for the sweet couple over there on the table for two. Do you think you could bring me a chair?'

The maître d' glanced over to where Molly and Daniel were halfway through their main course, gazing longingly into each other's eyes between mouthfuls. As Simon looked at Daniel, his heart rate soared.

'I am sorry,' began the maître d', in a thick French accent, 'there is no room on that table for another chair.'

'I see,' said Simon.

'Maybe you can wait for them at the bar?'

'You don't understand,' said Simon. 'I'm her brother. I've just flown in from Los Angeles as a surprise. Surely . . .' He smiled encouragingly.

The maître d' was stony-faced. 'Unfortunately it is not possible.'

'And I've got cancer,' said Simon, raising his voice so those around him could hear.

They looked at each other for a moment. Then the maître d's face softened, and he said, 'Just give me a moment. I will get a chair for you.'

'Thank you so much!' Simon beamed. 'And a bottle of champagne, kind of *maintenant*.'

A moment later he was squeezing on to a chair between Molly and Daniel, who stared at him, astonished.

'Hello, darlings! I just couldn't keep away!' he gushed, as the two lovebirds looked horrified. 'You don't mind if I join you, do you?'

'Simon!' said Molly, embarrassed. 'We're in the middle of dinner!'

'I know and I apologise,' said Simon. 'But as I was in the area I couldn't let the occasion pass without giving you both my blessing.'

Just then a waiter arrived with the champagne, whispering in Simon's ear that it was 'on the house'.

'Lovely,' Simon said. 'Just some fizz to toast you with, you gorgeous things.'

The waiter began to pour champagne into their glasses.

'Well, this is very nice of you,' said Daniel, handsome in a black linen shirt with the sleeves rolled up beyond his biceps.

'You've got a tattoo!' said Simon, touching the object of his desire with a forefinger. 'Is it a Celtic symbol?'

'No,' said Daniel. 'Arsenal coat-of-arms.'

Simon managed to stop stroking Daniel's arm and pick up his champagne flute. 'To the three of us! Congratulations on your first year together. Here's to many more.'

Molly and Daniel dutifully picked up their glasses and the three of them said, 'Cheers!'

'Great to see you, Si,' said Daniel.

'Yes, it is, love,' said Molly, looking happier now she could see that Daniel didn't mind Simon dropping by. 'Thank you for being such a good friend.'

'You're welcome.' Simon gulped back his champagne in a couple of mouthfuls. 'Now, I'd better be on my way.' He knew it was important not to outstay his welcome. Daniel would still be forming an opinion of him so, now that the heart-warming surprise had been delivered and both Molly and Daniel were beginning to enjoy his intrusion, it was time for him to leave.

'No!' protested Molly. 'Stay and finish the champagne with us.'

'Absolutely not,' insisted Simon. 'I shall leave you two to your evening together and disturb you no longer.' Despite their pleadings, Simon blew kisses to them both and disappeared as quickly as he had come.

I'm so naughty, he told himself, as he headed for the tube. But what harm can it do? It's just a fantasy. It won't come to anything. Oh. He's divine . . . Lucky Molly.

The popularity of Simon's *alter ego*, Genita L'Warts, continued to grow. He started to get enquiries from small theatres, and an agent from the alternative comedy circuit (a different world from the drag circuit) called Boris Norris arranged a meeting with him. Over lunch at the French House in Soho, he proposed a tour of universities and possibly a three-week run at the Edinburgh Festival. 'No good fiddling around with these pub gigs, mate. You need a strategy. Things could take off for you, big-time, if you want them to.'

Simon thought that Boris looked a bit like James Dean, and told him as much, adding, 'Before the car crash, obviously.'

'Thanks,' said Boris, flattered. He was tall and a little stout, married with two young children, and wore Fred Perry shirts and

Dr Marten boots. Simon hadn't a hope of seducing him, he realised, but then again . . . away from home, late at night in a hotel room after too many beers, anything might happen. He filed the delicious thought away for later consideration. Daniel was his current project. Boris's potential would have to wait.

'So, are you interested? Do you want to sign with me?'

'Hell, why not?' declared Simon. 'Where's the dotted line?'

Boris grinned. 'Great. We're going to be huge, I promise. You, me and Genita.'

Simon had decided to give in gracefully to the presence of Genita in his life. He wasn't the fighting type, after all. Like a triffid, Genita seemed to have a life of her own and a rapacious appetite for professional success and vodka that Simon could only wonder at. Besides, Grey Goose wasn't cheap. He needed all the work he could get to keep the cuckoo in his nest happy and sated.

And Genita L'Warts had, almost despite Simon, begun to evolve. She was still as vile as ever to her audiences and a large proportion of her time on stage was spent insulting and shouting and carrying on inconsequentially, but luck had given her new material. One night she found herself in a slanging match with a lesbian standing at the front. Genita grabbed her bag and began to rifle through it, looking for something to be withering about. (This was usually a fruitful exercise. Letters, clothes, diaries – all could be held up and ridiculed.) For some reason this particular woman had three fresh sardines zipped up in a supermarket cooler bag, complete with heads and tails.

'What the fuck is this, you disgusting dyke?' asked Genita,

picking up a fish between finger and thumb and waving it accusingly at her. The crowd were in uproar.

'That's my tea!' replied a gruff Geordie voice.

'Oh, it's your tea, is it? Are you sure it'll be enough for you? Or will you be tucking into your girlfriend's minge for afters?' Genita plucked another sardine from the bag and swung them around like a mad cheerleader. She stuck her fingers through their gills and began to improvise a mad puppet show. The sardines became a pair of lesbian lovers called Caroline and Caroline, billing and cooing and passionately expressing their love for each other. Then, just as a civil ceremony was imminent, the third sardine entered the fray. She was called Helga, and was determined to seduce Caroline. As the love triangle erupted in a violent climax, Genita juggled the sardines as best she could, bashing them together, tossing them in the air and catching them, slapping them on top of each other in a fishy orgy as she spat out the commentary like a wild, possessed Natasha Kaplinsky. Eventually it was all too much for Helga, who split dramatically in two, spilling fishy guts over the stage before she was hurled headlong into the crowd.

Just then the DJ, in an inspired moment, played Frankie Howerd's 'Three Little Fishes'. The excited crowd sang along lustily with Genita, who waved the triumphant, lucky-in-love Carolines above her head in time with the music. As the track finished she popped them back into the cooler bag and returned them to their rightful owner before she exited the stage to which she would return for no less than five encores.

Boris was the first person backstage. 'Brilliant!' he said. 'Fucking brilliant!' He paced up and down, clearly thinking aloud. 'Fish. That's the thing. You must make the sardines a regular climax to your act. Who knows? Maybe haddock, too. And a few sprats to throw into the crowd.'

'You really think so?' said Simon, bemused.

'Trust me,' said Boris, eyes glazed, staring into an imaginary future. 'Now we've got the sardines on board, I don't see any reason why it shouldn't be "Jongleurs, here we come"!'

'Imagine,' said Simon, deadpan.

'I have faith, my son,' said Boris, patting his discovery on the shoulder and smiling confidently. 'If you listen to me, I'll make you a household name. I guarantee that within two years you'll be selling out the Albert Hall. I'll take you on a journey from Camden High Street to the North Pier at Blackpool.' He paused for effect.

'Be still my beating heart,' said Simon, starting to remove his makeup.

'You're not listening to me,' said Boris, uncharacteristically earnest.

Simon was lost in thought. His mind swirled with adrenalin and post-show euphoria. Sardines. Who'd have thought they'd be the key to his future?

'I've got it!' said Boris. 'You're a performance artist! I shall call the Purcell Rooms first thing in the morning. I expect the *Guardian* will want to do a spread and *Front Row* will be gagging to get you on.'

'Okay, I'll do it!' said Simon. 'Anything to shut you up.'

Meanwhile Simon couldn't shake his desire for Daniel, which had grown to possess him like a succubus. Where only a short time before he'd been scolding himself for even looking at Molly's boyfriend, he was now plotting and planning to create opportunities where he might be with the object of his affections. He'd grown obsessed, erotically and emotionally. All he could think about was Daniel, and Molly was fast becoming little more than an irritating obstacle to his passion. He had taken to turning up at Molly and Daniel's flat late at night after he'd done a show, always in high spirits, a little drunk but full of post-show exuberance. 'But I bring champagne!' he'd screech down the intercom, if ever Molly said they were asleep and maybe another night would be better. He just wouldn't take no for an answer. A couple of times a week he was sitting on their sofa while Molly sat opposite him in her towelling dressing-gown, her eyes heavy with sleep, urging him to speak more quietly in case they woke Daniel – he had to be up at six.

'Oh, he could manage a glass of bubbly!' said Simon, as if it were equal to a few pennies for a blind beggar. Eventually, if he made enough noise, Daniel would appear like a vision, scratching his head, and join in the late-night drinking.

He knew he shouldn't . . . but the lust that possessed him was too strong to fight.

Then, one night, Molly excused herself at three in the morning and staggered back to the bedroom while Daniel slumped on the sofa dressed only in a once-white towel that clung perilously to his toned twenty-eight-inch waist. 'Don't be long, Dan,' she murmured, as she drifted by on her way to bed.

Simon saw his chance and pounced.

First he lowered the lights and turned up the central heating. Then he sat beside his prey for ten minutes while he nodded off to sleep. Daniel's head fell backwards and his arms splayed outwardly on the sofa, either side of his lap. As sleep took hold his knees relaxed and his thighs spread open invitingly. Simon sat on the edge of the armchair, poised like a panther about to spring.

When the moment was right, he lightly ran the back of his fingers over Daniel's chest. Simon gasped with delight, as Daniel parted his lips and sighed contentedly. This only encouraged Simon to stroke his chest a second time. After that, he allowed his fingers to fall, as if with the pull of gravity, downwards, to graze the knot in the towel. Daniel growled, so Simon proceeded, his fingers stepping inch by inch towards his Holy Grail, the one thing for which he would sacrifice everything: the aroused heterosexual penis.

He stopped for a moment, got up, darted across the room and listened at the bedroom door. Assured by the semi-snoring within that the coast was clear, he returned to the sofa, gently lifted Daniel's towel and eagerly set to work.

At the point of orgasm, the mannequin came to life. Daniel reared up, his panting, by the third expulsion, changing from pleasure to vocal distress. He roughly removed himself from Simon's mouth, pulling the towel back over his waist, the after-shocks of his nocturnal ejaculation causing involuntary moans of satisfaction. 'What the fuck is going on?' he said, fastening the towel, his expression shocked and angry.

'Sssh!' said Simon, holding his finger to his lips.

'Oh, Jesus, no, no, no!' said Daniel, rubbing his eyes, then his hair.

Simon sat back on his haunches and gave a wicked half-smile. 'Don't spoil a beautiful moment,' he whispered. 'I know I'm bad. But so are you.'

'I was asleep!' said Daniel, his voice croaking with emotion, like a schoolboy protesting his innocence. His fists clenched dangerously.

This was always a difficult moment, as Simon knew only too well. Things could go either way. He wasn't sure if he should expect a smack in the mouth, so he flinched slightly, still relishing that familiar salty taste. He looked contritely at the carpet and decided discretion was the best policy. 'I think I'd better be going,' he said. He let himself out of the flat and went on his way, guilty but rejoicing.

The next difficulty Simon had to overcome was to make sure that his 'affair' with Daniel continued. The moment his lust had been ignited, the entire energy of Simon's being had become focused on achieving his desire. There was no going back. He asked Molly if Daniel could come and give him an estimate for painting his flat.

'Sure, honey,' said Molly, blissfully unaware of her best friend's secret agenda. 'How about if he pops in on Thursday around six-ish? He'll be a bit knackered but I know he's looking for some more work.'

'I'll get him a couple of cans of Special Brew, shall I?' asked Simon.

'You know the way to a man's heart,' said Molly, oblivious.

Simon drew the curtains in his flat, even though it was still daylight outside. Daniel seemed on edge when he arrived, but he did his best to remain professional, looking over the flat and rubbing his chin, asking if it was to be emulsion or eggshell. 'Have you thought about colours?' he asked.

'I've thought about little else,' said Simon, staring at Daniel as he spoke. 'I'm into red and brown and sometimes yellow. Bold, I agree, but I know what I like.'

'Aha,' said Daniel, unsure of the subtext. 'Whatever you say.'

'Ready for another can?' asked Simon, brightly.

'Er, cheers,' said Daniel.

Simon was nervous too, but the extra-strong lager would ease the awkwardness of the situation, he hoped. He got the drinks from the fridge and passed one to Daniel, who was perched on the edge of the sofa.

'So,' said Simon, in his best Mae West voice, 'do you think you could fit me in? Can you sort out my interior?'

Daniel took a swig of lager and nodded. 'Okay,' was all he said.

After that the pattern was set. Things would nearly always commence with Daniel lying prone on a bed or settee. Even if he wasn't asleep he would act as if he was. It was important for his sexual status, Simon assumed, that what ensued was initiated by Simon and not by him. Simon would gently caress Daniel's chest and thighs, and sensual arousal would slowly envelop his subject. Simon's tongue and lips would come into play. Daniel simply responded to the stimulus, a slave, it seemed, to his body. No intellect, no thinking, just biological response. That was precisely what floated Simon's boat, what satisfied his thirst.

Thankfully, Daniel was not the sort to attempt any kind of analysis of his behaviour. A little discomfort, a mild display of post-orgasmic guilt and/or shame was gratefully received by his seducer; anything more articulate or insightful would ruin everything.

The arrangement, or rather the encounters, continued in this tenuous way. Each sexual opportunity took days of planning on Simon's part. The anguish of a 'near miss' would keep him awake for nights on end, but his suffering seemed to be in direct proportion to the joy and satisfaction he experienced when he hit the jackpot.

He was in bliss and rapture. And as for Molly – well, what she didn't know wouldn't hurt her.

Chapter Fifteen

Molly noticed the change in Simon straight away. Since the day after his gig at the Black Cap, he had been on the phone to her incessantly: how was she? Did she feel okay? Was everything all right between her and Daniel?

To begin with Molly was pleased. She thought Simon was making up for their short estrangement but also in need of true, trusted friends. The sudden success and popularity of his *alter ego*, Genita L'Warts, must have been a shock to his system. She was touched that he included Daniel in all his invitations, but she'd been surprised when he turned up at the romantic anniversary dinner when she'd specifically said it was an occasion for just her and Daniel.

Then he'd started wheeling up to the flat at all hours, armed with drink and begging them to get up and share it with him.

Whenever she told Simon that she and Daniel couldn't meet him because they were doing something on their own, his tone seemed to turn a little minty. 'Well, pardon me for intruding,' he would snap. 'Maybe you can fit me in some other night when you're not celebrating the romance of the century.'

'I'm worried about Simon,' Molly said to Jane, one afternoon soon after Christmas. They were taking tea at the Honest Sausage in Regent's Park after a brisk walk in the crisp sunshine. 'He's been a heavy drinker as long as I've known him, but now it's in a whole new league. He's working in pubs and clubs every night, drinking before he goes on stage, while he's on stage and even more afterwards.'

Jane looked thoughtful. 'Perhaps this new identity of his means he's losing touch with reality.'

'Reality has never really featured in Simon's life much,' said Molly. 'I love him dearly, of course, but he's so unpredictable these days.'

'In what way?'

Molly sighed, as if it was all too difficult to put into words. 'Well, just after we first saw him as Genita, he started turning up at our flat really late at night and getting us out of bed.'

'Looking for drinking companions?'

'Yes. But Daniel has to get up early for work, so it wasn't exactly convenient.'

'You had to nip that in the bud, then.'

'I tried to. But Simon wouldn't take no for an answer, and because I'd been away for so long and we'd had one of our fallings out, I found it really hard to say no.' Molly sipped her coffee. 'He was so wired and excited after performing, I think he was looking for someone – anyone – to be with. Anyway, all that seems to have stopped now.'

'Good.'

'But there are other things. He makes appointments with me and doesn't turn up. Four times recently I've been standing outside a cinema or a tube waiting for him, and he's left me dangling. It's not like him. He's never acted this way before.'

Molly sighed. 'I can sense so many other things that don't seem quite right. He doesn't seem to look me in the eye any more. He hardly ever kisses or hugs me, and he used to all the time. I'm so worried. He should join AA before it's too late.'

'I'll send some psychic healing,' said Jane, reaching over and touching Molly's arm reassuringly.

'I think I could do with some myself,' said Molly, suddenly tearful.

'I know. You don't have to tell me. I send you healing all the time,' said Jane, as two big tears rolled down Molly's cheeks.

'I'm sorry,' she said. 'It's just that Simon means so much to me. I hate to feel like I'm losing him.'

'Sssh!' Jane comforted her friend, giving her a big, love-filled hug. 'You'll never lose Simon. I can't imagine you two apart. Besides, you've always been there for him. Remember that time he got gay-bashed when he came on to some straight bloke under Charing Cross bridge? It was you who sorted him out and got him to casualty. He won't forget things like that.'

Molly started to sob. 'I'm just so fed up, Jane. I'm out of work and Dan's working all the time. Now that Simon's got a bit of money, he's decided to get his flat decorated. I can't deny that it needed it – it was a complete tip. So, of course, he asked Daniel to do it, and for the last few weeks he's been decorating Simon's flat in the evenings. I never see him. He comes back late, drunk and in a bad mood. I'm sick of it. We're usually so happy but he's been distant with me lately.'

'Why don't you go round there and spend some time with the two men you love most in the world? You could keep an eye on Simon's drinking.'

'I can't. Dan likes to be alone when he's working and Simon's out most evenings apparently. Besides, paint fumes are the worst thing for a singer. I sit at home, eating chocolate and feeling sorry for myself. I'm getting fatter by the week! I'll never get another job at this rate.'

'Come on, Molly, you're not fat. You'll get work soon. You're just in a negative state of mind.'

Molly sniffed. 'My agent says it's very quiet. There's nothing. Not even an audition. Not that I get to speak to him ever. According to his assistant, he's been in a meeting for the last three weeks.'

'It always seems like that between jobs,' reasoned Jane. 'Here, have a tissue and wipe your eyes.'

Molly did as she was told.

'Let's look on the bright side, shall we?' Jane continued. 'You're a beautiful young woman with a gorgeous voice. You have a dashing boyfriend and friends who love you. Isn't that more like the truth?'

'If you say so. Sometimes I think I'm a fat, ugly, penniless, unemployed wannabe whose boyfriend is never at home and whose best friend is becoming a star. I'm trying not to be jealous of Simon but it's hard. I've been striving for years to get somewhere and he's just stumbled into the limelight without even wanting it. It's not fair, Jane. When do I get my break, eh?'

'Hush now,' said Jane. 'Time to put a stop to all this. Jealousy is a very low emotion. Don't give it house room.'

As the weeks went by, Molly became accustomed to Simon's increasingly bizarre behaviour. But when he asked her to call him 'Genita' from now on, she was horrified. 'No!' she protested. 'It was Simon I met at college and it's Simon I care about. I'm not calling you Genita. For goodness' sake, get a grip!'

'That cabaret act is fucking with his mind,' she told Daniel, over macaroni cheese and rocket salad one evening. 'He needs to watch himself.'

Daniel only grunted.

'I mean, good luck to him and all that, but all this success is making him crazier than ever. Don't you think?'

'Dunno,' mumbled Daniel. 'He seems the same to me.'

'You don't know him like I do,' declared Molly.

Daniel frowned at his macaroni cheese.

'He's changed. I miss him! I don't want him to become some fame-crazed drag queen. And as for his delusions of grandeur – well, he could become the Archbishop of Canterbury but it doesn't mean his shit don't stink.'

'Please,' said Daniel, 'I'm having my tea. Can we change the subject?'

Simon will come back to me, Molly thought. He always has. One day, all this will be over and forgotten, and it'll be the same as it used to be again. I just hope it happens before he goes completely off his rocker.

'Fancy some ice cream?' she asked Daniel, who looked as if he needed cheering up.

Chapter Sixteen

Simon was now totally infatuated with Daniel and their sexual encounters were regular events. There was a kind of sweetness to the planning involved in each one. He had learnt that a number of crucial factors needed to be in place if he was to have his way with Daniel. Obviously the first, and in some senses the most difficult, was that they had to be alone. The greatest obstacle to this was Molly. Having his flat decorated was a particularly good wheeze: not only was Daniel's time accounted for but Molly had to stay well away from the perilous paint fumes. But once this job was done, Simon's imagination had to be artfully employed. A couple of times he had arranged to meet Molly for a trip to the cinema. Knowing she was standing patiently outside the Odeon in Leicester Square, he had dashed over to her place in the hope that Daniel would be home alone. But this plan was seriously flawed: Daniel might not be in, and if he was, time would be somewhat limited. When Molly realised Simon wasn't going to turn up she might jump on the tube and be home in half an hour. Hardly long enough for Simon to achieve his goal and get himself away from the scene of the crime.

And even if Daniel was at home the second factor might not

be in place: alcohol. Experience had taught him the painful truth that straight men rarely gave in to his advances when they were sober. The golden rules for the homosexual seduction of the utterly unattainable straight man were as follows:

1. He must be alone, with no risk of interruption or discovery.
2. Moderate amounts of drink should be consumed. (Too much and you risk impotence – an insult to your efforts.)
3. Cover of darkness can do half the work for you.
4. The more spontaneous and inconsequential you can make it seem, the greater the chance of a repeat performance.
5. Do things to him that his girlfriend wouldn't or couldn't.

What Daniel's thoughts were on the whole sordid business Simon could only guess. In the early days he had seemed uncomfortable and guilty, but as time went on he seemed to bow to the inevitable. Then, after several weeks, there came a moment when Simon knew he could, with just a moderate amount of connivance, have his way with Daniel. The object of his desire began to play along with the arrangements and, worst of all, to skip the pretence at semi-conscious seduction.

Once, they had been left alone for the afternoon in Molly's flat while she went to an audition. Daniel had smiled at Simon and unzipped his fly, pushing him down to his knees with a killer smile and a 'Go on, you know you want it.' Worse still, Daniel was stone-cold sober. Of course Simon obliged – it would have been rude not to – but his heart wasn't in it. This spelt the end. How could Simon believe that Daniel was straight if he was sober and awake, aroused and demanding? Reticence and a hint of disgust were vital components of the erotic cocktail and they were sadly missing. This was not how it worked. It was with a heavy heart that Simon wiped his lips after the deed was done. The deep, wide and everlasting well of desire began to dry up. The twenty–four–hour obsession with Daniel was reduced to an eighteen–, then twelve–, then six–, ever diminishing.

New conquests caught Simon's eye – the Turkish youth serving at the corner shop, who was always reading *Nuts* magazine, for example. Simon found himself in there several times a day, buying yoghurt and courgettes with as much significance as he could muster. Then there was the young husband who had scowled at his wife in the supermarket, given Simon a look that could only be described as 'significant' and disappeared in the direction of the gentlemen's latrine.

The joy of specialising in liaisons with straight men, Simon knew, meant there were never any painful, tearful, breaking-up scenes – on the part of the straight men, anyway. He never had to endure those 'difficult' conversations. He simply moved on. They would never admit to any emotional involvement or hurt, and if they did, the game would be up anyway. Perfect. No mess.

As Simon's focus drifted away from Daniel, so the reality of his behaviour towards Molly dawned on him. It was like waking up from a dream. How could he? What had he been thinking of? Molly was the most significant person in his world to him – like a sister. How could he have allowed such weakness to outweigh the value of their friendship? She understood him like nobody else did. Imagine how she would feel if she ever knew the truth! It made him cold with horror to think of it. What stupid risks he'd been taking, and all for fleeting sexual pleasure! Thank goodness the business with Daniel had run its course and they had not been discovered *in flagrante*.

What a filthy, dirty business gay desires are, he thought sorrowfully. He had very nearly sacrificed his best friend on the Altar of Cock. Simon felt ashamed.

Never again, he swore. I'll never risk our precious friendship like that, ever.

Meanwhile Genita L'Warts, a client of Boris Norris, had been promised a fast track to supersonic stardom by the never less than overexcited agent.

'Whatever,' said Simon. He was determinedly offhand about his so-called career, world-weary enough to believe things only when he saw them.

'There's a thirty-year career waiting for you, if you want it,' Boris said sincerely. 'Think about it. If you want to go to the ball I'll be your coachman.'

'I'm not Cinderella, you know,' said Simon tartly. 'And you're a piece of shit. You think you can make money out of me. Well, go on. Try! We'll scratch each other's backs.'

'I just happen to think you are the epitome of post-modern culture,' said Boris, clearly quite hurt by Simon's words. 'And you're right. My main interest in you is as a commodity. There's no sin in that. But I foresee a big future for you. There are things that could get in the way of my plan for you. Homophobia and your drinking. I'm not sure we can do anything about either, but why not give me a chance?'

Boris's plan was to transfer Genita L'Warts to a more middle-class, more educated audience. They would love this exotic creature, this vulgar horror, who made you splutter and gasp with shock but laugh so hard you felt slightly guilty about it afterwards.

'Here's your choice. Stay on the gay circuit and ride the crest of a wave for a couple of months, or break out, evolve onto the arts-theatre circuit. We'll conquer London first, maybe skip the provinces and go to New York in a couple of months.'

'Have an egg roll, Mr Goldstone,' said Simon.

Boris immediately put his plan into action. When one of his other acts was struck down with shingles, the opportunity arose to launch Genita onto the mainstream with a three-week late-night show at the King's Head in Islington. He visited Simon with the exciting news. 'I've got you the interview with the *Evening Standard*. You can promote the show.'

'My cup runneth over,' said Simon.

'You're cynical before your time,' said Boris.

'And you're rubbing your hands together rather tellingly,' said Simon.

As it turned out, no press was necessary: the run sold out within days. Simon didn't seem in the least perturbed by the prospect of a straighter audience. 'Look on the bright side. I'm less likely to get crabs. And if they don't like me? Fuck 'em if they can't take a joke!'

His confident attitude paid off. Confronted with a silent, seated audience of the mint-sucking middle classes, Genita excelled herself. She found new targets to lampoon. Her particular brand of anarchy seemed all the more shocking to the well-heeled and well-fed.

'Fancy people like you shelling out to see me!' she'd mock them, gently to begin with. 'Aren't you all saving hard for a holiday time-share in Tuscany? You're just the same as a gay audience but with worse haircuts.'

On her opening night she slipped a bit of raw liver into her mouth while doing a frenzied impersonation of Princess Michael of Kent. She then pretended to bite off her own tongue and spat it at the front row. Genita liked it best when she heard women weeping as they stumbled towards the exits. The reviews were ecstatic.

Boris brought on board a brilliant costume maker, who designed outfits with concealed panels. At a given moment Genita would freeze and the lighting would change so that she became a glowing blue silhouette. As 'The Ride of the Valkyries' boomed out of the speakers, she would discreetly pull a string and a cloud of white butterflies would appear to float out from under her luminous silk dress. By the time Genita had fulfilled Boris's expectations and sold out six nights at the Bloomsbury, the butterflies had been replaced by doves sprayed with iridescent glitter, and the sardines with a pig's head.

It was a week after these triumphant gigs that Simon had his final encounter with Daniel. It had not been planned and really shouldn't have happened at all. Simon was well on the road to success with the Turkish youth from the corner shop and had arranged for Halil to come round to his place one evening to give him a private Turkish lesson. Daniel hadn't entered his thoughts for weeks. But Molly had invited him for a celebratory dinner at her house, and Daniel had been there, looking particularly tasty in a white T-shirt and jeans, lit from behind by a lava lamp. After three bottles of champagne, Molly had been pie-eyed with tiredness. 'I'm completely sizzled,' she said, and Simon laughed.

'Go off to bed, darling. I shall let myself out. Thank you for a lovely evening. Delicious shepherd's pie.'

Molly stumbled over to the kitchen and filled a glass with water. She leant over Simon and gave him a sloppy kiss on his forehead. 'Congratulations on everything, darling. I really mean that. The world is your oyster now. The sky is the limit. Goodnight, love.' She blew a kiss to Daniel but staggered a bit in the delivery, and he jumped up to help her into the bedroom.

Two minutes later he returned, shutting the door quietly behind him.

'Out like a light,' he said, then flopped down on the sofa next to Simon and closed his eyes.

'Just the two of us left at the party, it seems . . .' said Simon.

Daniel smiled, saying nothing and keeping his eyes firmly shut. Seconds later his thighs drifted lazily apart and Simon knew what was expected of him. He set to work eagerly, happy to oblige now that Daniel seemed like a straight man again.

It was the sound of Molly's fist slamming on the bedroom-door panel that alerted them to their exposure. Daniel's automatic response was to leap to his feet and pull up his jeans in one movement lasting about two seconds. His hands clasped his now covered genitals protectively, like a fireguard. 'What's going on?' he said unconvincingly, looking around him as if he'd just been beamed in from a time-travelling experiment.

Simon's final position was less dignified: he was crouching on the carpet, naked from the waist down. He raised his head and looked at Molly, as thick drool lowered itself from his mouth to the hearthrug beneath him. The three of them stared at each other. The silence was deafening.

'I see,' said Molly, very slowly and quietly.

Chapter Seventeen

Molly couldn't remember afterwards what she threw first, but it was something breakable – either a lamp or a pair of seventies glass vases. It didn't really matter because everything followed in the end. The sound of shattering porcelain helped her to express her anger and distress and she lunged around the room, grabbing anything she could lift and flinging it at her lover and her best friend as they dived for cover. The TV set she couldn't lift, but she tipped it onto its side and it made a satisfying deadly thud. All of this was accompanied by shrieks and screams, expletives and threats. When she finally stopped – only, it has to be said, when there was nothing left to break and everything that wasn't nailed to the walls had been launched across the room – she realised that Simon and Daniel had left. The front door was open. She closed it behind them, turned and viewed the devastation. Stepping carefully over the shattered fragments and jagged edges, she slumped onto the sofa, too numb to cry.

After a good ten minutes of deep breathing, she felt contrastingly calm and cool, like a deserted street after a hailstorm. It was the middle of the night and she was still a bit drunk, but she knew she had to get out of that flat right away. The bedroom had escaped her rampage and she took her suitcase from the top of the wardrobe and opened it on the bed – the very bed she had been sleeping soundly in fifteen minutes before while her boyfriend betrayed her with her best friend. With this thought the tears streamed down her cheeks. Of course she'd known that Simon's lustful desires centred on attractive ultra-straight men, but she'd never imagined he would steal her boyfriend. How could he? They had been confidants, trusted and true soulmates.

With a sudden hot rush she remembered all the times Simon had engineered things to be with Daniel while she was otherwise occupied. The nights she'd waited outside the cinema, the evenings that Daniel was late home because Simon had been discussing the merits of Swiss or Roman blinds. And then there had followed occasions when she had reached under the duvet to initiate their lovemaking ritual and Daniel had uncharacteristically declined. It all became clear. She didn't for a moment suppose that that evening had been the first of their illicit trysts.

She had stood in the doorway for quite a few seconds before she'd banged the panel with her hand, and there was something very relaxed and comfortable about what was going on between them. Daniel's undulating hip thrusts and Simon's moans of pleasure had a musicality about them that was more of a waltz than a quickstep. They had been there before, clearly. She was completely amazed by the realisation. Daniel was, or so she'd thought, one hundred per cent heterosexual. She had never had the slightest inkling otherwise. She paused and shook her head with amazement. It just wasn't within the bounds of possibility. It was laughable. And so she laughed – a bitter, disbelieving laugh that soon turned into a cry of despair.

When the latest wave of emotion subsided, Molly seized the

window of opportunity and threw her belongings into the suit-case. She knew she would never return to this flat, so she chose with as much care as her hysterical mood would allow. She went into the bathroom clutching an empty Tesco carrier-bag and swept the contents of 'her' shelf into it. She plucked her expensive shower gel from its hook in the shower cubicle and threw in all of her cosmetics. Clothes were rifled through next, and tossed in a jumbled mess into the case. Within twenty minutes she was packed and couldn't wait to get out of there.

The suitcase had not been enough so the excess was in a black bin-liner. Her exit from the flat was not, therefore, as glamorous as she might have hoped. She paused long enough in front of the bathroom mirror to rearrange her curly hair, wipe the tearstains from her cheeks, apply some dark brown eye-shadow and some subtle tan blusher.

Then she walked out of Daniel's flat with her head held high, wearing four-inch heels and an expensive black mock-moleskin coat that made her look and feel a little like Kate Bush wandering madly over the moors. Molly knew she must be over the limit for driving, but the alcohol was only having a mild anaesthetic effect now, enabling her to act in her own best interests.

She threw her luggage into the boot and buckled herself into the driver's seat. She turned the key, started the engine and decided to wait while the windows de-misted. Trying her best to live in the moment, as Jane had advised, Molly thought about how much she loved her car. It was like a womb. When she was inside with the windows locked, it became her private world. It would have to take care of her now. Protect her. Molly pressed the button for the CD player and closed her eyes. Petula Clark's voice rang out, begging her sailor to stop his roaming.

Molly had no idea where she was going. The simple act of fleeing was enough to satisfy her for the moment. As she drove away, and out of Daniel's life, she opened the windows and let the cool, damp air invigorate her spirits. Then she had an idea.

'Lilia!' she said to herself. 'I'll go and see Lilia.'

An hour and a half later she found herself driving through the dark Northamptonshire countryside. The windows were firmly closed now and rain was hammering on the car roof. She was going very slowly down a narrow country lane. She didn't seem to need to direct her trusty car: it just took her, slowly and safely, to her destination.

She pulled up outside Kit-Kat Cottage and turned off the engine with a sigh of relief. She had arrived in one piece. The porch light was on but otherwise it was in darkness. What should she do? It was now four in the morning. Should she rouse the house, making a dramatic, tear-drenched entrance? Or should she wait until morning when there were signs of life within and her arrival would be more conventional?

Well, she figured, she was an actress. She would go for the more memorable approach. She applied some blood-red lipstick, tousled her hair to give it some lift and crept up the gravelled driveway like a burglar. She wondered whether to ring the bell or tap lightly on the front door but then had the bright idea of telephoning. She retrieved her mobile phone from her handbag and dialled Lilia's number. It rang ten or eleven times before an answer came.

'Yes? Who is it?' The accent sounded odd but it was clearly Lilia's voice.

'Lilia? It's Molly. I'm so sorry to disturb you at this time of night, but I'm outside your front door. Do you mind if I come in?'

'Molly, my child! What are you doing here?' said Lilia, reassuringly German once more. 'Of course – of course, you can come in. You poor thing! Something must have happened . . . I am coming now to let you in.'

The line went dead and within a few seconds the hall light came on. Then Lilia was standing before her in her embroidered kimono, arms outstretched in greeting, her face the epitome of motherly love. 'Molly! Molly! Come in, you must be freezing. Oh dear!'

Molly fell into the old woman's arms, sobbing already, a long-distance runner at the end of her gruelling journey, collapsing with relief. 'Lilia. Thank you for opening the door, for being here for me.'

Lilia pulled her in and led her distraught visitor into the lounge. 'Sit there,' she said, pushing Molly into the armchair and shuffling off to the sideboard to get two glasses and a bottle of brandy. 'You need a drink. Sit quietly, drink this, and when you are ready, tell me everything. Keep breathing at all times.'

Molly was hyperventilating, her inhalations rasping and raw.

'Sit still. Be calm,' Lilia commanded. 'You are home now. Relax!'

Slowly Molly's breathing returned to normal and she ceased flailing and rocking from side to side.

'Now,' said Lilia, 'tell me what has occurred. Your boyfriend Daniel, I suspect. Am I right?'

Molly wiped her eyes. 'How did you know that?'

They talked until dawn. Molly explained in great detail the relationship between her and Simon, and how she was now certain that the affair between him and Daniel had been going on under her nose for months. She recounted each and every occasion when

Simon had made arrangements with her just to be sure she was out of the way. She trembled in the recalling, she choked as she described the scene she had witnessed on the sofa, and she wailed her distress to a deeply sympathetic Lilia, who rocked her in her arms and told her everything would be all right.

'I am so tired,' said Molly, finally. 'I wish I could go to sleep and never wake up.'

'You will go to sleep. Your room is unoccupied and you need to sleep and heal yourself. Come.' Lilia, despite her fragility, pulled Molly out of her chair and hooked an arm round her waist. 'In the morning it will not seem so dark. It is the end of a chapter in your life, but by the same token it is also a new beginning. Better you find out the truth about Daniel and Simon now than in six months' or two years' time. All will be well. Come along now.' As she spoke she led Molly out of the door, along the corridor and into her old room. 'There now,' she said, releasing her grip and allowing Molly to collapse on the bed. 'Sleep well. Rest is what is required. You are home now, my dear Molly.' She stroked Molly's cheek and hummed a gentle, soothing lullaby. Molly went gratefully to sleep, escaping her misery in unconsciousness, the only true escape for the broken-hearted – apart from death, and that seemed a little dramatic, even for a musical-theatre actress.

PART TWO

PART TWO

Chapter Eighteen

Molly slept and slept, not opening her eyes until late the next afternoon. It took her a moment or two to remember the tumultuous events of the night before and her drive through the night to Long Buckby. She had cried in her sleep so the pillow was damp and her cheeks sore with salty tears. She blinked at the ceiling for a few moments before, as if on cue, Lilia tapped on the door and entered, carrying a mahogany tray loaded with a steaming mug of tea and a plate of digestive biscuits. She was wearing a navy dress with a white blouse underneath. 'Good afternoon, Camille,' she said. 'It is the day after the night before.'

'I'm glad to wake up here,' Molly croaked weakly.

Lilia peered over her. 'Oh dear. You are a little injured bird. Your wings are broken. It will take time, but they will mend.'

'There's no escape, even in sleep,' Molly whispered. 'I've had awful dreams. I didn't know I could hurt so much.'

Lilia patted her arm, then pulled the covers up and over Molly's shoulders. 'You've had a double-whammy. Lover and best friend. Daniel and Simon. At it like dogs in the street.'

Still lying and staring at the ceiling, Molly closed her eyes but fresh tears forced their way out and flowed down in tiny rivulets to bounce jaggedly on her tangled hair.

'Indeed!' said Lilia, tenderly. 'I did not mean to upset you, but we must squeeze a spot to get all the poison out. Now, so many tears are very dehydrating. Sit up, my dear, and try some tea.'

Molly wiped her eyes with the back of her hand and wriggled upright. Lilia handed her the tea and sat on the edge of the bed. She put her palm on Molly's forehead as if she was taking her temperature. 'Feverish.'

Molly sipped the tea. It was hot and sweet.

'That's right, drink up. I shall get you some water presently. A jug. I think you will need it. There will be more weeping where that came from. The pain will intensify, and you will keep seeing them together until the sordid image is tattooed on your consciousness for ever.'

'Do you have to keep reminding me?' said Molly, her lower lip trembling.

'Yes, I'm afraid I do,' said Lilia, nodding sagely. 'It will fester inside you otherwise. I will make sure, in the next few days or weeks, that it is flushed out of your system for good.'

Through her haze of misery and tears, Molly could hardly bring herself to imagine a future of any kind, but deep inside, some instinct for survival stirred, and she said, 'Lilia, I won't be a burden on you for that long, I promise. As soon as I can, I'll get myself together and leave you in peace.'

Lilia blinked at her. 'Don't talk nonsense. Where can you go? You have walked out on that life. You cannot go back. You have had a trauma and your mind and body need some tender, loving care.' She stood up to go. 'You will survive, my little bluebird. I shall see to that.' She went to the door, opened it and turned back.

'Eat the biscuits and drink the tea. But, most of all, you should sleep. It will help you to heal. '

'Thank you,' said Molly, managing a weak smile, although she had no appetite at all. Lilia bowed to her patient and left the room.

As soon as she was alone, wave after wave of sorrow washed over her and flattened her. She felt anger, jealousy and despair. She curled herself up in a ball under the sheets, weeping. What had she done to deserve this double betrayal? How could she bear the pain of losing her boyfriend and her best friend in one terrible moment?

Eventually she cried herself into an exhausted sleep, but she was tormented by terrible dreams that were vivid, stark and long. She was a little girl again, and she was cold, lying helpless on a kitchen floor. She screamed and shouted, but no one came to rescue her. She held her stomach with hunger. She wet herself. The policewoman who carried her down the stairs smelt of peppermints – Molly noticed this when the officer kissed the top of her head. 'It's all right. It's all over now,' said the policewoman, with a quiver in her voice. Was she crying too?

She woke, sobbing, in the darkness. It was night. She was vaguely aware of Lilia wiping her face with a wet flannel, and holding a cup of cool water to her lips.

She slept again. Now a doctor was examining four-year-old Molly, and someone else was taking photographs of her bruised legs. She had become mute with distress. She saw her mother wearing a coat and looking at her through a window. Her mother was a dark-haired, waxy-skinned woman with sad, simple eyes. Her coat was shapeless, beige, worn out and grubby. Then her mother was being dragged away, calling Molly's name, screaming as she went. The sound was clean and bright and piercing.

*

In the morning, Molly woke even more tired and weak than she had been the day before, wearied by her dark dreams and the flashbacks to childhood traumas. Lilia came in as soon as she woke and helped her to the bathroom, supporting her as she put one foot in front of the other. Her limbs felt heavy and stiff, and as soon as she was done she made her slow, painful way back to the comfort of the bed. 'It's a bit like having the flu,' she said. 'I feel terrible.'

'It's normal,' said Lilia, with a shrug. 'Your body shuts down to protect itself. Sleep – even if you have dreams as bad as yours – is a restorative thing. It would be very unwise for you to walk about. You would fall and hurt yourself. Just give in to it, my dear Molly. I will take care of you.'

Molly did as she was told. Lilia brought her some toast with a poached egg, and coaxed her into eating some. Hot tea and cool water revived her a little, but she still felt drowsy. Her thoughts were fuzzy and she couldn't remember anything much from the day before. Is this what a nervous breakdown feels like? she wondered. She really couldn't have moved just then, even if a fire had broken out.

When Lilia returned to collect the tray, she felt Molly's forehead and nodded. 'Another day of rest for you, my girl. Its only development will be me drawing the curtains. There. You can look out at the grey sky. Maybe the starling will hop on to the windowsill and peer at you. I will put a few crumbs there to encourage him.'

'Thank you, Lilia,' said Molly. Yes, it was a very grey, dark day, the clouds heavy with rain. 'How long am I going to feel like this?'

'When you see a sky like that, you wonder if the sun will ever shine again. But it will.'

'I suppose you're right. At some point, I need to sort my life out. I have nowhere to live, no job, no boyfriend . . .' Molly's voice trailed away.

'I will help you,' said Lilia. 'But there is no rush. Today you cannot even raise your head off the pillow. You must give yourself time.'

'How come you are so kind to me?' asked Molly.

Lilia sat down on the bed and gazed out of the window. At last she spoke. 'I see some of myself in you. I've known sadness and loss like yours. I, too, lost my parents. When they took my father away I was eight years old. My mother must have understood what was happening, but I did not and she tried to protect me from the terrible truth.'

'Who took your father away?' asked Molly.

'The Nazis, of course,' said Lilia, rolling her eyes. 'You really aren't with it, are you?'

'Of course,' Molly said hastily. 'I should have guessed.'

But Lilia was staring out of the window again, lost in her recollections. 'They knocked on the door early one morning when Papa was still asleep after a late-night show. We lived in a big modern flat on the corner of Jerusalemer Strasse and Schützenstrasse. It had big windows that let in lots of pearly white light when the sun was shining. My parents were very fashionable, but also disdainful of anything frivolous. We had simple cotton curtains and a glass table that was always kept spotless and gleaming, surrounded by metal chairs. There was a single shelf between the windows on which lived eight cacti in individual grey pots. My father's pride and joy. There were two small leather cup chairs but mainly I remember the table. I ran into it once and cut my head. Look, I have the scar.' Lilia pulled back her hair and showed a jagged line on her temple, its contours incorporated into the wrinkles her long life had earned her. 'I cannot remember any fuss when they took him,' she continued. 'There was no shouting. No guns.' She stared into the distance.

'How dreadful for you, Lilia,' said Molly. What was the misery of losing a boyfriend compared to something like that?

'Yes. All the more dreadful, really, because there was no drama. My mother and I were already up that morning, sitting at the glass table eating some rye bread for our breakfast. My mother had been working, too, of course, singing at the Palais der Friedrichstadt, but she always got up to make me my breakfast, dressed in her favourite silk kimono.' Lilia looked at Molly and raised her eyebrows expectantly.

'Not the same one you're wearing?' asked Molly, incredulously.

Lilia smiled. 'Correct. It was the only thing I managed to take with me . . . when the time came. This is the very kimono my mother was wearing on that dreadful morning – a little threadbare, but the genuine article. The knock – I can hear it still – was a rather gentle one, two, three. Nothing threatening. My mother was humming one of her tunes as she opened the door. There were only three of them. I can still hear their conversation, as clearly as if it happened this morning.

' "Good morning. Is this the residence of Otto Falckenberg?" said one.

' "It is," said my mother stiffly.

' "May we come in?" continued the man in uniform. He was polite and handsome. Quite young. He took his hat off, I remember. My mother backed away from the door, then turned to me. I could see the utter terror on her face.

'"My husband is asleep," she said. "What do you want him for?"

'"Just some questions," said the young Nazi. "For a few days." His voice was very reasonable, I remember that. He said something to his two comrades and they moved swiftly towards the bedroom. My mother stood behind my chair now and rested her hands on my shoulders. She said, "Now is not a good time to be a political satirist," and the Nazi replied, "Among other things."

'There was no noise from the bedroom either. But eventually the door opened and my father, his hair sticking up on end and still half asleep, emerged incongruously wearing a suit. He stopped in the doorway and looked helplessly at my mother. "These gentlemen will not allow me to kiss either of you goodbye." And then he went out of the door, with them at either side. They didn't close it behind them, just left it open, and we listened to the footsteps going along the corridor and down the steps. Fading away. He never came back, of course.'

Molly was speechless. The horror was too much. She reached out and gave the old lady a hug. Lilia slumped forward on to Molly's shoulder, breathing hurriedly, as if to stop a sob rising in her chest. Then, clearly with some effort, she pushed herself upright again, recovering herself. 'At this point, I would cry if I could, but I can't. I have dry eye. My tear ducts no longer function.' She sighed.

'Oh, Lilia, I'm so sorry.'

'Yes. I miss the release of tears. But my point is this: immediately afterwards, once the footsteps had faded into silence, my mother shut the door and told me to finish my breakfast. When that was done she said, "I'm tired. Are you? Let us go back to sleep now." And that is exactly what we did. We slept for ten hours. We escaped into unconsciousness. It is only natural. It is preferable, by far. You must do the same.'

'But what happened next?' Molly asked, eager to know the end of the story. 'What happened to you and your mother?'

Lilia stared at her, then spoke again. 'After my father was taken from us, my mother realised it was only a matter of time before they came back. I was just a little girl. I didn't understand what was going on. One afternoon she packed me a small suitcase containing a few clothes and, of course, the kimono. She knew it would be a comfort to me. She took me to the house of a friend of hers, a woman called Mary Tucholsky. Mama told me that she loved me, to be a good girl, and Mary would take care of me. I did not know I would never see my mother again.'

Molly gasped. However sorry she felt for herself, others had endured far greater tragedies. She could hardly recall her mother, but Lilia had known hers and loved her – and then to lose her like that . . . it didn't bear thinking about.

Lilia continued: 'When my mother left, Mary sat me on her knee and rocked me backwards and forwards for a while. "All will be well, little lamb," she said to me. She told me I should call her Mother, and that we would be going on a long, long journey together. She showed me my new passport, with my new name on it. Until we reached our destination, I was to be known as Bozena Tucholsky. We boarded the first train at Berlin, then travelled to Hamburg, Denmark, Oslo, Bergen, then got on to a boat to our eventual destination: England. Once we had escaped she brought me up as her own daughter. We lived in the East End of London, frugally, in a room above a tailor's shop. I went to school and Mary worked as a cook for a wealthy family in Clerkenwell. People were kind to us when they knew we were fleeing the Nazis.' Lilia looked at Molly. 'I owe Mary everything. She gave me a future. Unconditional love. She showed me that kindness is all we have.'

'What happened to her?' asked Molly.

'We were very close until she died of influenza when I was in my twenties.' Lilia stood up and moved towards the door. 'You do not need to ask me again why I am kind. That is the moral of the tale. Sleep some more. I will bring you cauliflower cheese at lunchtime. I will use Mary's recipe. She would be touched.' She shut the door gently behind her.

Molly slept, then ate some cauliflower cheese, which made her feel much better. In the afternoon, she read some of Lilia's magazines and dozed, amazed she could still sleep. Is this what it feels like to have a mother? she wondered. Someone totally focused on my well-being, someone I trust to look after me, and keep me warm and fed? Perhaps it is. It was a new sensation. Other people always seemed to have the option of escaping to the family nest when in need of some TLC, and Molly had always wondered what that felt like. If this was it, it was blissful.

When Lilia came back into her room in the evening, she looked up at her with a smile. 'I feel so much better,' she announced.

Lilia shook her head sadly. 'You are deluded, you poor thing. You actually feel much worse.'

'Oh.' Molly was confused. 'Do I?'

'Yes. You have experienced terrible pain and loss. You don't feel better at all.'

'But it's not as bad as it could be. The Nazis haven't come for me or my family,' said Molly.

'But your best friend has betrayed you. That is as bad in its way.'

'Is it?' Molly wasn't sure that it was really comparable.

Lilia leant towards her. 'Yes. It is a frightful act. The man you love and your best friend have laughed at you, spat at you, mocked you. Imagine the pair of them. Think about it.'

'I'm trying not to,' said Molly, the dread and panic rising again.

'But you must.'

'Why must I? It just makes me feel worse!' Molly felt tears spring to her eyes again. She covered her face with her hands as they fell.

'That's more like it,' said Lilia. 'No pain, no gain. You're not going to feel better any time soon, you know. It's barely two days since you found out that Simon and Daniel have been rogering each other senseless.'

Molly buried her face in the pillow, incoherent with misery once again. 'How could they do such a thing?' she managed to say, when the storm of sobs had died down.

'Homosexuals cannot easily be understood. It is best not to try.'

'I loved them both!'

'That I do not doubt. But they have instincts they cannot reason against. The cuckoo is a parasite. It lays its eggs in another bird's nest. The moment the cuckoo hatches it kills the other hatchlings. Nature has no morality. The poor host bird, the pippin, raises the cuckoo as its own. Feeds it, loves the vile, murderous infiltrator. We cannot even say it is unnatural, can we?'

Molly carried on crying.

'You must imagine Simon and Daniel writhing together in

their lust. You must imagine them scheming to deceive you, conniving to betray you so that they can lie together, caressing each other, moaning gently, taking each other to the peak, and screaming in the ecstasy of their ejaculations.'

Molly howled as she saw it, as plain as day, in her mind.

'That's better,' said Lilia, rubbing her shoulder. 'The poison is not yet out. The wound cannot heal until it is.'

Molly was crying so hard now that she was almost retching. All she could imagine was Simon and Daniel kissing passionately and it was agony to her.

'Mind you don't choke, my dear,' Lilia said, with concern. 'You are becoming delirious. Maybe I have encouraged you too much . . . Oh, my. I think I shall get you some medication.' She scurried from the room. A few moments later, she returned to Molly's bedside, holding a glass of water in one hand and a pill in the other.

Through her swollen, streaming eyes and hysterical sobbing, Molly was only vaguely aware of Lilia pushing the pill into her mouth, then tipping water after it.

'Swallow it, like a good girl,' Lilia coaxed her. 'It will help you sleep. Joey has generously donated it. It will bring you peace.'

Molly did as she was told. Her crying had peaked now and she lay on her back, disabled by pain but no longer convulsed by it. After a few minutes the pill began to work. Her limbs felt heavy and time seemed to slow down. 'What have you given me?' she asked weakly.

'Just a sleeping pill. You needed it, trust me. Relax now.'

Molly's mind began to swim. She didn't know if she was awake or asleep. She clutched Lilia's hand and tried her best to focus.

'How could Simon . . . how could he . . . after everything . . .?'

said Molly, her vision blurred and her limbs turning to lead. 'After what happened . . .'

Lilia brought her face close to Molly's and looked from one eye to the other. 'What is it, Molly?' she asked. 'What happened?'

Molly could only blink slowly, her eyelids like weights.

'There is something else, is there not? Something you want to tell me?'

Molly stopped blinking and stared questioningly at Lilia.

'You are afraid of something. Why can you not tell me?' Lilia's voice was no more than a whisper. With a few grunts and groans, she lowered herself into a kneeling position on the floor beside the bed. 'What is it?' Lilia reached forward and pressed her thumb gently on Molly's left collarbone, midway between throat and shoulder.

Molly exhaled. Her eyes fluttered as she slid into a semi-conscious state. 'I can't tell you,' she murmured. 'It's a secret.' She shook her head vaguely. Everything seemed very far away. Sleep rose up again, warm and inviting, a place of safety where she could forget all the bad things that had happened.

'Have no secrets from me,' murmured Lilia, pressing harder now, further immersing her guest in a twilight world, penetrating her resistance. 'I knew the first day I met you that you had a secret. Something terrible has happened to you, hasn't it? What is it? You can tell me.' She paused, allowing Molly to digest her words. 'Not your mother. Not Daniel. Something dark is flailing around inside you like an overgrown tapeworm. Tell me. Tell me what it is.'

Molly's thoughts were now distorted and her brain seemed unable to connect with her voice. She tried hard to speak, hanging on to the last thread of consciousness until eventually the words came. Once she had started, they fell from her mouth clearer and faster. She couldn't stop herself releasing the thing that had stayed locked inside her mind for so long. Her dark secret was finally free.

Chapter Nineteen

The next day Molly felt a little dopey when she woke. She remembered that she'd become hysterical the night before and Lilia had given her a pill. After that she could recall nothing, so she must have fallen into a deep, drug-induced sleep, which explained why she felt so groggy. Nevertheless, she was a bit more like her old self. For the first time she felt able to think about her situation without feeling as though she'd collapse with the agony.

It's over with Daniel, she told herself. That much is plain. I love him but he isn't the man I thought he was – in more ways than one. I can accept that, even though the pain is so terrible I doubt I'll ever fall in love again. But Simon . . . She closed her eyes. That betrayal was so completely unforgivable, so deeply wounding, that she didn't see how she could ever recover. Her heart was scarred for ever. She could hardly bear to think about Simon at all without dissolving into tears. The only solution was to put him as far from her thoughts as she could until she could cope with it.

She tried to focus on her immediate situation. Something had compelled her to come to Kit-Kat Cottage. Perhaps some innate sense of survival had carried her there, to a safe, kind haven. But now she was feeling better it was time to think about moving on. She must contact her agent and make a concerted effort to get some work. Maybe she could stay with Jane for a while, sleeping on her sofa. She had no money for the deposit on a new flat, and she'd need to find a bar job. She wanted to live somewhere far away from both Daniel and Simon – maybe west London. Shepherd's Bush, perhaps. She shuddered. Maybe she wasn't quite as recovered as she'd thought.

Despite herself, she couldn't help wondering what Daniel was thinking and doing now. Was he overcome with guilt? Was he worried about her? Would he try to find her and beg her forgiveness? Or would he recover in no time and get a new girlfriend? Maybe Daniel and Simon would move in together and put their relationship on a more legitimate setting.

No. Simon wouldn't allow that to happen. Or perhaps, for the first time, he'd want to have a relationship with the straight man of his dreams, even when he started acting gay. That thought was too terrible. Molly pushed it away and decided to get up.

One thing is certain, she thought. I never want to see either of them again. It's over as far as I'm concerned. I don't care what happens to Daniel or Simon, and that's that.

She had a long soak in the bath, washed her hair and even applied a little makeup. She pulled on a pair of jeans and a jumper and went into the lounge. There she found Lilia lying on the sofa with Heathcliff on top of her.

'That's one way to keep warm!' She laughed.

Lilia giggled from under the furry mountain. 'He's a big softy. Aren't you?' Heathcliff responded by giving his mistress a generous, slobbery lick. 'Now, up you get!' With an encouraging push, the dog slid off her and sat on the floor at her side. 'That's enough afternoon delight for one day,' said Lilia, patting his head. 'And look at our Molly! You look a hundred times better, my dear.'

'Yes. What a difference a day makes.'

'You are even able to attempt some sort of musical reference. A great improvement, I must say.'

'I think I might like a little fresh air,' said Molly.

'Goodness. This is more than I had dared hope for. Such progress!'

Molly went to the sofa and sat next to Lilia, taking her hand and holding it between hers. 'You really are a darling, Lilia. I don't know what I'd have done without you. Not only have you taken me in and looked after me, but hearing about what you have survived, and what your parents went through – it was really humbling. It made me realise how lucky I am. I mustn't wallow in self-pity any longer.' She gave Lilia a hug.

'You are a very wise, very special girl,' said Lilia. 'Why don't you take Heathcliff to the field? He'd love a run.'

As if on cue, Heathcliff stood up and looked hopefully at Molly.

'I'd love to. Come on, Heathcliff!'

'My boy knows the way. Take it easy and try not to push yourself too far too soon,' cautioned Lilia.

Heathcliff did indeed know the way. He dragged Molly there at such a pace she was out of breath by the time they arrived. As she leant over him to take his lead off so he could run free, Heathcliff gazed at her with grateful, intelligent eyes. 'There's a good boy,' said Molly, stroking his head and holding him under his chin. 'You look after Lilia, Lilia looks after me and I look after you.'

Heathcliff seemed to smile at her before running off into the undergrowth in search of rabbits. Molly began her walk, pushing herself a little beyond a gentle strolling pace once she got going. There was a well-worn narrow track right round the edge of the field, which occasionally branched off under a low archway of brambles. Clearly, the path was used by badgers as much as humans. Now and then Heathcliff would reappear, panting and full of excitement, as if he were checking on her. After ten minutes she was flushed and aware of the wind on her face. She felt an inner quiver of pleasure in her current activity. All of a sudden she engaged with the world again, sensed the moisture in the air and the spring in the turf beneath her feet. She tuned into the sounds of the trees rustling and the birds singing.

Her walk became a bouncy skip and, her hair flying about her like ribbons, she began to sing herself, a sure sign of her spirits improving. She returned to the cottage with rosy cheeks and a genuine smile.

Lilia greeted Heathcliff like a long-lost son, then looked Molly up and down. 'You must not run before you can walk, Molly. Beneath those rosy cheeks, you are still pale and wan. If we are not careful, you will have a terrible relapse.'

'Oh, no, I feel all right, honestly. The exercise has really perked me up.'

'Your feelings are deceptive. Yesterday you could not get out of bed,' Lilia said sternly.

Molly didn't want to argue. 'You're right, I expect, Lilia.'

'We have tomato soup for lunch. Then you must go back to bed. You are only at the beginning of your recovery.'

'I know,' said Molly, meekly. Lilia smiled at her, obviously pleased. 'I really don't feel I could sleep any more, though.'

'That's all very well but you are a long way from being able to face the future,' she said, shaking her head. 'Visions of Daniel and Simon locked in carnal pleasure will come back to bite you. The pain has dipped beneath the surface temporarily. It will return. What you are experiencing is a very severe case of post-traumatic stress disorder.'

'But I feel quite positive about my situation, in a way,' Molly argued. 'While I was out walking with Heathcliff, I had the chance to think things through and I've realised that now I have the chance to start my life over again. It's time to be on my way.'

'No!' snapped Lilia. 'You are in denial! You have a broken heart. This has caused your pulse to slow to such a rate that your brain is being starved of oxygen.'

'I'm not that bad, Lilia.' The old lady was talking nonsense now and Molly wasn't going to listen to it for much longer. 'I've taken enough of your hospitality and I should leave you in peace. By the way, I looked in my coat pocket for my mobile and I couldn't find it. Do you know where it is? I'm going to call Jane and see if I can go and stay with her for a bit.'

'But you are not ready, my child. I knew your phone would be full of calls from those traitors, begging you to forgive them, so I removed it temporarily. I cannot expose you to it. You can have it back when you're stronger.' Lilia rose to her feet. 'Now you are up and out of bed, I was going to suggest we do some therapeutic singing at the piano. I have plans for you.'

'I can't stay here for ever, Lilia. I'm so grateful to you, but I've made up my mind to go, so if you don't mind giving me my phone—'

Lilia interrupted her, a look of panic on her face. 'Oh, my goodness! I left poor Joey in the bath!' She dashed out of the room. A moment later, Molly heard a worrying thud from Lilia's bathroom and a horrified scream. She rushed to the room and saw Lilia sitting on the floor by the bath. Joey was naked, sprawled over the side of the tub, half in and half out of the wire-mesh hammock that lifted him from the water.

'The hoist got stuck,' said Lilia, her face red with distress. 'He fell out.'

Molly took charge of the situation. 'It's okay, Lilia, I'll take care of Joey. Everything's going to be all right. There, there, Joey, that's better.' She put her arms under his and, without much effort, lifted his sparrow-like frame out of the sling, then lowered him gently to the floor. She wrapped a towel round his waist, picked him up in her arms and carried him into the bedroom. Lilia got to her feet and followed.

'What a strong girl you are! Like a fireman,' she said, as Molly deposited Joey on the bed, laying him carefully down. She looked at her reflection in the dressing-table mirror, pulled her skirt straight, adjusted her pink crocheted waistcoat, and patted her hair. 'Thank you so much, dear Molly. How lucky you were here.'

'It could have been worse. Are you in one piece?'

'More or less. I know it could have been far, far worse. I left him there for a bit of a soak and then you came back with the dog and— Oh dear.' Lilia began to cry dry, tearless sobs.

Molly turned from Joey to comfort her. 'He's fine now, love, don't worry.'

'I try to be a good wife.' Lilia's voice was trembling. She picked up a giant disposable nappy from a pile next to the bed and handed it to Molly, wincing a little with the effort. 'I do not always succeed. He needs this putting on now. Would you mind? I'm still rather shaken.'

Molly hesitated, but then, as Lilia shuffled out of the room, moaning with discomfort, she saw she had very little choice. She attached the nappy swiftly, trying not to look at Joey's poor, shrivelled genitals. Then she spotted a pair of clean pyjamas folded on the pillow so she put those on him too, wrestling his delicate limbs, with skin like tissue paper, into the jacket and trousers. When that was done, she laid him down so his head was on the pillow, pulled the sheet and blankets over him and gave him a rub on the shoulder. 'All right, Joey? You just take it easy while I go and check on Lilia.'

The old man held her in his gaze, his face frozen with shock.

She found Lilia in the lounge, watching a quiz on the television.

'This woman will go home with nothing,' she declared, when she noticed Molly had come in. She gestured at the screen. 'You can see it in her eyes. She does not think she deserves the big money so her expectations will be fulfilled. Dozy cow. Look, I told you, she has lost the lot.'

'Joey's resting now, Lilia. Are you all right? Did you hurt yourself?'

Lilia tore herself away from the television screen. 'I bruise so easily. I think I landed on both my elbows. Tomorrow it will be worse.'

'Oh dear. Would you like me to call your doctor?'

'No doctors, please!' said Lilia, looking alarmed. 'I don't allow them in the house if I can help it. They will try to take my Joey away from me. He could not bear that. It would kill him.'

'I'm sure you should be entitled to some help caring for him. Have you spoken to your GP or the council? You could have someone come in and help you to bath him. Do the shopping and the cleaning.'

'No,' said Lilia, stubbornly. 'It would be the beginning of the end. Please don't tell anyone. It was just a silly mistake. Promise me?'

'It's a lot for you to cope with, Lilia,' said Molly, softly. 'No one wants to take Joey away.'

'We are fine!'

'You've bruised yourself. You said it would be worse tomorrow.'

'But you will help me, won't you? Just for a few days?' Lilia sounded like a helpless child. Molly didn't see how she could refuse. 'I've just seen how wonderfully you dealt with my husband,' continued Lilia. 'He is in very safe hands with you. You have a gift, my dear,' she said flatteringly.

Now she had decided to go, Molly was keen to get on her way. 'It's ever so nice to be asked but—'

Lilia turned the television off. 'I'm not asking, Molly dearest, I'm saying there is no alternative. I have badly bruised my tired old brittle bones. Surely you can help for just a couple of days?'

'I still think you should get some professional help. I'm sure you're entitled to—'

'I'll tell you what I am entitled to,' said Lilia raising her voice. 'A little gratitude. I took you in, in the middle of the night. You were a wreck, a ruin and a shrine to despair. I have fed you and nursed you and listened to your darkest ramblings—'

'I know, and I'm very grateful. But—'

'But what? Thank you and goodbye?' Lilia stared at Molly, her eyes hurt and angry.

Molly didn't want to upset her if she could help it. She knew she didn't really have a choice. How could she leave the old woman unable to care for her husband? 'Okay, I'll do it. I'll stay and help you look after Joey, just for a couple of days, until you're better.'

'Yes. Just a few days,' said Lilia, reverting to her helpless-old-lady voice. 'A week at most. Then I will be able to resume my wifely duties. Thank you, Molly. I know you'll make an excellent carer.' She pressed the remote control once again and the television came back on. 'Joey doesn't want to be in bed at this time of the day. Could you get him dressed and into his chair? *Neighbours* is on in fifteen minutes. It's his favourite.'

Molly returned to the bedroom where Joey lay on his back, his eyes still open. 'Hello, there, Joey. I'm going to get you up so you can watch some telly. I'll be standing in for Lilia for a couple of days while her bruises heal.'

In a wardrobe she found some trousers, a shirt and a jumper. She felt more comfortable if she chatted to him while she went about her task, taking off his pyjamas and getting his clothes on to him. 'Grey and blue? That will look nice, won't it? This jumper's ever so soft, isn't it? Should keep you nice and warm.'

She wheeled the chair to the side of the bed, manoeuvred him into it, then pushed him through to the lounge just as the *Neighbours* theme tune was playing. The three of them sat and watched it together.

When it finished, Lilia turned to Joey and said, 'Are you hungry, my dear?'

Joey stared blankly at the television screen.

'Yes, he is,' she said, turning to Molly. 'There are tins of Cow and Gate in the cupboard. Chicken and rice. He likes that. And Complan for afters.'

Molly went off to prepare Joey's supper, telling herself firmly that helping Lilia was the least she could do under the circumstances.

The next morning started rather differently from the previous three. Molly was woken at 7.30 a.m. by a brisk rap on her bedroom door. Lilia strode into the room and opened the curtains. There was no tea on a tray. 'Now then,' she barked. 'It is a brand new day and you have a lot to achieve. Chop, chop! A cold bath, I have decided, will wake you up. I have run it for you. Then you can walk Heathcliff after breakfast, which will be only fruit and black coffee. Your duties with Joey begin after that.'

'Fruit? Cold bath?' said a bewildered Molly, still only half awake. Is she joking? she wondered drowsily.

'You came to me a broken woman and, having mended you, I intend to test my patient,' said Lilia, standing with her back to the window, hands on hips and leaning over Molly in a matronly manner. 'You will eat fruit because it is slimming,' she continued, her chin quivering as she warmed to her theme and gathered pace. 'Let's face it, Molly. You are on the buxom side. Maybe you have convinced yourself that you can carry off this look, but I am here to tell you otherwise.'

Molly was aghast. 'Lilia, please!' she said, pulling the blanket up to her throat. 'I'm a healthy, big-boned girl.'

'I can't have some great heifer like you charging around the place. Think of my knick-knacks. We're going to slim you down.'

Molly sat up in bed, staring at her in disbelief: where had this martinet come from? Up until now, the old lady had always been contained and polite. But she wasn't done yet.

'You will have a bath because you stink of grief and sorrow and female hormones,' she announced. 'Wash them all away. And a *cold* bath to toughen you up and shock your mind and body out of their self-indulgence.'

At this Molly gasped. 'But I'm recovering from a broken heart!'

'Well, you are the one who announced herself fit and ready to return to normal life, my dear,' said Lilia, reasonably, tugging the bedclothes away from Molly, like a magician whipping a tablecloth from under a fully set table. 'We'll see about that, won't we? Get up. We are already behind schedule.'

With that, she marched out of the room, shutting the door so firmly behind her that Molly jumped.

She stared at the door in disbelief, then swung her legs over the side of the bed and pushed her palms across her forehead until they met at the back of her neck. Whatever was going on with Lilia, the line of least resistance was to humour her and do as ordered until she found out what on earth the old woman was going on about.

She staggered into the bathroom and found the bath waiting for her, full to the brim and stone cold. Perhaps she should just swish the water around and pretend to Lilia that she had got into it? No. Lilia would know, she was sure. I don't particularly want to get in there, she thought, but she felt programmed somehow by Lilia's instructions and unable to resist. She felt a stimulating mix of trepidation and wonderment. Gingerly she lowered herself into the tub. Sitting down was the worst bit, feeling the spikes of icy water reach slowly into every bodily nook and cranny. She didn't know whether to scream with laughter or shock. In the end, when she finally opened her mouth no sound came out.

After staying submerged for just a minute, Molly got out and towelled herself dry. Immediately she felt warm and energised. She caught a glimpse of her body in the mirror and stopped to have a look. Daniel had liked its generous curves, but maybe Lilia was right. A diet wouldn't do her any harm. Perhaps a new look would help the fresh start she was hoping for.

When she entered the kitchen, she half expected to find the old, smiling, kind Lilia there, stirring some warming porridge on the stove, and saying what a joke it had all been. But, no, it was still the new severe Lilia, barking at her to sit down.

On the plate in front of her sat an orange, an apple and a banana.

'Eat them all up,' said Lilia. 'The peel is optional, in the case of the banana and the orange.'

Molly was hungry and fancied her usual muesli and maybe some toast, but did as she was told. Lilia stood and watched her consume every mouthful, even offering her another cup of coffee if she wished. 'The caffeine will be effective in pulling you out of your sluggish state. We want to get your heart rate going. It is all for your own benefit. You will thank me one day.'

The coffee had indeed woken Molly up, and she found her voice at last. 'But, Lilia, I don't understand why you're behaving like this. I'm a grown woman, not some skivvy from the village that you can order around.'

Lilia shook her head. 'You are far from that. I understand you better than you think. I have your interests at heart.'

'Then why are you bullying me and ordering me about?'

Lilia sat down on the chair opposite Molly's, clasped her hands together and stared intently into Molly's eyes. 'Listen to me. You are special. Circumstances and Fate have thrown us together and

I have a vision, my dear. A vision of your future. So far you have lived a very dull and unspectacular life. With my help that can change. I can transform you. Your love was sprung and shot that fateful night, thanks to Daniel and Simon and their uncontrollable lust. If we are to derive some benefit from the situation then it is this: now you can join the ranks of the unlovable. We are the successful people in this world. We see things with a cold heart and we are all the better for it. We get on in life, live in nice houses and drive big cars. We are fearless.'

Molly frowned. 'I don't think I agree. Of course we can recover from sadness and heartbreak. Things can mend, can't they?'

'Only if you let them!' exclaimed Lilia. 'Now is your moment. Let these events change your life. What is the point of letting the wound heal and carrying on as before, on the same dreary treadmill of life?'

'But I'll learn from what has happened, won't I? I'll be older and wiser next time,' reasoned Molly.

'Of course you will. Such fighting talk! But under my steady guidance, I am giving you a makeover. A new look: slimmer, trimmer, wiser and more feline.'

'What do you have in mind?' said Molly, intrigued despite herself.

'Just imagine you have been put in hospital or sectioned for a few weeks. I will make all your decisions for you.'

'I don't know. It's a bit weird.'

'You can trust me. I will remould you. We will have acting classes and singing instruction, exercise with Heathcliff and a strict diet.'

'Are you a teacher, then?'

'When I choose to be. If I spot a special talent. I see great things ahead for you. Just let me show you a brighter future.'

'You sound like Mystic Meg.'

'Take me seriously, Molly. You are at a crossroads in your life. This way stardom, that way oblivion. Which are you going to choose?'

'You mean – you want to make me a star?'

Lilia nodded, her eyes glinting. 'A great singing star – rich, famous, a living legend. The usual thing.'

Molly couldn't deny this sounded appealing. 'So . . . what happens if I stay here?'

'I become your guide and mentor. I will make a timetable of recovery and transformation. I don't like to boast but Kate O'Mara passed through my hands once. She was a little minx at the time, but I could see the potential. Look at her now.'

'Gosh,' said Molly, impressed. 'But I have no money.'

'Neither did Kate. I never charge. She pebbledashed the house for me in gratitude. You will help me with Joey for a while. In return I will take you to the heights of greatness!' Lilia leant forward, her usually milky green eyes suddenly like steel. She licked her lips. 'Will you do it, Molly? Give yourself to me for six months – that is all I ask. Then you can return to your ordinary life if you wish. Do everything I ask. Become my creature. I promise you will not regret it.'

Molly bit her lip. The offer was tempting. Even the biggest stars in the world had to be discovered by someone – she couldn't just ask for a recording contract and expect to sell a million records overnight. Lilia must believe in her, she must really think she had the talent – and Lilia had been the first person to give credence to Molly's own certainty that she had a gift. So far her career had consisted of glorified pub singing and a few third-rate tours of badly staged musicals. It was a big leap from there to successful solo artist. Furthermore she wasn't getting any younger, and plenty of big stars were still in their teens. Lilia was offering her a chance. The worst that could happen was she'd waste six precious months. But she had nowhere to go, no home to return to. Why not embrace the idea and see what the outcome would be?

She took a deep breath. 'Yes, Lilia,' she said firmly. 'You have a deal.'

'Yes?' said Lilia, excitedly, clapping her hands.

'I am yours for six months to do with as you please.'

'I am delighted! You won't regret it.' Lilia reached a bony hand across the kitchen table. 'Let's shake on it!'

Molly's fleshy hand moved to meet Lilia's and the two women looked fondly into each other's eyes.

'I can't wait,' said Molly.

'Good,' said Lilia, 'because we are already behind schedule.'

Chapter Twenty

The lessons began as soon as Molly had finished getting Joey ready and put him in his usual seat in the sitting room. Lilia stood by the fireplace, looking stern, and when Joey was settled, she frowned at Molly. 'We will begin with some vocal exercises. Let me hear you hum.'

Molly did a bit of *The Mikado*.

'Not bad, but your tone is too clean, too musical theatre. We need to dirty you up a little.'

'Dirty me up?' Molly echoed, feeling worried. 'You mean, sing something more *risqué*?'

'Oh, no, something quite different.' Lilia went to the shelf to pick up something, then turned back to her. 'Here,' she said, handing her pupil a lighter and a packet of French cigarettes. 'Gauloises. I started to smoke these when I was on a tour of Syria. After a few packets, my voice developed a charming crack. You need to find that husky quality.'

'But I don't smoke,' declared Molly, moving away from the proffered packet as if it was going to bite her. 'I think smoking's disgusting.'

'Yes, but that is exactly what you need. There's a whiff of Julie

Andrews about you, and we don't want that.' Lilia took a cigarette from the packet and handed it to her. 'Pop it between your lips like a good girl.'

Molly stared at it, repelled.

'You want to be a star, don't you?' snapped Lilia.

'Yes, but . . .'

'You said you'd do anything I asked. You promised! Remember?'

Molly nodded and did as she was told.

Lilia picked up a box of matches and struck one. 'Suck!' she said, bringing the flame to the tip of the Gauloise.

Molly tried, but the smoke tasted bitter and it was hot in her mouth. She involuntarily blew it out, coughed and spluttered noisily, handing the cigarette hurriedly back to Lilia as if it were a loathsome living creature. Her eyes watered and her face reddened. 'Ugh! Yuck! No, thank you, Lilia. That's horrible, that is.'

Lilia rolled her eyes. 'We must persist. Take a few breaths and try again. Maria Callas smoked cigars and she sang like an angel.'

Molly took the cigarette back and gingerly put it to her lips.

'Gently this time,' instructed Lilia.

Molly screwed up her face as if she were about to take some unpleasant medicine.

'That's it. Be brave,' encouraged Lilia.

Molly drew gently on the Gauloise, inhaling until the acrid smoke was deep in her lungs.

'Now blow it out gently and smoothly. Good!' said Lilia, as Molly successfully completed the exhalation with just a small series of gunshot coughs.

'You see?' said Lilia, congratulating her pupil. 'That wasn't too bad, was it?'

Molly's voice sounded like a strangled ferret's. 'I feel a bit sick.'

'That is a natural enough reaction,' said Lilia, 'but only temporary. We will start with five cigarettes a day, and build to forty. Once the addiction takes hold, you will thank me. And your voice, my dear, will benefit enormously. This is a most exciting development.'

'My head's spinning,' said Molly, in a gruffer rasp this time, rubbing her throat.

'You see? You already sound far more Fenella Fielding. Congratulations.'

'Lilia—'

'This is, however, a no-smoking house, and I must ask you to take your filthy habit into the garden. There is a flowerpot full of sand that you may use as an ashtray.'

'Right,' said Molly.

'Next, brandy – or, more specifically, Courvoisier.' Lilia opened the ornate Chinese cabinet that stood by the piano and lifted out a bottle, which she then presented. She held it by the neck between the finger and thumb of one hand, while resting the base on the open palm of the other. 'Beryl Reid swore by it. It will, with time, add texture and resonance to the timbre of your singing.' Lilia lifted a cut-glass brandy balloon from inside the cabinet and poured a healthy measure. 'Just like the cigarette, it will burn your throat and make you feel queasy to begin with.'

'I have drunk brandy before, you know. Simon was very partial to it. Mind you, that was Sainsbury's cooking brandy.'

'A distant relative of this,' said Lilia, with a shudder.

Molly took the glass and downed it in one.

Lilia raised her eyebrows and smiled. 'I am very impressed!

You are clearly no blushing virgin where this particular lesson in concerned.'

'I could probably teach you a thing or two, if we're being honest,' said Molly, pouring herself another glass. 'Cheers!'

'That is the care and maintenance of the vocal cords dealt with: cigarettes and brandy.'

'This is going straight to my head,' said Molly. 'I've only had a bit of fruit for my breakfast.'

'That is all to the good, my dear. As well as improving your voice, alcohol will loosen you up and help you to access the emotions necessary for the songs you will sing. Let us begin.' Lilia moved to the piano and lifted the lid. 'We will try some scales now. Ready?'

Molly stood in the middle of the room, swaying slightly and feeling light-headed. 'Ready for action,' she replied.

With one finger Lilia played middle C and Molly sang the note perfectly.

'The right note but your voice is still too clean. Too bleached. Continue.' Lilia's fingers travelled up the piano keys and down again and Molly's voice followed suit. 'Not bad. Now squeeze the notes out for me, making an *eee* sound. Slide the note up as high as you can reach, then down again like this: eee-EEE-eee!'

Molly replicated the sound and this procedure was repeated higher and higher up the scale until her voice was just a squeak and then back down to a deep rumble.

'You have a good range, Molly. There is a lot for me to work with. Now pop out to the garden with some more brandy and have two cigarettes, then clean your teeth. It is almost time for Joey's lunch and we don't want you breathing Courvoisier and fags all over him.'

*

Molly's days were very full, beginning bright and early with the cold bath and the fruit for breakfast followed by at least three cigarettes smoked in the garden. After she had walked Heathcliff, she had to attend to Joey, feed him, bathe him, dry him, powder and dress him and get him into his chair for the day. Lilia's bruises proved too tender for her to attempt any shopping or housework so Molly ended up doing those as well.

The regime was far from easy: she felt permanently weak and hungry, and had the beginnings of a cough from the cigarettes. She longed for some chips, biscuits or bread, but these were all denied her. Lilia allowed her fruit for breakfast, salad for lunch and steamed vegetables with some fish or chicken in the evenings. She started on the brandy before lunch and they spent their afternoons at the piano. Joey had to be fed and bathed in the early evening while Lilia watched *Coronation Street*. After Molly's meagre dinner – which she often had to eat while Lilia tucked into delicious-smelling stews with buttery mashed potato, or juicy steak with chips – it was time for her acting lesson. Lilia would select scenes from Shakespeare, Bernard Shaw or Brecht, and make Molly perform them, reading the other parts for her. Then she would give her direction and advice on breathing, diction and posture.

A week passed, and by the end of it, Molly already found it hard to remember the life she had left behind, or any kind of existence outside Kit-Kat Cottage and her strict regime. It was curiously familiar, not unlike her institutional childhood, and comforting, with the absence of responsibility: all she had to do was obey.

*

One afternoon as they were doing their singing practice, Molly's voice suddenly broke into a jagged rasp. Lilia jumped up from the piano and clapped her hands. 'Did you hear that? Excellent! That is the very quality I have been looking for.'

'My throat feels like the bottom of a birdcage,' said Molly, hacking a little. She rubbed her temples. 'My head's throbbing.'

'I couldn't be more pleased for you,' said Lilia, delighted. 'Do it again.'

Molly's voice, once clear and bright, cracked a second time but remained in tune.

'You hear it?' said Lilia, excited. 'The voice of a woman, not a girl! Gritty, lived-in, broken like your heart. You see how it is all fitting together? We have made a breakthrough. Congratulations.'

Molly wasn't sure how thrilled she felt. She was permanently woozy and light-headed from the smoking, the brandy and the strict diet Lilia was enforcing. She had given Lilia control of her life, though, and it was amazing how quickly she became used to it. If Lilia was angry, she felt miserable; if she was pleased, Molly clung to the few, rare words of praise that came her way.

'There is a change to our routine today, Molly,' Lilia announced, the following morning. 'We are going into town. You need some new clothes. And I've been thinking about your hair. Now you are shedding all that blubber and your cheekbones are being given a chance to fulfil their potential, it needs attention.'

Molly looked down, surprised. Had she really lost weight? Now she thought about it, her jeans were getting looser and looser, and she was beginning to find her previously snug jumpers somewhat roomy. Then her hand went to her hair and she stroked her curls protectively. 'What do you have in mind?'

'Straight hair. More severe. And darker. I don't approve of the way you play with your curls all the time, as if they were seaweed. Obviously it isn't easy to find a stylish salon in Northampton, but I have secured an appointment at Hair Today. I shall come with you to hold your hand.'

After breakfast, they loaded Joey and his wheelchair into the car and Lilia drove them into town. She took Molly to the market first, and looked through some cheap tracksuits and poorly made skirts and T-shirts. 'It doesn't much matter what you wear for the next few months. Working clothes, that is what we are buying today. It is pointless spending much as your body shape will change dramatically in the next weeks and months. How do you feel about overalls? They're two for a fiver.'

They arrived at Hair Today in good time for the eleven o'clock appointment and Lilia immediately took charge, leaving the stylist in no doubt that Molly's curls were to be permanently straightened, and a dark-brown colour put on.

'And could you cut it, Eleanor, to just above the shoulder? A sensible length, don't you think?'

'Certainly,' said Eleanor. 'I'll take those straggly ends off. It'll be much smarter.'

Lilia wheeled Joey out for a walk around the town centre and a visit to the library while Molly was sat in a chair, swathed in a nylon cloak and given a battered old *OK!* to look at while Eleanor applied the various lotions and potions. It all took a very long time, and there seemed to be hours of waiting while the various chemicals took effect. Lilia and Joey returned and settled themselves in the waiting area, Lilia tittering over *People's Friend* while Molly had her hair washed and then cut.

'Your mum doesn't like it curly, then?' said Eleanor, as she began snipping off a good eight inches of Molly's now ramrod straight hair. 'It's funny, really. I get girls with straight hair coming in here who'd die for curls like you had. Then the people with the curls can't stand them. We're never happy with what we've got, are we?'

Molly said nothing but stared soulfully at her image as it altered before her eyes. When the cutting was done, the hairdresser got out her blow-dryer and set to work, brushing Molly's hair into long, glossy sheets as she blasted it with hot air. At last she switched the dryer off. 'All done!' pronounced Eleanor proudly. Lilia came trotting over, eager to see the results. 'It took some doing to get those corkscrews out, but we've managed. What do you think?'

Molly sat staring at herself in the mirror. She looked like the same person but now transported to a bygone age. Her hair hung to her shoulders in shining chestnut curtains. She had a sudden memory of her mother looking at her through the glass. It was just a flash but Molly gasped at the resemblance.

'Ah!' sighed Lilia. 'So much better. It was as if you had a bird's nest there before. You look sophisticated and serious.' She smiled at Molly. 'I consider that a success. Don't you?'

'I don't recognise myself,' said Molly. 'Is that me?'

'The new you,' said Lilia, proudly. 'The woman who is going places.'

'Bring it on,' said Molly, determinedly, giving in completely now, handing over her appearance to Lilia's charge.

*

When they eventually left the hairdresser's, they walked to the graveyard at the top of the high street and found an empty bench, parking Joey beside them. It was a bright, sunny winter's day. Lilia pulled a Tupperware box out of her bag and announced that it was time for Molly's lunch. 'Salad and pickled herring with pumpernickel and a hard-boiled egg.' She pulled out a flask. 'And strong black coffee, of course.'

'What are you having?'

'Joey and I ate earlier at a very pleasant café. This is only for you.'

Molly was so hungry she dived straight in, making quick work of her egg. Some tramps and punk rockers loitered nearby, but the bench they had chosen was on a path that seemed to be a cut-through. There was a constant stream of Northamptonshire folk going about their business.

Molly's lunch was interrupted by a familiar voice. 'Molly Douglas? Is that you?'

She looked up, her cheeks bulging with pumpernickel, to see Roger, the doorman from the Derngate, standing in front of her.

'I almost didn't recognise you – except that I saw Miss Delvard here and then thought it *must* be you. What you doin' here, girl? And, my God, you look so different. It's your hair! You've interfered with nature – and with spectacular results. So demure, so different!' He turned respectfully to Lilia. 'Miss Delvard. We met at your soirée a while ago. Such an enchanting evening. I'm Roger. Remember me?'

'Of course,' said Lilia coldly. 'You seemed to find something very amusing as you departed, if my memory serves me correctly. You laughed long and loud as you got into your car.'

'Why, I—'

'Still squandering your talents at the stage door?'

'Yes, still there.' Roger nodded. Then a cross expression came over his face. 'And do you know what makes me sick? I don't get no appreciation, no thanks and not so much as a whip-round when I passed my driving test at the sixth attempt. I thought, You know what? Fuck the lot of them. Not even a good-luck card.' He turned back to Molly. 'So, what are you doing back in this dump? And why are you loitering in a graveyard eating black bread as if you were auditioning for *Oliver!*? I fuckin' hate that musical. Too many kids in it. Kids can't act and I fuckin' hate them too. They shouldn't be allowed in the theatre in my opinion. So? Spill the beans.'

Molly swallowed the last of her pumpernickel. 'Hello, Rog. Lovely to see you. I'd give you a hug but I've got hard-boiled egg all over my hands. I've . . . er . . . I've come to see Lilia for a bit, that's all.'

'Come to Northampton on holiday?' Roger looked suspicious. 'I would have thought you'd be living it up in London with your boyfriend. What did you say his name was?'

'Oh, you mean Daniel . . .' said Molly, struggling to find the words to explain her situation without giving away too much.

'Finished,' said Lilia decisively. 'All over. So she came to stay with someone who appreciates her. To wit, me.'

Roger raised his eyebrows. 'I'm sorry to hear that. But if I'm honest, I can't say I'm surprised. I heard about you and Marcus on the last night of the panto. I mean, a woman of your age in a happy relationship does not go off into the night with an eighteen-year-old stagehand.'

'I'm sure he said he was twenty-one,' declared Molly.

'He was cross-eyed when he came to work the next day to do the get-out. I said, "Are you all right, Marcus?" He was nearly in tears. He said you were like some sort of wild, insatiable vampire. He's only a boy. How he had the sense to record some of it on his mobile phone I'll never know. Well, it's lovely to see you again. I'll call round and see you one of these days. It'd be nice to renew our acquaintance. 'Bye now, Molly. Take care.'

Lilia watched him wander off through the graveyard, his hands in his pockets. 'Hmm,' she said thoughtfully, her eyes narrowing. 'Yes. We shall invite Roger over very soon. I have a feeling he may be useful.'

Chapter Twenty-one

Molly had been living at Kit-Kat Cottage for a month when something extraordinary happened. The walls of Lilia's bedroom were a cold, watery blue, and her bedspread was a faded floral pattern, smooth and thinly padded on the flat surface, then ruched jauntily where it hung down towards the floor. Joey lay on the left-hand side of the bed, so still and delicate he hardly showed, just a slight incline and a bump, as if a cat were asleep there. Molly walked to his side of the bed and peered at him. His eyes were open and he looked at her fearfully.

'It's all right, Joey,' said Molly. 'I'm just going to get you up and washed.' She hesitated, not wanting to manhandle him while he seemed so scared. 'Is that okay? I'll try not to pull you about too much.' She gently peeled the covers back. Joey was lying on his side in a foetal position. She rolled him on to his back, then slipped a hand under his head and pulled him into a sitting position, resting his weight against her chest. She felt his breath on her neck.

'There . . . That wasn't too bad.'

With one arm round his back to support him she unbuttoned his pyjama top and slipped the first arm out. Then she pulled him away from her slightly so she could do the same with the other. 'Good,' she said. She laid him down and pulled off his pyjama bottoms.

'Excellent. No trouble at all,' she said, trying not to sound too businesslike. In the bedside cabinet she found a packet of wet wipes and a pair of adult incontinence pads.

'I'll just get a towel,' she said breezily, and nipped to the bathroom. When she returned, she rolled him to one side and placed the towel underneath him, humming a made-up tune to put him at his ease. 'That's good, Joey. You just try and relax.' Molly tried to imagine she was performing a simple domestic task as she undid the soiled nappy, pulled it off his pitifully thin body and wrapped it into a ball. She swiftly took a wet wipe in her hand, pushed his knees up and wiped him clean. She repeated the procedure a couple more times to be sure, then put the new nappy in place. Next she put on his well-worn grey tracksuit bottoms, then a long-sleeved T-shirt. 'Nearly done!' she said cheerfully, as she knelt on the floor by his feet to put on his socks and shoes.

'That's better, don't you think?' she asked, panting slightly and relieved that the job was done without any mishaps. 'Are you ready to get into the chair now?' She pulled him gently into a sitting position again, his head resting once again on her ample chest.

Suddenly Joey made a gurgling sound she had never heard before. 'You all right, chuck?' she asked, peering round to see his face. Joey's eyes rolled up to look at her. 'What is it, Joey, love?'

A sound came from inside Joey's throat. 'De-do . . .'

'Are you trying to say something?' asked Molly, shocked by what seemed to be an attempt to communicate. 'What's wrong?'

Joey's lips opened and closed and a bubble of saliva appeared in the corner of his mouth. 'Buh, buh . . .' he said weakly. 'Ah, ah . . .' It was barely louder than a twig snapping.

'You are! You're trying to tell me something, aren't you? Oh, Joey!' Molly clasped him tighter and touched his face affectionately. 'Do you want me to get Lilia? She wouldn't want to miss this moment.'

Joey seemed to shudder in her arms and his eyes widened. 'Naaa!' he said urgently. He even managed a very slight shake of the head, barely a millimetre or two to either side but still perceptible. Exhausted by his efforts, he gasped for breath and closed his eyes.

'All right,' said Molly, soothingly. 'Take it easy now. Just relax. If it takes all day for you to say only three words then it's still a friggin' miracle.' She patted his back.

They sat on the bed in silence for a few minutes. Molly's eyes filled with tears. How wonderful it would be if Joey could break out of the prison of his mute existence. Maybe his body was slowly healing itself. If he were to regain the ability to speak, then Lilia would have her beloved husband back. Everything would change for the better.

Joey began a series of cat-like coughs, which settled into a slow pulse of *g* sounds.

Molly bent her ear to Joey's mouth and whispered encouragement to him. 'You're doing very well . . . Gee? Gee? Do you want to put a bet on the horses?'

'Naaa!' said Joey, impatience distinctly discernible now.

'No, okay, not that.'

Joey began again, his *g* sound hard this time. 'G-G-Goooo!'

'Goose? That's a bit random. Er, Goon? Gawd blimey?' she asked, watching him closely, looking for an affirmative sign. 'This is like charades. Go?'

Suddenly Joey reacted, blinking like a Morse-code torch and raising his eyebrows.

'Go? It's go?' she asked excitedly, and Joey blinked some more. 'Right, I've got that, then. The first word is "go". What's the second?'

'Aravy,' said Joey. 'Array. Arraaay!'

'Harry? Go Harry?' asked Molly, without much expectation that she was right.

'Na,' croaked Joey, dismissively.

'I didn't think it could be somehow,' said Molly, cross with herself. 'Take a few deep breaths and try again.'

Joey did as instructed. 'Goo array.'

Molly looked nonplussed. She frowned and said, 'Go away?'

Joey blinked.

'Do you want me to go away?'

Joey blinked again.

'Oh,' she said, deflated. 'Go away. You want me to leave you in bed? You don't want to come and watch *Home and Away*?' Joey didn't respond. 'Or,' she said tentatively, 'do you want me to go away from this house?'

Joey blinked with such enthusiasm that Molly eventually raised her hand to signal that he should stop. 'I understand, Joey. You want me to go. I'm sorry if I've outstayed my welcome. Is there anything else?'

Despite the wonder of Joey talking to her, Molly couldn't help her clipped tone. She felt hurt. She had always had a problem with rejection, and when someone who had been unable to communicate for several years made the superhuman effort to tell her to 'Go away!' it was all the more upsetting.

She wheeled Joey into the kitchen and spoon-fed him his

breakfast. He made no further attempt to speak, and neither did she. When he was finished, she sat him in the garden as it was a sunny day and went to the lounge, where Lilia and Heathcliff were having their early morning cuddle on the sofa. Heathcliff was lying on top of his mistress as usual, his snout buried in Lilia's cleavage. He looked up when he saw Molly and wagged his tail.

'Ah, Molly!' said Lilia, a little flushed. 'Ready to take my boy out for his constitutional?'

'Yes. But can I have a word with you first?'

'Of course you can,' said Lilia, reluctantly pushing the dog off and straightening her dress as she sat up. 'What is it, my dear?'

'Joey just spoke to me.'

'Spoke?'

'Yes, honest to God. He said two words.'

Lilia looked almost cross. 'Those are just muscular twinges, you foolish, over-imaginative girl.' She tutted, as if Molly were a naughty schoolgirl caught swearing.

'Honest, Lilia! It took him a while, but he definitely spoke to me.'

'And what did he say?' Lilia sounded almost sarcastic. 'The Lord's Prayer?'

Molly could feel the colour rising in her cheeks. 'He told me to go. To go away, leave this house. He doesn't want me here.'

'Ha!' said Lilia disbelievingly. 'He sometimes makes strange gurgling noises and his eyes roll around, but you mustn't confuse him with Melvyn Bragg.'

'No,' insisted Molly. 'It took a great deal of effort but he can definitely speak. I'm telling you. "Go away," he said. He flutters his eyes for yes and keeps them still for no. He doesn't like me, he made himself very plain.'

'Listen to me,' said Lilia. 'My husband hasn't uttered a word for almost three years. The doctors say his brain is damaged beyond repair. Do you think you are Our Lady of Lourdes? And, anyway, he'd be a fool to send you away now, because without your helping hands he'll be swilling in his own excrement. I am sorry to be vulgar, but it is true. No. I will not believe it. I will increase his medication in case he is building up to one of his fits. We don't want that. He projectile-vomited with such velocity once that he broke a window. Not only that but I had to hose down my bird-bath afterwards, and that's at the other end of the garden.'

'But, Lilia—'

'Enough!' said Lilia, raising her voice. 'Now, Heathcliff is waiting. Perhaps he, too, will speak to you when you are alone. Maybe he will recite a Shakespearean sonnet.' She laughed derisively.

Molly gave up, and took the dog for his walk.

Lilia seemed a little irritable for the rest of that day, and even had a brandy herself after lunch. That evening when Molly gave Joey his bath, she tried to get him to speak again. 'Lilia doesn't believe you spoke to me this morning. But you did, chuck, didn't you? You told me to go away.'

Joey's eyes stared up at the ceiling without a flicker of understanding.

'She thinks I made the whole thing up.' Molly swished the water over his soapy arms to rinse them and gently turned his head to face her. 'I think you're more with it than you make out, Joey. What's going on in there, eh?'

Although he was only inches from her, Joey wouldn't look Molly in the eyes.

'If you can speak, Joey, but you don't want anyone else to know, that's fine. You and I could have secret little chats. Would you like that? No? You just want me away from here, don't you? You'd like me to go and leave you in peace.'

Joey did not respond.

Molly sighed, and finished the bathing in silence. She couldn't imagine what she had done to upset him. Maybe he didn't like anyone but Lilia to see him naked and vulnerable. Perhaps he was jealous of Molly spending so much time with his wife. Or was he missing Lilia's tender care? She would speak to Lilia about her taking back some of the duties. After all, her bruised elbows must surely be better by now.

Molly decided to wait to speak to Lilia until after they had eaten their dinner – steamed carrots and spinach (with potatoes for Lilia) and two grilled sardines each. Then she went to the garden for her compulsory cigarette, which she smoked pensively, gazing out over the garden and thinking about what she wanted to say. After that she washed the dishes and went into the lounge where Lilia and Heathcliff were sitting side by side watching *University Challenge*.

Lilia was back in her usual spirits. She pointed at the screen. 'They might be clever, these Oxbridge types, but it doesn't mean they don't have to wash. Look at that dirty bitch there! If she spent a little less time studying ancient Greek and a little more time washing her ugly mug, maybe her skin complaint would translate itself.'

'Lilia,' Molly began, 'I know you don't believe Joey spoke to me, but I'm sure he did.'

'Oh, not this nonsense again!' said Lilia, exasperated. 'Can't it wait? Wadham have just got some bonus questions on astronomy. That girl should do well – she's got more craters on her face than the surface of the moon.'

'He did, I tell you. Joey doesn't like me.'

'He doesn't know what he likes,' snapped Lilia. 'He doesn't have an opinion, any more than the carrots you've just wolfed down for your dinner.'

Molly took a deep breath. She'd come to a decision earlier, while smoking her cigarette, and now she had to tell Lilia. 'I think I should leave. Tomorrow.'

Lilia turned the television off and threw the remote control onto the floor.

'Leave? Don't be absurd!'

Molly held up a hand. 'I'm really grateful to you for all you've done for me, but if I'm making Joey unhappy, it's not fair for me to stay. His life is miserable enough as it is without me making it worse.'

'I am transforming you into a great artist. You cannot simply get up and leave because you imagine that pot plant I married has taken a dislike to you. It will ruin everything. You are not ready yet.'

'I've decided. Your bruises must have healed by now, and we can both get on with our lives. I'll pack my things and go in the morning.'

'Go where? You have nowhere to go!'

'I can stay with my friend Jane, I expect. If you give me back my phone, I'll call her.'

'No—'

'I've made my mind up, Lilia,' Molly said obstinately.

Suddenly the fire drained from Lilia's eyes and her shoulders slumped. 'Have you? Then I will not waste any more energy. Kit-Kat Cottage is not a prison. You are free to leave whenever you choose. I do not lock the doors.'

'I have to go. It's not fair on Joey,' said Molly. 'I'm sorry. I appreciate everything you've done, I really do. But I know what I want.'

'Very well. I shall return your phone to you first thing in the morning.' Lilia stood up and walked silently out of the room, Heathcliff at her heels.

Molly was surprised to find tears rolling down her cheeks. In her heart, she did not want to leave. Lilia had taken over responsibility for her life and, bizarre as the last month had been, she felt as if she was heading towards a future of some kind. Lilia had faith in her, she had a plan. To walk away now meant she would never fulfil Lilia's dream. True, she felt hungry all the time and was heartily sick of the cigarettes and brandy, but the results were plain to see. She was getting thinner every day and she loved her new look. She was suffering for her art and felt the pay-off was within reach. Her voice was, indeed, sounding grittier and lived-in – far more distinctive than the musical-theatre trill she'd had a few weeks before. With her slim figure, husky voice and dramatic straight hair, she was becoming a new woman. For the first time in her life she felt exotic and rather beautiful.

But go she must. The supreme effort that poor, defenceless Joey had made to tell her to 'go away' rang in her ears. She respected him. She could not go against his wishes. She would not be a cuckoo in Joey's nest.

Molly went to her room and packed her things. The atmosphere in the bungalow was sombre, so she kept to her room and went to bed early.

Chapter Twenty-two

It was four in the morning when Molly was awoken by terrible screaming. She leapt out of bed and stumbled down the corridor into Lilia's room where she found her in bed, reaching over her husband. 'Joey! Joey! My Joey!' she cried, then wailed some more.

'What is it, Lilia?' asked Molly, rushing to her side. Joey was still in bed, lying on his back as usual, and Lilia was in her blue-flowered nightie on top of the covers beside him.

Lilia stared up at her with wild, frightened eyes. 'I don't know, but look at my darling!'

Molly rushed to Joey's side of the bed and looked at him properly. He was deathly white, his mouth and eyes wide open, his tongue lolling out to one side. Molly felt his cheek. It was barely warm. 'Quick,' she said. 'I'll give him the kiss of life. You call the ambulance.'

Lilia seemed paralysed with distress and didn't move.

'Now, Lilia!'

Whimpering with distress, Lilia dragged herself away from Joey and left the room. A moment later Molly heard her quavering voice on the phone in the hallway, giving the details to the emergency services. Meanwhile, Molly struggled to recall everything she was meant to do when attempting resuscitation. Check the airways are clear! she thought. She tipped Joey's head back, opened his mouth and put a finger inside. It was clear, so she held his nose, took a deep breath and lowered her mouth to his. She exhaled as hard as she could three times, willing her own warm breath to fill the old man's lungs and bring him back to life. She pulled away, counting to ten and watching anxiously to see if his chest would rise. 'Come on, Joey, two, come on! Three!' she said urgently. 'Four . . . five . . .'

Lilia returned to the bedroom and stood shivering, her hands covering her mouth to stifle her cries. 'Oh, no,' she repeated. 'Oh, no, no, no!'

'Is the ambulance on its way?' asked Molly, not looking up from her task. She bent down to breathe into Joey's mouth again. Still there was no response.

'Yes,' said Lilia. 'Please help him – please don't let him die.'

'He's not breathing. I'll have to try pumping his chest.' She put her two hands crossed on his chest and pressed down. Then she went back to force another breath into his lungs. She was at the limit of her knowledge of artificial respiration now. Breathe in, watch for the chest to rise; if it doesn't, push down to expel the air, and keep going. In her heart she knew it was hopeless. With no warmth or response in the body, there was only one outcome.

Lilia let out another cry and turned away, the sight of Joey's lifeless body too much to bear.

Molly kept on with the mouth-to-mouth, followed by the pumping down on his chest, but after a few minutes more she stopped, panting. She felt something in her mouth and tried to spit it out. Then she put her fingers in and pulled out several coarse dark hairs that looked like Heathcliff's.

'Damn! It's no good, it's not working!' she said, her eyes filling with tears of frustration. She turned to Lilia and said softly, 'I'm so sorry, I'm afraid he must have been dead for a while.' She didn't want to distress Lilia further by telling her that Joey was already cool to the touch and beginning to stiffen. She pulled the sheet over him because she couldn't bear to look at his gaping, open mouth, then turned to Lilia, who fell heaving with dry sobs into her arms. Molly cried gently, her heart aching for poor Lilia, whose sobs soon turned to the high-pitched monkey-like screams of primeval distress. An ambulance siren, like a silverback gorilla wailing in response, sounded in the distance.

Molly pulled away from Lilia and led her out of the bedroom into the lounge. 'Come in here, love,' she said. 'Sit down and I'll deal with everything.'

A few moments later, the siren was right outside the house and the blue emergency light, showing purple through the cerise curtains, flashed round the walls. Molly gave Lilia a final squeeze and left her still whooping with grief on the sofa while she opened the door to the paramedics.

Two men dressed in green stood there, both holding medical-equipment bags and wearing serious expressions.

'Miss Lilia Delvard?' said the younger one, urgently. 'Ambulance service.' He was about thirty with dark hair and looked like a librarian. His colleague was in his fifties, with a ruddy complexion and a sombre demeanour.

Molly threw open the door and led the way to the bedroom, talking rapidly as she went. 'No, I'm Molly, a family friend. I've sat Lilia in the lounge, but come in here. This is where Joey is. It must have been a heart-attack, I think.' She stood in the bedroom doorway and let them rush past her, wrapping her arms round herself for comfort.

The paramedics immediately removed the sheet from Joey's face. The younger one lifted his pale, thin arm and tried to take his pulse while his older companion pressed his fingers to Joey's neck. They glanced at each other and stopped, withdrawing their hands simultaneously.

'He's dead, isn't he?' said Molly, needing to hear it confirmed by professionals.

'Yes, he is, I'm afraid,' said the man holding Joey's wrist. 'I need to speak to the gentleman's wife. Could you take me to her, please?'

Meanwhile the older paramedic stood up, turned away from Molly and began to speak into his radio. From what Molly could make out, he was requesting that the police attend.

A crackling reply came back, but Molly heard no more as she led the first ambulance man in to see Lilia in the lounge.

The old lady was sitting quietly now, her face buried in her hands, as if she was trying to keep the screams inside, just the occasional squeak escaping, as she juddered up and down with pain.

'Lilia, my name is Steve.' He squatted in front of her and put a hand on her arm. 'You won't mind if I just see that you're all right, will you? Only you've had a nasty shock.'

Lilia lifted her head and revealed two dry but bloodshot eyes. She peered at Steve, sniffing. 'This dry eye is agony,' she said. 'I want to cry but I can't.' She clutched at Molly's hand and said, with surprising calm, considering that only moments ago she'd been howling like a banshee, 'He's gone, hasn't he? Expired in the night, like a hibiscus.'

'My colleague is just seeing to your husband. I'm going to check you over and see that you're all right. Can you tell me how old you are?'

'Really,' said Lilia, crossly. 'I may be a widow but that doesn't mean you can molest me.' Heathcliff, sitting at Lilia's feet, growled menacingly at him.

'All right, love. Are you on any medication at the moment?' asked Steve, giving the dog a wary look.

'Leave me alone, I'm fine,' said Lilia.

Molly moved to Lilia's side and put a protective arm round her. 'It's all right, pet, he's just worried about you.'

Just then they heard a police siren, and a car pulled up outside the bungalow.

'I'll go and let them in,' said Steve. Voices spoke in the hallway, then moved briefly into the bedroom. Lilia buried her face in Molly's shoulder, sighing and moaning. There was a light knock on the lounge door. A remarkably short policewoman came in and introduced herself as Gail Jones. She spoke softly and kindly in a Welsh accent, and had her notebook at the ready. She had clearly been briefed by Steve and addressed her questions to Molly. She wrote down both their names and asked who had discovered Joey.

'I heard Lilia's screams about half an hour ago,' said Molly. 'I went to the room and tried, you know, to revive him, but it was no good.'

'If I could hear it from Miss Delvard, then, please,' replied Gail. She turned to Lilia. 'When did you discover your husband's condition?'

Lilia began to sob again.

'I'm sorry, but I have to ask.'

'I sleep very lightly, and my dog, Heathcliff, was having a very restless night. Anyway, at some point I put my arm round Joey – as it is every wife's right to do, I believe? – and became aware that his chest was not moving up and down. I have no medical training but something told me this was not right. I turned on the light and then I saw him.'

'What did you see?' asked Gail, determined to get the facts down on paper.

'Well, it wasn't Gary Barlow, I know that much. It was my husband and he was dead.'

'What time was this?'

'You'll be wanting the shipping forecast next. I don't know. It didn't seem appropriate to call the speaking clock. I was busy screaming.'

'I heard Lilia screaming at four o'clock,' offered Molly.

'Had Joey been unwell?' asked the policewoman.

'He had a severe stroke several years ago and was unable to move or communicate. He was very fragile.'

'I see.' Gail wrote all this down. 'And what position was he in when you found him?'

'He was on the bed on his back,' said Molly.

'Thank you both for your co-operation,' said Gail, when she'd finished writing. She snapped her notebook closed. 'Let me explain to you what will happen now. A doctor needs to certify the death. If he's happy that it's a natural death, you'll be able to call the undertaker and arrange for the body to be removed. If the doctor can't establish the cause of death or has any concerns, we'll have to have Joey taken to the hospital for a post-mortem examination.' She asked if there were any friends or relatives they could go and stay with.

'We shall stay here,' said Lilia, determinedly. 'This is where we belong.' She gave the policewoman a fierce look. 'Do you think someone could make me a cup of tea?'

Molly jumped up immediately. 'Good idea . . . I'll make a pot for all of us. I think I need a cigarette as well. Would you stay with Lilia while I'm gone?' she asked Gail.

'Of course,' said the WPC, leaning down to stroke Heathcliff, who was rubbing his back against her legs affectionately. 'So you're Heathcliff, are you?'

'He seems to like you,' said Lilia.

'Well, well, you're a fine fella, aren't you?' Heathcliff looked lovingly up at her as she patted his shoulder.

'He likes a woman in uniform,' said Lilia, smiling proudly at Heathcliff – just as he rolled over on to his back and revealed a huge, throbbing erection.

WPC Jones withdrew her hand sharply and took a step back. 'Jesus Christ! What the hell is that?' she said, her Welsh lilt accentuated.

Lilia suppressed a girlish giggle. 'Put that away now, Heathcliff. You're not her type.'

The policeman looked at Molly, nonplussed. 'There's an offensive weapon if ever I saw one,' she said.

'I'll be back in a moment with some tea, then,' said Molly, and left the room. While the kettle boiled she slipped into the garden and lit a cigarette, drawing the smoke deep into her lungs and holding it there for a few satisfying seconds before exhaling luxuriously, closing her eyes. It was almost half past five in the morning and the shock of the last traumatic hour was only just beginning to hit her.

Poor Lilia. It would be impossible for Molly to leave in the morning as she had planned. And it dawned on her that as she was only going at Joey's behest, the reason for her departure had expired with him. Had his dislike of her distressed him to such a degree that it had precipitated his death? Was it her fault?

She stubbed out her cigarette in the now-overflowing flowerpot ashtray and returned to the kitchen to make the tea. She heard one of the ambulance men open the front door and greet what must be the doctor before their footsteps moved to the bedroom. There were now seven people in the bungalow, but the teapot held enough for four cups. Too bad, she thought, but it was Lilia who mattered. She put just three cups on the tray and carried it back into the lounge.

Heathcliff was now sitting up, looking a bit grumpy, while the policewoman was eyeing him warily as she sat on the sofa beside Lilia, who was leafing through a photograph album. 'And this is Joey and me on our honeymoon. See what a strapping man he once was. You can hardly recognise him.'

'That's your husband?' said Gail, disbelievingly, as Molly put the tray on the table and began to pour the tea. 'It must have been a very severe stroke he suffered.'

'Oh, it was,' said Lilia. 'Like popping a balloon. I was left with a shrivelled bit of skin in comparison with how he used to be.'

'It doesn't seem possible that he was that tall,' said Gail.

'Your tea, Lilia,' said Molly, holding out a steaming porcelain cup and saucer.

'I think, after all, a spot of brandy, for medicinal purposes,' said Lilia, waving away the proffered beverage. 'Gail can have that.'

Molly swung her arm towards the WPC who held up her hand by way of refusal. 'Thank you, but no tea for me,' she said.

'I'll have it, then,' Molly said, with a sigh. She was raising the cup to her lips when Lilia spoke.

'Whenever you're ready with that brandy,' she said impatiently. 'Someone has just lost a husband here.'

'Oh, sorry, Lilia,' said Molly, putting her cup down so suddenly that some tea sloshed over the side into the saucer. She darted across to the Chinese cabinet and poured a generous amount of Courvoisier into a brandy balloon. It made a rich, glugging noise.

Lilia pointed out another photograph to Gail. 'And here is Joey competing in the 1948 Olympics. He was so proud of this picture! I didn't know him then, of course. He won a gold in the javelin.'

'Very handsome, very athletic,' she said, studying the picture.

'I never knew that about Joey, God love him,' said Molly, returning with the brandy for Lilia.

'We had to sell the medals to pay for his hoist,' said Lilia, sadly.

Just then the lounge door opened and a middle-aged Indian man entered. He smiled kindly at Lilia. 'Are you the deceased's wife?' he asked. Lilia nodded and took a sip of brandy. 'I am Dr Jabir,' he said. 'I am so sorry.' He bowed respectfully. 'I have completed the death certificate. You may go through and be with him now, if you'd like to.'

Lilia looked bewildered.

'It sometimes helps,' said WPC Jones. 'But you don't have to if you don't want to.'

'I don't think I could bear it. I'm sorry,' said Lilia, gulping her brandy, then pressing her free hand to her forehead. She handed her glass to Gail and dissolved into sobbing again.

'Of course,' said Dr Jabir. 'Then perhaps I might have a word with you, miss?' He looked at Molly. 'I understand you were present when the death was discovered.'

Molly followed the doctor into the hall. 'Was it his heart?' she asked.

'Are you the resident carer?' he asked her.

Molly didn't know how to reply. 'I've been staying here to help Lilia,' she said at last. 'She did a fantastic job of looking after Joey but, to be honest, it was getting a bit much for her, so I helped as far as I could.'

Dr Jabir nodded sympathetically. 'It is an increasing problem for the elderly. I see so many cases where they are too proud to ask for help.'

'It would be a comfort to Lilia to know that he died in his sleep. He didn't suffer, just drifted away.'

'Er, yes,' said the doctor. 'It looks like a fairly straightforward case of heart failure to me. How was the deceased's health?'

'Not good,' Molly said gravely. 'He had a stroke a few years ago and was left completely incapacitated by it. He's required full-time care and feeding since then. He's always looked terribly frail, I must say.'

The doctor nodded. 'Yes, that makes sense. I'm happy to fill out the death certificate with heart failure as the cause. I really don't want to give Mrs Delvard any more distress than is necessary, but—' He stopped.

'What is it?' asked Molly.

'I just wondered if the dog slept in this room – more specifically, on the bed.'

'Yes, Heathcliff often sleeps there. Why?'

'There are an awful lot of dog hairs around the deceased, that's all. All over the pillow and even some in his mouth.'

'Yes, I noticed that when I was giving him mouth-to-mouth,' Molly said, frowning.

'Hmm.' The doctor shrugged. 'Well, it doesn't have any bearing on the death. It's quite clear as far as I can see. Here is a copy of the death certificate. You may ring the undertaker whenever you wish.'

'Thank you, Doctor,' Molly said.

'Now, I shall have a quick with word with our paramedic friends and then join you in the other room.'

When Molly returned to the lounge, Lilia was showing WPC Jones her scrapbook.

'This is me with Noël Coward at his country estate in Kent. He wrote a song about me, called "Alice Is At It Again". Most amusing. And here I am with Princess Grace of Monaco. Such an elegant woman. She left me some trinkets in her will, but of course I never received them. Perhaps you could investigate for me.'

'The Monaco police would be the ones to contact about that,' said Gail, a slight weariness creeping into her voice, 'and I'd better go and see my colleague, if you'll excuse me. Molly is back now.'

'Good,' said Lilia. 'Maybe another small brandy wouldn't be too much trouble?'

The policewoman stood up, brushed down her uniform and nodded at Molly before leaving the room.

'Such a nice woman,' said Lilia. 'Quite engrossed in my old pictures and cuttings, she was.'

'How are you feeling, Lilia?' asked Molly, passing her a replenished glass of Courvoisier.

'You cannot imagine,' she said dispassionately. 'I am quite lost. I have nothing. No one. My life is over now, I am undone . . .'

There was a tap on the door and WPC Jones came back in,

followed by Steve and Dr Jabir. 'We'll be on our way,' said Steve, and Heathcliff immediately stood up and stared at the ambulance man, as if he might pounce.

'No, Heathcliff. Sit down,' said Lilia, sharply, and the dog reluctantly rested on his haunches. His eyes remained fixed on Steve, who moved back towards the door.

Dr Jabir stepped forward. 'I'd like you to get some rest, if possible. You've had a very nasty shock. Would you like a sedative to help you sleep?'

'I would not,' said Lilia, proudly. 'Molly is here. She is all the comfort I require.' She looked at Molly. There was a pause infused with expectation.

'Er, of course,' said Molly, aware that all eyes were upon her. 'I'm not going anywhere.'

'Good,' said Lilia. 'I have witnesses.'

'I'll telephone your GP in the morning and I'm sure he will be in touch,' concluded the doctor. 'I am so sorry for your loss.'

WPC Jones said, 'And I'll be contacting our bereavement-support officer. She will—'

'That will not be necessary,' interrupted Lilia. 'Thank you for the offer.' She reached out and squeezed Molly's hand. 'We will look after each other. Good morning to you, gentlemen, Miss Jones.'

It was almost seven o'clock by the time they had all left Kit-Kat Cottage, and a new day was dawning.

'I suppose it is an unusual time to go to bed, but that is what we should do. I know that would be my mother's suggestion – her solution to any problem.'

'If that's what you'd like to do,' said Molly, 'let me help you. We can call the undertaker later.'

'I cannot sleep in that bed, not with poor Joey still there. Do you mind if I come in with you?'

'No, of course not,' said Molly, aware that she couldn't refuse under the circumstances. 'You go to bed and I'll tidy up. Is there anyone you'd like me to contact?'

'Yes, there is,' said Lilia. 'Could you contact me?'

'What do you mean?' asked Molly, confused by the question.

'I mean, I'd like a bit of contact. Come and lie down with *me* and be there for *me*. For a couple of hours, at least. I need to feel the presence of the living, not the emptiness of the dear departed.'

Molly put her arm round Lilia and helped her up. 'Yes,' she said, 'of course I'll come with you.'

Ten minutes later they lay side by side on their backs in Molly's bed, staring at the ceiling. Heathcliff lay across their legs, pinning them down with his hefty frame. Only he snored. Every now and then one of them would sigh.

'Poor Joey,' said Lilia, quietly. 'Gone on his way. Wandered off like a restless tom cat.'

'On to the next life,' said Molly, philosophically.

'Where I hope he will be able to walk and talk.'

'Or fly,' said Molly, dreamily.

'Perhaps he'll be reincarnated as an albatross. That would suit him. He's had plenty of practice, after all.'

'Or a golden eagle,' said Molly, closing her eyes and imagining a magnificent bird soaring into the air, free and wild and beautiful. 'He's free at last.'

Chapter Twenty-three

The next few days were occupied with organising the funeral. Lilia was paralysed with grief, so Molly took care of the arrangements. 'Should I alert the Olympics committee that Joey has passed on?' she asked Lilia. 'Only I'm sure they'd want to honour him in some way. He was a gold medallist, after all. There's bound to be an obituary in *The Times*. There may even be a mention on the news. I expect some officials would like to attend and pay their respects.'

'Please don't,' said Lilia. 'I am very weak and the thought of all that fuss, the press, the phone calls from Buckingham Palace and the prime minister – it is too much.'

'Well, what about friends from the old days? I expect you and Joey knew so many people from your glamorous past. This would be the perfect opportunity to get in touch with them all again. I'm sure they'd like to pay their last respects.'

'No,' said Lila firmly. 'I can't face it. Let my Joey slip quietly into oblivion. That is what he would want, and what he had, in many senses, already achieved.'

In the end, there were only six people at the crematorium for

Joey's service, which took place a week after his death. Molly had felt she must invite someone else, so she'd asked Roger, who brought along his partner Freddie, a well-dressed but elderly gentleman who walked with a stick.

'I see Old Father Time is here,' muttered Lilia, under her thick black veil.

'Sssh!' said Molly. 'He's sitting right behind us.'

'What's Roger after? Some free sandwiches?'

'I invited him. I thought it would be nice for you to have some support.'

The other attendees were a strange middle-aged couple dressed in black who sat staring ahead throughout the brief service.

'Look at them,' hissed Lilia. 'Grief groupies. I expect they hang around here all day, going to funerals. Weirdos.'

It was the briefest of ceremonies with no personal tributes, and just a single dark pink rose on the coffin, from Lilia. She'd picked it herself from the garden.

'It's from my "Angela Rippon" bush,' she explained, as they filed out afterwards.

'Beautiful,' said Roger. 'Thanks for asking us. I didn't know Joey, but he was obviously a very special man who'll be sadly missed.'

Freddie muttered, 'So very sorry . . .' and shook Lilia's hand solemnly.

'He had a wonderful life,' said Molly, in an attempt to fill the awkward silence.

There was no wake afterwards. Molly thought they ought to ask Roger and Freddie back for a drink but Lilia wouldn't hear of it. 'I never feed vultures,' she said, when they were on their way home in a taxi.

'They came to pay their respects,' said Molly. 'I think it was very nice of them.'

Lilia just sniffed and stared out of the window through her veil.

Back at the house, every sign of Joey had, by now, been erased. The various slings and hoists that had been used to lift and transport him, the special mattress, the nappies, pills, lotions and dressings that were all kept on a big plastic tray had been returned to the hospital or donated to a hospice shop. Even his armchair had been thrown out and the furniture rearranged to fill the gap.

The morning after Joey's funeral Molly discovered Lilia staring out of the kitchen window, her face miserable. She put an arm round her and gave her a hug. 'You're missing him, aren't you?' she said.

'I do not understand,' said Lilia, her eyes searching the garden. 'The starling has gone. And I have not seen my little thrush since the night Joey died. I have put out bread for him, whistled for him, but he hasn't come to see me.'

'Ah, love,' said Molly.

'Sometimes, in my *People's Friend*, I read letters from widows. Their dead husbands revisit them in the form of a robin redbreast hopping around in their garden and fearlessly landing on their shoulders to give them an affectionate peck on the cheek. Why, in my case, has this happened in reverse?' Lilia turned to Molly for an explanation. 'Will my thrush ever return?'

'Mine never has,' said Molly, 'but I've got some very effective ointment if it does.'

There was silence for a moment, then both women laughed for the first time since Joey had died.

'Maybe he was Joey's bird, not yours,' Molly suggested. 'He's gone with Joey to guide him to heaven.'

Lilia shrugged. 'Either that or next door's cat got him.'

Despite the removal of any evidence that Joey ever lived there, Lilia talked about him constantly in terms that indicated how much she missed him and how badly she was coping. 'It is worst at night,' she would say, with a trembling voice, when Molly said she was going to bed. 'I reach out to touch him and he isn't there. I call his name but he doesn't answer!' she wailed. 'How can I go on? What is the point?'

Molly would smile and rub her back. 'Don't upset yourself now. You know you can always sleep in my bed.'

As a result, Lilia never did return to her own bedroom, but continued to sleep with Molly, clinging to her with her bony hands and sometimes weeping tearlessly on her neck. 'Do not leave me, Molly. Do not abandon me at such a time!' the old lady cried on her shoulder. Heathcliff slept on the bed too, and although it was hot and uncomfortable, Molly could see no way to ask for her privacy back.

The singing and acting lessons resumed on the day after the funeral and Lilia seemed happiest when she was giving her *protégée* instructions. In fact, without her time-consuming duties, getting Joey up and fed, Molly found that there were even more hours in the day to spend on her scales, diction and deportment. The cold baths and meagre breakfasts were reinstated.

Gradually Lilia became her old happy self again. Instead of looking for her starling and thrush each morning, she took to calling sweetly, 'Here, Pussy! Come to Lilia!' to next-door's cat while standing at the door with a bucket of water at the ready. The day she finally managed to drench him, she hummed to herself all afternoon and opened a bottle of port to celebrate.

'You are not smoking enough,' said Lilia one day, examining a half-empty packet. 'You should have finished these yesterday and be on to the next packet by now.'

'I'm trying my best but they're giving me a cough,' said Molly, defensively. 'Did you hear me this morning? I sound like Alf Garnett.'

'I heard just a polite clearing of the throat. We are aiming for the full consumptive lung rattle. You are a long way off. When I used to share a room in Paris with Edith Piaf, she filled half a bucket with phlegm before breakfast.'

'You lived with Edith Piaf?' exclaimed Molly. Lila's extraordinary life never ceased to astound her.

'Yes, my dear, I did. In the Grand Hôtel de Clermont, way back. We were like sisters. It was I who named her "Little Sparrow", as a matter of fact.'

'What was she like?' asked Molly.

'Rough. Always crying over one man or another. She stole Charles Aznavour from me.'

'Wow! Charles Aznavour!'

'I inspired him to write that dreadful song – "She". According to him, I could be the famine or the feast, the beauty or the beast – I've never been so insulted in my life!'

'Is that about you?' asked Molly, open-mouthed.

'I'm afraid so. Not that I get any royalties. Anyway, my point is that you must smoke a lot more if you are going to make progress.'

'Right,' said Molly, determinedly. 'I'll go and have a couple right now.'

'Excellent,' said Lilia. 'It is for your own good. Mucus is nature's honey. We shall increase your brandy consumption too, I think. And less food. You are not nearly thin enough.'

Molly stood in the garden and lit a Gauloise. It felt like sandpaper on the back of her throat but she didn't mind. Lilia's anecdote about Edith Piaf had inspired her to try harder. She smoked with gusto, and before she put out the cigarette, she lit another from the stub. She steadied herself on the wall as the strong cigarettes made her giddy and a little nauseous. But no one had ever said being a successful singer was easy. Lilia was teaching her so much. She must channel all the emotions and heartbreak of the Daniel and Simon affair into her singing, just as Edith had done. Lilia was a severe and demanding tutor but at least she had faith in Molly, had a vision. It was important to give herself over to her, to allow her mentor full access and to obey all her instructions. Lilia was going to mould her into something out of the ordinary. Otherwise she would just plod along, working in third-rate musical theatre all her life. What could be worse than that? This was a time of transformation and eventually, with Lilia's help, she would emerge from Kit-Kat Cottage a better person. A star in waiting.

Molly allowed herself to daydream for a minute or two. She saw herself on a big stage in front of several thousand wildly enthusiastic people, who clapped and whistled their appreciation. She was thin and beautiful and she bowed graciously several times as the applause went on and on. She sang songs of lost love and hard times in a husky, hauntingly melodic voice. She sang for all the sadness and heartbreak in the world and touched everyone in the audience. Tears ran down her cheeks, glistening in the spotlight, and rose petals rained down from her devoted fans up in the gods.

Eventually, all the cigarettes and brandy paid off. While Molly was singing her scales one afternoon, there was another sudden break in her voice, more dramatic than the last. This time, the note gurgled and shuddered. Molly was so alarmed she stopped singing, but Lilia rapped her knuckles on the piano and told her urgently to continue. Molly tried the same note and again her voice vibrated with a new, sticky tone.

Lilia clapped with delight. 'Yes! That is what I have been waiting for!' Her eyes shone with joy.

Molly clutched her throat and laughed, shocked by the sound that had emerged. Her voice had dropped a full octave. It was as if Aled Jones had changed, mid-sentence, into Joe Cocker.

'Again, quickly!' commanded Lilia.

Molly sang all the scales through twice, and the new voice became stronger and more resonant. When she finished she flung her arms round Lilia. 'Oh, thank you, Lilia, thank you!'

'At last,' said Lilia. 'Listen to the richness of your voice now, the depth of expression, the soulful pitch. Now we can put "vintage" on the label.'

'I have found my voice?' said an emotional Molly.

'The voice you need to express your inner self,' said Lilia, solemnly.

'Yes,' whispered Molly.

Lilia stood up and paced the room. 'I have such plans for you. It is all a question of alignment. We start with the broken heart.

This is essential for any great artist. We cannot experience the true depth, the divinity of human experience without it. I could not break it for you. It is a man's job. You came to me primed and ready to evolve. Now we have the voice, the rest is easy.'

'What is the rest?' asked Molly, eagerly.

'Aesthetics, mostly. Presentation, let's call it. Image.'

'Hair, makeup and costume, do you mean?' asked Molly.

Lila stopped pacing and studied Molly from a few yards away. 'Not exactly,' she said. 'Although it is very quaint of you to think so.' She opened the Chinese cabinet and took out the brandy bottle. 'We have a way to go yet, I can see. This is not a theatrical role we are discussing. A great singer is not an actress, paid to deliver someone else's lines while simulating emotions for the riff-raff in the auditorium. A singer of the calibre I fully expect you to become is giving of themselves. It is a major difference. When I sang at the Café de Paris, when I serenaded my public at an open-air concert in Central Park, even when I sang in the bath, I cried real tears of blood. It was a cry from the soul. We give and we give until it hurts, and then we give some more.'

'What happens now, then?' asked Molly, wide-eyed. She was aware that a crucial stage had been reached and it was time for something new.

'We shall begin work on a suitable repertoire of songs for you.'

'I love that idea,' said Molly, excitedly.

'I have already been in touch with Roger. I explained to him what our plans for your future are, and as he owed me for the pleasant afternoon he spent at the crematorium, he has given me the number of an excellent pianist who is available for the next few weeks. His name is Geoffrey. I hesitate to bring a man into the house, but needs must.'

'Why?' asked Molly, with a laugh. 'What are you worried about?'

'First, letting someone in on our secret,' replied Lilia. 'The golden goose could be stolen from me. Second, there is the danger of you forming an unsavoury liaison with him. He is a man, after all. According to Roger, Geoffrey is pig ugly, though. Forty-nine and balding, too. That should put you off, for a while at least.'

'He doesn't sound my type,' said Molly, with a shudder. 'Although,' she said impulsively, 'I'd like to think I'll meet a man one day and be happy again.'

Lilia looked worried. 'Happiness is always a great danger. It could ruin everything. Luckily for Edith Piaf, the great love of her life was killed in a plane crash. That kept her going for decades. Her misery vaults were full to bursting. Even so, she had to top them up with a couple of car accidents and the suicide of her best friend.'

'Do I have to be unhappy to be a great singer?' asked Molly, contemplating Lilia's words. 'Can't I just have an unhappy experience and move on with life? Maybe get married and have children.'

'Yes, that is scheduled,' said Lilia, matter-of-factly. 'But it is years away. You will marry someone interesting and rich one day.'

Molly smiled, pleased at the prospect. 'Oh, good!' she said.

'Put it out of your mind for now, though. We have work to do. Geoffrey will start tomorrow, and we will test your voice with some Jacques Brel. Now go for a smoke. Roger has also provided me with the telephone number of young Marcus.'

Molly's eyes widened with surprise. 'Marcus? What do you want his number for?'

'Apparently he knows where to buy drugs.'

'Drugs?' gasped Molly.

'Yes, indeed. You need to dabble. I have asked him to deliver six grams of high-quality cocaine, some skunk and a packet of Valium.'

'I've never taken drugs in my life!' said Molly, aghast.

'I know. A pitiful state of affairs. The cocaine we shall use as an appetite suppressant mainly. You are not losing weight quickly enough for my liking. It has the added advantage of being a depressant. Smoking joints will not only be beneficial to your new voice but will make you dreamy and other-worldly. They will also make you depressed,' added Lilia, happily, as if listing the advantages of a new skin-care range.

'And the Valium?' asked Molly.

'The same,' said Lilia. 'All in all, a fabulous combination. Think of it as your Judy Garland phase. Don't worry, I'll make sure you don't slide into hopeless addiction.'

Molly thought for a moment. Taking drugs was a serious matter – she'd seen the damage they could do – but this was a controlled environment, and Lilia was hardly going to let her do anything really dangerous. Besides, she'd said she'd do anything it took to become a famous singer . . . I'm fed up with being a good girl, she thought recklessly. Look where it's got me! Maybe it's time to live a little and find out what it's like on the other side. 'Okay,' she said, like a Girl Guide setting out to earn a new badge. 'I'll do it.'

'As to whether or not you should have sex again with Marcus,' continued Lilia, weighing the options, 'I am in favour of it. It will help to stoke up your emotions and therefore improve your singing. Particularly when he chucks you for someone younger and prettier. Your infatuation with his beautiful body followed by the unanswered phone calls will do you the power of good. I'm all for it.'

'I'll go for a cigarette,' said Molly.

Geoffrey, when he arrived, was indeed an unappetising man with the air of an undertaker. His hands and shirt collar were grubby and he had an unfortunate habit of grunting at the end of each song – a pig-like sound that signified its completion. His piano playing, however, was lovely, and his knowledge of torch songs encyclopedic. After a couple of days Molly and Lilia realised that he was eccentric rather than unfriendly, and if you could make him smile, which Molly's singing certainly could, then his face changed, lighting up with satisfaction. He carried with him a battered briefcase bulging with sheet music.

The first song that the new, improved Molly sang in Lilia's living room was 'Cry Me A River'.

'Exquisite!' pronounced Geoffrey, as Molly breathed to the end of the last, soulful note.

'It can be improved,' said Lilia. 'Curdle the words a bit more. You must spit when you sing that he says he's sorry. He *says* he's sorry, but he must *prove* it. Remember your own suffering! Cast your mind back to the night you were betrayed by Daniel and Simon. Sorry is not enough. Again!'

Geoffrey played the opening chords and Molly's voice quivered with the bitter memory.

Lilia interrupted her: 'No. You are still too kind and too gentle. You need to infuse the words with meaning, convey to me the betrayal and eternal hurt they inflicted on you that night. Sing it with irony. Find a way in. Again!'

Molly sang the song over and over until she was reliving the events of that terrible night with every phrase. Tears ran down her cheeks and her chest heaved with emotion.

'Good!' said Lilia, at last. 'That is what the song is about: the refusal to forgive or forget. Now you have it.'

Geoffrey said very little, but smiled encouragingly at Molly and adjusted his playing to accommodate her increasingly dark and dangerous rendition.

At the end of their two-hour session (punctuated with several cigarette breaks for Molly), Lilia handed the pianist a twenty-pound note and said, 'Thank you, Geoffrey. Your playing is very satisfactory. Most sensitive. We shall continue tomorrow at the same time.'

Geoffrey bowed respectfully. 'I would be very happy to. A fine afternoon's work.' He turned to Molly. 'Congratulations. A remarkable voice! And your teaching, Miss Delvard, is, well, inspiring.'

'You are most kind,' said Lilia, opening the lounge door to show him out. 'Tomorrow we will work on "The Man That Got Away" and Hoagy Carmichael's "Sky Lark".'

'Marvellous songs,' said Geoffrey, enthusiastically. 'I shall look forward to it.'

Molly was in the garden, smoking, where Lilia joined her after she had seen Geoffrey out, Heathcliff at her heels. 'You are going to be a great singer. I am already very proud of you.'

Molly tipped her head back and closed her eyes, blowing smoke up towards the sky. 'Oh, I hope so. I can begin to feel it.'

'Your destiny,' whispered Lilia, 'awaits you.'

Molly opened her eyes and straightened her head to look affectionately at the old lady. She smiled, raised her shoulders towards her ears, then dropped them down again. 'I'm so excited,' she said. 'I've suddenly got a purpose in life. It's a wonderful feeling.'

They gave each other a warm hug. Heathcliff collected his ball from the lawn and dropped it at their feet.

Chapter Twenty-four

'Tonight is special, Molly!'

They were sitting in the lounge. Lilia and Molly had not long finished their salad and were watching the news headlines.

'Really? What's happening? Am I going out?'

'In a manner of speaking. I've arranged for a delivery of drugs. You are going to try some, just as we discussed.'

'Lilia, what are you doing to me?' asked Molly, as if she was being tempted with chocolates.

'You cannot sing the blues if you are pure. You need to experience a few unnatural highs and lows to be convincing. You took to drugs after your lover betrayed you. You were trying to blot out the pain. You had nothing to live for. You were at an all-time low. Drugs were your only escape.'

'I get the general idea,' said Molly, considering the prospect.

'It will be good for your biography. Your singing talent sprang forth when you were in the very depths, and so on.'

Molly laughed. 'I can't believe all this. You really are re-creating me, aren't you? You're like Henry Higgins!'

She was amazed by the thoroughness of Lilia's vision. She seemed to have thought of everything.

At that moment, the doorbell rang.

'Ah!' said Lilia. 'The delivery. You stay here while I deal with Marcus in the kitchen. You must know nothing of it – he may try to sell his story to the press one day. Bastard.' And she left the room.

Molly heard the front door open and Marcus's monosyllabic tones as he and Lilia went down the hallway to the kitchen. Five minutes later Lilia opened the lounge door and announced, 'Marcus has come to see you.' Then she added significantly, 'I think I will have an early night.'

She retreated through the door and Marcus shuffled in. He hung his head as if he was embarrassed to see Molly, his hands dug deep in his pockets. His tousled hair had gone, replaced with a crew-cut and a few days' stubble. He didn't look at her until Lilia had closed the door behind him, but when he finally raised his eyes he did a double-take.

'Molly, is that you?'

'Hiya, Marcus. Yes, it's me.'

'What happened to the curls?'

Molly smiled nervously. 'Oh, I had it straightened. What happened to yours?'

Marcus stroked the top of his head as if he was only now aware of his new severe hairstyle. 'I let a mate cut it one night when I was pissed. How come you're still here? I thought you went back to your boyfriend.'

'I did,' said Molly, suddenly embarrassed at the memory of their night together. She felt a guilty twinge deep inside her. 'It ended rather messily so I came back to Lilia's.'

He nodded as though this made perfect sense, then stared at her again. 'You're a bit thin, aren't you?'

'I've been dieting.'

There was an uncomfortable silence.

'Perhaps I'd better go,' said Marcus.

'Would you like a drink, maybe?'

'I'm on the bike. Better not.'

Molly sipped her brandy. How could someone she had known so intimately seem such a stranger? She had devoured this boy a few months before, and he had twisted her body into all manner of shapes, but now there seemed to be nothing between them except mutual mortification. Despite Lilia's blessing there seemed little desire on either side to repeat their night of lust.

Marcus mumbled, ''Bye, then,' and left the room with unseemly haste.

Molly sat alone with her brandy and contemplated the feeling of emptiness she was experiencing. Seeing Marcus again and receiving the confirmation that sex with him had been a drunken fling, a physical release and nothing more left her vulnerable.

Was this what Simon went through after each of his many one-night stands? How desolate and lonely it must be. How damaging. All that was left was the memory of the moment. And because she had been drunk, that memory was all mashed up in her brain: she had flashes of moaning, tongue-stretching French kisses, the urgent uncovering and tasting of genitals and other animalistic acts. She and Marcus had been possessed and overcome, unthinking to the point of mindlessness. Maybe sensual pleasure alone was the point. It was foolish to try to analyse it in a rational way. Perhaps giving in to it, seeking out that liberating second of sexual ecstasy, was a life-affirming instinct – a self-contained triumph for nature to claim over rational, developed human analysis.

Her thoughts were interrupted by Lilia coming into the

lounge, now wearing her nightie and slippers. 'I heard Marcus leave,' she said, pouring herself a brandy and refilling Molly's glass. 'Rather lost his charm, I think. It can be so fleeting in young men, I find.' She sat down in her usual chair.

'We didn't really know what to say to each other,' said Molly.

'You were ships that passed out in the night,' concluded Lilia.

'I guess we were,' agreed Molly.

'How do you feel about that?'

'Confused,' said Molly, 'that something so intense can also be so meaningless.'

Lilia nodded knowingly. 'Ah, yes, indeed. There is a song called "Is That All There Is?" by Leiber and Stoller. I think you will perform it very well. Do you know it?'

'Was it sung by Peggy Lee?'

'After she stole it from me, yes.' Lilia closed her eyes and began to sing in her high vibrato: ' "Break out the booze and have a ball – if that's all there is." '

'Yes! I've heard it before,' said Molly. 'I'd love to sing that!'

'You will do it wonderfully,' said Lilia. 'Hang on to your feelings of confusion about Marcus. File them away. They will be very useful. It is a song about disappointment. Even death will fail to live up to expectations.'

'I can't wait,' said Molly.

'I shall call Geoffrey in the morning and tell him to bring the music with him tomorrow afternoon. It could be your encore, maybe.' Lilia got out of her chair and stood in front of Molly. 'Now put out your hand.'

Molly did as she was told.

'Here,' said Lilia, placing her clenched fist on top of Molly's hand and unfurling it.

Molly felt something small drop on to her palm. 'What is this?' she asked, examining a small, purple, diamond-shaped pill.

'Something to help you drift off to sleep,' said Lilia, soothingly. 'Judy's favourite.'

'Oh, I don't think I need it,' said Molly, resisting. 'No, thank you.' She tried to return it to Lilia, who put both hands behind her back.

'You do need it. Swallow it. You will lie awake for hours, otherwise, fretting about the indignity of your drunken fuck.'

'But I'm worried that—'

'There is nothing to worry about!' insisted Lilia. 'Trust me. Billie Holiday ate them like Smarties.'

Molly took the pill, put it into her mouth and washed it down with a gulp of brandy.

'There,' said Lilia. 'That wasn't difficult, was it?'

'What's good enough for Billie is good enough for me,' said Molly.

'We worked together in the fifties and, of course, she tried to embroil me in a lesbian affair, but I refused her. She wrote a song called "Our Love Is Different" about her feelings for me.'

'Gosh!' said Molly.

'Not one of her finest, but touching, I grant you,' said Lilia, casually. 'Now, then, you need to clean your teeth and wash your face before it takes effect.'

'Do I?' asked Molly.

'Yes. The fabulous thing about these pills is that your body goes to sleep before your mind does. It's a bit like sinking into a warm mud bath. You'll love it. Come on.' She tugged at Molly's arm and they tottered to the bedroom.

*

Lilia gradually introduced drugs into Molly's daily schedule, telling her it was a fun thing to do, not a chore. To be a torch songstress with no knowledge of amphetamines was nonsense, she declared. 'No one would take you seriously. It simply has to be done. Besides, Queen Victoria used to suck cocaine lozenges. How do you think those royals keep smiling all the time?'

To counteract the morning grogginess caused by the pills Molly was given at night, a healthy line of cocaine and a cropped straw were laid out for her on a plate after her breakfast. Lilia explained how to snort the white powder. 'It will make you feel perky and bright-eyed. You will whiz round the field with Heathcliff after this,' she said. 'What a treat!'

Another line was suggested before lunch, after which Molly could barely eat half of her steamed broccoli and tofu stir-fry. 'The thought of swallowing anything is disgusting. I'm just not the least bit hungry,' she said, pushing her plate away as Lilia looked on approvingly. The drug also gave her a confidence she had never known before. 'God, I'm good,' she said seriously, to Geoffrey, after she'd sung 'Lover Boy' one afternoon.

In the evening, after the effects of the cocaine had worn off she would sometimes feel a little fractious so Lilia rolled her a joint. 'It will take the edge off the come-down,' she said, as she sprinkled the powdery dried green leaves with some tobacco from a disembowelled cigarette. 'Enjoy!'

After her first experience of puffing a spliff, Molly felt so giddy and ill she was sick into a fruit bowl.

'Excellent!' said Lilia. 'The messier the better. You will have so much to talk about when you are a huge star giving exclusive interviews to upmarket magazines about your sleazy past.'

Molly retched again. 'I feel like shit,' she said queasily.

'Bravo!' said Lilia, with a chuckle.

'I think I'm going to pass out,' she said, her eyes rolling backwards.

'That,' rejoined Lilia, 'is too much to hope for.'

After a couple of days the nausea stopped and Molly was able to enjoy the mind-altering effects of her drug selection. Now she was overcome with a new-found creativity that inspired her to write some original lyrics of her own. In the evenings she would lie on the sofa, stoned out of her mind, and dictate to a vigilant Lilia, whose pen was poised over a smart new red notepad. 'I used to do the same for Bob Dylan,' she let slip.

'You knew Bob Dylan as well?' asked Molly, managing to raise her head at least three inches from the cushion. 'I thought you were more of a crooner than a folk singer.'

'Let's just say our careers brought us together and we were close for a while. After some weed he would close his eyes and think up songs. I wrote them down for him, and it's true that I improved them where I could. One evening he wrote a little trifle called "Like A Rolling Log". I decided a rolling stone would be catchier. Of course, he remembered nothing when he woke up in the morning.'

'Well,' said Molly, impressed, 'please feel free to improve on my words too. You obviously have an ear for such things.'

'Oh, I do,' agreed Lilia. '"Blowin' In The Wind" would have been a very vulgar little ditty if I hadn't worked my magic on it.'

'I feel a lyric coming on now,' said Molly, closing her eyes and moving her head from side to side.

'I am ready, my dear,' replied Lilia, as if they were at a séance and about to contact the other side. 'What is it you want to say?' She leant forward and tipped her ear to Molly's mouth as she began to mutter: 'I've got the blues . . . I just want to snooze . . .'

'No,' said Lilia, gently. 'Try a bit harder. What is making you blue? Think.'

'Daniel?' offered Molly.

'He done you wrong, did he not? Then you have the bad-boyfriend blues. Why don't you write a song about that?'

There was a long pause during which Molly's breathing became so laboured that she might have slipped into a deep slumber. But eventually she began to sing:

'Molly and Daniel were sweethearts,
Molly and Daniel were one,
Molly and Daniel shared everything,
They sure were having fun,
He was her man. He wouldn't do her no wrong.

'Along came Molly's friend, Simon.
Who was hardly as white as snow,
If he had his eye on Daniel
Then how was Molly to know?
He was her friend. He wouldn't do her no wrong.

'One night Molly drank too much brandy.
She had to hit the sack.
How was she to know that Simon
Would launch his vile attack?
He was her friend. But he did her wrong.

'This was a double betrayal.
Her mind just seemed to implode.
Her boyfriend making out with her boyfriend,
In her very own abode!
He was her man. But he was doing her wrong.

'She went completely doo-lally.
An understandable response:
She'd just seen her lover behaving
Like a low-down, dirty nonce.
He was her man. But he was doing her wrong.

'Her response was very dramatic,
She smashed everything in sight.
Daniel tried to reason with her,
But she was full of fight,
He was her man. But he was doing her friend.

'This story has no moral.
This story has no end.
This story only goes to show
That there ain't no good in men.
They'll do you wrong,
Just as sure as they were born.'

The creative flow seemed to dry up. Molly became distracted by the shadows on the ceiling and her eyes wandered. Lilia closed the notebook. 'Very promising,' she said. 'A work in progress, at least. Now it is time for your pill.'

Chapter Twenty-five

It was a cold, rainy afternoon and Molly had been at Kit-Kat Cottage for ten weeks.

The phone rang, and Lilia answered in her usual grand manner: 'This is Lilia Delvard. How may I help you?' There was a pause. 'One moment,' said Lilia, curtly. 'It's for you.' She handed the phone to Molly.

'Really?' Molly was astonished. She had begun to feel as though she had never existed anywhere except at Kit-Kat Cottage. Who from the world outside knew she was there?

A familiar voice said, 'Molly, it's Jane. Are you all right?'

It took Molly a moment to remember her friend from London. 'Oh! Yes, hiya, Jane! I'm fine. How are you?'

'I've been very worried about you. I called the flat loads of times. Daniel said you'd left after a row and he didn't know where you'd gone. You've been away for weeks and you've not answered any calls or texts. My psychic juices told me I needed to track you down and I found this number in my diary from when you stayed in September. I thought I'd try it on the off-chance.'

'Well, you've found me. How can I help?'

'Why haven't you been in touch, Molly? I've been frantic. We all have.'

'I'm having a break,' said Molly, a trifle petulantly. 'Things went wrong with Daniel and me. I needed a new start.'

'But you've not been in touch with anyone! Even Simon doesn't know where you are. Your agent hasn't got a clue either. If I hadn't found you by the end of the week, I was going to call the police. Didn't you think we'd be worried about you?'

'I'm entitled to run away if I want to,' Molly said, irritated. 'I am an adult, you know.'

'But why have you gone to Northampton?' said Jane. 'You've been there for months now. What do you do all day?'

'I'm fine, Jane, really. I'm looking after myself and finding my feet at the same time. I know it seems bizarre just to up and leave and never look back. But people do it all the time. It's very . . . refreshing.' Molly was slurring her words as the joint took effect.

'You don't sound refreshed. You sound washed out. Tired.'

'I am. Both of those things. But I would have been wherever I was. I needed a break. I'm perfectly fine here, honest.'

'Shall I come and see you? I could drive down tomorrow.' Jane sounded concerned.

'No, really,' said Molly. 'There's no need to do that. I'll be back in London soon and we can catch up then.'

Lilia had appeared in the hallway behind her, and was clearly listening to the conversation. She locked eyes with Molly.

'I'm needed here,' said Molly. 'I'm not needed anywhere else. It's just the way things have worked out. Keep in touch, won't you?' She hung up.

'Who was that? One of your musical-theatre friends?' asked Lilia, lightly, leading the way back to the lounge.

'Jane,' said Molly, following. 'Actress, actually. Still had my number here from when I stayed . . . the first time.'

The very mention of the past made Molly feel emotional, and the last few words caught in her throat. She saw herself as she used to be – a happy, flirtatious girl with bouncing curls and a curvy figure. Now she was thin, with heavy straight hair that didn't stir, even in a strong breeze. Lilia preferred her to wear it parted in the middle, dressed generously with wax and combed straight down at either side of her face. Molly had lost another stone in the last three weeks, since her introduction to cocaine, and occasionally a sticky strand would attach itself attractively (in Lilia's opinion) to her newly revealed cheekbones.

Lila sat down in her chair and looked at her watch. She reached down the side of her chair and produced a small enamel box. 'Just time for you to have a snifter before Geoffrey arrives.' She untwisted a small wrap of white powder, fished a silver mustard spoon from her cleavage and scooped some out, making sure she didn't spill any as she brought the spoon towards Molly's nose. 'Ready?' she asked.

Molly obligingly tilted her head and raised one hand to her face, using a forefinger to block one nostril.

'One, two, three,' said Lilia, and Molly, on cue, snorted with gusto.

Lilia returned the spoon to the bag and took another scoop. 'Other side,' she said, as if she were a nurse wiping a patient's face with a wet flannel. Molly swivelled her head and prepared the second nostril for its treat.

'Daniel told Jane I'd gone away,' said Molly, wiping her nose and feeling agitated.

'Today we are singing "I've Grown Accustomed To His

Face",' said Lilia, with a cheeky grin. 'Use it. Every day I teach you the same lesson. Use your pain to commercial effect. It is money in the bank. Remember that.'

Just then the doorbell sounded – the familiar two jaunty rings that indicated the arrival of Geoffrey.

'Here he is!' said Lilia, hurriedly closing the enamel box and stuffing it down the side of her chair. The spoon she returned to the safety of her bra. She patted her hair and stood up to answer the door. 'Enjoy your rush,' she said fondly to Molly.

The following afternoon, after Molly had popped one of her Judy Garland pills, she was lying on the sofa humming 'Lady Sings The Blues' while Lilia gave her a toe massage. They were both startled when the doorbell rang.

'Maybe I've won the lottery,' said Lilia, gently returning Molly's foot to the sofa. 'I will go and see.'

Molly sighed, feeling spaced-out and unwilling to move.

A moment later Lilia returned. 'There is a woman called Jane here to see you,' she said, sounding unnerved. 'I have told her you are unwell but she insisted—'

Just then Jane pushed her way past Lilia.'I need to speak to you—' She stopped in her tracks. 'Molly? Oh, my God, *Molly*!'

'Jane?' said Molly, only now registering that someone had entered the room. 'What are you doing here?'

Jane rushed forward and embraced her. 'Oh, Molly! I had no idea you were . . .' She trailed off, lost for words. She felt Molly's forehead. 'You're all clammy. And skinny. What's going on here?' She rested a hand protectively on each shoulder and turned accusingly to Lilia. 'She needs a doctor. Surely you can see that.'

'Don't be ridiculous,' said Lilia. 'Who are you to come barging into my house like the Keystone Cops? Molly is my guest and she wishes to stay here. You may leave now.'

'I'll leave,' replied Jane, swiftly, 'but I'm taking Molly with me.'

'Kidnapping?' said Lilia, derisively.

'I'm not here to argue about it,' said Jane, turning back to Molly. She addressed her as if she were a child. 'I'm taking you to stay with me for a few days, all right?'

'It's very kind of you but I think I'll stay here,' said Molly, closing her eyes and smacking her lips contentedly, like a Labrador.

Jane gave her a shake. 'Molly! Wake up!' She reached under Molly's armpits and, with a determined effort, pulled her now delicate frame upright. 'Let's go.'

Molly swayed and held her head with both hands to stop it rocking from side to side. 'Hang on.'

A furious Lilia stepped into her eyeline. 'Sit down at once!' she said. 'Do as I say!'

Molly wanted to, but she was too out of it to respond to any orders, however threateningly they were delivered.

'Come with me now,' said Jane, soothing and persuasive in contrast to Lilia's barks. She held Molly's hand and led her slowly towards the door.

'Okay. Let's go for a ride,' said Molly, stumbling vaguely in the right direction.

Lilia darted in front of them and spread her arms in front of the door. 'No!' she shouted shrilly. 'I will not allow it. Molly, we have classes tomorrow. You cannot leave!'

Jane let go of Molly with one hand and yanked Lilia out of the way with one firm pull. Within an instant, she had opened the door, pushed Molly through and followed her into the hallway. Lilia recovered quickly and scuttled down the corridor after Jane who was heading for the door, tugging a floppy Molly after her.

'Stop!' said Lilia, hysterical now. 'Molly lives here! She doesn't want to go. Stop!'

Jane opened the front door and, as if she were dancing with a rag doll, pulled Molly through after her. She turned to face Lilia, her expression fierce. 'Now back off! I don't know what your game is but your time with Molly is over. I'll look after her from now on.'

Jane walked down the gravel path, Molly's feet making a racket as they dragged behind her.

'Heathcliff!' cried Lilia, appearing at the front door. 'Heath*cliff*! See her off, boy!'

Jane was at the gate. 'Come on, Molly!' she said, fumbling with her keys. 'Just get into the car and we're out of here. You're going to need some crystals and a spiritual bath when we get home.'

'What's a spiritual bath?' Molly asked.

'Like an ordinary one but with herbs,' said Jane. 'Bay leaves, in your case, with a spoonful of taramasalata.'

Just as they got into Jane's Mini, a furious barking heralded the arrival of Heathcliff, who came racing out of the house in response to Lilia's cries. Jane jammed the ignition key in the lock and started the engine just as he bounded over the gate.

Molly, slumped in the passenger seat, was pushed back in her seat with the velocity of Jane's acceleration. She heard an assertive bark and even saw Heathcliff's profile as he leapt at the passenger window.

'Go, boy!' shouted Lilia. 'Stop them!'

The last things Molly heard were Jane crying, 'No!' the screech of brakes, and glass shattering.

When she came to a minute later, she was still in the front seat but Jane was leaning over her, asking if she was all right and dabbing her throbbing forehead. Lilia was kneeling on the ground a few feet away, wailing hysterically and calling Heathcliff's name.

'What happened?' asked Molly, groggily, blinking.

'The dog. He ran in front of the car,' said Jane, crying herself now. 'You banged your head on the dashboard. Are you okay?'

'Oh, my God. Heathcliff!' Molly pushed Jane away and staggered out of the car, which was now stationary in the middle of the road, the doors open and the headlights smashed.

Heathcliff was lying a couple of yards ahead in the gutter and Lilia was cradling him in her arms.

'Murder! Murder!' She threw back her head and let out a piercing scream. Then she turned towards Molly and Jane. 'He's dead!' she shouted. 'She killed him! She deliberately ran him over.' She hugged the dog to her chest, stroking his glossy black coat. 'Why?' she moaned. 'Why kill my innocent boy? How am I to live without him?'

Molly went to her and knelt beside her, stricken by the sight of Heathcliff's huge body limp and lifeless.

Two neighbours, a man and a woman, came out of their house to see what all the commotion was about. 'Are you all right, Miss Delvard?' asked the woman, as she approached. 'Shall we call an ambulance?'

'He's dead,' repeated Lilia.

'What happened?' asked the man. He looked round at the scene: the car, the dead dog and Molly's gashed forehead.

Jane came over, wiping her eyes and sniffing. 'It was an

accident. She set the dog on me and he threw himself under the wheels. It wasn't my fault, it was hers! Molly, get back in the car. I'll take you to hospital. You've had a bang on the head.'

Lilia let go of the dog and rose to her feet. 'You evil bitch. Do you realise what you've done here? You killed my Heathcliff!' With that she flew at Jane, whacking her across the head with her fist. Jane reeled to the right, bent double with shock, and Lilia grabbed hold of her hair with both hands. 'I'll fucking kill you for what you've done.' She held Jane's head tight and raised her knee, cracking it into Jane's face several times, grunting with the effort, then threw her to the ground and kicked her head like a football.

'Hey!' shouted the neighbour, rushing forward to restrain her in a bear-hug. 'That's enough of that. Come on!'

Lilia stood, breathing heavily through clenched teeth. Unable to continue her attack, she spat at the figure on the ground.

The woman helped Jane upright and sat her on the kerb out of reach of Lilia, who was kicking out wildly again. Jane's nose was pouring with blood. 'Aah!' she moaned. 'Keep her away from me!'

Molly stood between them, not sure who to comfort first. 'Lilia! Jane!' she said, helplessly. 'Stop it!'

'Get into the car, Molly,' said Jane, dabbing her nose with a tissue. 'You can't stay here with this mad woman. Can't you see she's insane?'

Lilia was crying loudly now, strange, tearless weeping, looking down at Heathcliff. 'Oh, my baby, my boy. How could this happen? What am I going to do now? Molly, help me!'

Molly stood between her old friend and her mentor, not sure which of them had the greater call on her.

'Molly,' begged Jane, her eyes pleading, 'you can't stay here. Please come with me.'

'Molly . . . Molly,' moaned Lilia. 'Help me . . .'

Molly screwed her eyes shut, wishing all the nastiness would go away. She just wanted it to be quiet and peaceful and everything to be all right, as it had been before Jane arrived. She opened her eyes and walked towards Lilia, who prised herself free of her neighbour and collapsed into Molly's arms, burying her face in her shoulder. 'Come on,' said Molly. 'Let's get you in.'

'Don't leave me!' wept Lilia. 'Please don't leave me.'

'It's all right,' said Molly. 'I won't leave you, don't worry.' She walked Lilia back towards Kit-Kat Cottage.

Jane called after them. 'Molly? You've got to get away from her. Come with me, I'm begging you.'

Molly turned to her. 'No, Jane. Go – go now and don't come back. You've caused enough trouble.'

Jane stared at her, hurt and baffled.

'Heathcliff!' cried Lilia. 'I can't leave him.'

'Would you carry him into the house for us?' Molly asked the bewildered neighbours.

'Er, yes, of course,' said the man. He bent over the dog and lifted him by the front legs. 'I can't manage him on my own,' he said to the woman, who took hold of Heathcliff's back feet. Together they hauled him up and, with considerable effort, shuffled towards Lilia's home. He swung between them, like a freshly killed stag being brought to the hunting lodge.

Left on her own, Jane managed to get to her feet and, holding her still-bleeding nose with one hand, walked unsteadily to her car. 'Goodbye,' Molly heard her call, as she went into the bungalow with Lilia. 'I'm always your friend if you ever need me.'

Inside, Molly led Lilia into the lounge and sat her on her chair.

The neighbours were struggling down the hallway with Heathcliff. 'Could you put him in the back bedroom?' asked Molly. 'Thank you so much for your help.'

Too out of breath to speak, the couple nodded. Heathcliff was placed on the bed that hadn't been occupied since Joey had lain there, and the man kindly offered to come back in the morning with a shovel to bury the poor dog in the back garden.

'Thank you,' said Molly, solemnly. 'Lilia would appreciate that. You've been very kind.'

The neighbours left and Molly went to the back door for a much-needed cigarette. The drama of the last half-hour had quite sobered her up. She touched the tender bruise on her forehead and felt a wave of compassion for Lilia. She had doted on Heathcliff. They had seemed to share a special understanding, and she would be lost without him. And why was Jane being so dramatic, hunting her down to Long Buckby and trying to get her away so urgently? Molly had been rather stoned when Jane arrived and maybe she had looked a bit of a mess. But there was no need for her to be so heavy-handed. No doubt her dubious psychic skills were telling her something. Jane was always trying to rescue people, cure them, change them, help them to see the light. Well, this time it had gone horribly wrong. Within a few terrible minutes Heathcliff's life had been snuffed out and Molly had been forced to choose between her old friend and her new mentor. She couldn't leave Lilia now, even if she wanted to.

Molly finished her cigarette and went to Lilia's bedroom. Heathcliff was laid on his side on the bed. His eyes were closed as if he was asleep, his big, pink tongue just poking out between fleshy black lips. 'I'm sorry,' she said quietly, rubbing his chest the way he'd liked. 'We're going to miss you, old boy, more than you know. God bless.' She gave him a final stroke, covered him with a sheet and returned to the lounge.

'A brandy, love?' she asked Lilia, who was staring into space, her hands twisting in her lap. There was no response, so Molly poured her one anyway, and one for herself.

'I'm sorry, Lilia,' she said, placing the glass in the old lady's hand.

Lilia's eyes flickered. 'Why?' she said flatly. 'Why did she come here and ruin everything?'

'I don't know,' said Molly, her voice full of pain. 'She was worried about me.'

'If she had taken my life it would have been easier to bear.'

'Don't say that.'

'First Joey and now Heathcliff. Everything is being taken from me.'

'I'm still here,' said Molly, giving Lilia's hand a reassuring squeeze.

'For how long?' asked Lilia, hopelessly. 'And then what is to become of me?'

'I'm going to stay with you,' replied Molly. 'Seriously. You and I are a team. We have plans, remember?'

'You are not going to leave me?' asked Lilia, clutching Molly's arm, a faint glimmer of hope detectable in her voice.

'Never,' said Molly.

'Do you promise?'

'I promise. I love you, Lilia.'

The two women embraced and then Lilia wiped her eyes.

'Could I have a line, please?' asked Molly, who was feeling the vague, panicky beginnings of cocaine withdrawal. 'I need something for my nerves.'

Lilia reached down the side of her chair and produced her enamel box. 'I'll tell you what I am going to do with this,' she said. 'I am going to flush it down the toilet.'

'Why?' asked Molly, alarmed. 'What would you do that for?'

'Because you've had enough,' said Lilia determinedly.

'But I . . . It seems such a waste,' said Molly, flustered and feeling the need for a line more strongly now that the supply was being removed.

'If you hadn't been so drugged up, Jane wouldn't have been so overcome with sisterly concern. She would not have barged in here and Heathcliff would not be lying in the next room dead.'

'Yes, but—'

'Yes but nothing,' said Lilia, standing up. 'Your drug-taking is to blame for all this. Plain and simple.' Lilia left the room, and a few moments later Molly heard the toilet flush. Her palms felt moist and she felt suddenly irritable and trapped.

When Lilia returned she wore a look of triumph. 'All gone!' she said. 'No more pills, powder or puff. Welcome back to reality.'

Molly managed a tight smile. Probably, in the long term, it was just as well. She had only been on the stuff for a few weeks, but it was remarkable how much she had come to enjoy it. Depend on it, even.

'You will be going cold turkey, my dear,' continued Lilia. 'Just as I will be suffering withdrawal symptoms from the passionate love and affection Heathcliff brought to my life, so will you from the drugs. Depression, sweating, panic attacks, sleeplessness: we will be in perfect harmony with each other.'

Molly said nothing.

'Now,' said Lilia after a pause, 'I am going to light some

candles and burn some incense in my bedroom. I intend to spend one final night with my dear boy.'

'Shall I come with you?' asked Molly.

'No. It is a private matter,' replied Lilia, grandly. 'You take a hot bath, and put some disinfectant on that bruise on your forehead. We have spent months working on your looks and the murderess has ruined them. Hopefully, it is just temporary.'

'But I won't be able to sleep without a pill,' said Molly.

'No, you won't. Here,' said Lilia. She passed her pupil a pile of sheet music. 'Study the songs. Learn the lyrics, absorb them into your very being.'

'Yes, Lilia,' said Molly, meekly.

'We will soon be ready for the next phase of your development.'

'What's that?'

'A public performance. I am ready to reveal to the world the remarkable creature I have created.'

'Jeepers,' said Molly, feeling a surge of nervous excitement wash over her.

Chapter Twenty-six

Lilia was true to her word. Just three weeks after they had buried Heathcliff (in the middle of the lawn, she had insisted), Molly was given a trial for a job singing at a restaurant opposite the stage door of the Derngate called the Snappy Italian. Roger had told Lilia of the vacancy after the resident entertainer, Betty Swollocks, had eloped with a Lost Boy from *Peter Pan*. He came round to tea one day to tell them the news. 'An odder couple you will never see than Betty and that pimply youth,' he said. 'Well, good riddance, that's what I say. If she thinks a nineteen-year-old pouf from Southampton is going to stay with her for more than a fortnight, she's got another think coming. Anyway, Luigi needs somebody for Thursday, Friday and Saturday nights. I told him he should go upmarket. The bingo night wasn't to everyone's taste. I told him about you and he'd like to give you a trial. Am I the Angel Gabriel or not?' Roger laughed, pleased to be the bringer of such happy tidings.

Lilia gasped with excitement and clasped her face. 'Oh, darling you!' she declared, leaping up to kiss Roger on both cheeks. 'This is just what I wanted.'

'It's been a while since I sang in restaurants,' Molly said

uncertainly. She was still recovering from an unpleasant few weeks of cold turkey and found it hard to muster much enthusiasm. 'Isn't this a step back for me?'

'No. Forget your old life. This is your new life. It is the perfect place for you to work on your performance,' Lilia declared. 'We have the voice, we have the body, now we need to work on presentation. The Snappy Italian will be just the right training ground. You shall see.'

Molly was more nervous than she'd expected on her first night. Lilia dressed her carefully in a plain black dress and high heels, pulled back her hair into a tight ponytail and gave her simple but effective makeup: pale eyes, swooping black lashes and a dark crimson mouth. Molly looked at herself in the mirror: the woman who stared back at her was a million miles from the plump, curly-headed girl who had belted out Broadway hits and Gilbert and Sullivan. What a strange path I'm on, she thought, feeling the pleasurable anticipation mixed with nervous dread that always came before a performance. I wonder where it's leading . . .

'Chop, chop!' urged Lilia, obviously pleased with how Molly looked. 'It's time.'

With the faithful Geoffrey on the piano, Molly sang her selection of sultry and bitter love songs to the largely theatrical clientele. They played two half-hour sets, one at ten forty-five and another at midnight. Her now deep and husky voice impressed the audience, and they whooped and cheered at the end. The moment she finished Lilia came into the tiny dressing room and congratulated her. 'Excellent, my dear. Very well done. The songs are working nicely. But it is a mistake to look too happy when taking your applause – indifference would be more suitable. Remember, we are peddling misery here. It is not Butlins. Try not to smile until we have had your teeth fixed. Look at your audience as if they are low-life.'

Molly was buzzing with adrenalin. 'You are funny, Lilia! I had a ball out there. I can't believe how much I enjoyed myself.'

When Luigi came in at the end of the evening and offered her a permanent booking, singing three nights a week, she was delighted. The money was pitiful, but that didn't matter. They returned home to Long Buckby in triumph.

Now Molly had something to live for outside Kit-Kat Cottage and she adored it, from the careful preparations, the selection of her outfit and the application of her makeup, to stepping out into the glare of the spotlight and hearing the first tinkle of the piano, knowing that she would open her mouth, begin to sing, and the restaurant would fall silent to listen to her astounding voice.

Lilia managed to secure a table at the front for herself each night as part of the deal and sat, pen poised, taking notes and occasionally instructing Molly, in a loud whisper, to leave her hair alone or relax her shoulders. Generally the punters were respectful. The majority were performers or post-theatre diners, who listened appreciatively and applauded after each song. If, as occasionally happened, a few people talked loudly or laughed raucously, Lilia would 'ssh' loudly until others joined in and they were shamed into quiet.

One night when they'd arrived back at the bungalow, after Molly had been performing regularly at the Snappy Italian for a fortnight, Lilia suggested they settle down for a brandy and chat. 'Chin, chin,' she said, raising her glass.

'Cheers!' Molly took a sip, then let out a deep sigh. 'Ah! That's better.'

Lilia produced her pad. 'I took some very thorough notes tonight,' she said. 'It's time for a review. You have settled in well, but that doesn't mean you can stop trying.' She peered down at her scribbles, then said briskly, 'Remember to walk slowly when you first emerge on stage. No bounce. Your soul is full of despair, remember. You are Our Lady of the Camellias, a tragic, wasted beauty who can only alleviate the pain by singing.'

'Right,' said Molly, paying rapt attention.

'I have decided to change your name, too. Molly Douglas is all wrong.'

'Not very torch song, is it?'

'No. Sounds like a cleaning woman.'

'What do you suggest?'

'First, let's get rid of Douglas. How about . . . for want of something better . . . Delvard?'

'Oh, I love it!' said Molly, excitedly. 'Molly Delvard,' she said, trying it out. 'I'd be honoured to perform under your name.'

'Now. The Molly part. We need to do something about that too. I suggest something a little less chambermaid. How about . . . Mia?'

'Oh.' Molly blinked. She hadn't expected to lose her name entirely. But she liked Mia. 'Yes . . . Mia Delvard. That's good. I like it.'

'Excellent. That is settled. Next we come to your hair. It looked a little dull under the lights, and I think we should go for some colour.'

'I've always wanted to be platinum blonde.'

'I have some henna in the bathroom,' replied Lilia, ignoring Molly's statement. 'We will try that on you tomorrow.'

'So I'll be a redhead like you.'

'Redheads are more worldly wise. It was Leonard Cohen who advised me to go this colour.'

'When did you work with him? I love his music.'

'We met at the Trident Studios in 1967. We sang a duet together on his album *Songs of Hate*. "Lilia," he said to me, "a woman such as yourself should have hair like fire!" The next day I bought my first tub of henna and I have never looked back.'

'I can't imagine you any other colour,' said Molly.

'Leonard was right, of course.'

'What was the duet you sang together?'

'A song he wrote for me called "Lady Lilia". A pretty ballad, it was. They didn't put it on the album in the end. I rather out-sang poor Leonard on the track, so the producers cut it.'

'How amazing,' said Molly.

Lilia returned to her notes. 'Your clothes are not suitable either. We will take a trip to London on Tuesday and go to Chanel.'

'Chanel – how fabulous!'

'As Coco said to me once, at the Ritz in Paris, "Simplicity is the key to all elegance."'

'You knew Coco Chanel?'

'I was her muse for several seasons. In my modelling days.'

Molly shook her head in amazement. 'You've done everything, met everybody.'

'I've led a glamorous life, it's true.'

Molly was worried. 'But isn't Chanel terribly expensive?'

'Yes. No matter. I have a few pennies left from auctioning

Joey's Victoria Cross. Chanel is the only place suitable. We will see what Jasper Conran has to offer as well while we are in town. He is the only modern designer with taste, in my opinion. A tight cashmere dress with a belt. All black. You must only ever wear black. And some serious heels.'

'Oh, yes, yes!' said Molly.

The trip to London passed in a haze of excitement and pleasure. They took the train to Euston and then a black cab to the West End, where they spent a couple of happy hours in the Chanel boutique. Molly was astonished to find that she was now a slip of a size eight, and that clothes she'd never have dreamt she could wear now fitted beautifully.

As she stood in the soft gold lighting of the boutique, studying her reflection in the flattering mirrors, she could understand why these clothes were so expensive: they were exquisite, designed to enhance her figure with elegance and structure.

'Two dresses, a classic suit and some cashmere knitwear. All monochrome or shades of grey and pearl,' declared Lilia. 'And while we're here, we may as well take a look in Prada.'

When it came time to pay, Lilia opened her handbag and brought out packets of twenty-pound notes, stacking them up on the counter. The staff showed only a flicker of surprise as they accepted them.

'Thank you, Lilia,' said Molly, on the train home, looking at her smart shopping bags. They'd also bought a black dress in Prada, some shoes in Gina and put her name down for a black Kelly bag in Hermès. 'What incredible generosity. I don't know how I'll ever repay you.'

'I enjoyed it too. A taste of my old life,' said Lilia, smiling. 'And don't worry, my dear. You will repay me many times over and in many different ways – I can promise you that.'

By the time of her next appearance at the Snappy Italian on the following Friday, Molly was even further transformed, with startling red hair, a beautiful figure-hugging dress and six-inch stilettos.

'You look amazing!' declared Roger, congratulating her after the show. 'You're too good for this place, girl. Northampton isn't used to such class. And your singing's fantastic. You had me in tears!'

'Thank you,' said Molly.

'And you're a Delvard now,' he said, with a giggle. 'Lilia is re-creating you in her own image.'

Lilia, too, dressed up for these evenings at the restaurant. Her hair was swept up in a raspberry-coloured meringue, and she would wrap a beaded pashmina round her shoulders, later revealing a low-cut vintage evening gown. She always sat in the same place at the front, elbows on the table, chin supported by her knuckles, watching Molly closely, smiling sagely, blinking and nodding after every song. Occasionally she would frown and break her pose to write something on her pad with a silver Mont Blanc fountain pen. Together they made an enigmatic pair, dripping style, talent and a distant, haughty air.

Within weeks, word had got round, and the Snappy Italian was packed whenever Mia Delvard was due to appear. After a month of full houses and a huge surge in bookings for the restaurant, Lilia requested a meeting with Luigi. 'We want more money,' she told him bluntly, 'or we will leave. I also want large framed photos of Mia both inside and outside the premises. Furthermore, Miss Delvard's second set will not be until one a.m. We will keep them waiting from now on.'

Luigi didn't hesitate. 'Of course, I shall see to it. A very good idea. None of this is a problem,' he said, even bowing slightly to Lilia as he spoke. 'And perhaps you'd consider double the fee?'

But despite Luigi's willingness to please, three weeks later Lilia cancelled Molly's appearances at the Snappy Italian altogether. 'I'm sorry,' she told Luigi one Saturday after the show. 'Molly is an artist. I can no longer allow her to sing in front of people who are chewing microwaved spaghetti carbonara.'

'How dare you?' said Luigi, furious. 'Everything is freshly cooked.'

'Whatever,' said Lilia, picking up her fur stole. 'So long, baby. We've got bigger fish to fry.'

During this conversation Molly stood meekly by. It was the first she'd heard about leaving but she trusted Lilia implicitly. Whatever she said was right – must be right. She'd be sad to leave the Snappy Italian, but she had absolute faith that something better was about to come along.

Roger came over when he heard. 'Is it true you've sacked Luigi?' he asked disbelievingly.

'Yes, Molly's leaving,' Lilia announced grandly. She flung her shawl round her shoulders. 'We're moving on.'

'Fuck me,' he said. 'This is turning into Gypsy fucking Rose Lee.'

'We're leaving here as well,' said Lilia. 'Molly and I will be renting out Kit-Kat Cottage and moving to London. So it's goodbye, I'm afraid.'

'Charming,' said Roger. 'Is that all the thanks I get?' He turned to Molly. 'Well?' he asked petulantly. 'Is it? You're fucking off to London and you don't have the good grace to tell me?'

'I didn't know we were moving to London,' said Molly, a trifle bewildered. 'Lilia?'

'Well, we're not going to conquer the world from Long Buckby, are we? Even Jane McDonald had go south eventually to fulfil her potential.'

'Oh, my God, I'm going home,' said Molly, beginning to feel excited at the prospect. 'Oh, yes, Lilia, this is fabulous news.'

'Well, I hope you're both very happy in throbbing London,' said Roger, tartly. 'Some of us have done that dump and moved on.'

'We are not, as far as I am aware, committing a crime by going to London. We are not taking up a life of vice or joining a cult. It is a sensible move, essential to Molly's career.'

'It makes sense, Roger,' said Molly, softly. 'You've got to be in London if you're in showbusiness.'

Roger thought for a moment. 'I know,' he said sincerely. 'I'm only angry because I'll miss you. You're the best thing that's happened to Northampton since Julian Clary appeared here in panto.'

'Julian Clary was at the Derngate?' squealed Molly. 'I just love him. He's so funny. I wonder if he went into my dressing room?'

'That *was* his dressing room, come to think of it,' said Roger.

'That's amazing!' said Molly. 'Wow! Did you hear that Lilia? I actually occupied the same dressing room as Julian Clary!'

'He was a dirty queen, if you don't mind me saying so,' said Roger. 'I've seen chorus boys coming out of that dressing room bow-legged.'

'Please,' said Lilia. 'Do stop this nonsense. We're leaving at the end of the week, Roger. You're welcome to come along if you want, but I can't think what you'd do to amuse yourself. So I suppose this is goodbye.' She offered him her cheek and Roger kissed it.

'Take care,' he said, and turned to hug Molly. 'You look after yourself, girl. I've got mighty fond of you. And I know you've got what it takes to be a star, so go out there and get 'em. Just don't forget your old pal Roger, all right? I shall expect tickets to your first nights.'

Molly relaxed into his warm embrace, surprised by how emotional she felt. She'd grown to like and trust Roger. He seemed a voice of sanity in the curious fantasy world she now occupied with Lilia. She would miss him. 'Bye-bye, Rog. I won't forget you, I promise.'

'Fame and fortune, here we come,' said Lilia. 'Again.'

Chapter Twenty-seven

Lilia and Molly moved to a studio flat on Charing Cross Road. It felt minute after Kit-Kat Cottage. 'It is ideal,' said Lilia, satisfied. 'We can walk home late at night after work. Soho is our world. It is perfect that you live here.'

The flat was in a 1930s block built above the Phoenix Theatre, and consisted of one large room with a separate kitchen and bathroom. It took them a while to get used to the cramped space and adjust to their new proximity. They still shared a double bed, which they folded up into a sofa during the day. Sleeping with Lilia didn't even feel strange to Molly any more, she felt only gratitude towards the old lady, a remarkable woman who had, via a series of fateful happenings, become her mother in every sense other than the biological. She still felt a little uncomfortable that she was so much under Lilia's control but everything that had happened so far – the new look, the success in Northampton, the miraculous new voice she had found – was down to Lilia and her sense of purpose, which made it all worthwhile.

Molly could sense that she was in very real danger of becoming a star. She had to go with the flow now. The journey might be weird, but it was wonderful too.

Lilia moved a baby grand piano into their tiny flat for them to rehearse with and set about finding gigs for Molly. Even though they were almost in Soho, there were none there yet. Molly's first booking was in a community centre in Plaistow, and Lilia got her a late slot at a once-weekly jazz club in Luton. Then, as Christmas approached, more opportunities came their way. Lilia had business cards printed, photographs taken, a sample CD made, and went round knocking on doors or phoning every contact she could make. The results were good: as the party season approached, Molly performed at a string of Christmas dos, then at the 606 club in Chelsea's King's Road and the famous Vortex in Stoke Newington. Wherever she played, she was a sensation.

'Word is building, my dear,' Lilia said, as they sat together at their tiny table, eating the Christmas lunch Molly had cooked for them. 'People are beginning to come to me, asking if Mia Delvard is available. Your reputation is spreading. Believe me, we will soon leave all this behind.'

'Do you really think so?' Molly knew in her heart that Lilia was right, but she wanted to hear it again. Every morning she woke up with her stomach churning excitedly, knowing she was a day closer to her dream.

'I know so. It is your destiny. It is unstoppable.'

'I owe it all to you. Happy Christmas, Lilia.' Molly gave the old lady an affectionate kiss on both cheeks. The tiniest Chihuahua puppy, hardly bigger than a gerbil, nestled in Molly's arms, Lilia's Christmas present. 'And to you too, precious Pancho.' Molly gave him a peck on the top of his head, and Pancho closed his eyes contentedly. His pink tongue, no bigger than a sixpence, licked her cheek.

'He's an albino, which is very rare,' said Lilia, gazing at their new pet admiringly. 'He'll go very nicely with your black Chanel two-piece, the one with the daring grey buttons.'

'We can carry him around in my handbag!'

'Once he's house-trained, maybe.'

'I'm so thrilled with him,' said Molly.

'I never thought I'd look at a dog again, but there was something about Pancho that I couldn't resist.'

'He's adorable.'

'You needed an outlet for your emotions. Pour your love into Pancho, not some good-for-nothing two-legged man.'

'I'd take a one-legged man,' said Molly, returning to her native accent momentarily, despite Lilia's rigorous elocution lessons.

'That is where you are wrong,' said Lilia, politely. 'You are no longer a rambling rose. I have pruned and cultivated you. Now we are waiting for the right man to come along and pluck you.'

'Will he be long?' asked Molly, earnestly. 'Only I'd rather like to know.'

'We are not yet moving in the right circles, my dear. There are no fish worth diddly squat in our current pond. We will bide our time until circumstances change. How long that takes is really up to you.'

Early in the new year, Lilia set about securing the services of an agent. She had persuaded Molly to sack the previous one a few months before, when she had agreed to Lilia's experiment. 'If he was any good, you wouldn't need me,' Lilia had said dismissively, and Molly could see she had a point.

Now, though, Lilia had changed her mind. 'I've almost reached the limit of what I can do,' she explained. 'You need a proper agent, with access to the highest show-business echelons. But I must be careful who it is. I must find someone who shares my vision for you.'

One afternoon she returned to the flat in a state of some excitement. Molly was washing up in the tiny kitchen.

'Molly!' cried Lilia. 'Come and listen. I have found us an agent. You are now represented by none other than Boris Norris, agent to the stars.'

'Oh, good,' said Molly. She reached for a tea-towel and dried her hands. 'Is he the bee's knees?'

'He heard you last night at Pizza Express on Dean Street and he's mad about you.'

'Are you sure he doesn't just want to be my agent because I've been in the same dressing room as Julian Clary?'

'Don't be silly,' snapped Lilia. 'Boris Norris is the best in the business. Shirley Bassey, Nina Simone, Kathy Kirby – he's heard of them all.'

'Great,' said Molly. 'If you think he's right for me, then I'm happy.'

Lilia removed her gloves and coat. She sat down on the simple brown sofa and looked seriously at Molly, who came over and sat opposite. 'In another month, we will reach the end of our six-month agreement. I would like to propose that, before you sign with Boris, we make a pact. We will extend our partnership indefinitely, and there will be certain terms I would like you to agree with – to do with my status as your mentor and manager. When you begin to earn money, I will need to be sure that my efforts are rewarded. That is fair enough, is it not?'

'Of course, Lilia! I'm your creation so of course you must share in the rewards when it begins to pay off,' said Molly. The idea of their agreement coming to an end appalled her: she couldn't imagine living without Lilia now. To put it simply, she needed her.

'Good. I will have a lawyer draw up our agreement – it's best to have these things done properly. It can save much heartache in the long run. Now . . .' she looked mischievously at Molly '. . . I have other news, too. There is something else that Mr Norris would like us to consider.'

Molly recognised her portentous tone. Something major was about to be announced. 'What is it?' she asked, almost nervous. She sensed that whatever Lilia was about to say would change her life.

'How would you like to play a week at Ronnie Scott's?'

Molly gasped and her hands flew to her mouth. 'Really?'

'Really,' said Lilia. 'Ronnie Scott's. The most famous jazz club in London. The world and his wife will be there. Press. Reviewers. Record labels. Boris will make sure of it. Mia Delvard will perform her heart out and everyone – the whole world – will fall in love with her. Everything we have ever wanted is about to come true.'

'Oh, Lilia!' said Molly, overcome. 'Thank you. Thank you so much! I knew you could make this happen. I always believed you.'

'This is it, my little canary,' said Lilia, gravely. 'This is your big chance. We are an unbreakable team and you are about to become a star!'

PART THREE
Eight years later

Chapter Twenty-eight

A delicate-looking man with yellow skin and a stoop shuffled through the excited crowds outside the London Palladium. Despite the mild autumn weather, he was wearing a woollen coat and scarf and would stop occasionally to allow a rumbling cough to work its way out of his lungs. He checked his coat pocket and found the single ticket for the back row of the stalls. Yes, it was still there. In a little less than an hour he would see the legendary Mia Delvard on the final night of her world tour. He had followed her career with interest over the years: he had listened a million times to all of her recordings, watched her rare television appearances (Mia was disdainful of the medium) and avidly read all the articles and interviews he could find. But he had never, until now, experienced her live.

Simon had made a special effort to be there that evening. He rarely went anywhere, apart from the off-licence, and felt decidedly panicky about being away from his flat. It had taken great discipline and courage to get himself a ticket and then to the Palladium, relatively sober, in time for the performance.

Outside the theatre, touts were asking everyone in low, urgent voices if they had any tickets to sell. This night had been sold out for months, and if he had been interested, Simon could have sold his single ticket for several hundred pounds. But he had no intention of doing that. He suspected, and rather hoped, that he did not have much time left, and one thing he wanted to do before he became incapable was see his old friend Molly in action.

Simon stopped for another cough and studied the poster for the show he was about to see. At the top, in huge gold letters, it read, 'MIA DELVARD World Tour 2009', followed by the title of the show: *Losing My Mind*. Across the right-hand top corner a sticker proclaimed, 'Last Sensational Night!' Above Mia's name were the small but important words: 'International Artists in grateful association with Lilia Delvard present . . .'. The rest of the poster featured a full-length image of Mia standing, sylph-like, in a single spotlight, dressed in her usual figure-hugging black dress. She held a microphone in one hand while the other was stretched out towards the camera. Her eyes, heavy with charcoal, were closed and her mouth open as she sang one of her show-stopping, anguished notes. At the bottom there were a few choice words of praise from her many rave reviews. 'A star of the brightest and most illuminating kind,' gushed the *New York Times*. 'Her voice is the eighth wonder of the world,' opined the *Guardian*, and 'A star for our times,' said the *New Statesman*.

Simon pondered this last quote. The title of Mia's show was indeed clever. She was touring at a time when most of the world was in the grip of an ominous depression, and people were indeed losing their minds, their jobs, their homes or their pensions. Mia Delvard's dark songs expressed their mood. She seemed to speak to all of them individually. But no one could know her the way he did.

Like most of her fans, Simon knew all of Mia's recordings by heart. But, unlike them, he had a window into her past. Sometimes he would get out his old photos and compare the groomed and sculpted Mia with the bubbly Molly he remembered. There was one particular photo of her and him sitting on the steps of the National Portrait Gallery. He remembered that afternoon, soon after they'd left Goldsmiths. They'd been in high spirits after drinking a bottle of rosé in St James's Park and had just been curtly asked to leave the gallery for laughing at a Beryl Cook exhibit.

'What on earth were we expected to do?' Simon had said indignantly, as they sat on the steps to recover themselves. Between howls of laughter he had stopped a passing Japanese tourist who had obligingly taken that picture of them. They had clearly tried to stop giggling while they posed for the camera, but their faces were tipped up towards the sun and their eyes were shining with suppressed amusement. Molly's mass of wild dark-blonde curls framed her pretty, round-cheeked face and she was stunning, in a friendly, northern sort of way. He looked back to the show poster. You would never guess this was the same girl: Mia was all cheekbones and pouting lips, with soulful, sorry eyes.

But then, he thought ruefully, lighting a cigarette, I've changed a bit myself.

The cigarette only made him cough again, but he persisted and was eventually able to inhale the invigorating smoke. The coughing set off a burning sensation in his stomach that spread in all directions until he had to close his eyes and clutch at his waist, willing the agony to subside, which it did after about thirty seconds. He sighed with relief and popped two Gaviscon Extra Strong tablets into his mouth. The excruciating stabbing pains happened all day and all night now, and he lived in fear of them.

Time for a drink, he thought. He threw his half-smoked cigarette into the gutter, then elbowed his way through the theatre doors and eventually into the heaving bar. This was really a bit much, he thought. He wasn't used to crowds or, indeed, to physical contact of any kind, these days, and being pressed against all and sundry made him irritable.

He had almost reached the bar when he got wedged between a big actressy woman in a vintage floral dress with an unfeasibly large red handbag, and a small-framed wiry little man wearing a pork-pie hat. Simon studied his options and decided he'd stand a better chance if he pushed in front of the man. He took a deep breath and lunged, thrusting the pork-pie hat into the people behind him, and got one hand, clutching a ten-pound note, across the bar.

'Oi!' said the pork-pie hat, squeezing angrily back. 'I was before you!'

'Oh, piss off, you little runt,' said Simon.

The man looked ready to punch him, but suddenly his expression changed and he stared at Simon, astonishment on his face. 'Simon?' he said. 'Is that you? It is, isn't it? I remember those eyes! Well, fuck me pink. Still as rude as ever, I see. You haven't forgotten me, have you? It's Roger. How are you?'

'Roger?' Simon blinked, then realised that the face of his old friend was beneath the ridiculous hat. 'I don't believe it! Roger. It's been years.' He shook his head. 'You can buy the drinks, then.'

'That's bloody typical, that is.'

'I knew something awful would happen if I came out tonight. But I had no idea it would be as bad as this. I'll have a large vodka and tonic.'

Roger appraised his old friend. 'You all right, girl? How's life treating you?' He seemed concerned now.

Simon shrugged. 'I have endured. And you? Did you tire of the Midlands, or did the Midlands tire of you? Didn't you move there in pursuit of everlasting love? Please don't tell me it didn't last.'

Roger managed to get served and they moved away from the bar scrum to stand in the corridor.

'Freddie developed dementia,' Roger confided, handing Simon his drink.

'Oh dear. You don't want that.'

'The maisonette became too much for him.'

Not a sentence you'll hear very often, thought Simon.

'I had to put him in a home,' Roger continued. 'He kept mistaking me for John Barrowman.'

'We all have our snapping point. That must have been hell for you,' said Simon, resting a hand sympathetically on Roger's shoulder.

'It's all been rather awful, actually,' said Roger, his eyes filling with tears. 'I visit at weekends but he keeps asking me if I've ever worked with Denise van Outen.'

'You poor thing.'

'So I moved back to London. There was nothing for me in Northampton once Freddie was in the home. I'd had enough of my stage-door duties, so I decided it was time for another fresh start. I'm a window dresser.'

'How glamorous. Who for?'

'Poundstretchers,' said Roger, looking momentarily uncomfortable. 'But it's just a stepping-stone. What about you? What have you been up to in the last eight years?'

'Nothing. Absolutely nothing. My father left me some money so I bought a flat. I've got a roof over my head and that's enough for me. Other than that, I please myself.' There was much more to tell but Simon couldn't begin to go there.

'You're looking a bit yellow, if you don't mind me saying so. And you've put on a bit of weight by the look of your stomach. You sure you're okay?'

Simon drew his coat closed over his distended belly. 'Of course I am. I'm fine. I had that motherfucker of a flu virus that's been going round. Shall we have another drink before we go in? I'll buy.'

'All right, then. Thanks. You must be a Mia Delvard fan as well. Have you seen her before?' asked Roger.

'Er, no. First time. I'll be back in a tick.' Simon went to get the drinks but the bar was far more crowded now, and no amount of pushing or shoving seemed to help. By the time he returned to Roger the two-minute bell was ringing, and they were both anxious to find their seats.

'Thanks for this,' said Roger, taking his drink. 'Listen, meet me after the show, outside the front. All right?'

Simon agreed and the pair separated.

As he made his way to his seat in the stalls, Simon felt a sudden rush of nervous excitement. How extraordinary. On the very night he was to see Molly in the flesh for the first time in eight years, he had bumped into an old cruising chum he hadn't heard hide or hair from in almost a decade. You might almost think it was meant to be, he thought.

Just then an excited buzz filled the auditorium, and people craned their necks to look up at the royal box. A small red-haired old lady wearing a glittering gown and a modest tiara was taking her seat. She waved regally in all directions, then the house lights went down and darkness fell.

Simon didn't recognise her face. Maybe minor royalty, he thought. Never mind that, though: the show was about to begin.

Unusually there was no opening act and no interval. Mia Delvard would sing her most famous songs for forty incredible minutes – and then the show would be over. The purity and intensity of Mia's performances were what her fans adored. They had no need of a warm-up act: they were hot for Mia.

Seven or eight musicians made their way into the pit and soft pink lights came gently up on the stage. The atmosphere was tense with anticipation. Then a lone figure emerged from the shadows and the audience erupted into rapturous applause. Before Mia had sung a note, she received a standing ovation. She stood centre stage, slender and beautiful in a figure-hugging dress and high heels, and gazed out at them all, as if she were slightly distracted by a buzzing fly. Eventually she managed a half-nod. When the applause finally subsided, the first chords of 'Spring Will Be A Little Late This Year' floated up from the pit. The audience were on the edge of their seats, the desperation to hear her almost tangible. Then she opened her mouth and sang.

Hers was the most extraordinary voice anyone had ever heard: clear and pure but cracked and world-weary too. It caused a collective intake of breath from the audience, sending them in two completely opposite directions: up into a blissful state of rapture at its effortless beauty, yet simultaneously to the depths of human despair and disillusionment. Here was a singer as sweet as straw-berries dipped in honey, but as sad as a stillborn baby and as bitter as a mouthful of Campari for breakfast.

She's stupendous! thought Simon. He'd heard her voice on

CD thousands of times, but to see her in the flesh and to hear her live sent goose-bumps up and down his spine. When she finished her first song, he joined in the riotous applause, hollering and cheering from the back, almost swooning with delight at her bitter-sweet singing. The high notes of their college days were long gone, he noted, but her husky, soulful new singing, not to mention the fabulous figure and the long, straight red hair, were entrancing. No wonder she was a star. She was truly special.

Mia never spoke between songs, simply nodded her mild appreciation of the fans' enthusiasm. Occasionally she would look towards the upper circle, slowly down to the balcony, then the stalls. Finally she would drop her head and rest her gaze on the stage just in front of her feet. This constituted a bow.

The nearest Mia got to singing a happy song was her rendition of 'What A Difference A Day Makes', but even this was performed at a funereal pace, the sun and flowers given far less emphasis than the rain. After that brief declaration of happiness rediscovered, she retreated to bleaker territory, wowing her public with 'Goodbye, Little Dream, Goodbye', 'One Less Bell To Answer' and 'The Party's Over'. The last two songs of her set were a dark and deathly rendition of 'Falling In Love Again' and finally the inevitable 'Losing My Mind', sung so convincingly that everyone was in tears of sympathy and concern.

After a stunned, magical silence, the audience was on its feet, roaring its love and approval as she left the stage. She returned a few moments later to sing 'Maybe This Time', but even then they wouldn't let her go. There were five minutes of tumultuous, foot-stamping applause before Mia returned to screams of delight.

For her second encore, Mia sang her world-famous signature

song, 'Daniel And Simon', a bleak, bluesy number that reached a peak of emotion when she sang of how Molly was done wrong. It brought the house down, as it always did, and afterwards she was showered with long-stemmed deep-red roses, thrown from the adoring multitudes up in the gods. She placed her microphone on the stand, made her graceful bow once again, but this time continued downwards and swept the roses up into her arms, burying her face in the blooms, then rolled her head backwards as if the heady scent was overpowering her. As the wild applause and shouts of her public reached a crescendo, Mia Delvard managed a wan smile. It was only momentary, and not wide enough to reveal her perfect white teeth, but it sent them into deafening, almost hysterical heights of rapture. Such a smile was like a snowdrop in spring, the first glimmer of the sun at dawn. It gave the audience hope. If Mia Delvard could be happy then maybe they could too, one day.

Then, to the astonishment of all, Mia went back to her microphone and spoke into it, her voice low and husky. 'Thank you. Thank you so much. You are amazing.' She blinked her smoky eyes at the audience, who fell in love with her all over again. They hardly dared to breathe in case it stopped this unheard-of happening – Mia speaking to her public. 'Tonight is a very special night – the last night of my world tour. I've visited fifteen countries and travelled many thousands of miles, but that journey is nothing compared to the one I've come on in the last eight years. It would not have been possible without you.' She blew kisses to the audience, who laughed and applauded lightly. 'This is the last time I shall be on stage for some time. I'm going to withdraw from the spotlight for a while . . .' There were cries of 'No!' but Mia hushed them with a wave of her hand. 'Not for ever, just long enough for me to regain my strength and renew my spirit. I'm sure you will allow me that. And so goodbye for now. But this is *au revoir* and not *adieu*.'

With that, she smiled again at her audience and walked slowly into the wings, managing a final wave before the curtain came down and the house lights went up. Still the applause continued, even after some people had made their way out of the theatre. A few sobs were audible.

Simon was almost the last person to stop clapping. He suddenly realised he was exhausted. He sat down and wiped his cheeks, which were streaked with tears. How he longed to see Molly and congratulate her on her amazing success and her stunning talent. He wanted to apologise for the terrible thing he had done and the pain he had caused her, make everything all right between them. But he couldn't. Had Molly Douglas not become Mia Delvard, it would have been a lot easier to approach her. Now he had left it too late. They could never be friends again.

He got up to leave the theatre and shuffled out in the wake of the last few audience members.

'There you are!' said an impatient voice, as he emerged from the stalls.

Simon looked up and saw his old pal waiting for him. He was in such a daze from the performance that he'd forgotten they were meeting.

'I thought you'd disappeared into the Gents like you used to,' Roger said.

'Hardly,' said Simon. 'Not in my condition.' His once-hectic sex life had dwindled to a standstill a couple of years previously. 'I don't feel the need, these days. I rather like the way life dovetails itself together. Just when you become less likely to pull, your desire to conjugate correspondingly decreases. It's one of nature's little marvels, don't you think?'

'If you say so,' said Roger. He took Simon's arm as euphoric punters swirled around them, saying what a marvellous night it had been. They went out through the foyer towards Great Marlborough Street. 'Anyway, I stopped all that when I moved to Northampton. Some of us grow up, you know. Did you enjoy the show?'

Simon lit a cigarette. 'I was blown away. She's amazing. And fancy meeting up with you. It's been a really weird night.'

'Can I have one of your snouts?' asked Roger. 'I've given up but I could just go a Marlboro right now.'

'Here you are.' Simon handed the packet to him. 'The lighter's inside.'

Roger lit a cigarette and blew out the smoke contemplatively. Then he turned to Simon with a smile. 'Hold tight, love. Your night is about to become even stranger. I've got tickets for a very select after-show party. And I mean *very* select. A private room at the Ritz. Mia will be there. You're coming with me, girlfriend!'

'Oh, no, I couldn't,' said Simon, flustered. As much as he longed to see Molly again, he couldn't face her – not the way he was now. Not with everyone around her clamouring for her attention. It wouldn't be what he wanted at all. 'I have to go home.'

'Come on,' said Roger. 'Don't be a misery. There's a free bar. You said you loved the gig. Wouldn't you like to meet the star? I can introduce you.'

Simon's mouth twitched. 'I can't, really.' He was just puzzling over how on earth Roger could have tickets to Molly's exclusive after-show party when the pain hit. He moaned as it gathered and ripped through him with such force that he clutched his stomach and bent forward involuntarily, his face distorted with agony.

'Simon!' said Roger, clutching his friend to steady him. 'Are you okay? What's wrong?' He supported Simon as his weight fell on him. 'It's all right, mate. I've got you. Take it easy.'

After a full minute of torture, the pain at last ebbed away, leaving Simon sweating and panting. He pulled himself upright and let go of Roger. 'I'm fine, thank you. There's no need to fuss.'

There was an excited buzz from the people around them, and Simon realised that they had ended up in the crowd outside the stage door, which had opened, causing the ripples of excitement. The crowd of a hundred or so was about eight deep and, with his stoop, Simon couldn't see over their heads.

'She's coming!' several people shouted. There was a flurry of flash bulbs and applause and cries of 'Bravo!'

Roger ignored the activity behind him, focused only on Simon. 'You don't look well at all,' he said. 'When did these pains start?'

'Don't fuss, Roger, I'm fine.'

Just then, the crowd began shouting and shoving. Mia Delvard had emerged from the stage door, her burly bouncers making a path for her from the theatre to the road where a blacked-out Bentley awaited her. Surrounded by her entourage, her face shielded by huge dark glasses, head bowed as if she were just a commuter homeward bound, Mia moved quickly through the throng as people cried her name or clapped their hands, lit by the flashes of cameras and the lights from mobile phones that filmed her. Simon caught a glimpse of red hair and a whiff of jasmine perfume as she passed within a few feet of him. Then she was blocked from view by her hangers-on and squealing fans as she climbed into the waiting car.

'Look at the colour of you. Something's seriously wrong. Have you seen a doctor?' said Roger.

'Have *you*? You're not exactly pork-sausage pink yourself,' snapped Simon. He watched the Bentley glide down the road, carrying Molly away from him. The crowd began to disperse. Just then another, stronger wave of pain engulfed him and this time knocked him off his feet.

Roger caught him just before he hit the pavement. 'That's it,' he said. 'Something's very wrong here.'

Simon could hardly hear anything above the agony that had him in its clutches. Is this it? he wondered. Am I actually dying, at long last? Here on the pavement where Molly just trod? The pain grew and grew until there was nothing else in the world.

He heard the distant sound of Roger's voice. He was saying, 'Yes, emergency services? I need an ambulance as soon as possible . . .'

Chapter Twenty-nine

The afternoon sun was lowering in the sky, and the chill of a September evening was rising up from Romney Marsh nearby. Molly picked up the tattered bamboo stick she kept by the back door and made her way down the acre of garden towards the mulberry tree. The three hens and Blake, the cockerel, usually dozed in the shade under the low-hanging branches. When she reached the tree, Molly stirred the leaves above them with her stick, and after a few indignant burbles, Blake popped out, alert and outraged as only a cockerel can be. Jodie, Jordan and Maureen followed. They were big, brassy, white Sussex Light chickens, although Blake had a handsome, tapering dark grey collar of feathers and a spray of dramatic dark blooms at his tail.

'Come on, girls!' she called. 'Let's be 'avin' you. Bedtime!'

Familiar with the routine, the four birds squawked and scuttled across the croquet lawn and into their pen. Molly flung a handful of corn after them and fastened the gate with a sturdy Y-shaped stick stuck through the padlock catch.

'Be good. I'll see you in the morning,' she said. She left the chickens to their roosting, envying them their simple existence.

She felt like roosting herself, drawing in, closing her eyes and sleeping for days on end. The night before had been more draining than any performance she could remember, perhaps because it was the last on the tour that had taken her round the world over the last six months. Or perhaps it was because she knew that she had stored up trouble for herself with the announcement she had made. Lilia had been so livid that she hadn't spoken a word to her at the party afterwards, and Molly had come home alone. Where Lilia was now, she had no idea.

She made her way back across the lawn and up the crazy-paving pathway towards the house. A patio nestled against a semi-circular bay, around which grew a profusion of ice-white roses. There she paused. From inside the house she could hear the children laughing with Michelle, the nanny. In a minute she would go in and see them, but first she wanted to savour a few more peaceful moments looking out over the garden on a perfect late-summer evening.

Her life had turned round so dramatically, and her happiness had blossomed so much, that she had trouble taking it all in. It had all begun eight years before, when she'd stepped out onto the stage at Ronnie Scott's. Moments before she was due to go on, Lilia had come to her dressing room with the terrible news that Pancho, her little Chihuahua puppy, was dead. He had leapt from Lilia's arms in front of an approaching tube when she was waiting for the Bakerloo line train to Oxford Circus. 'He gave just one little yelp and was gone. Under the wheels like a dropped sandwich. I'm so very sorry,' Lilia had said sadly.

'Oh, poor Pancho!' Molly had cried. 'That's just dreadful. I feel sick!'

'I know,' said Lilia, comforting her with a hug. 'Such a

sweet, loving little chap. How about we get you a kitten? Would you like that?'

Tears flowed down Molly's cheeks but just then the stage manager knocked on the door to tell her it was time to go on.

'Be brave,' Lilia had said, helping her dry her eyes and pushing her towards the door. 'Be strong. You know you can do it.'

When she had stepped out into the spotlight, she had sung with such sensational sadness and heartbreak that the whole audience was moved to tears. The next day, she woke up to rave reviews and an ecstatic agent whose phone wouldn't stop ringing. She was, overnight, a star.

The next few years passed in a whirl of hard work, dressing rooms, stages, studios and all the other places her career required her to be. There was hardly time to breathe. More than ever she depended on Lilia to advise and guide her, to help her manage her overcrowded diary, to sit at her side in interviews or just to book her hair and beauty appointments. Molly Douglas gradually disappeared completely as Mia Delvard took over. Sometimes it was hard to remember who she really was. It was only when she was here, at home with the children, that she felt she was Molly again.

Sighing, she turned to go inside. Stooping slightly, she went through the bleached-oak door that led into the half-timbered Elizabethan house. She crossed the boot room, then the small lounge, which led into a rambling drawing room and from there to the office and TV room, where she heard her sons gurgling and laughing with Michelle.

Four-year-old Leo was a ray of joy, as happy as the day was long, forever smiling and amused by life. He jumped up as his mother came in, leaving the puzzle he was doing, and rushed over to her for a hug. 'Leo! Hello, gorgeous!' said Molly, taking him into her arms. 'How have they been, Michelle?'

'Wonderful.' The nanny was holding eighteen-month-old Bertie, who was clutching a toy train and chattering happily at the sight of Molly. 'They've both been very good.'

'Great.' Molly smiled at her nanny. They had formed a strong bond over the last few months when she and the boys had accompanied Molly on various parts of the tour. 'Why don't you get off home now? I'll do bath and bed.'

'Are you sure?'

'Of course.'

'I'll see you in the morning, then.' Michelle kissed the children and said goodnight to them, while Molly set about getting their tea, humming as she bustled about the kitchen. She loved this humdrum domesticity after the weeks of hotel rooms and planes. She savoured these moments, filing them in her memory under 'blissful contentment'. She would never have guessed that marriage and motherhood would suit her so well.

Molly had met her future husband at the Jazz and Blues Awards at the Grosvenor House Hotel where she had won the Best Newcomer trophy. Lilia had grabbed her by the arm and led her through the crowd of fashionable people until they were elbow-to-elbow with a good-looking well-upholstered man in his early forties.

'Oh, Mr Shawcross!' declared Lilia. 'What a pleasure. May I introduce you to my client, Mia Delvard?'

Molly smiled while Rupert Shawcross looked at her appreciatively. 'Of course. The pleasure is mine. Congratulations, Miss

Delvard. I'm so glad you won. I was rooting for you,' he said, with a generous smile.

'Thank you,' said Molly, swimming in his handsome brown eyes.

'Mia, this is Rupert Shawcross, the well-respected producer.'

'Of course.' Molly smiled at him. 'Congratulations to you, too.'

Rupert was clutching his own award for his inspired musical version of *Gaslight*. 'Thank you. Will you join me for a glass of celebratory champagne?'

Molly considered. She'd heard, of course, of Rupert Shawcross, successful theatrical entrepreneur and producer, not just because of *Gaslight* but because of his high-profile divorce, which had only just faded from the front pages. She knew that his wife Sheila had separated from him after he'd had an affair with the leading actress in one of his shows, and it had cost him dear. He'd lost the family home in Chalfont St Giles, complete with stables, swimming-pool and staff bungalow in the grounds, with the second home, a state-of-the-art villa in Ibiza, and had to pay annual allowances amounting to several million pounds each year. Sheila had revelled in her triumph, and been interviewed sympathetically on several daytime TV programmes about her love-rat multi-millionaire ex-husband and the effect of it all on their son. Did Molly really want to get involved with someone who had so much baggage, even if so far he was just offering her a glass of champagne? She could already feel the crackle of chemistry between them and, if she was honest, she was desperate for romance, sex and a little sensual stimulation, and was likely to fall wildly in love with the first man who gave her a good seeing-to.

'Yes, please!' Lilia said eagerly. 'We'd love to.'

To Molly's delight, Rupert was nothing less than utterly charming to Lilia, and didn't seem to mind that their drink together was a threesome. He toasted Molly with champagne, and when he went to order another bottle, Lilia grabbed her arm. 'He is the one!' she said urgently. 'He is the man we have been waiting for! He has love in his eyes, love for you. A man might have everything, wealth, fame, success, looks, even, but if he does not have that fire, that longing for you in his soul and his loins, then he cannot help you. Rupert is yours for the asking. Look at his teeth. He is worth a fortune!'

'Really, Lilia, how can you tell he has love for me? We've only just met!'

'I can see it, believe me. He fulfils all our requirements. Don't let this one get away.'

When Rupert returned, Lilia made her excuses and left them together. They fell in love that night over champagne and success. He kissed her before dispatching her home in his chauffeur-driven car, then sent white roses at dawn and more roses every hour on the hour for the whole of the next day, then three times a day for the next week.

'What a gentleman!' said Lilia. 'Such tenacity! Such taste! What a life he is offering you! All we can hope is that he soon abandons the theme of roses and takes up diamonds instead.'

Molly hardly heard her – she was in love.

After a whirlwind romance Molly, too, had known that Rupert was the one, and she was pregnant almost as soon as their relationship was consummated. They were married just a month before Leo was born, in a quiet ceremony with only their closest friends present and the paparazzi outside, hoping for a glimpse of the very pregnant bride.

Molly had always thought that Simon would give her away at her wedding but, as it was, she asked Lilia to do it. Jane, reconciled to her old friend after Molly had called and begged forgiveness for the episode at Kit-Kat Cottage, was her bridesmaid, and Boris Norris attended with his family.

Lilia made a memorable speech at the reception. 'I know that Molly's parents would be very proud of her and very happy for her on this day. They are not here, so I speak for them.' She closed her eyes, as if channelling the thoughts of Molly's absent mum and dad. 'Rupert, they say, "We give you the precious gift of our daughter, and entrust her to your keeping. To have and to hold, to keep and cherish, spoil and lavish. Spare no expense in the care of our beloved Molly." A top-of-the-range BMW will do very nicely for starters. Pension schemes and life insurance are something I'll discuss with your secretary.'

Now Molly had the life Lilia had promised her. Slumming it (as Rupert said) in darkest Kent, they nevertheless lived in a romantic and imposing house, all rambling roses and latticed windows.

Lilia lived on the top floor of the picturesque home. The sweet, cosy, self-contained flat had been the deciding feature when Molly and Rupert first viewed the house. 'This is perfect!' Molly had said, clapping her hands in pleasure. 'Lilia can live with us but we'll have our privacy. What do you think, darling?'

Rupert had already been charmed by Lilia and was aware that his wife came with an attachment. He had been thinking about buying a cottage down the road from wherever they moved into, but the granny flat upstairs solved the problem and saved him a few bob too. 'I think it's the one,' he replied.

When they'd first moved in, Lilia had been happy to keep to herself, pottering about her kitchenette. In fact, Molly had had to insist that she dine with them in the evenings. 'I don't like to impose,' Lilia had said graciously. 'Thank you for thinking of me, but you and your husband need time alone together. You couldn't possibly want me sitting between you like the Shroud of Turin. I shall stay upstairs alone and nibble an oatcake. Maybe a radish too, if I have one.'

All of this carry-on only made Molly more insistent. Before long, she had persuaded Lilia to join them for dinner each night, and thereafter the old lady would enter the dining room at precisely eight o'clock every evening. She was always slightly overdressed in something elegant but fussy, with freshly applied makeup and her ruby-red hair combed up into several improbable curls, lacquered to the resistance of a wicker basket.

With Lilia in the house, and then the arrival of Bertie, Molly had what she'd always dreamt of: a family. Just when she thought life couldn't get any better, it had trumped itself: first weight loss, sudden professional success, fame and financial rewards beyond her wildest dreams. Then falling in love. Marriage. More wealth. A dream home in the country. Motherhood. Whatever next? Ascension to heaven?

'Come on, boys, time for tea!' called Molly, dishing up spaghetti Bolognese. The children giggled and shrieked as they ran and toddled for the table, their blond heads gleaming in the early evening sunshine. Molly let out a long, contented sigh and smiled.

But after a moment or two the smile faded and her forehead puckered into a frown. Despite her wonderful husband, her gorgeous children and the beautiful house they lived in, Molly couldn't hide her growing anxiety any longer.

Over the years, as Molly's success had grown, Lilia had become grander and grander, declaring herself solely responsible for her student's professional triumphs. 'You came to me a frumpy pantomime actress and you left a charismatic firework! All this is down to me and me alone.' In the meantime, she was trying to work some of her transformative magic on herself and was no stranger to the surgeon's knife and the sumptuous Harley Street practices where physical perfection and eternal youth were on offer at the right price. The various procedures she had undergone had plumped and smoothed her skin, any deeper wrinkles removed with fillers, so that she looked much younger than a woman in her early eighties. Her hair, though still thin, was persistently red and enhanced with a selection of weaves and clip-in tresses that added lustre and fullness. She wore a corset, more to hold her upright than to hold her in, which gave her the posture of a much younger woman. She made the most of her new 36C breasts, and the killer heels gave her height with a feminine totter. She was certainly a world away from the bent, limping old lady who had opened the door of Kit-Kat Cottage all those years ago.

Her desire to be close to Molly was stronger than ever. Whenever she went shopping with Molly in Bond Street, it had become her habit to order two of everything, one in each of their sizes. Lately she had even taken to appearing in the identical outfit that Molly was going to wear that day, though how she could predict it so accurately, Molly had no idea.

'Not again!' Lilia would say, with mock exasperation. 'It must be a psychic link between us. Like twins!'

But Molly found it irksome to have a much older German double alongside her each and every day. The relationship had become stifling, and the truth was that Molly didn't want it any more. She appreciated what Lilia had done for her, but she no longer needed her. She had Boris to negotiate her deals, a publicist to look after her image, and she was perfectly capable of managing herself. If it was her lot in life to look after the old lady and humour her until she passed away, then she would do that, but she didn't feel the attachment to her that she had in the old days and was irritated by Lilia's constant presence and interference.

She was married now, with two sons, and she wanted to make her own decisions, call her own shots. It might not have been so annoying if Lilia had fulfilled the role of sweet old grandma, but with her new looks and her ever-more ferocious ambition, it was like having a discontented teenager in the house.

It was an awful thing even to think, but Molly was beginning to daydream about life without her old friend. She was not as obsessed with her career as she used to be. She had enjoyed phenomenal success but now she wanted a break. Her children were still very young and they needed their mother. She didn't have the heart to leave them constantly in the care of others. What was the point in that? Hadn't she earned the right to take a couple of years off?

She knew Lilia would never agree. She seemed to feel that unless they toured constantly, continuing to perform and record a new selection of heartrending songs every six months, the public would forget them and move on to someone else. Things had come to a head one morning a week ago, as soon as Rupert had left for the office.

'Lilia, I've come to a decision. I don't want to work for a while,' Molly had announced, as they sat drinking their breakfast coffee together. Michelle had taken the children down the garden to the trampoline. 'There's only a week left of the world tour – just five more London dates. Once it's over, I'm taking a break. I need to spend more time with the children.'

Lilia stared at her, aghast. 'What sort of talk is this? A break? We are just at the beginning of our journey. We cannot stop now, just because you are consumed with nauseating maternal feelings. What about nurturing *me*?'

'I've been working flat out for eight years,' Molly said softly. 'I've done everything you've asked of me. I've made us both rich and successful. Surely I'm entitled to some time off.'

Lilia put down her coffee cup crossly. 'But Boris is in talks with Paramount! We would be mad to throw it all away now.'

'Hollywood can wait. The boys are growing up so fast. I don't want to miss it.'

Lilia narrowed her eyes. 'How can you be so arrogant? I have sacrificed everything for you. Now you throw it all back in my face. Ingrate!'

'Please calm down, Lilia. I have other responsibilities. You are not the only person in my life.'

Lilia got up with slow, wounded dignity. 'I see. You've made yourself quite clear, Molly—'

'Oh, Lilia, I'm sorry – you know I love you . . .'

Lilia held up a hand. 'No, no, Molly, I quite understand. Others come first in your heart now. I cannot compete with a silver-haired husband or vomiting children.'

There was a pause. Then Molly said, 'I need a rest, that's all. A little time off. I'll be ready to start again soon, I promise.'

'I beg you to think about this seriously. We have poured everything, *everything*, into your career. Do not abandon it now, I beg you. Please, Molly, think about it before you do anything you may regret.'

Molly had promised she would. But then, last night at the Palladium, she had been possessed by something greater than herself that had spurred her on to make her announcement. She had felt calm and liberated afterwards: now she was free to live a real life for a while. Today it had been all over the papers that she was retiring for good, and she'd not seen or heard from Lilia since.

Molly sighed. No doubt she was furious. Well, they would sort it out in good time. They always did.

Chapter Thirty

On the way to hospital Roger had held Simon's hand and kept repeating, 'You all right, girl? You all right?'

'Am I going to die?' Simon had asked weakly. The pain-relieving drugs administered by the paramedics were already taking effect, but he knew that he was very ill.

'Well, we're all going to snuff it one day, let's face it,' said Roger. 'I've always fancied a brain haemorrhage. Dead before you hit the ground. Not yet, though. You're only in your thirties. Pull yourself together. You're not going yet, do you hear?'

But some of us will die sooner than others, thought Simon now. He was lying in his bed on the ward, curtained off from the other patients and awaiting Roger's return. The fresh-faced consultant, wearing an expensive shirt with rolled-up sleeves, had paid a visit that morning, and after he'd examined Simon thoroughly, had taken Roger into a side-room to talk through his treatment. Simon had been in hospital for five days now and had rather surprised Roger by naming him as his next-of-kin on the official forms, which meant that Roger was kept abreast of his progress and medication.

'I simply refuse to take on the responsibility,' Roger had said, when Simon told him what he had done. 'I'm sorry, but I've got enough on my plate. Visiting is one thing, getting the results of your stool samples quite another.'

'Go on, Rog. The consultant's a dish. This way you'll get lots of one-on-one time with him,' said Simon, persuasively. 'They earn good money, you know . . .'

'He hardly looks old enough to operate a Bunsen burner,' said Roger, but he went off all the same to hear the latest verdict on Simon's health.

He had been gone for such a long time that Simon was beginning to wonder exactly how much the consultant had to confide when the curtain round his bed was pulled back and Roger came through.

'So – am I dying after lunch or before?' quizzed Simon, as Roger sat on the chair next to his bed.

'If you can get through *Loose Women*, you have a very sturdy constitution,' Roger mused. 'I spent most of the time mentally undressing the dear doctor. Dreamy, intelligent eyes and a very trim waist, but the upshot is he seems to think you're rather ill. That was the gist, anyway.'

'Go ahead. Make my day.'

'You have cirrhosis, hepatitis and ascites – that's dropsy to you. It's why your stomach's so swollen – full of retained liquid. You also have an inflamed pancreas, glycogen deficiency, high blood pressure, damage to your nervous tissue, and alcohol dependency, obviously. Not to mention an overload of poisons and toxins in your system and mental-health problems. Apart from that, you're fine. They can't do anything about your vile personality, unfortunately. I did ask.'

Oh, well, thought Simon, philosophically. That's my life, then. It really hadn't turned out to be as spectacular as he'd expected. Like many a tortured queen, he had simply drunk himself to death. He had sacrificed everything for the dubious pleasure of getting smashed. The eternal, fervent need to forget, to get out of it, was giving him, finally, what he craved. Death would be the ultimate oblivion, the night of nights to remember.

What would I have changed? Simon wondered. What *could* I have changed?

But he knew the answer to that.

Simon had always drunk to excess, but after the night Molly had discovered him with Daniel, his drinking had taken on new, gargantuan proportions. If the answer to life's problems before had been to drink, now it was to drink much, much more.

He'd got home, bedraggled and befuddled, and immediately consumed almost a full bottle of vodka. He drank until he passed out. He knew all too well that he had very probably just shattered his friendship with his soulmate – the look on Molly's face when she saw him and Daniel together was burnt on to his consciousness. Her utter despair had frightened him like nothing else in his life ever. He drank to blot that picture out of his mind, but no matter how much vodka he poured down his throat, he couldn't forget it.

He woke up full of self-loathing. How could he have risked the trust and love of the only person who really understood him? A future without Molly was unthinkable. What on earth was he to do without her? The answer had been to drink.

He had drunk all that day too, desperate to call Molly but too scared of the pain he had caused her and of what she might say to him.

So he had gone out and got drunker still.

The next night he was booked to perform as Genita L'Warts at the ICA. It was a very high-profile gig, and Boris, the excitable agent, had invited television producers and commissioning editors to view the startling new talent everyone was talking about.

'This is your big chance,' he'd told Simon, when the gig had been confirmed. 'I mean it. This is your stepping-stone to the big-time. Get this right and we're made.'

In a bid to show how upmarket his star turn now was, Boris ordered the sardines from Selfridges for the performance.

It was three o'clock in the afternoon when Simon woke up, feeling sick and dehydrated. There was still so much alcohol in his system that he also felt unsteady and uncentred. Shit, he thought, staring at his watch through bloodshot eyes. I've got a sound check in two hours.

He tried to roll on to his side and ease himself into an upright sitting position, but ended up lying in a heap on the floor. 'Oh, bollocks,' he said. 'I can't even stand up.' He reached up to the overcrowded bedside table and blindly grasped whatever he could reach in the hope that it was a glass of water. Instead his hand clutched a vodka bottle.

'Oh, well,' said Simon. 'Why the fuck not?' He put it to his lips and drained the remnants. Then he flung it across the room. It smashed against the wall, spraying the room with shards of glass. His head rolled back on the dusty carpet and Simon fell into another deep, impenetrable sleep.

He slept through all of Boris Norris's frantic phone calls and never heard the incessant ringing of his doorbell. When he next opened his eyes it was midnight and he had missed his important gig. After he had staggered into the kitchen to drink a gallon of water straight from the tap, he phoned Boris's number. 'Boris, it's Simon. I—'

'Where in the name of Jesus have you been? Abducted by aliens?'

'Er, well, I . . . I . . .'

'This had better be good, Simon. I've had to deal with four hundred angry punters, theatre management, unimpressed journalists and photographers, and more TV executives than you could fit into a toilet cubicle at Soho House. Where the fuck were you? Tell me.'

'I was asleep.'

'Okay. That's not great. I phoned and rang your doorbell for two solid hours.'

'I remember having a dream about Santa and I thought I heard sleigh bells,' said Simon, stifling a yawn. 'I'm sorry about the stupid gig. Sorry you were left in the shit. I messed up.'

'You most certainly did,' said Boris. 'What am I supposed to do? Employ some kind of minder to ensure that you're able to fulfil your contractual obligations?'

'Oh, I like the sound of that,' purred Simon. 'Maybe an Eastern European with ice-grey eyes and a tattoo of his girlfriend's name on his torso.'

'This is no joking matter.'

'But unfortunately,' continued Simon, 'the girlfriend is back in Poland and my swarthy minder has to spend twenty-four hours a day with me. What's a boy to do?'

'Get a new agent,' said Boris.

'Oh,' said Simon, thoughtfully. 'It's like that, is it?'

'Yes, I'm afraid it is,' said Boris. 'I have my reputation to consider. You've made me the laughing stock of the industry. You're a talented man but you have no future in this business. You are that most terrible of things: unprofessional.'

'Are you sacking me because of one unfortunate evening?'

'I am sacking you before there's another. My nerves can't take it.'

'What if I say there won't be another?'

'I wouldn't believe you. Good luck with your career. Goodbye, Simon, goodbye, Genita.'

Simon was undaunted by the departure of Boris. Despite his no-show at the ICA, plenty of agents were panting to get him to their books. He eventually signed with Worldwide Artists, under the guidance of Portia Thomas. His first and last booking via Portia was a high-profile appearance at the British Comedy Awards. Such was Genita L'Warts's profile at the time that the producers broke with tradition and scheduled a seven-minute slot for one of her rants.

He'd felt the danger signals while preparing in the dressing room. As he'd applied his makeup and sipped his Grey Goose, he hadn't felt that other personality possess him as it usually did. When the time came and he took to the stage, Genita was nowhere to be found. Instead of the glorious, triumphant crowning of the mistress of post-modern comedic genius, twelve million people watching live saw Simon mumbling, 'Genita? Where are you?' as he stared, mortified, into the close-up camera. 'I'm sorry,' he said, once the excited shouts and jeers had died down. 'I have nothing to say.'

Because they had time to fill, and maybe because they thought this was all a prelude to a hilarious bit of comic genius, the director kept the camera on Genita's face. There was a silent stare-out between Simon trying to summon Genita and the cameraman. Eventually they cut to Jonathan Ross who did what he had to do to reignite the audience.

That was the end of Genita L'Warts. She never appeared again. Her spirit departed Simon for good, just as he had predicted. She had evaporated into thin air. Strangely, he didn't mind. He wished her well and took great delight in cancelling all his future engagements.

'Genita has gone,' he told all bewildered enquirers. 'May she rest in peace. Goodbye.'

Simon withdrew from the world of showbusiness. He screened his calls and simply ignored all messages and post. He was amazed by how quickly he was forgotten. Once the bookings and appearances dried up, so did the invitations to parties and first nights. He was even refused entry at the Shadow Lounge one night, even though he explained who he was. He blended back into his old life, which meant he stayed at home.

The years passed and gradually Simon's world grew smaller. He spent the money he had made as Genita, then lived off social security and a small allowance that came in from an investment his father had left him. Now poor, he could no longer afford Grey Goose vodka so resorted to supermarket own brands.

Drinking began to take its toll on Simon's body: he gained weight and his startling eyes were lost in puffiness and jowls. He knew he was becoming increasingly unappealing, with his bloodshot eyes and musty breath. All his pretty hair fell out, leaving hanks on the pillow and in the shower. His skin looked awful, his fingernails became coarse and yellow, and he could see red cracks creeping over his cheeks and nose, like sparrow's footprints. He felt unattractive. His sexual desire decreased and eventually he hung up his cap as far as cruising was concerned. Without ever renouncing his former lifestyle, he just couldn't be bothered.

'I don't have the stomach for it any more,' he told a concerned Charles, when he bumped into him one day in Sainsbury's.

'That's an unfortunate choice of words,' said Charles, perusing the fresh-meat section. 'But I know what you mean.'

'I've had enough cock to last me a lifetime,' said Simon, failing to lower his voice and rather shocking an elderly lady, who tutted, then scurried away with her trolley as quickly as her legs would carry her.

'You're not withdrawing your dance card, are you?'

'Yes.'

'Is that just because you're getting fat?'

'How dare you?'

'I'm being honest.' Charles looked worried. 'You're not looking at your peak, let's put it that way.'

Simon didn't want to hear it. The road back to his vibrant youth was too long to travel now. He could only go forward into an alcoholic, fuzzy, almost unreal future. By now he was in a permanent state of bleariness, incapable of caring much about anything other than the next drink. He needed Molly more than ever, but she had disappeared. What was he to do? He drank to calm himself. Sobriety was one extended panic attack and he wanted nothing to do with it.

Then one day he heard of Mia Delvard, whose fame and talent eventually pierced his tiny, self-absorbed world. He heard her voice in a shop coming over the sound system, and was at once fascinated by it. He asked the assistant who was singing and she blinked at him as though he must have come from another planet not to know that this was Mia Delvard. Simon scraped together enough pennies for a CD and bought a Mia Delvard recording.

Back home, he listened to the album while he sipped a glass of wine. Something about the girl's voice touched him like no other ever had. It was nostalgia and bitter-sweet regret made into sound, a voice at once familiar and yet quite new to him. Then he froze. The voice on the album had begun to sing 'Molly and Daniel were sweethearts, Molly and Daniel were one . . .' He could hardly breathe. When Mia sang 'Along came Molly's friend Simon', he grabbed the album cover and stared at the picture of Mia on the front. He suddenly saw who stood behind the heavy-lidded eyes, glossy lips and long red hair. He listened to the entire song, then drew a shuddering breath and wept.

The chest pains had started as a vague, irritating burn in his chest, usually the day after a particularly heavy session. Then he noticed that the pain spread, in gentle ripples, up to his ears and down to his groin.

Simon increased his water intake, assuming it to be the righter of all the wrongs he had done to his body, though he didn't reduce the amount of alcohol he drank. He couldn't now. He was beyond that.

Gradually the pains got worse, taking over his whole body. He simply ignored them, coping with them when they came and forcing himself to forget them when they passed.

By the time he went to see Molly at the Palladium he was on two bottles of wine before lunch, his stomach was hugely swollen and as tight as drum, and the abdominal pains alarmed him.

Hurry up, was all Simon had thought. This must be the slowest, most protracted suicide there is.

Now he knew the lie of the land. His body was shattered – beaten, scarred and pummelled – by years of neglect and abuse. His system had done its best in the face of the poisonous onslaught, but eventually it had had to crumble. No part of him, it seemed, was unaffected by his alcoholism.

God, he thought. I need a drink.

Roger was staring at him, pity in his eyes. It was obvious now that time was short.

At last, Simon said, 'Roger, how well do you know Mia Delvard?'

'I've known her for yonks. I got her a singing gig at an Italian restaurant and she's never forgotten. There's always a ticket and an after-show invitation for me, although Lilia, the old bird, her manager, would happily have dropped me. Not one for tender friendships. Why are you asking me this now?'

Simon turned his head so he could look Roger in the eyes. 'I need a favour. Could you call her? Tell her Simon needs her. Tell her how ill I am.'

Roger frowned. 'Do you know Mia?'

Simon smiled sadly. 'I know Molly. We were at college together many moons ago and we were friends.'

Roger was clearly puzzled. 'Yes, her real name is Molly – but I had no idea she was friends with you, Simon . . . Oh.' Roger's expression changed as he made the link between Molly and Simon and the words of Mia Delvard's famous song. 'I don't believe it. So *you*'re Simon. You done her wrong.'

'I did. I must speak to her. Please, Roger. Tell her Simon's dying and needs to see her. Bring her to me before it's too late.'

Chapter Thirty-one

Lilia appeared back in her flat the following day with a suspiciously red face, which meant she had been having facial peeling at her favourite dermatologist's. Molly was relieved to see her. She had worried that her announcement of a temporary retirement might have made Lilia so furious that she would be impossible for weeks on end. But she came down to breakfast quite happily and seemed her old self.

Molly tried to mention her break but Lilia would hear none of it, and brushed away her attempts to discuss with it with a breezy 'Come, come! If you need a rest, you need a rest. I'm not Pol Pot, you know.'

Molly was delighted that harmony was restored.

A few nights later, Lilia came down to the lounge to join Molly and Rupert for a quick drink before dinner. 'Good evening, Rupert, my dear,' she said, going over to peck his cheek. She looked elegant in a light blue dress with a glittering diamond brooch. 'I trust you have had a good day?'

'Hello, Lilia,' said Rupert, cheerfully. 'Not bad, thank you. I think we've got Tara Palmer-Tomkinson to play Ophelia at Regent's Park.'

'An excellent choice.'

'It's what the punters want. Can I get you a drink? Your usual?'

Lilia went to sit down opposite Molly. 'I very rarely . . .' she said, as she always did '. . . but it would be rude to refuse. Just a small brandy to wake up my tastebuds, if you insist. And when I say small, I'm talking continental measures. Don't just show the bottle to the tumbler if you don't mind.'

Rupert half filled the glass with Courvoisier and handed it to Lilia, who held it up to the light and examined it as if it were an old donkey and she the keeper of the knacker's yard. 'Well, it's a start, I suppose.'

Molly accepted another top-up from Rupert as she said brightly, 'How was your day, Lilia?'

'Rather marred by worry, if you must know.'

'Really? What about?'

'It's the children.'

'What about them?'

Rupert looked over from the drinks table, his eyebrows raised.

'I can't help wondering if your nanny – Michelle, isn't it? Such a pretty girl! – is altogether wise to let the boys play in the way she does.'

'What do you mean?' said Rupert.

Lilia raised her shoulders. 'It's probably nothing. I'm an old woman. What do I know of raising children? Except in my day we didn't throw them in the air, let them fall into ponds or eat chicken shit.'

'What?' exclaimed Molly, sitting up straight. 'What are you talking about?'

'Nothing, really,' said Lilia, demurely.

'No. Explain to me what you mean, please. What's Michelle done?'

'I spent most of the day in my flat and every now and then I looked into the garden. What I saw shocked me. At one point, Michelle was throwing each child up in the air like a Frisbee. Higher and higher she tossed them, catching them as they plummeted to the ground only by the most fortuitous of good fortune. Perhaps that was just good fun and high spirits and I'm silly to be concerned.'

'But what's this about the pond?' asked Rupert, coming over.

'Oh, they both took a tumble into the fish pond. Michelle seemed to be encouraging them to balance on the ornamental edging. Naturally, at only four and almost two, the boys hardly have the skill required. Luckily she hauled them out of the freezing, filthy water before too long.'

Molly gaped at her, open-mouthed. 'But I didn't see any of this!'

'You were on the phone for a while today, weren't you? Three hours, I think it was.'

'But . . .' Molly had been chatting to Jane for rather a long time but could she really have missed both boys being soaked to the skin?

'Then, when Michelle fancied a rest, she simply shut the boys in the chicken run and went off for a sleep on the sun-lounger. That's when I'm sure I saw Bertie eating chicken shit. Of course I went down immediately and let them out. Poor little things, poo smeared all over them.'

'My God!' said Rupert, horrified. 'Are they all right?'

'I just can't believe it,' Molly said, appalled. 'It doesn't sound like Michelle at all.'

'This is serious,' Rupert said grimly. 'We can't leave Leo and Bertie in the care of someone we don't trust to look after them.'

Molly was amazed. 'But she's a marvel! The children love her. What would I do without her?'

'You heard Lilia. Michelle's been dangerous and reckless when she thought no one was watching.'

'But that can't be right,' said Molly. 'She's very responsible. I trust her implicitly.'

Rupert shook his head, his eyes grave. 'I don't think we can take the risk. If we have the least doubt, she has to go. Luckily for us, Lilia is on hand to see things we can't. We've had the warning and must heed it.'

'But how will I cope without her?' said Molly, becoming distressed.

'My dear, you are not to worry,' said Lilia. 'I will pop down after *Trisha* to help you for a while. It will be no trouble.'

'There,' said Rupert, looking relieved. 'Lilia can help you. You wanted more time with the children and now you can have it. We ought to think seriously about letting Michelle go.'

'But, Lilia . . .' said Molly, helpless to express what she was thinking. How could she tell her that she was both too old and unqualified to care for the children?

'I am glad to be of use,' said Lilia. 'It gives me a reason to carry on. Especially now you are *on a break*.'

Molly felt sure that something was going badly wrong but she couldn't see exactly what it was. Just then the telephone rang and Rupert went to answer it.

'It's for you,' he said, holding the handset towards Molly. 'Someone called Roger wants to speak to you. He says it's urgent.'

Roger was waiting for Molly at the grand glass-fronted entrance of University College Hospital on Euston Road when her driver dropped her off. 'Molly!' he called.

'Oh, Roger,' she said breathlessly. She hugged him.

'Thanks for coming,' he said.

'Don't be silly. Of course I had to come. How is Simon?'

'I'll take you up to see him. He's on the sixth floor.'

'Is it very serious?' she asked, as they made their way to the lifts.

Roger looked grave. 'Yes, I'm afraid so. They've done a lot of tests and an ultrasound scan. Basically he has all the symptoms of end-stage liver failure: jaundice, hepatitis, abdominal swelling – they're draining off litres of fluid. He's also suffering from alcohol withdrawal so he's got the shakes and is a bit delirious. They've given him some sedation to help that.'

Molly closed her eyes. It was too terrible. 'Oh dear. How on earth did he get into such a state?'

'When did you last see him?'

'Years and years ago. We fell out rather badly. We were incredibly close once.'

'He was never the easiest person to get along with.'

'When we were young and carefree, I adored him. Couldn't imagine my life without him. And I've thought of him often over the years. Every day, really. And now this . . .' Sadness washed over her, and her voice trailed away as she became lost in memories.

They fell silent as they entered the crowded lift. Molly's ordinary clothes, lack of makeup and the pair of dark glasses she wore protected her from being recognised. Once they stepped out on the sixth floor, Roger touched her arm. 'Prepare yourself. He's not a pretty sight. Go through the doors and he's in the second bed on the right.'

Molly hung back, stomach churning. Of all the places in which she'd imagined meeting Simon again, his deathbed had not been one of them. She was frightened now of seeing him and of not knowing what to say. 'Are you sure he wants me? I'm terribly nervous.'

'You're the one he keeps asking for. Go on. I'm going to stay here. Let you two be reunited without me being in the way.'

'Thank you, Roger,' she said, and impulsively kissed his cheek. 'You're a dear, kind man.' Then she gathered her courage and walked slowly down the ward to Simon's bed. As she approached, she saw that the curtains were partly drawn round the bed and a male nurse was busy, probably taking his patient's blood pressure. She waited awkwardly until he'd finished, then drew a deep breath and walked into view. Simon was turned away from her, trying to plump up his pillow, and didn't see her straight away, so Molly had time to register his appearance and hide her shock. His scalp was drawn tightly over his hairless skull, his cheeks were hollow and his skin looked dry but glowed a luminous pumpkin yellow, as if lit from within. He sighed with frustration and lay back. Then he saw her. Their eyes locked.

'You came,' he said quietly. 'Thank you.'

Molly was filled with pity for her old friend. He was just a frail, sick shell of his former self. 'I almost didn't but once Roger explained how serious things are and how much you wanted to see me, well . . . I had to come. I'm so sorry you're ill. How are you feeling?'

He lifted up his arm and turned his head so she could see the various tubes and drips that entered his body via wrist and neck. 'There's another tube under the covers that is draining what they call my morbid retention of fluid. And yet another darling little tube up my tired old penis to save me the bother of going to the lav. I don't need to miss a moment of *The Paul O'Grady Show*. It's bliss.'

The very mention of his sexual organ embarrassed them both. The unspoken subject of Daniel and the rift between them loomed large in their minds.

Molly sat down on the chair next to Simon's bed. 'Is it God's way of telling you to stop the drink? I always told you to cut down.'

'Unfortunately I didn't listen. My liver's had some sort of hissy fit, it seems. Refusing to play ball. The good news is they've given me Librium to stave off the withdrawal symptoms.'

'Lucky you,' said Molly, remembering her own fondness for the Valium with which Lilia had once supplied her. 'It's been eight years,' she observed.

There was a silence between them and Simon's eyes turned serious. 'I'm sorry, Molls.'

'What for?' she asked, needing him to say the words.

'You know what for. Daniel, that's what. I'm more sorry than you'll ever know.'

'It was pretty unforgivable,' she said. 'Kind of final, don't you think, as far as friendship goes?'

'There was a woman on *The Jeremy Kyle Show* who ran off with her sister's husband. She said they couldn't help themselves, that it was animal lust. And when the husband came on, I quite understood.'

'No regrets, then?' said Molly, briskly.

Simon fixed her with sad eyes. 'Of course I regret it. I lost you, didn't I? The most important person in my life. You were the one person in the world I knew inside out. When you wrecked the flat and threw us out, I knew I'd done something unspeakable and I've been consumed with self-hatred ever since. I thought I would never, ever see you again.'

'Well, I'm here now. I've missed you too,' she said, softening. She had never seen Simon so sincere and his vulnerability touched her.

'You're a star now. Living in another universe. And you got the handsome husband, the two adorable children, the house in the country . . . The magazines think you have a perfect life.'

'I'm very lucky. Look.' She pulled a photograph out of her handbag and showed it to Simon. 'Leo and Bertie.'

He looked at it, a half-smile on his lips. 'Gorgeous. Well done, Molls. I'm glad you got your dream. You deserved it.' Then he said softly, 'At the end of the TV show that woman went off arm in arm with her sister.'

Molly reached out and squeezed Simon's shoulder affectionately. 'A happy ending, then.'

'She forgave her. Say you forgive me?'

Molly blinked back some tears. 'I wonder if I have it in me. I can't say it if I don't mean it.'

'You can, as far as I'm concerned.'

Molly half laughed. She could see how very ill her old friend was. Death hovered about him like a cloud of midges. Of course she forgave him. In fact, would she have the life she had now if it weren't for him? Perhaps, paradoxically, she was in his debt. She said quietly, 'I forgive you, Simon. I accept your apologies. You did a terrible thing but you've punished yourself enough. Look at you. What have you done to yourself?'

'Seeing you and hearing those words is like the sea rushing over the sand and smoothing away all the bumps and footprints. Thank you.' Simon closed his eyes and exhaled contentedly. 'The guilt is dissolving and draining away, just like the bile from my gut.'

'We need to get you better, Simon.'

'The professor told me if I ever drink again my liver will pack up altogether. There's just a sliver still working. What they call a window of opportunity.'

'And do you understand that it's serious?'

'I know I must stop the drink and start looking after myself. Those are my orders.'

'And do you intend to obey them?'

'I shall now. You've given me the will to live.'

They smiled at each other. Then Simon fell back on his pillows, sighing.

'You're tired. I'll go now.' Molly stood up.

'Come back soon, won't you?' Simon said, through half-closed lips.

'Of course. I promise.' She left quietly and Simon was already sleeping as she slipped through the curtain.

Chapter Thirty-two

Simon soon became accustomed to the hospital with its rhythms of doctors' rounds, meal trolleys, medication times and visiting hours. It was soothing in a way. In fact, he hadn't had such a bustling social life for years. At every hour of every day nurses and medics came to check on him and administer various drugs. He learnt their names and flirted with them, making them laugh and charming them.

He began to feel something he hadn't experienced for a very long time: hope.

Typical!' he thought. Just before I bow out for the final time, I start enjoying life!

After ten days and more tests, including a very unpleasant examination of his gullet and stomach with an endoscope, Simon began to turn a corner. He was still very tired but the jaundice was retreating, his skin a little pinker and less yellow. One day he even got out of bed and wandered down to the hospital shop to buy the *Guardian*. His catheter had been removed and he was gradually weaned off the Librium. He was given a selection of new medication to take throughout the day.

Molly visited him almost every afternoon, bringing him fruit, yoghurt, books, papers and magazines to occupy his empty hours. His favourite was the volume of selected poetry. 'Tennyson and Librium go fabulously together,' he announced.

It was amazing how quickly they resumed their former friendship. They chatted away as they had in the old days, catching up on everything that had happened in the intervening years. If she couldn't visit, she telephoned. Very often they would laugh and howl together, but Simon had his serious moments too. He wanted to be totally honest and up front with Molly about everything. He didn't want to shy away from painful memories. Soon he found himself talking about his life in a way that he had never done before. Molly sat and listened quietly, as though she knew that Simon was talking to himself as well as to her.

'You know, Molly, I'm far from sure about the wisdom of my life's course. My particular niche on the sexuality gamut, for the illicit pleasure it has brought me, seems now to have left me high and dry. The outcome I find most irksome is my solitude. My relationships, such as they were, never developed because commitment was anathema to me. The very mention of it would curdle my blood, I swear. I would lie awake at night, eyes aflame with dastardly plans to snare my next victim. Quick, dirty, dangerous sex was my only motivation in life. Back then, a conveyor-belt of deliciously unattainable men was forever running through my mind. My laughable career was an exciting diversion, I admit. While I was hot, and the flavour of the season, I felt as if everything I touched would turn to gold. But after you left Genita left too. It was back to sex and drink to fill the hours.

'And when you lose the imperative urge to go looking for the next notch on the bedpost, you're fucked in the other sense – left in some sort of vacuum. Poverty, in all its forms – financial, creative and emotional – is suddenly to be heard scratching at the door. One day it sounds like a gerbil, but within a week there's a wild boar out there and the timber's splintering. After a while there's nothing to do but stare at the walls and listen to your inner dialogue – never an enticing prospect in my case. A dark and dirty tale. With only drink as a friend, you become socially inept. The thought of conversing, having eye contact and "enjoying" company of any sort withers. The part of the brain that deals with interaction and intimacy on every level dies from lack of use, and desire is replaced with fear. So it's goodnight, Vienna.' He came to the end of his speech and smiled wanly.

Molly took his hand and squeezed it. 'That's why you must get better,' she said. 'To make up for the lost years.'

Three weeks after he had been admitted to UCH, Simon was told he would soon be able to go home. The idea of returning to his flat filled him with dread, and he was considering Roger's offer of the sofa-bed in his small apartment when Molly came up with her own suggestion. 'I want you to come and stay in Kent. It's beautiful – fresh country air, new-laid eggs and me to look after you.'

'Really? Could you stand me?'

'Of course I could. I want you to meet my boys. I've told Rupert all about you and he insists you come.'

'And will I get to meet the famous Lilia?'

'Oh, yes.' Molly frowned. 'Lilia, too, of course.'

'If the magazines are to be believed, you don't cross the road unless she tells you to.'

Molly laughed a little uncomfortably. 'It's not quite as bad as that, even if Lilia would like it to be.'

'Is everything all right?' Simon asked, quick to pick up on Molly's emotions even now. 'You seem a bit troubled.'

'I'm fine,' Molly said, but she couldn't quite meet his eye. 'You've got enough to worry about without my woes adding to it. Things are not quite as easy as they might be. Lilia and Rupert have taken it upon themselves to sack the nanny, and Lilia's looking after the children.'

'Really? Isn't she about a hundred?'

'Not in the first flush, despite all the help money can buy. She's been wonderful to me over the years, an absolute rock. She guided me to where I am today . . . but she's being a bit odd at the moment. She won't hear of a new nanny, and every time I get a CV from the agency, she finds a reason why this one's no good. She's taken to whispering to Rupert constantly about goodness knows what, and spending all her time with the children. I'm being selfish, probably. I'm used to having her attention focused on me.'

'Mmm. Well, I can't wait to meet her,' said Simon.

'You'll probably love her. She's a scream, even if she's a bit strange sometimes.' Molly smiled. 'Good! It's settled. You're coming to Kent to rest and get healthy. Let's tell Roger the good news.'

A few days later Molly's driver arrived at the hospital and Simon was transported, with his goody bag of pills, to the secluded peace of Molly and Rupert's country home. It was a blustery autumn afternoon, and as the car made its stately way up the gravel drive towards the house a cloud of crisp burnt-orange and red leaves flew up and over them like confetti.

Simon was impressed by the beauty of the rambling red-brick Elizabethan house. As the car drew to a halt on the driveway, Molly appeared at the door, jumping up and down with excitement, dressed in jeans and a stripy cardigan.

She welcomed him with an affectionate kiss. 'You're here! Let me take your bag. I'll show you upstairs.'

He followed her up the staircase to a large, light bedroom on the first floor. 'This is gorgeous,' he said, looking at the mahogany bed, then up at the beamed ceiling and out through the latticed window to the vegetable garden below. 'What a wonderful house.'

'I love this room,' said Molly. 'In fact, I gave birth on that bed. Twice.'

'Darling, I'm recovering from a near-death experience. I don't want that vision in my head.'

'Too late,' laughed Molly. 'Have a rest, and when you're ready we'll have tea in the drawing room. That's down the stairs and follow the sound of children. They're dying to meet you, and Leo is wearing his Spider-Man costume in your honour.'

'How touching.'

'Lilia is here and Rupert will be back soon. He's been having lunch with Craig Revel-Horwood so he'll probably be wrecked.'

'What's he seeing her for?'

'He's trying to persuade Craig to take on the role of Ariel in a stadium tour of *The Tempest*. They've already cast Bruno Tonioli as Caliban, Len Goodman as Prospero and Arlene Phillips as Miranda. He's the last piece of the jigsaw, really.'

'It'll be a sell-out. See you downstairs when you're ready.'

Simon did his meagre unpacking and arranged his pills by his bedside. He already felt the calm and warmth of the house entering him and comforting him. He didn't stay for a rest but went downstairs quickly, eager to meet Molly's children. In the drawing room, two blond boys were playing, one in a miniature red Spider-Man suit and the other, who was smaller, in overalls caked with Play-Doh.

'Here's Simon!' announced Molly. 'He's come to stay with us. Say hello!'

The boys approached him, a little shy.

'Why doesn't he have any hair?' asked Leo, taking off his Spider-Man mask.

'Leo!' exclaimed Molly. 'You mustn't be rude like that.'

'It's all right, Molls.' Simon gazed down at the wide blue eyes looking up at him. He sat down on the sofa. 'If you really want to know the truth, I donated my hair to a very good friend, Arthur the Spider. You see, Arthur needed to spin an extra large web one day and . . .' The next minute he was lost in the tale he was making up, and both of the children were leaning on his knees, listening intently. Once the story was over, the boys shrieked with excitement and climbed all over Simon until Molly had to tell them off.

'Careful, boys! Simon hasn't been very well.'

'It's all right, Molly, I don't mind,' he said, wincing a little as Bertie's foot landed on his skinny thigh. Then he noticed a small, stiff, red-haired old woman standing in the doorway, wearing a blue apron over a silk tea-dress and recognised her: she'd been in the royal box at the Palladium that night. The famous Lilia. Molly saw where he was looking. 'Lilia, please come and meet Simon.'

'I've heard so much about you,' he said, giving her his most charming smile and standing up.

Lilia approached slowly. 'Yes,' she said, shaking his hand

weakly. 'Pleased to meet you. If I'd known you were coming I'd have baked a cake.'

The words were uttered with such casual sincerity it took him a moment to realise how withering they were really intended to be. He watched her as she clucked round the children, gathering them up to go through to the kitchen for tea. What struck Simon most was the similarity between Molly and Lilia. Their hair was exactly the same shade of coppery, vibrant red. Lilia even seemed to have adopted some of Molly's mannerisms, tossing her head backwards when she laughed, if a little more stiffly than Molly did. Before she left the room with Leo and Bertie, she turned back to Simon and said, 'I'm preparing dinner tonight. Are there any allergies or restrictions I should know about? I take it I should leave the sherry out of the trifle.'

'Yes, thank you,' Simon said politely. 'I'm an alcohol-free zone, I'm afraid. Apart from that, I'll be delighted with anything.' He turned to Molly when Lilia had left the room. 'Blimey. She's a game old bird, that one.'

'I owe her everything,' said Molly.

'She's had a bit of work done, hasn't she?'

'A bit! She's had her eyelids done, her forehead, chin, neck and boobs, then liposuction, and more Botox than an entire front row at London Fashion Week. It's all tax deductible, she keeps telling me.'

'Is she trying to be you or are you trying to be her? I can't work it out.'

'Well, it used to be me being styled by her in her own image. But lately I seem to be leading the way. She copies me.'

'I can see that. But she's not quite pulling it off. Camp, though, I'll give her that.'

'Oh, Simon,' said Molly, smiling, 'it's so good to have you around again. You've always had a way of looking at the world that makes everything seem okay.'

Simon was too tired to take much notice of what was going on around him that evening. Rupert came home and was welcoming and friendly, and Simon thought he seemed lovely, but he really only wanted to get to bed.

Over the next few days, though, he began to feel better. He had nothing to do but sleep, eat and rest, while Molly made sure he had everything he needed. The children already adored him and were keen to play and have more stories, but Molly had to shoo them away when Uncle Simon was too tired to be boisterous, which was quite often.

He watched with interest as the family dynamics swirled around him. Rupert was gone early in the mornings and returned just in time to read his boys a bedtime story. He seemed very affectionate to Molly, always gathering her up in a hug or giving her a tender kiss. Molly was an adoring if somewhat chaotic mother, making as much mess when she was trying to clear up as there had been to start with, and the boys were happy, healthy and energetic.

But the person who interested him most was Lilia, the old lady who had changed Molly's life so profoundly. She was constantly in the background, watching and observing, making herself indispensable. She did most of the cooking and looked after the practicalities of the children. A cleaner-cum-housekeeper came in for three hours a day, and Lilia was decidedly brisk with her, making sure that standards were maintained, the laundry and ironing properly organised, the cupboards stocked and meals planned.

She spent the day in a pinny, but when Rupert came home, she changed into a smart dress, makeup and jewellery and became a charming woman, eager to make sure that Rupert had everything he wanted and playing the flirtatious, pampering housewife to the master of the house. She's the hub of this household, thought Simon. She's made herself the heart of the place.

All the time, he noticed that Lilia was watching him. Her green eyes were always fixed on him but she was never smiling. She rarely spoke to him, except on the memorable occasion when she stopped as they passed in the corridor and glared at him.

'I must ask you to stay away from the children,' she said, with the tone and authority of an experienced police officer.

'Excuse me?' said Simon.

'Whatever you have, it may be catching,' she said matter-of-factly. She turned and carried on down the passage, leaving Simon speechless.

'Ignore her,' Molly said, when he told her.

'I don't think she likes me.'

'You're not alone. It's only me she likes.'

'And Rupert,' Simon said, looking at Molly carefully.

'Oh, yes, she loves Rupert.'

'She certainly does. To distraction,' muttered Simon, but Molly didn't seem to notice the implication behind his words.

One day, a week after he had arrived, Simon was enjoying the warmth of the afternoon sunshine as he reclined on one of the patio sun-loungers. He closed his eyes, feeling the heat fill his bones.

'Excuse me,' said a low voice.

He opened his eyes to see Lilia standing next to his chair. She was staring at him with flinty green eyes. 'Yes. I want to speak to you.'

'I'm all ears.' Simon gave her a small, tight smile. He'd been expecting something like this.

The old woman sat down in the chair next to his and folded her hands together. 'Why Molly has allowed you back into her life I cannot imagine. I guess you played your trump card. Made her think you were at death's door. Well, you don't fool me. I put the poor, shattered Molly back together after your sordid, selfish affair with Daniel. She may forgive you but I do not.'

'I'm here because Molly invited me. We've put the past behind us.'

'Have we?' she said threateningly. 'How convenient for you.' She gave a sinister little laugh. 'I, on the other hand, know all about *your* past. And I have no intention of forgetting a single thing. What goes around comes around.'

'What do you mean?'

'If you hang around here longer than is good for you, you'll find out. And don't go blurting silly tales to Molly – you'll only frighten her and, besides, she'd never believe you.'

'I have no intention of upsetting Molly,' Simon said. 'She thinks you're just a sweet old lady. You and I both know there's more to it than that. As long as you have her best interests at heart, we have nothing to argue about.' He pulled on a pair of dark glasses and lay back on the sun-lounger. 'I'll be heading off in due course, don't you worry about that. I have outpatient appointments to keep. But I'd just like to add that if you hurt Molly, you'll have me to answer to.'

'I am shaking in my boots,' snorted Lilia. 'What will you do? Strike me with your Lucozade bottle?' She got up and he heard her chortling gently to herself as her heels tripped across the stone patio.

Chapter Thirty-three

Molly loved being at home and looking after the children. It was true that life was not as easy as it had been with Michelle but, after all, she had wanted more time with Leo and Bertie and, anyway, Lilia wouldn't hear of another nanny. She was surprised that Lilia was proving so useful around the house: as usual, she was able to manage everything perfectly. She could tell that Lilia didn't like having Simon about, but she might have expected that. It gave Molly so much pleasure to be able to look after her old friend and help nurse him back to health. He was far from well and there was no guarantee he'd ever be anything more than a sickly, pill-popping invalid, but she hoped that the countryside, good food and sleep would work its magic on him. He looked healthier and happier every day.

One afternoon, as Molly came in from the garden carrying a wriggling boy in each arm, Lilia got up from her armchair. 'I was just wondering, my dear,' she said, 'which flight you would prefer to Toronto. There is one at nine in the morning with BA or another in the afternoon with Virgin. Maybe the later slot would suit you better.'

'Toronto?'

'Yes. We have a six-date tour there just after Christmas. If we go on the later flight you will at least have the morning with the brats.'

Molly put the children down and they ran off, then turned to Lilia. 'Don't call them brats, please. And what trip to Toronto? I told you to cancel all my engagements.'

'Don't be silly,' said Lilia, with a light laugh. 'We can't simply call a halt to your career. Besides, this has been in the diary for a year or more. I assumed you would want to honour it.'

Molly took a deep breath. 'No. I'm not going. I told you, I'm exhausted and I need some time off.'

'You are nothing of the kind. We shall go to Canada and then on to Hollywood to meet some very important movers and shakers. Boris is organising it.'

'No,' said Molly, simply but firmly. 'I'm sorry for the inconvenience but I'm staying put here, with my husband, my children and Simon. They all need me.'

Lilia frowned. 'Don't you see, Molly? If you take your eyes off the ball and allow vulgar domestic matters to interfere with your superior destiny then you might as well retire and become a session singer. We were on a journey, you and I. We have not yet reached our destination.'

'I can't argue my point any more. I'm tired, and I'm staying here. Nothing you can say will alter that.'

Something like a snarl seemed to pass over Lilia's face, but then she relaxed. She shrugged helplessly. 'You're wasting your time over those children. What can they add to your career in the long term? They're very sweet and ideal for a photo opportunity, but let's keep it real. It's not as if they're sextuplets. However, if that's your choice—'

'It is,' Molly put in firmly.

'—then you must live with the consequences,' finished Lilia.

It was Molly's turn to cook that night, and while she was not an accomplished chef, she always did her best. Rather ambitiously she attempted pork chops in Gorgonzola, but the meat was a little undercooked and the cheese seemed to curdle a bit once it was melted.

'Delicious,' Rupert said manfully, swigging down a gulp of wine after each mouthful.

'My appetite hasn't really come back,' said Simon, apologetically, as he put his fork down on an almost untouched plate.

'Unusual,' Lila pronounced, as she pushed hers away, 'but, then, so are shark bites. Now, is that a Pavlova I can see winking at me? More of a Wayne Sleep from the look of it, but shall we make a polite attempt?'

She approached the sideboard where Molly's burnt offering rested on a glass dish, like an elderly tortoiseshell cat asleep in a fruit bowl. 'Shall I be mother?' she asked, picking up the pie knife and clutching it like a dagger above the scorched meringue. She made tutting noises as she spooned it into the Victorian glass dessert dishes. She even tasted a tiny morsel, scooping it up with her little finger and saying, 'Poo!' quietly and discouragingly, wrinkling her nose at Rupert. She carried three dishes over to him, Molly and Simon, then sat down in her chair and crossed her arms.

'Are you not having any?' said Molly, her voice trembling. The failure of the main course and now this attack on her Pavlova had quite undermined her self-esteem. First she had been judged negligent in allowing Michelle to care for the children. Now she couldn't even rustle up a decent meal.

'Delicious though it looks, I shall decline. Gooseberries do not agree with me,' said Lilia.

'They aren't gooseberries, they're kiwi fruit,' said Molly, defensively.

'Well, they look like genetically modified gooseberries,' snapped Lilia.

Rupert, meanwhile, had swallowed his first mouthful. 'It's very nice,' he said.

'Well done, Molly,' said Simon, eating some of the less burnt bits.

'I don't understand!' burst out Molly, her eyes filling with tears. 'I cooked it at the lowest heat as usual. How could it have burnt?'

'Perhaps it was another of those long phone conversations you so enjoy,' Lilia put in sweetly. 'You were talking to your publicist today, weren't you? Two hours, I think it was.'

'I was on the phone for two or three minutes,' protested Molly.

Lilia shook her head. 'Dear Molly. So lost in her showbusiness world. She can talk about herself for a hundred and twenty minutes and it seems like five!'

Rupert gave Molly a quizzical look. 'Were you really on the phone for two hours? What about the children?'

'They were with me,' said Lilia, 'at the doctor's surgery. Bertie hurt himself badly on Molly's luxury home-manicure set, which she left carelessly on the sofa. I took the boys to have an anti-tetanus injection. I thought it best.'

'What?' said Molly, surprised. 'Bertie's hurt?'

'Didn't you even notice?' Rupert said, sounding cross. He pushed his pudding away. 'What are you playing at, Molly? I thought you wanted time off to look after the children, not while away your time chatting on the phone.'

'Nothing, I . . . I . . .' She looked at Simon. 'Did you see Bertie get hurt?'

'I was asleep most of the afternoon. Sorry.'

Molly thought she caught the ghost of a smile flutter across Lilia's face.

The next day Simon had an important hospital appointment in London and Molly offered to go with him. 'How was it?' she asked, when Simon got back from his examination.

'Sobering,' said Simon, ironically. They turned and walked towards the hospital exit. 'Apparently my liver is heavily scarred. I felt rather proud, when the doctor told me. Battle-scarred, I was thinking. Scars to be worn like trophies, testimony to my internal organ's tenacity in the face of two bottles of vodka a day. But it seems these scars are not as decorative as I'd thought. After this it all gets very technical, but suffice to say that my darling liver has fought bravely on, but now, sadly, is facing a future of special needs.'

Molly grasped his hand. 'I'm sorry, Simon.'

'I'm thrilled!' said Simon, jocularly. 'I've always wanted to say, "I don't have long"!'

'That's not true, though, is it?'

'Well, I haven't done myself any favours.' They walked out of the hospital, headed across Euston Road and towards Camden Town.

'But you're recovering, I can see that.'

'Yes,' Simon concurred. 'I do look better. My skin's gone from healthy tan to magnolia, then rather suddenly into sunflower, and now I've emerged a pleasant Sahara sand. Very on trend. The tests show the liver has some function, bless it. But it's a bit like Kenneth Williams towards the end: miserable and doesn't want to be here.'

'How sick are you?' asked Molly.

'Well, let's just say I'm not putting anything away for the future. There was talk of a transplant. Just think, I could have some leather-clad motorcyclist's organ inside me at long last. But it may not come to that. I'm booked in for a counselling session tomorrow morning. I expect they're going to say the dreaded words "Alcoholics Anonymous".'

'Does that mean you can't come back to Kent with me?'

'So it seems. I must return to my bachelor flat and face reality.'

'What about your medication?'

Simon held up his canvas messenger bag. 'I've got most of what I need with me here. If you could send the rest of my things up by car later, I'd be most grateful.'

'Of course.' Molly nodded, then shot him an anxious look. 'I'm worried you'll go straight to the pub the moment you're out of my sight.'

'Only if I feel like dropping dead on the spot – and *Hollyoaks* is particularly gripping at the moment. So, no. I'm quite keen on living all of a sudden.'

'Come on, then. I'll get my driver to drop us off. I'd like to see where you live.'

'Er, I don't know if that's a good idea. It's a bit of a mess.'

'Then I can help you to tidy up.'

'No, really. I'll be fine. Just drop me outside.'

'You're being shifty, Simon. What is it?'

'You can't see my flat. It's a disgrace. I'd be embarrassed.'

'Don't be. I'm your friend.'

When they got to the front door, Simon paused. 'I haven't been here since the night of your concert at the Palladium. The night I had my dramatic collapse. I didn't really have time to tidy up. Brace yourself.'

The flat was like a bombsite. The hallway wasn't too bad, but as soon as they entered the lounge they were confronted with a six-foot mountain of paperwork – letters, bank statements, poetic jottings, ideas for plays and final demands for household bills. Plates of half-eaten food led the way into the kitchen, which was piled high on every surface with more dirty plates, saucepans, empty tins and thick, greasy grime on and beneath everything.

In Simon's room the bed was unmade. Indeed, it was naked – a bare, stained mattress only partially covered with a similarly naked but dramatically bloodstained duvet. An incongruously luxurious eight pillows were piled at one end, under the window; they were relatively new but strangers to a pillowcase. Beside the bed there was an overflowing ashtray, a packet of Marlboro and a lighter. Next to them a heavily fingerprinted wine glass held an inch of stale brandy.

'Oh, my God,' said Molly, looking about. 'You weren't joking. How on earth did it get like this?'

'I can make you a cup of herbal tea without too much risk to your health, if you wish. I must apologise for the state of my home. I wasn't expecting visitors.'

Molly peered at the mess that surrounded them. 'Fuck me, Simon. Quentin Crisp said to ignore the dust, not garbage of every known perishable kind. This flat's a health hazard. What's the matter with you?'

'What isn't?' said Simon, quietly, to himself. The shapes and swathes of the mess spoke clearly of many nocturnal dramas, much as the ripples and dunes of a damp beach tell all about the previous night's storm. He must have done full-on King Lears every other night, swearing at the sky and the universe, invoking chaos. Domestic anarchy was the result.

Molly looked at her friend, quivering before her. She couldn't help herself – she put her arms round him. It was Simon's turn to cry. It was as if the dirty protest he had been making for ages had finally been noticed and help was on the way. He cried tears of thanks.

'I've been so frightened,' he said. 'I thought I was going to die here and no one would notice. Thank you for coming to my rescue.'

'Oh, Simon,' said Molly, 'I wish I'd known. I wish you'd told me. We've wasted so many years not speaking to each other. Thank goodness we're together again. I'm going to look after you. I'm going to help you to get better. Now, then,' she said, pulling away from him. 'Let's get this sorted. Bin-liners, scrubbing brush, bleach. It's just like the day we moved into the squat together. Remember?'

The clean-up operation took several hours. They filled ten bags with rubbish, threw everything out of the fridge and cleaned the oven. They sorted the mountain of paperwork, placed the books in stacks against the walls and made up the bed.

'Well, it looks better than it did,' said Molly, wiping the sweat from her brow. 'You don't expect to see that sort of domestic filth north of the river.' When she came to leave, she said, 'I'm worried about you being here on your own. You'll be okay, won't you? Promise me you'll call if you need anything at all.'

'I'll be fine,' Simon said stoutly. 'You've been wonderful and I've loved my time in Kent, but I have to stand on my own two feet, you know. And Roger's promised to come over and keep me company. I'm lucky to have two such good friends.'

They hugged again, then Simon gazed earnestly into Molly's eyes. 'There's one thing, though.'

'Yes?'

'Lilia. Stay on your guard. I know you love her, but she's trying very subtly to undermine you at the moment.'

'She's angry with me because I won't go to Toronto. I think she imagined that after a week or two I'd be dying to tour again. But I'm not.'

'Just watch out, okay? I'm sure you can handle her but she's a funny old thing and you don't know what she's capable of.'

'I will. Be strong and take care, Simon. I'll see you soon. I shall miss you. Make sure you come back to Kent as soon as you can.'

Chapter Thirty-four

Simon found it strange to be alone and back in his flat. Although he was much better than he had been, it was still just a matter of weeks since he had collapsed outside the stage door of the Palladium. Molly was so concerned that, in his old environment, he would take to the drink again – with fatal consequences – that she had arranged for him to see a cognitive behavioural therapist twice a week.

'It must be costing you a fortune,' he said to Molly, on one of her weekly visits. 'The place reeks of very expensive carpets.'

'Never mind that. As long as it's helping you.'

'She is rather brilliant, actually. We're doing the Twelve Steps.'

'Is that an AA term?'

'Well, it's not a song by Robbie Williams. I've already admitted my addiction. I got a gold star for that.'

'Good boy.'

'I'm dreading next week – I have to make a searching and fearless moral inventory of myself.'

'Hmm. That should keep you busy till the end of the decade,' said Molly.

Simon studied her as they sipped their tea. 'You look like you could do with some counselling yourself. What's up?'

Molly rubbed her eyes. 'Oh, well, it's Lilia again, seeing as you ask.'

'I knew it would be,' said Simon.

'Perhaps I'm being paranoid but it feels like she's taking over everything: the cooking, bathing the children. I came in the other day and she was giving Rupert a back massage. I feel like the au pair.'

'You've got to fight back,' said Simon, decisively.

'How, though?' said Molly. 'She's unstoppable. She had me fetching her slippers yesterday. And nothing I do is right – I'm a disaster round the house at the moment. I seem to leave a trail of burnt food, broken china and crying children wherever I go.'

Simon raised his eyebrows. 'You're hardly Mrs Beeton, Molls, but that sounds extreme.'

'She's eighty-two but she's the one up a ladder hanging the Christmas decorations.' Molly sniffed, wiping her eyes. 'I don't mean to cry, but I feel so useless. As if I'm just in the way all the time. She's taking the children to a carol service on Saturday and I'm not allowed to go. It would be a good chance for me to wrap the presents, Lilia told me.'

After Molly's tearful goodbye, Simon sat and worried. One of the things he relished about his new alcohol-free life was the ability to think clearly. There was something mysterious and sinister about the overbearing old lady. He needed to find out what secrets she was hiding.

He called Roger. 'You know where Lilia's old house in Long Buckby is, don't you?'

'I think so. Just along the lane from Costcutter's.'

'Are you busy today? Could you drive me there?'

'Well, I did pass my test eventually, and I drive a rather

depressing Polo, but my diary appears to be clear. What are you up to?'

'There's something I don't quite trust about Lilia. My hackles rise whenever I'm in the same room as her. I have a feeling it would be worth knowing a bit about her. Let's go back to when she first appeared in Molly's life.'

Roger said he was doubtful how much they could learn from staring at Kit-Kat Cottage but he'd take Simon there if he wanted to go. By two o'clock that December afternoon the intrepid pair were travelling up the M1. 'This is very Miss Marple, if you don't mind me saying so,' remarked Roger.

'It'll be dark soon,' said Simon. 'Are we nearly there yet?'

'Don't start whining. I'm doing you a favour here!'

Finally they peeled off the motorway and wound their way along picturesque roads to the village of Long Buckby.

'Turn right here, and there's Costcutter's!' exclaimed Roger, triumphantly, driving into a narrow lane. 'Jesus!' he exclaimed, as they parked outside the bungalow. 'Her bush needs a trim.'

'It's deserted,' said Simon.

They climbed over the gate, which didn't open any more, and walked up the overgrown garden path.

'It's like Miss Havisham's gaff,' said Roger, peering through the grimy windows. 'So they never did rent it out.'

'I'm going round the back,' announced Simon.

'That's not like you,' quipped Roger. 'Wait for me. This place is giving me the creeps.'

At the back of the bungalow they waded through thigh-high brambles stiffened with frost to the back door.

'Look at that,' said Roger, reaching down to the moss-covered doormat. He lifted up the dry skeleton of a bird by its feet and slung it into the dense mass of undergrowth.

Simon knew how to pick a lock from his days as a squatter, and within a minute he had the door ajar.

'Girlfriend, this is illegal!' hissed Roger.

'We're not going to do any harm. I just want to have a look round, see if Lilia's hiding any secrets.'

Simon was in the kitchen now, shining a torch he'd produced from his pocket on a Welsh dresser stacked with plates, dishes and cereal boxes, now covered with dust and strings of cobweb.

'We're in a scene from *The Avengers*,' said Roger. 'Is Emma Peel going to leap out of the larder?'

'Which way is the lounge?' asked Simon, ignoring Roger's schoolgirl excitement.

'It's through there. At the front on the right.'

The room smelt musty and sweet. Simon swung his torch round, illuminating it with the beam.

'I don't want to spoil your fun, but wouldn't it be easier if we turned on the light?' Roger flicked the switch. Now the room was a lot less eerie, if still grimy. Two empty brandy glasses, covered with dust and fungus, stood like candelabra on the table.

Simon picked up a dry, yellowed *TV Times* and blew on it. 'April 2001. Nicky Campbell's on the cover.'

'No wonder they left.' Roger sniffed.

Simon looked about. So this was where Molly had spent all those months learning to be Mia Delvard, locked behind those pink curtains and sitting next to her teacher on the chenille sofa to receive her lessons. Everywhere he looked, he saw old show posters and photographs. The room was dominated by a dusty oil painting of a foxy redhead holding a cigarette. Was that supposed to be Lilia? It didn't look much like her – for one thing, the woman in the portrait had blue eyes. And a much bigger nose.

'Let me get this straight. Lilia claims she was a big singing star in the sixties.'

Roger nodded. 'Oh, yes. She sang at the Café de Paris, toured London, Paris and Vienna. She met everybody, all the greats. She gave it up for love when she met her husband.'

'Really?' Simon shook his head. 'Then how come I've never heard of her?'

'The world's full of forgotten stars,' Roger replied. 'Look at Mike Smith. All right, the old bird milks it a bit, but you know what these girls are like: they can't quite accept that it's all over, can they? Besides, look what's she done for Molly. Silk purse out of a sow's ear or what? You can't deny Lilia knows her onions.'

Simon reached up to a shelf in the alcove and pulled out a photograph album. 'This should be interesting, then.'

He opened it and flicked through the pages. There were dozens of black-and-white photographs, mostly of glamorous, well-dressed showbiz types at parties. Nearly all had Lilia, bat-dark of eye and backcombed of hair, somewhere in them.

'Well, well. Maybe you're right,' he said. He took the album to the sofa and sat down with it. Roger perched next to him.

'Isn't that her with Peter Sellers?' said Roger, impressed.

'Yes, but she appears to be wearing Britt Ekland's coat.'

Roger pointed at another photograph. 'Here she is with Grace Kelly!'

'Let me have a look. This light's rubbish,' said Simon. He switched on his torch and shone it directly on to the image so that he could inspect it even more closely. There was Lilia, aged about twenty, standing alongside Grace on the set of *Rear Window*.

'How remarkable!' said Roger.

'Wait a minute,' said Simon. He began to pick at the middle of the photograph.

'What are you doing?' asked Roger. 'I can't be party to vandalism.'

'There,' said Simon, suddenly lifting Lilia's head up from the picture and proffering it on his fingertip as if it were the body of Christ.

'Ugh! What's that?' asked Roger.

'Salome – I give you Lilia's head!' said Simon, triumphantly. 'The woman is a fake. Look there,' he said, eyes shining brightly. 'Who do you see? Whose face was underneath Lilia's?'

'Thelma Ritter's,' said Roger, the penny dropping at last. 'Oh, my God! You're right!'

'And this isn't her with Katherine Hepburn, either. Wondered why she was wearing a suit and tie. That's because it's Humphrey Bogart. The deceitful old bag! And this! It isn't Lilia with Peter Purvis at all, it's Valerie Singleton,' said Simon.

'That's too much,' said Roger.

Simon put the album down crossly and moved into the hallway to look at the posters and framed playbills of Lilia's glittering career. 'Fakes. Every one of them.'

'My God,' said Roger. 'I always had my doubts, but I thought she'd been more of a chorus girl than a leading lady. More Stephen Gately than Stephen Fry, if you catch my drift. Fancy going to all that trouble with scissors and Pritt Stick!'

'I don't think she ever stepped on a stage in her life.'

'Wait till Molly hears about this,' said Roger, relishing the thought of Lilia's exposure.

Simon shook his head. 'No, we can't tell her. Who knows what it would do to her confidence if she learnt that her whole career is based on fraud? I have some more detective work to do first. Lilia's harmless for now, but if she's exposed, we'll have to watch out. There's no knowing what she might do.'

'Get me out of this madhouse,' said Roger, who was pale with shock. He shuddered. 'It's all beginning to feel distinctly spooky.'.

'One final snoop in each room and then we'll go,' Simon said grimly.

Chapter Thirty-five

That Christmas, there was little evidence of the recession in Bond Street. The rich were spending their cash with reckless abandon and Molly was one of them, the Bentley kerb-crawling along the street beside her, ready to receive the various packages as she left each shop. She bought Rupert a gold Rolex, the boys a mountain of toys and expensive clothes, and Lilia a delicate string of seventeenth-century black pearls from Asprey's. For Simon, she found a signed first edition of Muriel Spark's *Memento Mori* and a diamond-encrusted friendship ring by Cartier.

Satisfied with her afternoon's shopping, she checked into Claridge's to freshen up for the smart party hosted by her record label at Century, a private members' club. It would be fun to dress up and forget her domestic woes for an evening.

Molly was taking a rare visit to her old life and, for a few short hours, it was pleasant to be fêted, spoilt and treated with deference and respect. There was precious little of that at home, these days. She got a bit drunk on champagne and was pleased to be able to snuggle down with a blanket on the back seat of the Bentley while her driver steered her expertly home.

By the time they got back to Kent, it was just past midnight.

The driver dropped her at the main gates and, to avoid waking the children, she walked up the frosty lawn rather than across the gravel driveway. The front door had been left on the latch and she slipped silently into the hallway. She deposited her black-and-silver pashmina on the hall table and walked over to the drawing-room door. She had seen smoke rising from the ingle-nook chimney and hoped Rupert would still be up, maybe asleep on the sofa, so she could snuggle up to him and tell him how much she loved him. It seemed ages since they had had any time alone together.

As she got to the door, which was ancient pockmarked oak with creaky black hinges and a big iron latch, she heard Lilia's voice:'I am sorry to be the bearer of bad news, but I thought it best to tell you what was on my mind.'

'But I don't understand. How do you know all this?' said Rupert, sounding deeply shocked.

'Some of it I have deduced from Molly's behaviour. You must have seen her scattiness, her remoteness. Her mind isn't here even if her body is. And some she has told me. But it is only now that I know you and, if I may make so bold, like you that I feel compelled to share my fears. I believe that lately Molly has got much worse – I've seen such signs in the past, of course, before her previous breakdown.'

'Breakdown?' said Rupert.

'I assumed you knew.'

'What breakdown?'

'Did she never tell you about her psychotic episode seven years ago? Oh dear. I shouldn't have mentioned it.'

'I'm glad you did, Lilia.' Rupert sounded weak and tired. 'It's just so much to take in. It's a shock. But you're right – Molly has been behaving oddly recently. She does seem distant and she can't manage the simplest things.'

As Molly listened she had no real idea what they were talking about, but instinct told her to stay put and listen on for a few moments. What she heard next left her in no doubt.

'I'm afraid that the truth is Molly doesn't love you any more. It is not her fault, she is just incapable. She is fond of the children, of course, but her first love is herself and always has been.'

'But she seems so loving most of the time!' Rupert said, bewildered.

'No. You are just a stepping-stone to her. You have a five-year shelf-life, to my mind, and you've already enjoyed four of those. I don't think she realised quite how costly your divorce had been and you are simply not wealthy enough for her. She'll be wanting someone along the lines of Damien Hirst or Richard Branson next – the big guns. No disrespect.'

'It's still so hard to believe,' Rupert said sadly.

'I may be wrong,' Lilia said quickly. 'But where is she now? Cavorting about London like Eliza Doolittle. Leaving her precious children in my care. Me. An elderly, disabled, not to mention unpaid and unqualified friend. Are these the actions of a devoted wife and mother?'

'But what would I do without her?' cried Rupert's anguished voice.

'I will take care of everything for you,' said Lilia, in a matter-of-fact voice. 'We must do what is best for those dear, dear children.'

Molly, her hand clasped over her mouth to stop herself scream-ing, backed silently away from the door. She wanted to burst through the door and yell at Lilia, slap her and tell her get out of her house. She wanted to throw herself into Rupert's arms and reassure him that of course she loved him and Lilia was the mad one. But wouldn't a hysterical reaction just confirm everything Lilia had just told him? Would such actions make her look like a fit and dutiful mother? No. She needed to get Rupert on his own, away from the evil serpent Lilia was showing herself to be. She would try and explain everything to him then. She must be calm. Then she could confront Lilia later.

She took a few moments to get control of herself, then she entered the drawing room where Lilia and Rupert were sitting in silence together.

'Hi,' said Molly, smiling broadly at them. 'Did the boys go to bed all right?'

'Yes, fine,' said Rupert. 'Did you have a good time?'

'Lovely, thanks, but it's nicer to be home. I think I'll go up and look in on them. You coming up?' she asked Rupert.

'Yes. Let's go,' said Rupert.

'I will turn the lights out and put the fireguard in place.' Lilia stood up.

Molly couldn't bring herself to say goodnight to Lilia. She just turned and left the room.

Upstairs she kissed her boys' foreheads and stood in the doorway for a few minutes, watching them sleep, illuminated by a soft orange night-light.

By the time she entered her own room, Rupert was already in bed, his big form turned away from her, the duvet pulled up round his shoulders. Nevertheless, when she climbed into bed beside him she couldn't resist slipping an arm round his waist and pressing herself to his bare back. But Rupert remained as still as a statue, his breathing steady, and while she doubted he was asleep she could tell he wanted to give that impression. 'Rupert?' she said softly. She longed to explain that he'd been told a pack of lies, and to offer her side of the story. 'Rupert? Please, can we talk?' But there was no response.

Lilia, what are you doing? she thought, staring into the dark. I thought we loved each other. Why do you want to destroy my marriage? What is it you want?

She woke with a start and looked at the clock beside her. It was just after eight a.m. She had had the old dream of her mother being dragged off screaming, calling her name. Breathing deeply to calm herself, she noticed that Rupert's side of the bed was empty. Suddenly filled with foreboding, she got up, stumbled out of the room and ran the short distance along the landing to Leo and Bertie's, but they were gone, their unmade beds staring at her accusingly. She gasped, then told herself that of course they would all be downstairs at this hour, having breakfast. Except that the house was eerily quiet.

She ran down to the kitchen. No one was there. Next she raced to the front door and flung it open. Rupert's black Land Rover was gone. The gate was open.

Oh, my God! thought Molly, horrified. Could he really have believed what Lilia said about me last night? Has he taken my babies away?

Desolate, she returned to the kitchen, terrible thoughts racing through her head. On the table, she spotted a folded piece of paper with her name on it in Rupert's handwriting. She snatched it up.

Molly,
I have taken the boys to the zoo for the day.
See you later.
R

She breathed out with relief. The note was curt, but that was to be expected – no doubt Rupert wanted time away from her to think. She had to act quickly – get to him before Lilia did any more damage and explain herself. She saw it clearly now: Lilia had become her enemy and was working to destroy her. But why? Right now she could only deal with facts and solutions. Too much was at stake. She would tell Lilia she had to go, she decided. Tough action was called for. Like vermin, a parasite or fungus, Lilia had to leave the house as soon as possible – today.

'Good morning,' said a familiar voice behind her. 'Still in your nightie? You must be cold. Winter draws on, as they say.'

Molly turned slowly towards the door and saw Lilia standing there. It was like looking at a vision of herself: the bright red hair, the makeup exactly as she did hers, the grey cashmere dress identical to the one that hung in her wardrobe, the breasts exactly her size. As she looked at Lilia, she felt fear for the first time.

'Good morning, my dear!' said Lilia, cheerfully, coming into the room. 'No children to worry about today – what a relief for you.'

'Morning,' replied Molly, with equal brightness. 'Yes. They've gone to the zoo with their father.'

'Port Lympne, I expect,' said Lilia. 'They have a baby giraffe. Most opportune for their fund-raising activities.'

Molly went to make herself some tea, aware that her hands were trembling. Could this be the same sweet old lady she had heard telling such wicked lies to Rupert, making him believe she didn't love him, causing a terrible rift between them? Was divorce what Lilia wanted? Did she intend to tear Molly away from her children? As she thought of these things, she contemplated throwing the kettle at Lilia. She restrained herself, but kept her fingers on the handle just in case. 'What are your plans today?'

'How funny. I was about to ask you the same question.' Lilia came round the kitchen table and stood inappropriately close to Molly. 'I want to ask you again about whether you're willing to go to Toronto. Think carefully. This will be the last time I ask you.'

'I've told you.' Molly put a teabag into her mug, trying to hide her trembling hands. 'The tour is cancelled.'

'Oh, no, my dear. The tour will go ahead with or without you,' said Lilia, coldly. She turned to look at herself in the mirror on the far wall and softly patted her hair.

'What's that supposed to mean?'

'Well, it's simple, really. *I* shall do it.'

Molly stared at her, astonished. 'You?'

'Yes. Me. I shall go in your place. We look identical and have practically the same name. Only a small typographical error, in truth. Who will tell the difference? You have never been to Canada before, after all. I shall go out there, slay them and bring home the bacon.'

Molly laughed. Was she teasing? It was too absurd. 'Don't be silly. You don't have my voice for one thing.'

Lilia spun round to face her, livid. 'How rude! Your cracked vintage voice is indistinguishable from mine. I have already done several telephone interviews on your behalf. The Canadians can't wait to see me.'

'You're mad,' said Molly. 'You can't be me!'

'Why not?' answered Lilia. 'You have become *me*, after all. Fair exchange is no robbery.'

'Let me get this clear. You think you're going to appear on stage as me in Canada and no one will notice the difference?'

'I did the same thing with Anne Murray in the seventies.'

'You're a raving lunatic,' Molly said again. As she said it, she realised it was true. She'd always known Lilia was eccentric and, over the years, she'd learnt to take her stories with a pinch of salt, but suddenly she knew for certain that the old woman must actually believe her own lies.

'It happens in showbusiness all the time. Tracy Barlow in *Coronation Street* – they had a different actress every other week. And there have been at least five Tony Blackburns to my knowledge.'

Molly wrapped her fingers round the warm mug of tea, feeling suddenly vulnerable in her light nightdress. 'What is it you plan to do, Lilia?'

Lilia stalked to the window and stared out over the garden. It was the dead of winter – the lawn was a dull grey and the geraniums that had flourished until a few weeks ago were now blackened entrails twisting, agonised, down the side of their pots. The trees were bare and frozen against the sky. She turned back to Molly. 'You had to know eventually, my dear. And the time is now. I have a feeling that you're about to ask me to leave your house and your family. Well, I have a little surprise for you. The one who is going to leave is *you*.'

Molly felt cold and shivery. 'Don't be silly,' she managed to whisper, through trembling lips.

'You see, I won't leave. I refuse to,' said Lilia, defiant and proud. 'I have made a life for myself here now. Here, in this house, with Rupert and Leo and Bertie.'

'You don't mention me. Am I not in the picture?'

'Not for much longer.' Lilia smiled amicably. 'Please don't think I'm not grateful. I couldn't have done it without you. You have been the host, the chariot that has wheeled me to my rightful place in life. I give you my grateful thanks, but you may go now.'

'I heard what you said to Rupert last night,' countered Molly. 'That I don't love him, that I'm a heartless money-grabber who's going to move on to the next man very soon, that I'm a bad mother.'

'I was simply paving the way for your departure. The last thing I want is him being all heartbroken and trying to get you back.'

'So, you think that not only are you going to step into my career, you're somehow going to replace me in my own home? Take over my husband and children?'

'We will have to change the lighting, obviously. I'm not unaware of the unseemly age gap, and I can't expect Rupert to get used to it immediately.'

Molly's mouth dropped open and a cold chill swept over her. 'You can't do such a thing!'

'Of course I can. There's a very well-stocked lighting shop in Canterbury. I'm just waiting for the January sales.'

Molly began to laugh in a high-pitched tone, with an edge of hysteria. It was utterly absurd. Lilia must be completely deluded. 'I'm sorry, Lilia, but we need to get you some help. You're a sick woman.'

Lilia's expression changed. It became hard and determined. 'No. I have been preparing for this day for eight years. Everything is now coming to fruition. I will not let you stop me.'

'Except for one thing. I am not going to disappear into thin air.' Molly set her jaw. She was going to fight every inch of the way. Once, she had submitted to Lilia, done everything she wanted, subsumed her identity to realise the old woman's dreams. Not now.

'I was thinking about that,' said Lilia, as if this were a happy reminder. 'It would not be healthy for the children if you did. Visitation rights will be arranged. You will not be completely exiled. You will be their mother in the same way you are stepmother to Rupert's other son – a distant, benign presence who dutifully sends cards and presents at Christmas and birthdays.'

'And where am I to go?'

'Obviously I have considered this. It occurred to me that Kit-Kat Cottage is empty. I never did rent it. You may go and live there.'

'A home full of such lovely memories,' said Molly, her voice dripping with scorn.

'We can sort out the terms of your rent once you are settled in. It is a property of considerable historic interest so we are not talking peppercorn. I expect the garden has become horribly overgrown, so sorting that out will obviously occupy you for a good few weeks. I wonder if my bird-bath is still standing.'

'You ramble on for as long as you want,' said Molly. 'When Rupert comes back we shall see about getting you some help.'

Suddenly Lilia raised her voice. 'I want you to leave this house. Within the week.' There was a pause as the two women studied each other.

'I will not,' said Molly. 'There is nothing you can say, no threat you can make, that will induce me to leave.'

'What about the truth?' asked Lilia, jutting out her chin bullishly.

'What about it?'

'I have an ace in my hand,' said Lilia. 'I know something that will have you walking out of that door as swiftly and meekly as a whipped dog.'

'What?' demanded Molly. 'Bring it on.'

'The secret. The secret about what happened that night, years ago, down by the river. You and Simon.'

Molly gasped. Her hands flew to her mouth. She tried to scream but no sound came out.

Lilia smiled with satisfaction. 'Yes. That's right. You see, I know all about it.'

'Wh-who told you?' stammered Molly.

'You did, my dear.'

'No!' Molly managed a quiet, terrified scream this time, and then she ran out of the kitchen, away from Lilia, as fast as she could, towards the safety of her bedroom. But Lilia came after her, slow but steady, like a yeti, bellowing at the top of her voice as she went.

'So much for a devoted wife and mother! I know every detail of your sordid secret. You told me when you were delirious that first night at Kit-Kat Cottage. You're a murderess! A callous killer!'

'No, no!' cried Molly, as she ran up the stairs. 'I won't listen, I won't!'

But Lilia's words followed her, impossible to shut out.

'Your words were quite disjointed that night. It took all my powers of deduction to piece things together. Then I did a little research to see if such an outlandish tale could be true. Local news archives, a bit of research. And, yes, your story hung together very well.'

Molly raced along the landing to her bedroom and ran inside, slamming the door. She turned the key in the lock and leant against it, sobbing with fear and horror. Did Lilia really know about that terrible night? She had never told another soul! She had erased it from her memory, locked it far away inside her mind. The awful voice kept droning on, getting closer and closer, spilling out the details she'd tried so hard to forget.

'Murder. A boy found with his head caved in floating in the Thames. March 1996. Remember? That thug had lured your best friend Simon under a bridge with the promise of sexual congress while you sat on a bench, waiting impatiently. You heard a scuffle and ran to the rescue.'

Lilia had reached the bedroom door now and her voice came through it clearly. Molly covered her eyes and sank to the floor.

'He was sitting astride Simon, beating him to a pulp. He had robbed him and stolen his St Christopher medal and now he was enjoying himself. Beating the life out of the dirty, pretty queer boy. Gay-bashing. Dear, fragile Simon was already unconscious. He knew nothing of what happened next.'

'Please, stop,' moaned Molly.

'According to the newspaper archive reports, which I have taken the trouble to read, the deceased was called James Bellwood, from Sheffield. He was twenty-one years of age and had come to London that day to watch the football. Open the door, Molly.'

'Enough, Lilia, I can't bear it!' Molly was sobbing now.

'His girlfriend was eight months pregnant at the time of his death. Open it!'

'He was trying to kill Simon,' Molly managed to say. 'He had his hands round his throat!' She picked herself up, beaten. She turned the key and opened the door. Lilia came in, a half-smile on her face. She patted Molly's arm with something like sympathy.

'I expect he did. And who could blame him? He was a simple northern lad on his first trip to London and had somehow become separated from his friends. Being propositioned by a grinning queen was outside his field of experience.'

'It was dark under the bridge. All I could see was this man on top of Simon. I didn't even have time to think. I picked up the first thing I could see to stop him.'

'A brick?'

'Yes, that's right.' Molly was talking softly now through her tears, as if remembering that terrible evening for the first time. Lilia helped her into the chair by her dressing-table. 'I panicked – he was killing Simon and he wouldn't let go even though I was screaming at him. So I picked up a brick and hit him as hard as I could, to make him stop, not to hurt him. Then blood poured out of his head and he groaned and let go of Simon. He got up and I thought he was going to attack me, but he seemed dazed, as if he couldn't see straight. He staggered to the river edge and the next moment, he'd fallen in – just vanished into the water as if he'd never been there at all. I didn't mean to . . .' She couldn't finish the sentence.

'So Simon has no idea of the brave, foolish thing you did to save him?'

'No. By the time he regained consciousness the boy had sunk into the water. I got him to his feet and away from there as quickly as I could.'

'So. The secret is out now,' said Lilia, with a subdued air of triumph.

'And I told you all this?'

'You did. You unburdened yourself while in a vulnerable state. The police suspected a local gang of the murder. Turf warfare. But it was you – sweet, theatrical Molly. Who'd have thought you were capable of such a vicious, bloodthirsty murder?'

'And you'll tell all of this if I don't comply with your wishes, is that right?'

'Yes.'

'But how will you prove it? The police investigation would have gone cold long ago.'

Lilia shrugged. 'I have two things in my favour. First, when James Bellwood was pulled from the river, he still had Simon's St Christopher in his pocket. The one you bought him for Christmas and engraved with his initials. An unfortunate detail, but enough to sway the case, should it come to court, in favour of the prosecution when records show that Simon attended hospital the day after. The second is the recording of your confession I've just made on my new mobile phone.' Smiling, she held out a square, luminous iPhone. 'In fact, I have filmed the whole thing. Your tragic confession could be on YouTube in minutes, if I so desire.'

There was a long pause while Molly stared at the tiny lens on the phone. She could see now that she was trapped. 'What do you want me to do?' she asked, in a small voice.

Lilia smiled and turned off the phone. 'Good girl. Follow my instructions and you will retain your liberty and see your sons again. Any funny business and you'll be on the bottom bunk below Rosemary West. Understood?'

'Yes,' said Molly, hopelessly.

'Call me a sentimental old fool, but I have decided that I wish you to have a final Christmas with your family. So you have two more weeks with your family culminating in Christmas Day – a joyous occasion, though poignant for those of us in the know. On Boxing Day, you have breakfast as normal, then announce that you are going to pop out in the car to deliver a festive greeting to some nearby friends. In fact you go to Kit-Kat Cottage and begin your new life as an eccentric recluse.'

'Why?' she asked. 'Why are you doing this?'

'To survive,' said Lilia, simply. 'Jungle law, you understand. I want your life – after all, I've worked hard enough to get it. And for that to happen, you have to go.'

'You can't expect Rupert to believe all this,' said Molly, incredulous. 'He knows a vindictive, evil harridan when he sees one. Suppose I tell him what you're planning?'

'He'll never believe you. I've already done the groundwork so he sees me as a kindly adviser and regards you as unreliable, unstable and selfish. He'll soon realise he's better off without you. Anyway, any hint of the truth to another soul and this phone goes straight to Scotland Yard. Will your darling husband feel the same way about you when he learns you're a murderess? Will he really want to bring his sons to prison to visit their mother? I don't think you should risk it, my dear. Your options are plain. Do as I say and see your children. Disobey and lose them for ever. It's make-your-mind-up time.'

'Keep away from my sons!' shouted Molly, with all the primal ferocity she could muster. 'You can't get away with this! Do you really think you can expel me from my own family? Run me out of town?'

'Don't be so dramatic!' said Lilia, striking a mocking pose. 'I envisage a very agreeable and modern solution. Web cams are marvellous, these days.'

'Bitch!' cried Molly.

'When I'm not touring as Mia Delvard, I will remain in the marital home to add the feminine touch. I will happily feed your children, play with them and put them to bed at night and, of course, see to Rupert's masculine needs. It is the perfect arrangement, don't you think? Our swap-over is complete. Don't forget to pay your TV licence when you get to Long Buckby, will you? And you might as well put yourself down on the electoral register as Lilia Delvard. That way you can claim my widow's pension. It only seems fair. I'm going to be using your bank account from now on, after all.'

'I thought you were my friend, my mentor, but you're nothing of the kind. You're a monster!' said Molly, suddenly grasping Lilia's utter resolve. 'You're the devil!'

'The devil? Yes, maybe I am. But I am the devil in disguise,' said Lilia, looking decidedly pleased with herself.

Chapter Thirty-six

Simon's phone chirped to announce the arrival of a text message. It was from Molly.

I need to see you URGENTLY.

At once he was filled with worry. He had been sensing for some time that a crisis was approaching. Was this it? He called her at once. 'Molls? Are you all right?'

'No,' sobbed Molly.

'Where are you?' He could hear the sound of a car engine running.

'I'm driving.'

'What's happened?'

'I'm going to lose everything! Lilia's going to take it from me. What am I going to do?' Molly was hysterical, and Simon could hear angry car horns and screeching brakes.

'Pull off the road, Molly, before you kill yourself. Where are you?' He tried to sound calm but firm.

'I don't know – I don't know. I just got into my car and went.'

'Is there a road sign or name? A postcode?'

'I'm in SE4. Breakspears Road,' said Molly, after a pause. 'Oh, my God. I'm just along from Goldsmiths.'

'Stop the car and wait for me. I know where you mean. I'll be there in half an hour.'

In fact, it took him forty minutes to get there from Camden Town, but Simon eventually jumped out of the minicab and into the passenger seat of Molly's car. She had calmed down now and was listening to a CD of the Priests singing 'Ave Maria'.

They hugged each other.

'Oh, my God,' said Molly, desolate now. 'What a mess everything is. I've been such a fool. I've walked blindly into her trap and now there's no way out.'

'Whatever you have to say, hear me out first. You have to get Lilia out of your house. She is not who you think she is. She's a con merchant. She never was a successful cabaret singer. All her showbiz stories are just lies. She's a pathetic fantasist who's no more a faded star than my sofa cushions.'

Molly closed her eyes and sighed deeply.

'I went to Kit-Kat Cottage. She's fabricated her entire career. I don't think a word of it is true.'

Molly said slowly, 'I think I've always known that. At first I believed her, but gradually, over the years, I've guessed that she made most of it up. Her stories became more and more out-landish. And then, at the Ivor Novellos, I took her to meet her old pal Julie Andrews, who didn't know her from the waitress. I guessed then she'd embroidered her past but I made excuses for her because of the trauma of her childhood and what she suffered. But now it's gone too far.'

'Throw her out!' declared Simon. 'Right away! You don't need that old vampire – you've got everything you need on your own.'

Molly gave him a stricken look. 'That's just the thing. I can't throw her out. It's too late.'

'What's happened?' said Simon, placing his hands on Molly's shoulders and giving her an encouraging shake. 'Why are you in such a state?'

'She's ordered me to leave. She wants everything for herself – my career, my husband, my house, even my children. I'm supposed to resume her old life in her cottage in Long Buckby in some kind of sick swap. I have one last Christmas in my home, and then I must go.'

Simon was shocked. 'But that's crazy! She's in her eighties – what makes her think she can possibly have your career? Not to mention the idea that Rupert might find her in the slightest bit attractive. You're right, Molly, she's gone mad. Mad and dangerous, from the sound of it. She should be sectioned.'

Molly said nothing but stared at her steering-wheel. At last she muttered, 'No. I have to do as she says.'

'Why? She's a nutter. Throw her out. Call the police and have her removed.'

Molly sighed again. 'There's something you don't understand. She has a hold over me because of something I did. Something you don't know about.'

'What do you mean?'

'Do you remember that night you were beaten up on the South Bank?'

'Of course. I followed that dream under the bridge and it all turned nasty, but you scared him off after he stole my cash and my St Christopher. What of it?'

Molly looked at him with frightened eyes and said, in a stumbling voice, 'Well . . . it wasn't just a case of pulling him off you and him running away. He was sitting on you, beating you viciously, he was about to kill you and so . . . so . . .'

Simon felt a chill crawl over him. 'So what, Molly?'

When she spoke, it was in low, quiet voice. 'There were some bits of rubble under the bridge. I picked up a brick, ran at him and hit him with all my strength. I was terrified, panicking, sure he was going to kill you. All I knew was that I had to make him stop, but I must have hit him very hard, or at some weak spot on his skull because he got up, and it looked like there was jammy rice pudding running down his face. It was so unreal, I could hardly believe it was happening, but as I watched he staggered over to the water and fell in. Within a few moments, he'd vanished under the surface. I was in shock. I didn't know what to do so I sat there crying and shaking until I managed to gather my wits. Then I dropped the brick into the river and went to your side. You looked terrible and I thought you were dead but suddenly you began to gurgle and sat up. I got you home somehow and the next day, once we'd sobered up, we spent the afternoon in A and E, where you were eventually patched up. That's what really happened that night. I know I should have gone to the police and explained how it happened, how I didn't mean him to die, but I was too much of a coward. I thought they'd never believe me, and I'd be locked away for the rest of my life.' Molly covered her face with her hands. 'So I shut it away inside my head and tried and tried to forget all about it. But it's haunted me ever since!'

'You saved my life. You never told me.' Simon touched his forehead. 'I still bear the scars. But why are you telling me now?'

Molly looked desperate. 'Lilia knows. She gave me a pill the night I arrived there, after you and Daniel . . . that night. She knows what I did, and this morning she confronted me with it. I was so shocked and upset, I blabbed out what I've just told you. She was recording it all, of course. If I don't do as she says, she's going to the police.'

'Dear old-fashioned blackmail,' said Simon, with a hollow laugh. 'Bette Davis would bite your hand off for this role. Can we buy her off?'

Molly shook her head. 'She doesn't want money. She wants nothing less than my life, to shut me away like the man in the iron mask.'

'No,' said Simon decisively. 'She can't get away with this.'

'There's nothing I can do,' said Molly. 'Talking about it now, I don't understand how I let it happen. I had no idea she was so dangerous.'

Simon clenched his fists with rage. 'You felt sorry for her. For people like Lilia compassion is a sign of weakness. A tool they use to their evil advantage.' Simon thought hard, plans and schemes whirling about his now clear, free-thinking head. 'Right. We have to be business-like about this. We have two things to achieve. The first is to persuade Lilia to go away. The second is to make sure she doesn't have that recording or you'll never be able to rest easy.'

'How on earth are we going to do that?' Molly turned huge, tear-filled eyes on him. 'She's holding all the cards. The only reason I dared to come out and see you is because she's convinced I won't tell another soul about all this.'

'Yes,' Simon said thoughtfully. He was acutely aware that his dearest friend was on the point of meltdown. 'She really believes you're still the meek, submissive Molly who did everything she wanted for all those years. That can work to our advantage.' He grasped her hands and looked her straight in the face. 'My darling Molly, I'm so much in your debt it's hard to know where to begin.

Now I know I owe you my very life. Relax. You can be sure I won't let that vile old woman succeed in robbing you of everything you care about.'

'But how can we stop her?'

'I don't know yet. But I'm sure she has a weakness, something we can exploit. I may need to go back to Kit-Kat Cottage and see what else I can find. Lilia is hiding something, I'm sure of it. I will stop her, though, I promise. The important thing is that you go home and don't arouse her suspicions. Make her think you've realised you have to obey her orders. Don't let her suspect that you've told me.'

'I won't. I'm sure she believes I'd be far too frightened of risking all this coming out. At the very least, she would tell Rupert what I did.'

'Can't Rupert help us? Can we confide in him? He loves you, doesn't he?'

'He did.' Molly looked close to tears again. 'But I daren't say anything to him. Lilia has poisoned his mind against me so effectively that I'm sure if he ever learned about what I did, it would destroy our marriage for good. She's been so fiendish at laying the groundwork that I'll condemn myself out of my own mouth no matter what I say. I can't believe I've let Lilia do this – we used to be so strong! And now he thinks I'm capable of anything . . .'

Simon gave her a sympathetic look. 'Don't worry, Molly. You'll get it all back – your home, your life, and your husband. I promise. I'll use the time between now and Christmas to work out what must be done.'

'You're my only hope,' said Molly.

'I won't let you down.'

She began to sob quietly. 'Thank you, Simon, thank you.'

'Don't be silly. It's the least I can do. It'll be fun spoiling that evil old trout's scheme.' He smiled at her.

'I'm sorry, bringing all this trouble to you when you have your own problems . . . your health . . .'

'Don't be silly – I'm getting rosier-cheeked by the day. My liver's making a spectacular comeback.'

'But I'm scared. Lilia's so formidable.'

'My dear girl, so am I. But true bravery comes naturally to the homosexual. Think about it: Stonewall, civil rights, anal sex. Now, before we part it's important that you tell me everything you can remember about your time with Lilia, starting at the very beginning . . .'

Chapter Thirty-seven

In accordance with Simon's instructions, Molly returned home and pretended she was willing to go along with Lilia's plans: yes, she surrendered. She had no choice. She would go on Boxing Day as suggested and, no, she would not make a fuss. All she wanted was to spend a happy last Christmas with everyone.

'I'm so glad you've seen sense,' Lilia said. 'Such a bright girl. There is no need for all this to end nastily, after all.'

It was torture for Molly, as Lilia began to take over more and more of her life. She was no longer allowed to get the boys up or put them to bed, and she had to pretend she had little interest in them. Before and after dinner, she had to leave Lilia and Rupert alone, shut out of their discussions.

It was difficult to remain hopeful. Rupert grew colder and colder as, under Lilia's instructions, Molly stopped communicating with him and the boys. She could see her husband was hurt by her growing remoteness and the way she no longer seemed to care for her children, but she didn't dare disobey her orders. It pained her deeply to think what must be going on in his head and what he must think of her. Was he already contemplating divorce? Was his love for her dying as a result of Lilia's malevolent machinations? Sometimes, when they were alone at night, she longed to confide in him and explain the real reasons for her behaviour but she couldn't risk it. One false move and she might lose everything. She had to hold firm to her trust in Simon.

After a week, Rupert moved to the spare room anyway, and then her chance was gone.

As Christmas approached, she felt constantly sick and unbearably miserable. The gaily decorated tree, the tinsel and lights seemed to mock her. The boys' growing excitement as they opened the doors of their Advent calendars and talked about what they hoped Father Christmas would bring caused her intense pain. The very sight of Lilia sent prickles of fear all over her.

She heard almost nothing from Simon. They had decided it was too dangerous to be in constant contact, in case Lilia overheard them or checked Molly's mobile. She began to panic in case he couldn't think of a way out of her dilemma. What if he'd decided he didn't want to help her after all? Perhaps he'd had a relapse and was now unconscious in hospital, unable to come to her aid.

Then she had a text message:

> Hold firm, dear heart. I have the
> solution. I'm coming Xmas Eve and will
> tell all. Keep mum until I get there.
> Delete this message at once.

Christmas Eve came at last. The children were overexcited that night and took some time to settle. It was agonising for Molly, not being allowed to share in bathtime and hanging the stockings, but Lilia had forbidden it. She loitered on the landing where she could hear Lilia's voice coming from her sons' room, reading them a story called *Sharing a Shell* by Julia Donaldson. Then she heard the front-door knocker slamming against the old oak surface and hurried down to answer it.

Simon stood on the doorstep, wrapped up against the winter chill. He smiled at her. 'Happy Christmas, Molly, my darling. Santa's here.'

'Oh, thank goodness. Quick!' hissed Molly, throwing an anxious glance up the stairs. 'She's reading a story to the boys. We've got a few minutes to ourselves.'

She led Simon into the lounge, where he sank down into a chair, clearly exhausted by his journey. 'Well?' she said, trying not to appear as nervous and tense as she felt. 'Is everything all right? What's your plan?'

Simon smiled happily. 'Don't you worry about a thing. Remember you told me about how, when you were living at Kit-Kat Cottage, the husband, Joey, told you to go away. It was obvious to me that that was a warning. You were determined to go, and told Lilia so. When you said he'd died from heart failure *that very same night*, I knew it was no coincidence. You mentioned dog hairs in the poor man's mouth . . . How on earth had those got there? So, back in Northampton, I tracked down a copy of the death certificate, and from that the name of the doctor who'd signed it. He remembered that night, because the inordinate amount of dog hair around the body had struck him as odd. The rules of his profession prevented him from discussing the specifics of the case, so when I put it to him, hypothetically, that a dog could have been coaxed to lie on the old man and suffocate him, he admitted it was possible. Lilia had a dog, didn't she?'

'Yes, yes – Heathcliff. She adored him and he did anything she said.' Molly looked astonished. 'Lilia killed Joey?'

Simon nodded. 'To keep you at the bungalow. If I take my allegations to the police, they'll be forced to investigate.'

'Oh, heavens!' cried Molly, anguished. 'That explains everything! Of course, I should have guessed . . . Oh, poor Joey. He was such a dear, helpless soul. Now I've got his death on my conscience too.' Molly sat down and covered her face with her hands.

'It's not your fault, Molls. She's the wicked one, not you. What happened to the man who attacked me was an accident, you know that. And Joey's death was not in vain – it's just what I need to send her on her way. What are the plans for tonight?'

'Dinner, then Midnight Mass. I'm not supposed to be going – just Lilia and Rupert. My orders are to prepare port and mince pies and go to bed.'

'Hmm, not quite what I'd hoped.' Simon looked thoughtful. 'We need to find a reason for Rupert to stay here. Then I'll take Lilia on my own and confront her with her crimes. I'll offer to keep quiet in return for the mobile phone, then tell her to sling her hook. Premeditated murder of an innocent disabled man in her care is far worse than your crime of trying to save me from a vicious hooligan. She'll see my point, I think.'

Molly jumped up, her eyes shining. 'Oh, Simon, do you honestly think so? Will you really be able to get rid of her?'

'Trust me,' declared Simon. 'She'll be gone by morning, I promise. We'll be able to enjoy Christmas without her rancid presence. Leave it to me. Play your part well, but rest assured that you will not be leaving this house. Trust me to do the right and proper thing. Know that I love you.'

'I love you, too, Simon.' Molly heard footsteps descending the stairs. 'That's her. Storytime's finished. Look casual.'

Lilia greeted Simon with cool surprise. She frowned as she said, 'I didn't know you were joining us for the festive season.'

'No one did,' answered Simon, cheerily. 'I've just dropped in. I hope that's all right. It's important to be with your loved ones at Christmas, isn't it?'

'You're very welcome,' Rupert said hospitably, while Molly, pale and nervous, tried to act normally.

They gathered to drink mulled wine in the lounge before dinner. Lilia, looking wonderful in dark-green satin with delicate emerald earrings that glittered against her hennaed hair, sat regally on a stool by the fire. She sipped her drink, looked into the flames and smiled at her private thoughts.

As they all sat down for dinner, Molly was relieved to see that Simon and Lilia seemed to be getting on rather well, sparring together, laughing at each other's catty jokes and swapping companionable glances every now and then. Lilia seemed completely at ease, and only criticised the roast beef once, lamenting the absence of a bloody centre. 'You've overcooked it, Molly. Never mind,' she said breezily. 'There's a lot to be said for a crusty exterior, don't you think, Simon?'

'You would know,' replied Simon, and the pair of them laughed drily.

Can this really be the last time we'll have dinner together? wondered Molly, watching her old mentor through the candlelight. It's hard to imagine my life without Lilia in it. But she must go. It's her or me.

She would trust in Simon.

'You have certainly made good progress since I last saw you,' Lilia was saying to Simon. 'I shall pray for your swift recovery at Mass tonight. Will you be coming?'

'Oh, yes,' said Simon. 'I come alive at midnight. I wouldn't miss it for anything. I love a Midnight Mass.'

'The Catholic Mass is at eleven thirty in Bilsington.' She turned to Rupert. 'I suppose we should be setting off soon. Molly, I believe, will stay at home.'

Molly nodded meekly, while Rupert gave her a cold look and said nothing.

After Molly had cleared the plates, the other three put on their coats and got ready to set out into the night. As they stood in the hallway, Molly said suddenly, 'Rupert, I don't feel at all well. I've had champagne, port, mulled wine, brandy and then three glasses of Merlot. Would you mind staying with me? I'm worried that if I'm ill and the children wake up, I won't be able to look after them.'

Rupert looked cross. 'Really, Molly, we're just about to leave . . .'

'I honestly don't feel well.' She stared at him with pleading eyes.

'But I'm going to drive us in the Land Rover—'

'Don't worry,' said Simon, piping up. 'You stay here with Molly. I can drive the Land Rover – that is, if you don't mind and your insurance policy covers it.'

Lilia frowned at Molly, a flicker of suspicion crossing her face.

Rupert thought for a moment. 'Yes, that's fine. It would be very kind of you, Simon. Sorry to put you to all this bother.'

Lilia watched Rupert hand Simon the car keys and relaxed a little.

'Shall we?' Simon offered her his arm.

She hesitated for a fraction of a second, then took it. 'Thank you, Simon.'

Simon turned to Molly. 'I'm sure you'll feel better very soon. My Christmas present to you is very special.'

'As are you,' said Molly, in a weak voice, as Simon and Lilia went outside. She closed the door behind them, her mind reeling. Now it was a question of waiting. Whatever Simon had in mind, she hoped he did it quickly. She wasn't sure she could bear the suspense. She turned to look for Rupert, but he was padding upstairs already.

'Night,' he said, with all the expression of a moody teenager.

Chapter Thirty-eight

In a moleskin coat, with matching hat, black leather gloves and a sensible black handbag, Lilia stood on the driveway, a picture of gracious elegance. Simon reversed the black Land Rover, complete with privacy windows and a fridge, from the car port and parked it in front of her.

As she made her way to the passenger door, he produced a water bottle from his coat pocket and took three healthy swigs. 'Mmm,' he said to himself, as he felt the vague stirrings of something familiar flapping, like a moth, inside him. He waited for Lilia to get in, but it became apparent that she was waiting for her chauffeur to open the door for her. He went round, opened the door and offered a hand, which she declined, stepping nimbly into the luxury interior unaided.

Back in the driver's seat, he said, 'All set?'

'You're most kind,' said Lilia, resting her handbag on her knees and patting the brim of her hat. 'Are you a regular churchgoer?'

'Not even my bowel movements are regular any more, unfortunately,' replied Simon. He drove the Land Rover smoothly on to the main road.

'Turn left here and follow the signs.'

I'll wait until after the service before I get down to business, he decided. Attending church first seemed poetic and correct, so he followed Lilia's directions and a short while later they arrived at Bilsington. The twelfth-century church was pretty but crowded. They managed to get a seat, and sat in silence for a few minutes, inhaling the smells of damp and incense and listening to the sad, tuneless organ trying its best to be jolly and festive.

'I must light a candle for Molly,' whispered Lilia. She got up, stepped out of the pew and made her way to the back of the church. She fished in her handbag for some coins, popped them into the metal money-box, lit a night-light and put it with the many others already flickering on the three-tiered candelabra. She stood in thoughtful silence for a moment, crossed herself and nodded, her prayer complete. Simon was behind her, waiting patiently for her to finish. He purchased two night-lights, lit them and placed them next to Molly's candle. Lilia looked at him inquisitively.

'For you and me,' he said, lowering his head and closing his eyes in silent contemplation. When he opened them, Lilia was still studying him. 'Hmm,' she said. 'There are tears in your eyes.'

'What a shame you can't mind-read,' said Simon. 'Come on. Let's go back to our pew. The priest is on his way. Lovely robes.'

They scurried back to their seats just ahead of the procession, which consisted of four pre-pubescent altar-boys followed by two portly, bald, stooping men, with simple faces and pale, waxy skin. Behind them, holding aloft a large, decorative crucifix, was a tall, beautiful youth, with full lips, a tangle of brunette curls and broad, athletic shoulders. The priest, a fresh-faced forty-year-old with a pleasing smile and a surprisingly smart but trendy hairstyle, brought up the rear.

Simon leant over and spoke softly in Lilia's ear. 'Get her,' he said.

'It's like a scene from *Death in Venice*,' murmured Lilia.

When it reached the altar, the procession fanned out to either side of the tabernacle. Once the priest was in the central position, they took their cue from him and turned as one, like a Busby Berkeley chorus, to face the congregation.

Simon snorted. 'It's Girls Aloud,' he said softly to Lilia, who lowered her head and shook with companionable laughter.

In another life, we might have been friends, Simon thought, almost wistfully, as the rusty choir groaned into life. I must remember that she is evil incarnate.

The singing over, Mass got under way. Father Edmund's sermon was about the sanctity of the family, as highlighted by the birth of the baby Jesus. 'The family is God's way, the Christian way. And you and I are part of God's family, too. The Nativity teaches us to cherish our children. The miracle of birth is always worthy of celebration but the miracle of God's own birth, of God made man, without stain on Mary's immaculate soul, is the happiest, the most joyful of events and we thank the Lord our God. Let us pray.'

I'll drink to that, thought Simon.

During the Mass, Lilia took communion. Simon watched as she went up to receive the Holy Sacrament while the choir sang 'The Holly and the Ivy'. Having swallowed the paper-thin wafer and sipped the sweet red wine, Lilia turned, head bowed, and returned down the aisle to her seat next to Simon. When she arrived at his side she knelt, resting her elbows on the back of the pew in front of her, clasping her hands and pressing the knuckles to her forehead. Her eyes were closed and her lips quivered a little, like cat's whiskers.

Is she confessing her sins? he wondered. Does she seek forgiveness for what she intends to do? A line from *Hamlet* floated into his mind: '. . . am I then revenged, To take him in the purging of his soul, When he is fit and season'd for his passage?'

Considering his plan of action, Simon felt that attending Mass was appropriate, a kindly final gesture, in light of what was to follow – but it also delayed matters and made the immediate future a more calculated act. Would he have the gumption to go through with it?

I must, he told himself, looking at Lilia's saintly profile. It's the only way to be sure that Molly is safe. It's the most sensible, foolproof course to take.

He must think of Molly whenever his nerve faltered. *Dear Molly. The things you've done for me. The debt I owe you. We are a part of each other.*

Once the Mass had finished, the procession made its stately exit down the aisle to more carol singing.

'That was like a gay Moonie wedding,' said Simon. 'Talk about mince pies.'

'Happy Christmas, Simon,' said Lilia. 'Now, shall we go home?'

'Merry Christmas. Yes. Let's.'

Outside, it was cold, with a sharp wind and dusted with frost, but the sky was clear. Simon, without thinking, placed a protective arm round Lilia's back and guided her to the passenger door. Once they were both safely strapped inside the Land Rover, they pulled out on to the dark country lane that led back to the village.

'It's Christmas Day,' said Lilia. 'What a lovely service. Now let's get back. Mince pies and port. Delicious.'

Simon turned on Radio 2 and, without Lilia noticing, silently pressed the child-lock button on the dashboard. Instead of turning right at the T-junction, he turned left.

'No,' Lilia said at once, raising her voice above the sound of a cathedral carol service. 'It's the other way.'

'This is just a bit of a diversion.'

'A diversion? But it's one o'clock in the morning!'

'Let's take a drive, Lilia.' Simon lifted his water bottle to his lips and drank heartily.

'What do you want?' Lilia cried. 'I don't want to go for a drive. Take me home at once.'

'I want to explain a few things,' said Simon, taking another swig. 'I have been Molly's close friend since the day we met. I love her and there is nothing I wouldn't do for her.' He stopped talking for a moment. He wanted his words to sink in but also he had had a moment of revelation. The dull ache in his chest, the source of painful misery that he had carried with him for as long as he could remember, was gone. He inhaled deeply: before, when he'd done this, the pain would intensify as his lungs neared capacity. But this time there was nothing. It was as if someone had left the room. He tried a few more deep breaths to make sure. No, it was definitely gone. He felt almost giddy, definitely excited.

'Are you having a heart-attack?' asked Lilia.

'No, I think not,' he replied. 'Quite the opposite, in fact.'

'Can we please turn back now? You're making me feel most uncomfortable.'

'That'll be the body of Christ glowing within you.'

'What was it you wanted to explain to me?' asked Lilia, plainly. 'Presumably you're not driving me around Kent at this time of night just to discuss our health.'

'Not exactly. But I'm ill and you're old. I thought perhaps we could find some common ground.'

He turned the car on to the main road towards Folkestone and Dover. He checked the rear-view mirror, then drank some more from his water bottle. He sent out a psychic summons. Hurry up! We're almost there!

The signpost did not go unnoticed by Lilia. Before the car gained much speed, her hand darted towards the door handle. She pulled it and pushed her shoulder against the door but she was trapped. She turned, wide-eyed, to Simon. 'Why are you doing this?'

'Why? Come on, Lilia. I know all about you. I know everything! And I know your plans for Molly, how you want to steal her life.'

'So she told you,' spat Lilia. 'I should never have trusted her – she was bound to tell somebody. And you want to come to her rescue, make amends for your betrayal all those years ago? How quaint. But it doesn't change anything. I have proof that she murdered that poor boy.'

'It's all a bit pot and kettle, isn't it? If you want to start talking about murder, how about poor old Joey?' Simon said jovially. 'The point is, it doesn't matter what proof you've got or whether you're willing to give it to the police. You see – you're not going to get the chance.'

Lilia looked alarmed. 'Where are you taking me?' she whispered.

'Have a guess. I was contemplating Beachy Head but I'm afraid it's in East Sussex and I try not to go there. I fell in love with Brighton once and we moved in together. But it didn't last.'

'I'm sorry to hear that,' said Lilia, adopting a soft, soothing tone. 'But at least it wasn't Eastbourne. Now, please stop the car and let me out.'

'Oh dear! I seem to be accelerating!' said Simon, breezily. He swigged down the last of the contents of his water bottle.

'What's that you're drinking?' Lilia asked, suddenly suspicious. 'That's not water!'

'No.' Simon tossed the empty bottle over his shoulder into the back seat. 'It's vodka, as it happens. Grey Goose, if you must know. If ever there was a need for a special reserve, it's now.'

'But you're a recovering alcoholic – you can't drink!'

'I'm having a brief relapse. Most unfortunate, yet somehow predictable.'

As they sped through Hythe and Sandgate Lilia said nothing, just gripped the dashboard and looked about, like a caged animal searching desperately for a way out.

As they began to climb upwards towards Capel-le-Ferne and the famous White Cliffs, Lilia could not contain herself. 'You fool! Everyone knows I am with you. If you kill me, you'll be the obvious suspect.'

'Do shut up,' interrupted Simon. 'Of course I know that. But I don't have to worry about the future. My life expectancy is short enough as it is. I don't care what happens to me. I am getting rid of you as a final act of love and devotion towards Molly. I am the self-appointed angel of death. It is time for you to go. Molly told me all about your plans to get rid of her. Well, I'm afraid it's backfired. It's you who are being dispatched, and in a much more thorough and final way.'

'Just take me to Dover,' said Lilia, pleading now. 'I'll get on a ferry to France and never come back.'

'But you'll only slither into someone else's life. I have a public duty to dispose of you.'

'Why spend your last months in prison? I swear I'll disappear into thin air as surely as if you threw me over a cliff.' Saying the words caused Lilia to break down in tearless cries. She reached out to him, clawing at his arm and neck as she moaned and sobbed.

Simon flicked her away with his arm as if she were an annoying fly. 'I'm driving, stop it,' he said, as he turned right at Abbots Cliff House on to the Old Dover Road, a narrow sandy track named Saxon Shore Way. It was pitch dark, and Lilia took on the look of a queen on the way to her execution. She was the picture of terrified dignity, quivering with fear but sitting bolt upright, shoulders back. Simon knew not to trust her. If she sensed the vaguest glimmer of an escape route she would attack.

After a bumpy mile, Simon took a right fork in the direction of the fierce wind, towards the big, dark sky and the gaping expanse that led towards the cliff's edge.

'North Downs Way. Here we are,' he said, before letting the car slow down and stop. 'There,' he said, nodding out of the driver's window towards the rough, wind-flattened grass illuminated by the broad beam of the headlights. There was about thirty yards of this before the sudden, terrifying drop. He turned to look at his victim.

Lilia was crouched over, her arms clasped at the back of her neck, rocking slowly backwards and forwards. 'No, no, no. Please, no. I don't deserve this. It is too cruel. Let me out and I will run to my death. Give me a fighting chance. I'm begging you. Just drive off and leave and I promise – I swear – neither you nor Molly will ever hear from me again.'

'Oh, I see. Do you hear the wolf's howl of obscurity calling you?'

'Yes, yes, I do!'

'You never were a famous cabaret star, ever, were you?'

She stared him, panting with fear. 'All right, all right, you win. I wasn't.'

'You've never been bosom pals with the rich and famous either, have you?'

Lilia struggled to speak, as though her desire to maintain her pretence, even now, was overpowering. Then she stuttered, 'I once sat next to Jan Leeming on the bus.'

'That's the sum total of it? No chinwags with Grace Kelly? No Tupperware nights with Barbra Streisand? You disappoint me. And did you ever actually sing anywhere to anyone at all?'

Lilia shot him a look of pure hatred. 'Let me out!' She banged her fists on the window, trying to smash the glass and escape.

'I see. A phoney from beginning to end. No wonder you needed Molly and her genuine talent to get anywhere. Now we're on a roll, you'd better confess *all* your sins. Did you kill your husband?'

She growled with distaste at being forced to admit it. 'Yes! I had to! There was nowt else for it.' Her German accent seemed to be veering further and further off course, flying up the British Isles towards the north.

'Admirably frank. It's too late for honesty now, unfortunately. You see, I have some bad news and some good news.' He felt the fluttering inside his chest grow and grow, ballooning inside him until it possessed him utterly. He knew that feeling, and welcomed it. His back straightened, his eyes brightened and he turned his head to look at Lilia. Then he opened his mouth to speak.

'I am the patron saint of homosexuals,' said Genita. 'And you're the fucking bitch that's going to die. That's the bad news. The good news is that I'm coming with you. I'll hold your hand as we drive over the edge. Fair play, don't you think? Any last words? In a minute, I shall release the handbrake, turn the steering-wheel hard right and accelerate at full speed towards the abyss. I don't know about you, but I feel a strange mixture of excitement and calm. This is like crystal meth without the scabby nose.' Genita smiled happily. 'The terrain is rough and we must expect a bumpy ride for the few seconds that we're crossing from here to . . . there. I'm not sure how much speed we can build up from this distance. Don't expect too much James Bond nonsense. Once we drop over the edge, that's the fun part. A sudden smoothness, probably a somersault, but it will be fast, like a fairground ride. Then, I imagine, a crunch, a millisecond of pain and that will be more or less that. We'll be a smouldering wreck, visible on a night like tonight from Calais, I'll be bound. I'm sure we'll make the local papers but I'm very hopeful that the nationals will pick it up, too. I was a minor celebrity once, after all. Ready?' Genita moved her foot from the brake to the accelerator and pressed her foot to the floor. The Land Rover leapt forward with a roar.

'Heathcliff!' cried Lilia, the velocity pushing her back in the passenger seat, her fragile body shaken violently by the journey over rough terrain. Then, suddenly, they were floating. 'Heathcliff, it's me!'

'Whoooaaaeeeee!' screamed Genita, in those final, free moments before impact.

Postscript

It was five o'clock on Christmas morning when the Kent Police knocked on Molly and Rupert's front door with the grim news.

With Boris's agreement Molly cancelled all engagements for a year. The story of her double bereavement was front-page news for weeks, and the sympathy for Mia Delvard was unprecedented. Her place in the hearts of the public as a torch-song singer with an impeccable pedigree was firmly established.

With the canker in the house gone, Molly and Rupert managed to recover their relationship and re-establish their marriage, and they agreed tacitly never to talk about those terrible months when they had nearly been driven apart. Life became almost normal again.

No one except Molly ever knew why Simon had driven Lilia to their deaths. At Simon's funeral, Roger said to Molly, 'He knew something, didn't he? I'm nobody's fool. I can't sleep at night. This is like your TV breaking down halfway through an episode of *Murder She Wrote*.'

But Molly, pale and grief-stricken, said nothing, except 'I loved him, Roger. I'm so glad he knew that.'

*

It wasn't until several months after Lilia had been buried in Northampton in the same grave as Joey that Molly felt able to enter Lilia's upstairs flat. She had just returned from the official opening of the Mia Delvard Music Room at Goldsmiths, and her mind was full of Lilia. It was time to face what the old woman had left behind.

Molly went in and walked tentatively through the abandoned rooms, just as Lilia had left them. In the bedroom, draped across the bed, was her famous blue silk kimono, lying where Lilia had flung it on the last, carefree evening.

She felt a throb of grief. Lilia might have wanted to destroy her at the end but for years there had been real love between them, too. She was, after all, the closest thing to a mother Molly had ever known. A sob rising in her throat, Molly collapsed on the bed and buried her face in the soft, comforting folds of Lilia's mother's robe, the one lasting connection the old lady had had with her extraordinary past.

Once the tears had subsided, she pulled away to inhale some cleaner, fresher air. It was only then that she saw the label. It took half a second to read it, but several moments to register the implications. The label on the kimono said 'Dorothy Perkins'.

'No,' said Molly to herself. 'How can that be?'

In a daze, she opened the bedside drawer and pulled out a sheaf of documents. Leafing through it, she came upon a crisp, yellowing bit of paper, which, when she opened it, revealed itself to be a birth certificate with the following information: 'Name: Maureen Watkins. Date of birth: 20 April 1928. Place of birth: Grimsby, Lincolnshire.'

She stared at it, unable to take it in. She saw again the little German woman opening the door to her, breathing,

'*Wilkommen*,' and spinning stories of her magnificent heritage of Berlin cabaret and her heartbreaking past.

'Well, I never.' Molly started to laugh. 'The lying cow!'

A moment later she glanced out of the window and saw a flock of migrating geese on the horizon.

'But if Lilia Delvard never existed,' she wondered out loud, 'then who was Maureen Watkins? And what on earth was *her* story?'

An exclusive interview with
Julian Clary:

What was the inspiration for Devil in Disguise?

Of all the experiences life has offered me so far, love, friendship
and betrayal have been responsible for the greatest highs and lows.
This book is my attempt to explore the agony and the ecstasy.

*Lilia is a truly fabulous – if distinctly evil – creation. Is she based on
anyone you've ever encountered?*

Lilia is based on someone a friend of mine knew for many years: a
seemingly kind, quaint, fragile old dear who turned out to be full
of evil and malicious intent. All of the main characters in the book
transform by the end, either by artistic endeavour or because they
were concealing the truth about themselves.

*Dream casting time: who in the movie of Devil in Disguise would
play Molly and Simon? What about Lilia?*

Lilia is easy to cast – as I wrote it I was imagining the fabulous
Angie Richards who played Frau Schneider in Rufus Norris'

production of *Cabaret* at the Lyric Theatre. (I was playing the part of the Emcee for 7 months while gestating the ideas for the novel.)

Molly is a tricky part – Amy Nuttall (Sally Bowles in the same production) has the right qualities but would need to put on about 3 stone to play the early, buxom Molly and then lose it again towards the end.

I'd quite like to play Simon myself, but, sadly, I'm too old. Someone pretty who used to be in Hollyoaks perhaps. Is Henry Luxemburg available?

This year you've been doing a stand-up tour for the first time in years, but which comedians make you laugh?
I'll laugh at almost anyone. Even those straight blokes who wear awful shirts and talk about their girlfriends endlessly can raise a smile. I'm not fussy.

Which book would you never have on your bookshelf?
Jim Davidson's autobiography.

Is there a particular book or author that inspired you to be a writer?
Muriel Spark.

What is your favourite word?
Obfuscate.

Why do you write?
Escapism. I love creating a fictional world where I control everyone's destiny. It's like being God.

Which book are you reading at the moment?
Jack Dee's *Thanks For Nothing*, which is highly entertaining.

What are you working on at the moment?
My next novel is in the gestating period. I'm like a broody hen sitting on her egg. In a few month's time the book will start to hatch out and that's when I actually put pen to paper. It should be rather epic – it involves two different story lines set fifty years apart, and the two world collide in a surreal and ghostly climax that I haven't quite worked out yet. It's quite a big egg, let's put it that way.

MURDER MOST FAB
Julian Clary

'My fame might have looked easy to you, but getting to the top of the celebrity ladder took talent, beauty, commitment and a number of unfortunate deaths. If we're being picky you might describe me as a serial killer, but I really don't see myself that way. It sounds trite to say 'one thing led to another' but it's true…'

Johnny Debonair is Mr Showbiz - Mr Friday Night. Only his past isn't so clean cut as his image. Once a hugely popular rent boy with a talent for S&M, he has more skeletons in his closet than the average political party. But Johnny also has a ruthless streak – and he'll stop at nothing to stay at the top…

The dark, very funny story of the world's first showbiz serial killer…

Praise for *Murder Most Fab:*

'A slick page-turner, darkly funny, incongruously believable . . . you are completely swept along by it' *Guardian*

'With his high camp and filthy humour, Clary is as entertaining on paper as he is on stage.' *Observer*